FINDING HOME

HOME SERIES
BOOK 1

MELISSA WHITNEY

ABOUT THE BOOK

Sometimes you have to go back to move forward.

Eleanor "Elle" Davidson has avoided going back to her hometown. Out of excuses, she's back home for thirty days to confront the ghosts of her past, including the mother she hasn't spoken to in eighteen years. Soon, Elle discovers that sometimes going back can help you move forward.

In the search for her authentic self, she finds an unexpected passion with the village's handsome veterinarian, Dr. Clayton Owens. Will her feelings for Clayton be enough to free her heart from the prison of her past, or will she do what she's always done...run away?

Finding Home
Copyright © 2024 by Melissa Whitney
All rights reserved.

Digital eISBN-13:9798990433403
Print ISBN: 979-8-9904334-1-0

*To everyone who ever felt their tattered pages
made them unreadable…
You are a goddamn masterpiece.*

A NOTE FROM THE AUTHOR/CONTENT WARNINGS

My Dear Reader,

Finding Home isn't just a small town romance with the swoon, sexiness, laughter, and heart we want from our love stories but a true labor of love. This is the very first novel I wrote and a deeply personal story. In so many ways, Elle Davidson's journey and mine intertwine, minus the handsome veterinarian (I got an adorable special education teacher). Like myself, and so many others, Elle is a survivor of sexual trauma, parental neglect, and emotional and literal abandonment. Despite a weary heart, she, like so many of us, traverses the choppy waters of her painful past to find her way to her happy ending.

This is a work of fiction. Actual places discussed in this book may have fictionalized details. Any resemblance to real people or places is just a coincidence. While the book does take place in my hometown of Perry, New York, much of the description and places highlighted have been fictionalized. This is not a true story based on anyone, though it is deeply personal for me to have written. I had all the feels over the three months of writing and year and a half of editing this story.

This is a romance with a guaranteed happy ending, but this story explores some sensitive topics and themes that may be triggering for some individuals, such as sexual assault (not on page), parental abandonment, parental emotional neglect, post-traumatic stress disorder, impact of divorce, grief/loss, self-image, and attempted suicide (not on page). As a trained social worker with a history of working with individuals that have faced traumatic situations and as a survivor of sexual trauma, I aimed to tackle these topics in a thoughtful and sensitive manner.

This story will explore these themes, but it will also provide laughter, swoon, consensual on page sexy time (sorry, Uncle Mike), an adorable pug, and a lot of heart. However, please take care of yourself when reading. Your mental health is important.

Sincerely,

Melissa Whitney

ONE

"Ah! There is nothing like staying at home,
for real comfort."
~Jane Austen, Emma

"Explain this to me like I'm four," Viet said, one dark brow arched. "You'll go to your hometown for a week for your cousin's wedding, fly back here, and then fly back again for another week for your uncle's fiftieth? All within the same month? Do I have that right?"

Willa ran a manicured finger around the rim of her glass. "Why don't you just stay in New York the entire time?"

"I can't take a month off!" Elle scoffed.

Eleanor "Elle" Davidson regretted her rare decision to leave her downtown L.A. office before seven to make happy hour with her friends, Viet Vo and Willa Andrews. Their badgering was akin to the Spanish Inquisition. Only with more rosé and less physical torture.

"Aren't you the boss?" Willa signaled the server to bring another round.

"Yes." Elle looked around as if Sloan-Whitney, the

healthcare system she worked at, had secret HR spies at the bar. She bent closer and whispered, "I'm the boss bitch." And there it was… She was officially tipsy.

"Yes, queen!" Willa snapped her fingers.

"I may lose my feminist card for that one."

"More importantly, aren't you the National Director of *Virtual* Medicine? If anyone should be able to work remotely, it should be you." Viet tipped his glass toward Elle.

Willa shimmied and raised her hands in the air. "Brilliant! Would you Airbnb your place? My cousin is a visiting nurse and needs a short-term rental in August. I can guarantee he's very clean."

"What?" Elle tried to blink away the rosé fuzziness.

"Your cousin Ned? Yes, please! He's hot, despite his old man name." A pale blush swept across Viet's face.

"You're a married man." She *tsked* and then turned to Elle with a wink. "But Ned is single and hetero-leaning."

Like a modern-day version of Jane Austen's Emma Woodhouse, Willa was ever the matchmaker. Just like Emma, she was bad at it. *Really Bad.* Over the years, Elle had been subjected to a string of Willa curated meet-cutes. None of which were cute.

"I do love that Ned is a boy nurse." Elle batted her hazel eyes, the rosé warmth spreading across her limbs.

"He prefers man nurse."

"And what a man!" Viet raised his Old Fashion.

"Thank goodness he's my cousin by marriage or this would feel a little Lannister Family Rules to me," Willa joked.

"Back to my opening thesis. Elle, it makes sense. You've been trying to get your headquarters to be more open to remote work. You could pilot it." Like the highly paid corporate lawyer that he was, Viet laid out his argument.

"You just want to use your spare key to catch Ned in his underpants." Elle aimed her now empty glass at Viet.

"I think Willa may be more apt to do that as she mentions how they aren't related by blood each time his name comes up." Viet waggled his finger at Willa, who flipped him off in response.

"Besides, you *hate* flying. When we went to London last summer, you needed three glasses of wine to get on the plane. You especially hate non-direct flights. Don't you have to take two flights and a wagon train to get to Perry, New York?" Willa mocked.

It was unoriginal, but Elle gave her the finger.

"Also, Uncle Pete," Viet murmured, playing his trump card.

Damn it. Elle closed her eyes. Guilt churned in her belly.

Her best friend of eighteen years knew Elle better than anyone. Even if he didn't know all of her. Who did, after all?

He knew how important her surrogate family of Uncle Pete, his wife Janet, and their son Tobey were to Elle. A simple silver framed photo of Elle in a cap and gown beside a grinning Pete and Janet, while a smirking Tobey gave her bunny ears, was the lone family picture displayed in her condo.

Pete, Janet, and Tobey were far too important to Elle to be dealt the last fourteen years of bad excuses that she used to not visit. They deserved better.

"Ok," she whispered her defeat.

"Hand me your phone." Viet held his hand out, palm up.

"*Why?*"

Viet's forehead puckered. "Eleanor Marie Davidson."

"Oh, you got full-named." Willa laughed, sipping the fresh cocktail that had poofed into existence without Elle noticing.

Perhaps, the wine fairy would bring Elle a fresh glass to numb the dread of being forty minutes from the nearest cocktail bar for a month. More importantly, to dull the anxiety about being in a town where painful phantoms haunted each corner. How much rosé could she pack in her luggage?

"Fine," she muttered and dropped her phone into Viet's hand.

"I'm texting Uncle Pete to tell him the news."

"Wait, I need to get my boss to sign off." Elle reached for the phone.

But Viet was faster. "You're a boss bitch. You'll make it happen."

"Fine." She puffed out a breath. "Willa, let Ned know he can stay at my place."

"Oh, I texted him five minutes ago. He's pumped."

"What if Viet's emotional terrorism hadn't worked?"

"Plan B was for you to fall in love with Ned via close proximity."

"You read too many romance novels." Elle took Willa's drink from her and sipped.

Stupid alcohol. She narrowed her eyes at the cocktail, scrunched her nose, and handed it back. It was the three glasses of rosé's fault that she was doing this. At least, that's what she'd tell herself.

"No such thing! I've had some of my best orgasms thanks to Denise Williams." She fanned herself with the card-stock menu. "Anyways, I'll find you a *dream* Airbnb to live in while you're in Perry-dise. I wonder if I can find one with a hot farmer waiting for a city girl to melt his pants off with her steamy sass!"

"Check the filter options," Viet deadpanned.

"This will be more like a Stephen King novel, only Carrie returns to get doused with even more buckets of blood." Elle rested her head on the table, its cool smooth surface sobered her to what a terrible idea this was.

"Except in this version Carrie returns as a badass health-care executive with killer fashion sense and a hot bod." Viet placed Elle's phone beside her head.

"Totes! Also, you style your hair *way* better than in high school."

Face pinched, Elle raised her head. "Why did I show you my senior yearbook?"

"It will be fine." Viet covered Elle's hand with his, warmth seeping through her. "You're going home."

Only she wasn't going home. She was going back to where she'd grown up.

TWO

"My idea of good company...is the company of clever, well-
informed people who have a great deal of conversation; that is
what I call good company."
~Jane Austen, *Persuasion*

I *'m back.* Deboarding her flight, Elle sucked in the sleepy
airport's stale air. It was day one of thirty back in Western, New York.

Rows of closed coffee shops, restaurants, and gift shops
greeted Elle as she made her way through the Buffalo-
Niagara Airport. "This is what they mean by ghost town," she
mumbled to herself.

Even the car rental counter wouldn't open until eight
a.m. With a sigh, she ambled toward baggage claim. Uncle
Pete had offered to pick her up, but she'd opted to rent a car.
It made no sense for him to drive an hour to pick her up.
However, that meant waiting for the next two hours until the
rental counter opened.

"Eleanor!" A deep voice boomed when she emerged into
the main terminal.

Elle winced. She'd been home for five minutes and was Eleanor, again. Shaking away the revulsion, she blinked at the tall stocky man with thinning blond hair.

"Uncle Pete?" she gaped.

He waved.

Of course, he'd come. Her mouth curved into a grin.

"Kiddo!" Pete wore a big smile along with the *Life's a Beach* T-shirt she'd bought him during his last visit to Long Beach.

"I told you—"

"Pish posh." He scooped her up in his arms. "It's not every day *my* favorite niece flies in."

"I'm your only niece. This is sweet, but unnecessary."

"Hertz doesn't open until eight. Was I going to have my *only* niece sit in an airport for two hours? What kind of favorite uncle would I be?" He took her laptop bag and slung it over his shoulder.

"You're my only uncle," she teased, looping her arm with his and strolling to the escalator.

"One and only." His blue eyes twinkled. "I figured I'd take you to breakfast, bring you back here to pick up your rental, then follow you to your Airbnb to inspect it."

After Pete grabbed her two oversized suitcases at baggage claim, they drove to a restaurant down the road from the airport. It had been at least fifteen years since she'd eaten at a Cracker Barrel.

"What are you thinking?" Pete asked, his gaze not leaving his menu.

Elle hesitated, her eyes fixed on her own menu. To those that didn't speak Pete, it would appear he was just asking what she wanted for breakfast. However, she was fluent and the unsaid beneath the spoken words volleyed within her. *How are you feeling about being back? Have you thought about what I said about seeing your mom?*

"Eggs of some sort," she replied, choosing not to engage.

"I'm glad you didn't go vegan living in California." He peered over the menu top.

Her stare met his, a small smile curving her mouth. "I've experimented. I do love oat milk."

"How do you milk an oat?" His chuckle eased the awkward tension between them.

Despite religious adherence to Saturday morning calls, it had been two years since she'd sat in the same room with him. Those visits had been on her territory in Long Beach. Playing tour guide for five days, once every two years, was easy. So were the almost scripted weekly chats about Elle's work, Tobey and Janet, and whatever TV show each was binging.

That nagging voice in her head, which sounded far too like her high school PE teacher, hissed that she may only be a good-on-paper niece. A failure in the flesh.

She fiddled with the silver pendant of her starfish necklace. "So, Aunt Janet's planned a BBQ for today?"

"Yep." He patted her hand. "Speaking of the BBQ—"

"Hey folks, what would you like?" The gray-haired server appeared, interrupting Uncle Pete mid-sentence.

"I'll have the veggie omelet, crispy bacon, no toast, and can I get fruit instead of the potatoes?"

"Do you want a biscuit or pancake instead of toast?"

"Nope."

The waitress huffed. "You girls and your no carb diets. What will your lover grab on to?"

"My niece is a nun, so nobody is grabbing anything."

"I'm not a nun."

"I'd say. Although, I'm sure folks wouldn't mind you slapping them with a ruler, while wearing that tight little skirt," the server crooned.

Pete's hands flashed up. "Uncle present! Bring me her

biscuit with the Lumberjack Breakfast. Eggs scrambled and sausage, please. I have three and a half weeks to enjoy the metabolism of my forties."

"You got it." The server sauntered away.

"Thanks for letting me eat your biscuit." He winked.

Elle's eyes widened. "Please don't wink while speaking of my biscuit."

"Is biscuit dirty?"

"You sweet innocent man," she cooed.

"I'm glad you're here. It's been too long." He reached across the table and squeezed her hand.

"Me too." The guilt prickled. It *had* been too long since she'd sat across a table from him. She knew it was her fault.

He sloshed a long breath. "Your mom called. She'd like to see you."

"No." It was almost a growl.

They'd had this conversation before. A truce was brokered for Tobey's wedding and Pete's birthday. Her mother agreed to not approach nor speak to Elle, who agreed to attend both events in return.

"I know you don't want to talk about what happened with your mom, but she's hurting."

"She's hurting?" Elle hissed, crossing her arms over her chest.

Elle was all too aware of her mother's *hurting*; that pain had been an unwanted sibling for much of her teens. Before *that* day twenty-four years ago, fragile was a word used to describe her grandma's porcelain doll collection, not people. That day Elle learned people could break. Dolls could be put back together with glue or tossed and replaced. What did you do with broken people? At twelve, Elle didn't have a clue. At thirty-six, she still didn't know. What she did know was if you were too close to something broken, the sharp edges could cut.

"She's not as strong as you." His voice was soft.

"*Clearly.*"

A furrow creased his forehead. "Eleanor."

"I don't want to have this discussion again. I don't want to argue with you. Can we just stick with the plan? I'm here for Tobey and you, not her… I love you, you're my favorite uncle."

"I'm your only uncle." The skin around his eyes crinkled.

"My one and only."

Such an uncle! Before leaving for Perry, Pete haggled with the rental car clerk to get Elle a discount and inspected the vehicle.

"I want to see this place. I heard Doc Owens did a great job with the renovation." Pete held open her car door for her to get in.

"Dr. Owens owns the Airbnb?"

"Yeah, he bought it two years ago after the divorce."

"Divorce?" Her jaw slackened.

Dr. Owens, the village's sole primary physician, and his wife had been together for forty years. They had three kids: CJ, a year older than Elle, and Natalie and Evan, who were younger. For god's sake, they'd held hands in the stands during CJ's football games.

"Mrs. Owens was so disappointed."

"I bet." Elle's reply was more sarcastic than she meant.

"Next stop, Perry!" he cheered, walking to his SUV.

With her hands on the steering wheel, Elle sighed. "Here I come Perry-dise."

THREE

"The more I know of the world, the more I am convinced that I shall never see a man whom I can really love."
~Jane Austen, *Sense and Sensibility*

Lush green hills, leafy trees, pastures with potential "Happy Cow" models, and rivers painted the landscape as Elle drove the hour toward Perry. Western New York's boundless beauty was decadent compared to the drought-soaked landscape of Southern California.

Loose gravel pinged on the car as she steered the rental down the long driveway. Below a *Little Red Barn* sign, a white arrow pointed her to the right. A blue farmhouse with a turquoise front door claimed the other half of the maple and pine tree lined property. In between, there was a kidney-shaped pond and a small dock.

"This is like something out of a Hallmark movie." Elle inhaled the air's perfume of freshly mowed grass.

Pete parked behind her and jumped out of his SUV.

She dug through her purse. "I have instructions on how to get the key to this place."

"No need." He dangled a paw-shaped keychain from his thick fingers. "I have them. Doc Owens gave them to Janet. He gets flowers for guests from the Village Rose. When he put the order in on Monday, he gave Janet the keys."

"Small towns." The eye roll was involuntary.

For the next month, she'd have more moments like this. It wasn't just a small town thing; it was a being the niece of Pete and Janet Coates thing. They were the Beyonce and Jay Z of Perry. Pete had a construction business, which oversaw most of the village's renovations, and coached the high school football team. Janet worked at the Village Rose, Perry's sole florist.

"By the way, Janet told Doc you don't eat carbs, so no basket of baked goods. I told her not to mention it, in hopes of getting the spoils, but she has me on a diet for Tobey's wedding." Dread overcame his calm face. "Don't tell her about your biscuit!"

"What biscuit?" Elle winked.

With a relieved breath, he placed the keys in her hand. *Wipe your Paws* written in fancy black script on a tan mat welcomed them as they reached the white-trimmed red barn door.

Airbnb listings often deceived. There were always little things missing, or certain angles used to make things appear more impressive. But pictures hadn't captured the fresh citrus aroma that enveloped Elle upon entering and the way the sunlight kissed every crevice.

"This place is gorgeous." She slipped her white heels off, leaving them by the door.

"Let's not be fooled by a pretty face, let me check this place out," he said, rubbing his hands together.

This place is perfect. Elle skated her fingers along the smooth surface of the antique desk tucked against the front window. Its sheer curtains offered a perfect view. Vibrant maple trees swayed in the gentle breeze outside. It was heaven until…

A shrill alarm burst her moment of Zen. "What the fu—"

"Smoke detector works!" he shouted and turned off the alarm. "Sorry." Pete's mumbled approvals filled the barn with each completed item from his safety checklist.

As he worked, Elle wandered the space. A small island with a sink served as a barrier between the living room and kitchen. A white envelope with *Eleanor* written in neat hand-writing sat propped against a glass vase of sunflowers on the kitchen table. Opening it, she read.

Eleanor,
Thank you for making the Little Red Barn your home for the next 30 days. There are staples from the farmers market in the fridge. Fresh flowers will be delivered each Friday. I live in the farmhouse, if you need anything, please knock or text/call. You'll find my number on the front of this.
I hope I passed your uncle's inspection.
Best, Clayton.

"That Doc is a class act," Pete whistled, walking over to the TV for the last item on his checklist; to ensure ESPN and Hallmark, his two favorite channels, were available.

"I didn't know his name was Clayton."

"That seems odd that you didn't know." His eyes brightened. "Score! *The Golden Girls* are on Hallmark. Your aunt says I'm a Rose."

"I'm a Dorothy."

"As long as you're not Blanche." His arm looped around her shoulder. "Thanks for coming back."

An emotional lump formed in her throat as she melted into his broad chest.

Elle pulled away. "Enough mush. We have reputations to uphold."

"I'm a modern man… I embrace the mush."

"Barf." She pushed him. "Alright, you take *that* mush home to Janet."

"Yep. Don't bring anything to the BBQ."

"Show up empty handed to the house of the woman who pounded it into me to *always* bring a gift when you are invited to someone's home? I think not."

"Text if you need anything." Pete kissed her forehead, then moved to the door. He paused. "Lock this after I leave."

"You know I live alone, right?"

"Don't remind me," he groaned, stepping out of the door.

Elle locked the door, knowing that Pete would check the doorknob from the other side in 3…2…1…

"Good girl!" His muffled voice wafted through the door.

With that, she was alone. Elle walked up the steps to the large sleeping loft. A queen-size bed with a cream-colored duvet dominated the room. Two dark oak tables that matched the headboard flanked the bed.

A leather-bound copy of *Persuasion* lay on one of the bedside tables. It was one of the faux antique looking classics from a chain bookstore. Kneeling on the bed, she grabbed the book and flipped to a random page. A smile stretched across her face as she read the moment Anne Elliot first reunites with Captain Wentworth, her first and only love.

"Austen? This place is perfect. Nice job, Willa."

Elle placed the book back with a long sigh. The anxiety-tightened muscles of her body screamed for relief. She changed into workout clothes from her suitcase. Tugging on a simple black tank, her favorite purple yoga pants, and sneakers, she headed out.

At the property line, she started a slow jog toward town. As her pace clicked faster, salty sweat stung her eyes and her muscles twitched alive.

With a steady stride, she hugged the narrow shoulder between the blacktop and fenced-in pastures lining the quiet country road. The morning's coolness morphed into that sneaky New York summer humidity. It wasn't Birmingham or Atlanta, but the moist air was oppressive, nonetheless.

After running a mile and a half, she stopped and stretched against a weathered fence post near downtown Perry. Lifting her head, she looked past the full parking lot and realized she was at the Owens Family Clinic. The medical practice had always been open on Saturdays, when Elle was a kid.

The once brightly colored clinic had faded to a dull yellow. It looked the same, but different. Patients hurried in and out of the clinic, including a familiar petite woman with short blonde curls.

Mom. A sharp ache burned in Elle's chest.

She seemed not to see nor sense her daughter who stood mere feet away. If she had turned, would she have recognized Elle? At thirty-six, Elle was so different from the eighteen-year-old girl her mom had last seen. In that moment, she was more teenaged Eleanor than adult Elle.

Her pulse raced. *Why is my mother here? Is it just a check-up? Is there something wrong?*

"Enough! It's not your job to worry about her anymore," she snapped at herself.

With that she turned and jogged away.

The further away she ran from the village, the more her tension uncoiled. Before she reached the Little Red Barn, she slowed to a power walk. Placing her hands on her lower back, she breathed in the grass, weeds, and blacktop's blended aroma.

A sound drew her attention to the right. A small gray goat had poked their head through a gap in the fence bordering the pasture.

"Well, hello to you," she cooed, approaching the animal.

With careful movements, she bent to rub her hands along the coarse fur of its neck. The goat-like purr in response was so sweet.

"You are adorable. Where're your goat people? Are you alone?"

He answered with a lick. The startling effect of his rough tongue caused her to stumble backwards. She tripped and landed on her butt.

Laughter burst out. Brows furrowed, she rose and dusted dirt off her behind. Several goats in the distance captured her gaze. A man in a gray T-shirt that stretched over a muscular back was in the center of the goat cluster. He leaned over, examining a small, brown speckled goat's hooves. Elle stepped closer, her breath hitching as she drank in the man's defined physique.

The baby goat nuzzled her waist through the fence gap, but she was focused on the man. Straightening to his full height, he lifted his baseball cap and then pulled the hem of his T-shirt above his waist, wiping sweat from his face and revealing a taut stomach.

Hot farmer! Elle licked her lips then bit down on them. Those brief seconds of exposed tan skin elicited a flutter in her stomach, something she hadn't felt in a long time.

The tall figure lowered his shirt and plopped back on his navy ball cap. His features were shadowed beneath the hat's brim, but a boyish grin peeked out as he waved at her.

Dear god, I've been caught ogling. The breath whooshed out of her.

The man took two steps forward. Elle turned to leave but halted with a jerk. The traitorous goat had the hem of her top gripped in their teeth, grunting and yanking.

"Seriously?" she gritted, tugging her shirt.

With a final grunt, the goat let go. Elle crashed to her butt…again. The goat let out an annoyed bleat.

"Worst meet-cute ever," she grumbled under her breath.

"Are you okay?" the man hollered. His long strides ate up the ground between them.

"Totally. No need to worry. Just go about your goating." She tied the tank top's tattered fabric into a knot at her navel.

"*Goating*?" He stopped with a huff of laughter.

"Yep." She doubled down, popping the p.

Her vision pulled to a wisp of dark ink dotting his right forearm. What was it about masculine forearms that made her stomach clench? One of the sexiest thing a man could do to attract Elle was roll up his shirt sleeves.

"I do enjoy a good day of goating." His mouth quirked.

"Yeah?" The question came out breathy.

Without thinking, she twirled a damp auburn strand around her finger. Cringing, she let go of her hair. Dirty and sweaty, she stood in front of the hot farmer come to life from one of Willa's romance novels.

"Well, you'd best get on with your goating and I'd best get on with my—"

"Running?" he laughed, finishing her sentence.

"It's the new walking." She grinned, walking backwards, praying she didn't fall for a third time.

Waving to her mystery hot farmer, she pivoted. With a glance over her shoulder, she found him leaning against the fence, a smirk playing on his lips. Eyes forward, she ran away. His shouted, "see you soon" and something that may have been, "welcome back" or "watch the crack" followed her.

Hours later, she stood in front of the full-length mirror in the sleeping loft mentally preparing for Janet and Pete's BBQ. Her sky-blue sundress's flirty A-line skirt enveloped her in a sense of delicate confidence. Time spent washing, drying, and straightening her auburn waves further buoyed her.

Grabbing the bottle of Aunt Janet's favorite wine she'd bought at the store after her run, she headed out. At the store, she'd also purchased a gift for her Airbnb host, a mug with *Making your own path* scrawled beneath tiny rainbow paw prints dancing across its ceramic surface. A red pickup parked in front of the blue farmhouse hadn't been there earlier when she'd delivered the gift, leaving it in a gift bag on the porch.

On her way to the BBQ, Willa called to inquire how her Airbnb recommendation turned out. She also used her psychologist Jedi mind tricks to get Elle to let it slip about the encounter with the hot farmer.

"Make sure you ride *that* tractor," Willa purred.

"You have a one-track mind." Elle laughed.

"And what a track... A track *you* could run once in a while."

Despite the eye roll, a smile remained on Elle's face. "Goodbye, Wills."

Hanging up, she pulled into Pete and Janet's tree hugged property. It had been fourteen years since she visited the sunshine yellow country cottage rimmed with pink rose bushes. Her sandals slapped against the stone walkway that led to the front porch, overflowing with potted plants.

"Isn't that dress a little tight around your bosoms?" Aunt Janet tutted with a cheeky grin. The barely five-foot dynamo with brunette hair cut pixie-short, had the presence of someone twice her size.

"Hello to you too."

"Don't sass me." Face puckered, Janet descended the stairs. Meeting in the middle of the walkway, she wrapped her arms around Elle's waist. "I'm so glad you're here, Eleanor." Her soft rose fragrance twined around them.

"I almost forgot what a good hugger you are."

"Come home more than every decade and a half and you wouldn't forget."

Elle moved to pull away with a snappy retort, but Janet clenched tighter.

"Oh no you don't. I'm your aunt and I get to nag you about tight dresses, not coming home enough, and hug the hell out of you. It's in the job description and I'm good at my job."

"At least you're not nagging about me being single."

"Oh honey, that comes with dessert." Janet's deep belly laugh vibrated her entire body.

"Hey! I want in on this action," Jerome hollered, bounding out of the front door.

"Me first!" Tobey's shout erupted from inside the house before the door smacked shut, cutting off his rich baritone.

Tobey's fiancé, Jerome, dashed down the stairs. Where Janet was fun-sized, as her son teased, Jerome was king-sized. Both Tobey and Pete were six-foot, but Jerome still towered over them with his bulky physique and height.

"Look at the blushing groom." Elle gushed as Jerome folded his muscular arms around her.

Jerome hugged with his whole self, never giving throw-away hugs, sometimes making it hard to breathe.

"Bear, stop mauling them." Tobey approached the trio, his blond brows knitted together.

"Aw, my future husband, do you feel left out?" Jerome pulled Tobey in without releasing Elle and Janet.

"No." Tobey scowled and squirmed.

"You know you're the only one I want to maul." An oversized grin took up residence on Jerome's face.

"I know," Tobey murmured, pink kissing his cheeks.

"No mauling 'til you're married!" Janet slipped free from the group hug.

"You know they live together. There's probably been some light mauling."

"Eleanor Davidson, no mauling before marriage for them or you. Now, let me go open this wine." Janet snagged the wine bottle. "Pete has the grill going. My future son-in-law will help me bring things out."

"You got it, little mama." Jerome looped his arm around his future mother-in-law and escorted her into the house.

Admiration shined in Tobey's eyes locked on his mom and fiancé as they slipped inside the house.

"You're *so* gone." Elle nudged Tobey's side.

He just grinned.

"This time next week. Are you excited? Is she really making you wear white?" She looped her arm through Tobey's as he led her to the backyard.

"That she is." He smirked.

The backyard hummed with the traits of a standard Coates' barbecue. Beneath shady canopies, picnic tables had been draped in blue checkered tablecloths, mason jars filled with yellow daisies at their center. Children giggled and shouted on the wooden swing set, while several adults played yard games.

Atop a small patch of brick, Pete stood flipping burgers, their mouthwatering scent perfumed the air. Beside him, in hopes of rescuing any grill droppings, was Lt. Scout. Elle stopped in her tracks and gave Tobey the same look that a teenager would have upon seeing a member of BTS.

"Oh my god!" Elle fell to her knees, arms flung wide.

With a low whistle from Tobey, the black lab ran into her arms. "You are adorable. I love you so much!"

Lt. Scout licked Elle's face with fevered kisses.

"Did you squeal? Is that allowed at your age?"

"Who wants belly rubs?" Elle ignored Tobey, stroking along Lt. Scout's velvety chest.

He barked and flopped on to his back giving her full access to his belly.

"Sir, you're an officer of the law. Show a little decorum." Tobey wagged a finger.

When Tobey's police dog partner wasn't in uniform, he was a lovable goofball. Despite the protest from Tobey, the many selfies of the two of them sharing vanilla ice cream cones showed that her sometimes buttoned-up cousin could be just as playful as his canine colleague.

"You're going to get dog hair all over you," Aunt Janet called from the deck, holding two glasses of wine.

"Worth it! I'm in love."

"Scout!" A tiny voice shouted from the swing set.

His floppy ears perked forward, and he dashed off to investigate.

Elle laughed, walking up the four steps to the deck where Aunt Janet handed her a glass of Riesling. Sipping her wine, she took in the playing children and chatting adults. A gentle breeze stirred the trees, the sky was a slightly darker shade of blue than Elle's dress. Fat, cotton ball clouds speckled the sky. The almost too-perfect picture was reminiscent of something out of an allergy commercial.

"Eleanor, you get the first cheeseburger. We have brioche buns, Hawaiian rolls, or lettuce. Your aunt said lettuce may fit your lifestyle better. Please don't make me wrap this perfectly medium-well angus beef in lettuce." Pete dramatically pressed his hand against his heart.

She lifted one brow. "My lifestyle?"

"Carb-free." he said with a horrified expression.

"I prefer the term carb-challenged." She winked. "I'll have a brioche bun. Today's my cheat day. I get one a week and I saved it for one of your famous cheeseburgers and whatever dessert Aunt Janet has whipped up."

"And wine." Tobey clinked his glass against Elle's.

"Oh, that's not a cheat. It's a necessity."

"I didn't make a dessert," Janet chirped.

"What?" Elle gasped. "I flew in from California!" She almost pouted.

"Don't worry. Doc Owens is bringing dessert," Pete said.

"Dr. Owens is coming?" Forehead creased, she tilted her head.

"He's Jerome's best man."

"*What?*"

"Yeah. Didn't we mention that?" Tobey ran his hand over his cropped blond hair.

"You said his partner at the veterinarian clinic was his best man."

"Yeah, Doc Owens. Speak of the devil." Pete swung the spatula in the air in greeting. "Doc! We were just talking about you."

Elle's gaze darted to where Pete pointed with his spatula. Her breath hitched as a familiar figure approached. "That's not Dr. Owens."

Dr. Owens was in his sixties. More salt than pepper colored his hair. He wore bow ties, even to picnics. He was *not* the man strolling across the yard toward her. A man who was now as far away from her as he'd been in that field of baby goats.

FOUR

"It is a truth universally acknowledged that a single man in possession of a good fortune, must be in want of a wife."
~Jane Austen, *Pride and Prejudice*

"That's *not* Dr. Owens," Elle repeated, shaking her head. The man that strode across the yard wore a muscle-hugging black T-shirt, khaki cargo shorts, and a navy Yankee's cap she'd last seen earlier that morning.

"It's Doc, Dr. Owens' son."

Each clue clicked into place like pieces of a puzzle she had no idea she was putting together. Uncle Pete's shock that she didn't know his first name was Clayton. CJ stood for Clayton James; she had forgotten that.

"Mrs. Coates. Coach." CJ smiled, reaching the bottom of the steps where Elle and Tobey stood, a pink pastry box in his hand.

"Call me Pete."

"You can call me Countess Coates," Janet joked, descending the stairs with her head raised like a member of the royal family.

"Yes, madam," he chuckled, giving Janet a quick bow before handing her the pastry box.

That was sweet. Elle's lips lifted.

"Eleanor, nice to see you again." The brim of his ball cap hung low, hiding a wink that Elle detected with a tiny movement of his cheek.

A flood of annoyance tinted with something else she chose not to examine heated her face, while he stood across from her apologizing to Jerome for being late because he was stuck "goating." Elle nearly spit out her wine.

"Goating?" Jerome and Tobey asked, faces pinched in confusion.

"It's the new sheeping." He smirked.

Prickles of embarrassment heated her skin. "Oh, look. I'm empty." She drained her glass. "I'll get more."

Elle turned, swung back, and for some unknown reason curtsied as if addressing royalty. At Tobey's slacked mouth and CJ's bemused expression, Elle realized what she'd done and ran into the house.

Laughter followed as she stepped through the sliding glass door into the house. Placing her wineglass on the kitchen's granite countertop, she headed to the bathroom at the back of the house.

Behind the bathroom's closed door, she leaned against it and waved a hand in front of her face. It wasn't like her to get tongue-tied at boys from her past. With his tattoo and muscles, Clayton James Owens AKA Doc AKA CJ was not a boy.

The most verbal interaction they'd had in school was at the Winter Ball her junior year. It was the first time she'd felt pretty thanks to her purple lace dress. Well, until Summer Michaels had squeezed her once plump arm, squishing Elle's fat.

Upset, she sat on the school bleachers watching everyone else dance until someone touched her arm for the second time that night. Turning with a growled, "Asshole," she had found CJ Owens. Angry, at herself, at Summer, even at CJ, she'd pivoted to leave, but a misplaced foot sent her sailing. Only the hard floor below hadn't caught her. CJ had. For a moment he just held her until a group of boys made a joke about him doing better. He mumbled "Shut up" and righted her. They stood quiet until she walked away.

Elle blew out the memory with a long breath. As she opened the door, CJ and Janet's voices drifted from the kitchen where they discussed the dessert he'd brought.

"Frosted sugar cookies are Eleanor's favorite."

CJ cleared his throat. "I know."

He knows? Elle's mouth dropped open.

She paused in the hall as Janet lamented the strict diet Elle had embraced thirteen years ago to lose the extra weight she'd always carried.

"We just worry," Janet said.

Elle's mouth grew dry. They didn't need to worry. She was in control. She was Elle.

"Is there something to worry about?" CJ's tone dripped with concern.

"No, not like that. We're parents. We worry about every-thing. Let's take these outside and grab some grub."

Elle waited for the shuffling of feet and slide of the door, before emerging. Her empty wine glass was filled. *Janet must have refilled it.* Wine in hand, she peered outside at the people she loved, adored, and who worried for her and, in return, people she worried for. So, why did it feel easier to stay on this side of the door?

Pete appeared, plate in hand, motioning her to come out. Spine straight, she stepped out.

Elle took the seat next to Tobey at the small four-person patio table. Tobey's arm slung over his fiancé's shoulder, his fingers slow danced across the soft cotton of Jerome's T-shirt. Contentment brightened their faces.

It tickled Elle's heart to see their happiness. At seventeen, Tobey had come out to his parents, but never really dated. Ten years later, he'd met his person. As far as Elle was concerned, it had been worth the wait.

"Here you go." A forearm obscured Elle's view. Small paw prints prowled toward a bottle of water clutched between lean, sexy fingers. "I thought you'd want to hydrate. It's warm," CJ offered, warmth filled his expression.

Claiming the other seat beside her, he flipped his baseball cap backwards revealing a boyish grin and bright eyes. Eyes so different from what she remembered. Still gray, but now soft like the early morning sky. The citrus smell from the Little Red Barn drifted off him, making her wonder who owned that fresh scent.

"How are you finding the Airbnb?" Jerome asked, forking a bite of potato salad.

"It's perfect."

"See, I told you not to worry." He pointed his food-covered plastic fork at CJ. "You've been renting out that place for over a year."

"Being nervous means you care. I still get nervous before big projects or meetings. Even if I have done it a million times," Elle said, her gaze meeting CJ's.

"She gets it." CJ grinned, tapping Elle's upper arm with the palm of his hand.

A tiny current of electricity spread from where his hand touched her. The brush of his skin over hers was so different from the last time he touched her when the long lacy sleeves of her dress served as a barrier.

The foursome fell into a mixture of comfortable silence and superficial conversation typical of barbecues. Uncomplicated conversation, about the wedding, the reception, the honeymoon destination. Perfect for a summer evening.

Of course, no family barbecue could be without its controversy. As a not-so-serious argument about the flowers broke out, Elle found herself watching Jerome and Janet square-off over their four-months-long battle about carnations versus roses for the wedding centerpieces. Both their bemused and, perhaps, a tad beleaguered other halves joined in as their backups or referees. It was likely the latter, not the former.

Happiness fizzed in Elle's belly at the sight. "I love them."

"They love you." CJ placed his warm palm on hers.

Again, with the prickles.

"Jerome has been talking for weeks about how excited they are that you weren't just coming back for the wedding but that you'd be here for a month. They've missed you."

"It's hard to..." She paused to think of the next words. What she wanted to say is it's hard to come back here, but instead she said, "...take time off work."

"It's hard." His eyes seemed to say, "I get it."

She shifted in her seat. "At what point did you realize it was me? Was it with the goat or when you arrived here?"

"When you lost the tug-a-war with Feta."

"Feta?" Elle choked on a sip of water.

"Naturally the goat would be named that."

"Naturally." She smirked. "I'm surprised you recognized me. It's been almost twenty years since we saw each other."

"Your hair is straight. You don't wear glasses and you dress differently, but you have the same smile." An infectious grin played on his lips.

The same smile? Heat flamed her cheeks. "I had no idea that was you."

A playful knowing glint sparked in his eyes.

"So, are those your goats?" she asked.

"No. Just checking on some patients. We service some of the county's farms."

"How long have you been a veterinarian?"

"About ten years."

"Do you like it?"

"I love it." A full-face grin lit his expression.

She returned that big smile. "I guess that explains all the paws. The welcome mat, key chain, and that." She pointed at the tattoo on his corded right forearm.

"Yup. Speaking of paws; Thank you for the mug you left on my porch."

"You're welcome."

"Although, from what Pete said, it sounds like you thought you were giving it to my dad. I'm happy to drop it off to him if you'd prefer."

"My superpower seems to be the ability to embarrass myself in front of you without even trying or even knowing you are you." Elle raised her hands, covering her eyes. "I guess I haven't done a good job keeping up with most people from Perry."

"Nothing to be embarrassed about. Although, you never answered my question. Do you want me to give my dad the mug?"

"No. It's for you."

"Thank you." His smile got just a little bigger and something fluttered in her chest at that.

"I know you said not to be embarrassed, but there were so many clues that it wasn't your dad. They call you Doc. Nobody ever called your dad Doc. He was always so formal with his bow ties." She motioned with her hands.

"Those bow ties. He even wears them golfing."

"More evidence of my foolishness. The name Clayton on your note. The divorce," she blurted, then winced at her misstep. "Sorry."

"It's okay. I'm the Doc, not the doctor. I'm the Clayton, he's the Chris. I'm the one with a failed marriage."

"I wouldn't call it a failure." She squeezed his forearm gently, her tone soft. "Janet would be overjoyed if I was divorced, because it would mean I dated someone long enough to get married. You shouldn't call it a failure. You tried. Some of us don't even do that. Plus, failure is just success preparation."

"Success preparation?" One eyebrow arched, his head tilted. "That's smart. Did you come up with that?"

"It was Kevin Smith."

"Silent Bob? Are you spewing life advice from the director of *Clerks*?" he guffawed.

"Hey, the guy that brought us the phrase 'snoochie boochies' has much wisdom to bestow."

He threw his head back in a full body laugh and her nerves hummed as if hearing a favorite song.

"I am sorry you got divorced, especially if you're sad about it." She placed her hand on his.

"Thank you." He rested his other hand on top of hers.

"I'm glad you love what you do. It makes sense."

"Most folks thought I'd be a people doctor like my dad."

"Well, most people are morons."

CJ barked out another laugh that matched his big smile.

She beamed. "I remember how green you were when I sliced my finger while we volunteered at the Nursing Home in high school. You were ready to play medic until you saw the blood. Also, you did 4-H and were always raising farm animals."

"Didn't realize you noticed all that in high school." Bemusement glinted in his gray eyes.

Raking her teeth against her bottom lip, she shrugged. *I hadn't either.*

"I remember you were always taking the lead on school

projects and organizing activities. It makes sense that you're in management."

Elle shifted in her seat, now aware of how he saw her, then and now. "Yeah. I'm the National Director of Virtual Medicine for Sloan-Whitney. I'm assuming Jerome has mentioned that."

"He and your whole family. Pete tells everyone you're a big wig."

"*Hardly.*"

"He's always bragged about you. In high school, Coach sang your praises." He smiled, deepening his voice in an accurate impression of Uncle Pete. "Eleanor is taking twelfth grade classes and she's only a junior. Eleanor collected one-hundred pounds of canned food for the food bank. Eleanor saved Christmas from the Grinch."

"Enough." She raised her hands, giggling.

"It's sweet. He's proud of you, Eleanor. As he should be. You're impressive. You always have been."

"Thank you, CJ." Their gazes wove together. "My friends call me Elle."

His mouth quirked. "My friends call me Clayton."

"Clayton," she said his name slowly, allowing her lips to try it out. Elle held her water bottle up in a toasting gesture.

"Elle." He pressed his water bottle against hers. A simple toast to them.

FIVE

"The person, be it gentleman or lady, who has not pleasure in a good novel, must be intolerably stupid."
~Jane Austen, *Northanger Abbey*

Sleep was more of a journey rather than a destination for Elle. Most nights she tossed and turned between intrusive thoughts and vivid nightmares of the past. Last night was no exception. As she lay watching daylight tiptoe into the room, she willed sleep to come.

"I give up," she huffed, kicking off her blankets.

A good sweaty workout would purge the previous day and reboot her to tackle today. Almost twenty-four hours in Perry left her battered from a tornado of emotions. Bubbles of happy reunions vied with the sharp pang from seeing her mom in front of the Owens Family Clinic.

Changed into black yoga pants and a purple tank top, she sucked in the dewy morning air. Elle strolled to the dock for some pondside yoga. Flip flops kicked off, she spread her mat on the dock's wooden planks.

Even before nights of challenged sleep, Elle was an early riser. It started with Grandma Coates, who'd wake her before the first crack of dawn. They'd sit in the living room, a bowl of sugary cereal in Elle's lap, watching the news before school.

That childhood morning ritual dissolved away after grandma got sick. The cancer consumed the once vibrant woman. At eleven, Elle got herself up and sat, cereal bowl in her lap, alone watching the news before school.

Not alone. Elle had herself. That self-reliance bolstered her to not just care for herself, but for the broken doll that was her mom after Elle's dad had left.

Eyes closed tight, she moved into the workout and away from the haunting pull of the past. Around her the world hummed with the morning playlist of chirping birds and a distant happy bark.

Lowering into corpse pose, she ended her yoga routine. The glow of ache and energy radiated within her. Controlling her breaths in time with the gentle breeze, she closed her eyes for a moment, then opened them to golden rays streaked between fluffy clouds. The sunshine the same color as her mom's blonde curls. Her throat choked with sudden emotion.

Those phantoms were dimmed in Long Beach. In Perry, they burned bright.

I see you ghosts. Now fuck off. She closed her eyes tight.

"Oof," Elle gasped as the weight of something round, furry, and squirmy hit her chest. Her eyes shot open and met the dark eyes of a rogue pug, its wrinkled black and tan face drawn into a curious pout. "Well, who are you?"

The pug wiggled its roly-poly body. Raising to a seated position, she placed him on her lap. Before she could read the bone-shaped name tag dangling from his collar, he attacked with wet kisses.

"I see you've met Fitz." A tall shadow and that familiar citrus scent fell over Elle.

"Sure have. Morning, Clayton." A fluttery sensation formed in her belly with each syllable of his name. It was like fresh brewed peppermint tea, soothing and warm.

"Good morning, Elle."

She craned her neck to study his features, which were shaded by that same Yankees cap. Elle was tall for a woman, but Clayton towered above her by seven or eight inches. A light blue shirt molded over his muscular frame, discolored with drying sweat spots along his armpits and collar.

Any self-consciousness about the pieces of her sweat soaked hair dissolved. Both wore the signs of recent exercise. Except, only one of them carried that fresh citrus smell after working out. No doubt her aroma was not as appealing.

"He's a bit of a flirt." Clayton pointed at Fitz, who'd flipped on his back to be cradled like a baby in Elle's arms.

"Is he yours?"

"I think I'm his."

"I like that. How long have you been with him?"

"About two years. I volunteer at the county shelter. He came in. He was so little. Not little like tiny and cute, but skinny and sunken into himself…and so scared. They couldn't get him to come out of the crate. He's stubborn, but I lured him out." Clayton lowered to his haunches near Elle.

"He's not skinny anymore," Elle teased, rubbing Fitz's squishy belly.

"Don't fat shame my dog." Clayton teasingly tutted, leaning over to pet Fitz. The heat of his body caressed her flushed cheeks.

"Did he come with the name Fitz, or did you name him?"

"I named him."

"Why Fitz?" She turned her gaze from the sleepy pug to

his human. That flutter in her stomach kicked up as her hazel eyes met his gray ones.

"His full name is Fitzwilliam, but Fitz for short."

"Fitzwilliam? Like Colonel Fitzwilliam?" Her eyes widened. "Mr. Darcy's cousin?"

"It's also Mr. Darcy's first name," he added with a boastful tug of his lips.

"I would never take you for a Jane Austen fan."

"Why, because I'm a man?" There was an air of playfulness as he bumped his knee against hers.

"No. I once dated a man that read Austen, so I know men can read Austen," she playfully scoffed.

"A boyfriend?"

"Hardly." She swatted away the idea like a mosquito. "So, you read Austen."

"Among other authors. I'm a big reader, always have been."

"Really?" Searching her memories of Clayton, a fuzzy image of him sitting quietly in study hall, nose in a book, appeared. She'd assumed the book was an assignment, but perhaps not. "Naming your dog after Mr. Darcy is not a casual Austen reader move. That's some serious fanboy stuff. What made you start reading Austen? Was it a girl?" She wiggled her eyebrows.

He averted his gaze.

"Why Clayton James, did you try to woo a young lady with Jane Austen?" She tapped her bare foot against him, drawing his eyes back to her. "Lucky lady. I think the most romantic thing a man has done for me is pick me up at LAX during rush hour and that was my gay best friend, so it doesn't count."

"So, no Mr. Darcy waiting for you?" he asked, wincing immediately, as if stepping in mud.

"No Darcys, Knightleys, or Colonel Brandons. Certainly, no Wickhams or Willoughbys either."

His lips curled into a grin. "No Miss Bennets, Watsons, or Dashwoods for me. Certainly, no Caroline Bingleys."

A charge zinged in the air between them. The listing of characters from Austen's novels offered the masquerade of letting each other know they were available without the words being said.

Am I available? There wasn't anyone waiting for her, but that didn't mean she was open. For the first time she wanted to be, but wasn't sure why.

"My first Austen was *Pride and Prejudice*," he said.

"It's the Austen gateway drug."

His lips quirked. "I got it from the school library. I was hooked. I loved the relationship between Lizzie and Jane. I saw myself in Darcy. As I read more Austen, I saw myself in more characters. I re-read them every couple of years, they're like old friends. I discover more things I like about them each time." His smile was wistful. "I didn't understand why you were always reading her books until I read Lizzie and Darcy's story. Then I got it."

Her forehead wrinkled. "Wait. Me?"

He rubbed at his nape. "At football practice in high school, you'd be sitting on the bleachers, waiting for Coach. You were always reading. Sometimes books from English and a lot of Jane Austen. Your face would tell the story of what was happening on the page. Like I knew if something was good, bad, sad, or silly was happening just by looking at you. You're very expressive when you read."

"I didn't know you were watching."

A strange sensation bloomed within her at the idea of this man being so enamored with her teenaged facial expressions that he'd read Austen, the romantic primer for so many young women. Goosebumps skipped across her skin. Who knew a conversation about Jane Austen would elicit the heat cascading through her?

"Not in a creepy way," he was quick to clarify, a tinge of pink on his cheeks. "Just curious. When I read my first, I got it. So, thank you. My mom also thanks you, because I am the one person in our family that will watch a Jane Austen movie with her."

"To think we could have let you join our little Jane Austen Sisterhood in high school. Although, you would have grunted just like you did in Spanish class," she joked.

"Probably. I wasn't a big talker then."

"Like Fitzwilliam Darcy. Is *Pride and Prejudice* your favorite?"

"That's a tough question. I think it changes depending on, well, life. What remains constant is I relate the most to Darcy. I know, I'm a cliché. I have a literary crush on Elinor Dashwood. I would love to have a beer with Mr. Knightley. But the story that gets me every time is *Persuasion*."

"Is that why it's on the bed-stand in the Little Red Barn? Is your Airbnb a brilliant ploy to get guests to read your favorite book?" She smirked.

"I wish I was that devious. I left it for you. From one Austen fan to another."

Their gazes twined together in the quiet beat that stretched between them. Elle's heartbeat sped with the intensity of his stare.

"What's your favorite?"

Elle let the simple but loaded question simmer. A favorite book revealed so much about a person. Clayton's favorite hinted of a desire for second chances at happiness. Her eyes waltzed from the little blue farmhouse to the Little Red Barn and down to the snoring love nugget in her arms. Was this

his second chance or was it still out there? Was he Captain Wentworth returning, transformed into something more, ready to claim his happy ending?

Maybe she was reading too much into this. What she wanted to say was she related the most to Elinor Dashwood, had a literary crush on Mr. Darcy, and wanted to sip mimosas with Mary Crawford. Who wouldn't? The lady knew how to party and was, perhaps, a very misunderstood character. Instead, what she said was, "*Sense and Sensibility* is my favorite."

"That's my mom's favorite too."

It grew quiet again. Not uncomfortable, but thoughtful. Both lost in their own musings or in each other's answers.

"So, you do yoga." He motioned to her mat.

"I run most days, but yoga is my daily centering."

"I have some favorite trails. If you want to join—" He paused for a second. "—or if not, I can show you where they are so you can run on your own. The trails are safer than running on the roads." He tugged at his hat's brim.

Sweetness dripped from the nervous way he asked her to go running and the concern for her safety. It all blended in an adorable package. Even if that package was wrapped up with all those muscles.

"That would be nice."

"Which?" he asked, hope sparking in his eyes.

For a moment, she also wanted to know which… To run with him or on her own? Her normal response would be to run alone, but those rambunctious butterflies said otherwise.

"Will I get Fitz-time after?" She batted her lashes.

"That could be arranged."

"Have his people call me." A throaty quality underscored her response. It was like the ghost of Marilyn Monroe possessed her. Elle imagined what her teenaged self would think about CJ Owens asking for her number, and how aghast she'd be about thirty-six-year-old Elle giving it to Clayton, hoping he'd use it.

SIX

*"I cannot fix on the hour, or the spot, or the look or the words,
which laid the foundation. It is too long ago. I was in the
middle before I knew that I had begun."*
-Jane Austen, *Pride and Prejudice*

Starting the day off with a run was not unusual for Elle.
Every morning in California started with her solo treadmill jog, looking out her window at the pre-dawn sky. That
was normal. What wasn't normal was running with a former
classmate turned hot farmer turned hot veterinarian Airbnb
host.

Despite the veterinarian clinic being closed on Mondays,
Clayton insisted on sticking with a six a.m. start time.
Opening the door, she was startled to find him standing on
the porch.

"Sorry. We never said where we'd meet this morning, so I
just came to you." He threaded his fingers into his short
sandy strands. "I got here a bit ago but didn't want to knock
too early. I didn't want you to feel rushed."

With a nod, she smiled.

Walking to his pickup, he outlined the plan. Just knowing he had a plan made her knees wobble. She always had a plan. Her plans had plans. It was nice having someone else hold the map for once, even if she itched to take it back.

They drove to the Greenway, a former railroad track refashioned as a running trail cutting across several nearby towns. Two reusable water bottles sat in the cupholders filled with water for them. One of the bottles a simple black, the other with the words *Go Pug Yourself* in white lettering skating over a pug silhouette. Clayton explained the bottle had been a gift from his sister Natalie.

Elle claimed the plain bottle for herself, his thoughtfulness making her stomach somersault. Being near him was reminiscent of sitting too close to a campfire on a cold evening. The flames' hot breath a comforting blanket wrapped around you, but if you get too close, you'll burn, and if you step too far away, you'll freeze. It was a complicated dance to experience his thoughtful fire while reminding herself she was only here for a month.

"Thank you. Just don't tell Fitz. I don't want him to think I'm anti-pug."

"That's a tall order. He's my best friend, even if he hogs the bed."

"How big is your bed?" The innocent question sounded more suggestive than she meant. Blushing, she twisted and looked out the window.

"Big enough." He cleared his throat, making her turn, wide eyes meeting his winking ones.

Oh dear.

The morning air was already thick. The forecast called for near ninety-degree temperatures for the next few days. She'd dressed appropriately, but her running shorts and exposed sports bra strap poking out from her tank top somehow made her feel naked. Elle tugged the hem of her shorts, feeling the caress of his side-eye gaze.

He's so checking me out. Wait, do I want to be checked out?

"Fitz must be so disappointed in Natalie for becoming a human doctor," Elle said referencing Clayton's sister, who was completing her residency in Boston.

The joke was an attempt to ease the sexually charged energy in the pickup, but there was a new tension punctuated with the clench of Clayton's jaw. Everyone, including Elle, had assumed he'd grow up to be his dad. Even if she'd witnessed him go green in the gills at the sight of her blood in high school, it had seemed a pre-destined role for him. Only he hadn't fulfilled that prescribed destiny.

Questions swirled within her at his mournful expression. She bit the inside of her cheek, fighting back the urge to ask.

"Belly rubs soothe all of Fitz's disappointments," he said, his tone quiet.

"I may need to try that." She shot him a smile, which he returned. "I always liked your little sister, even if she used too much glitter on her projects at day camp. She'd insist everything needed sparkles." She wiggled her fingers like jazz hands. "Didn't matter what it was. She once made a football mobile with rainbow glitter. Glitter was everywhere but on her. Somehow, I had it all over me, even in my bra. No idea how it got there, but I had bedazzled rainbow boobs."

The tense muscles lining Clayton's face eased, a rumbling laughter erupting as she gestured to her breasts. She grinned, choosing not to be embarrassed by the motioning to and speaking of her breasts. The relief that came with the relaxing of his rigidity was worth it.

"She used to do the same thing with frosting. Mom would find smudges and globs everywhere. We'd be covered, but she'd be spotless. I swear she's made of Teflon. Nothing sticks to her."

"I think I've heard you speak more since the barbecue than in the entire time I knew you growing up," she blurted. "I'm not saying you talk too much. I'm not complaining, not at all. I like it, it's nice. Now, I'm talking too much." A line creased her brow. *Where's my filter around this man?*

"I have a stutter," he whispered.

What? Elle shifted in the seat to face him.

"It was pretty bad when I was a little boy. It's why I went by CJ. Clayton was too hard to say. I would just stumble through my own name. My mom started introducing me to people as CJ, because I could say it without stuttering. My parents put me in speech therapy and slowly, very slowly, I learned to manage it. But it was easier to just not speak and to give one-word responses," he explained.

"I had no idea. I just thought you were grumpy and didn't like me. Well, that you didn't like anyone but Noah. I feel bad that I used to call you Oscar behind your back." Elle scrunched up her face in self-reproach.

"Oscar?"

"The Grouch."

"Makes sense." His eyes warm. "Noah's mom and my mom are best friends. I've known him forever. I have no memories of a life before Noah Wilson. My stutter never bothered him. He'd say it was just how I talked. He knew it bugged me though, so he never forced me to speak. When I did speak, he never looked at me in the way my parents or teachers did." A sad smile covered his face.

An uncomfortable fullness bloomed in Elle's chest. She placed her hand on her heart, picturing a tiny, stern-faced Clayton, his mouth drawn tight at the expectant stares of adults. Some waited for this little boy's words to stumble, while others for them to smoothly flow out of his mouth. Either way, a losing battle of expectations.

"We both had Ms. Lane for Kindergarten. I had to do

show and tell and was terrified. When Ms. Lane called on me, I remember feeling like I was going to puke. I got up, looked at the faces of the other kids, and already imagined their laughter in my ears. I just stood there. Then the whole class began laughing, but not at me. At Noah who was making fart noises against his arm. It distracted everyone and by the time Ms. Lane got control of the class, it was time to go to Art. He saved me."

"He had your back."

That uncomfortable fullness in her chest filled with a warmth for the dimpled-smile Noah Wilson coming to the rescue of his best friend. The sweet-natured boy that by default received the role of Mr. Bingley in her imagined high school version of *Pride and Prejudice* lived up to that role. The boy with ocean-blue eyes was one of the kindest boys she knew. Where other boys teased, Noah complimented. Where other boys were hard, he was soft. Where other boys' moods seemed to sway with the winds like flimsy tree branches, he was steady like an immovable oak.

"He always has. We're still good friends. I'm not close to most people from high school, but Noah…" he paused, shaking his head. "I can't get rid of him. My stutter sometimes comes out if I'm over-tired or emotional. You can't cure a stutter, but you learn how to deal."

"That's so true for so many things. What about Evan, your little brother? Is he as impressive as his big brother and little sister?"

The air shifted again as the pickup rumbled down the gravel road to a parking area. Turning off the engine, he fiddled with the keys while his throat bobbed up and down with unsaid words.

"He died." With Clayton's whispered response an ache grew in her heart.

The pale grey of his eyes darkened to weary storm clouds.

He clenched and unclenched his hands around the steering wheel as if locked in an inner debate; stay and speak or run.

Like a familiar book, she could read the question with each flex of his hand. She didn't know when she learned how to read him, but she could. She didn't ask how or when. She didn't offer any condolences. Words always failed in moments like this. Evan was dead and Clayton was sad. How do words fix that?

Pulling his hand off the steering wheel, she threaded their fingers. "We can sit here. We can be quiet. I could listen. Or we can run. You choose." She stared forward, not wanting to steer him in any direction but the one he chose to go.

"Thank y…" he started then stopped as he stumbled over the word.

She made no movement in recognition of his stumble. At that school dance so many years ago, his waiting arms caught her when she almost fell, and she would now catch him. Viet once told her that sometimes catching meant allowing someone to fall without saying anything.

Exhaling a shaky breath, he found his footing. "Thank you. Let's run."

"Ok." She reached for the door with one hand, while his hand held her other.

There was a tug as each reached for their doors bringing them to a halt. Elle was surprised to find she didn't want to let go.

SEVEN

"Now I must give one smirk, and we may be rational again."
~Jane Austen, *Northanger Abbey*

Elle sat at her desk at the Little Red Barn daydreaming about a boy like a teenaged girl. *Nope, not a boy. Clayton. A man.* She hadn't done that since high school when she fantasized about Noah Wilson. This was not the behavior of a thirty-six-year-old woman. Groaning, she dropped her head to the desk's surface knowing that at sixteen or thirty-six, a woman could be susceptible to infatuation. And she was infected.

The vibration of her iPhone disturbed her internal debate. Raising her head, she read the latest updates in her group text with Willa and Viet.

Viet: How's day one of teleworking from the sticks going?
Elle: Good. *Smiley emoji.*
Willa: Did you have to use carrier pigeons for your emails?

Elle: No, we have pony express.

She silently laughed, inserting a racehorse emoji.

Willa: Glad it's going well. How's hot farmer?
Viet: HOT FARMER?!

Her fingers hovered, as she thought how to respond.

Elle: We went running this morning.

Within seconds her phone buzzed with a video call request from Willa, which Elle accepted. "That was quick."

"I'm adding Viet, so hold on," Willa said.

Elle could make out the picture of the red sailboat drifting on calm waves that was a focal point of Willa's office.

Viet's angled face appeared. "I repeat. Hot farmer?"

"Turns out hot farmer is not a farmer, but a veterinarian, my temporary landlord, and Jerome's best man. I know him from high school."

"OMG! You're living in a Hallmark movie!" Willa swooned, throwing her head back dramatically, caramel locks tumbling.

"Wait, there's really a hot farmer?" Viet's mouth puckered.

"Dude! Keep up. She met him when she was attacked by the goat."

"You were *attacked* by a goat?" He bounced like he needed to pee.

"Yup."

"Welcome to Perry," Viet chuckled.

Unlike Willa, Viet had been to Perry a few times when they were in undergrad. They would drive down for a quick dinner or family event once in a great while. By the end of their four years of college, Elle chose to travel to Perry less and less often.

"So, you went running with the…I'm still going to call him hot farmer… this morning? Did you get sweaty?" Willa's voice dropped low and her face contorted to suggest something far more vigorous than a morning run.

"We ran. We talked. It was nice." Elle touched the petals of the large golden blooms basking in the afternoon sunshine. It was sweet how he got fresh bouquets for his guests each week. Sunflowers were perfect. They were simple, lovely, and grew wild. Like Clayton.

"What's that?" Willa pointed.

"What?" Elle twisted, half expecting someone or something behind her.

"That look on your face."

"What look?"

"That 'there's a piece of cake I want' look," Viet joined in.

"And by cake, he means dick." Willa held up a highlighter in a lewd gesture, making Viet and Elle groan.

"I don't know if I want the cake," Elle paused, taking in a slow breath. "I also don't know that I *don't want* the cake."

"Now I want cake." Willa nibbled her bottom lip.

"You always want cake," Viet taunted.

Willa lifted a manicured middle finger in reply.

Waving off Willa's non-verbal insult, he continued, "I know you and cake, Elle. You'll find any excuse not to have it. Too many calories. Not enough calories. It will go stale. It has—"

"Tiny coconuts," Willa interrupted.

"Exactly! Although, that one is valid. Elle, have the cake or don't. Just be open to cake."

Should I? It had been so long since Elle had cake. The metaphor stirred hunger pains in her belly and a clenching in her lady bits.

EIGHT

"Think only of the past as its remembrance gives you pleasure."
~Jane Austen, *Pride and Prejudice*

Elle's sling back sandals clacked against the pavement as she walked toward the front door of the Wine Down, the town's only wine bar. The red brick building the bar now occupied had sat unused throughout much of Elle's childhood. Just like many of the buildings along Main Street. After the textile mill, which had once employed most of the town's residents, moved its operations elsewhere, many people moved to find work and the mom-and-pop shops that had inhabited downtown disappeared.

In the last eight years, revitalization pushed into the village with new businesses opened by Elle's fellow Perry High School alumni. All spearheaded by the town's mayor. Perry may not be home, but she was impressed with its scrappiness. The renovated and thriving downtown spoke of a feisty will to succeed.

As Elle walked through the bar's wood framed glass door, a tall spiky red-haired man with a name tag proclaiming him

Todd greeted her. With little ceremony, he presented her with a single-page glossy menu and motioned around the mostly empty bar.

"Good luck finding a seat," he snarked.

It was seven on a Tuesday in Perry. There'd be none of the hustle and bustle of Long Beach. Despite the town's rebirth, most businesses buttoned up by eight during the week.

Elle perused the menu. Everything originated in the area. She, of course, ordered the rosé from a small winery in the Finger Lakes.

"Rosé the night away," Todd said, lips raised in a wry grin as he deposited the glass on the oval-shaped table Elle sat at. Like everything in Perry, there was something both familiar and new about him.

Elle sipped the sweet rosé and scanned the bar. The space was lit by a single chandelier and the evening sun streaming in from oversized windows. Todd stood flipping through a book at the mahogany bar. Silver framed pictures of Perry-ites toasting wineglasses in various locations around the village dotted the violet walls.

"Ms. Lucas!" Carmen's musical voice waltzed into the quiet bar.

"Ms. Bennet!" Elle replied, using their old nicknames.

In high school, her two best friends, Carmen Herrera and Beth Lake, formed the Jane Austen Sisterhood. Their deep love of everything Ms. Austen led each to adopt the name of the character that best fit their personality. Carmen was the Jane Bennet to Beth's Lizzie and Elle's Charlotte. Jane Austen had both brought and kept them together. Anything Austen or Austen-adjacent facilitated a text, call, or email.

"I can't believe you are here." Carmen squeezed hard, swaying in a dancing hug, her floral scent twining around them.

"Ditto."

Elle pulled away, examining Carmen. Dark curls tumbled over her slim shoulders and her brown skin glowed against a sunshine-yellow sundress. Carmen had always been gorgeous, even when nobody else saw it. She was also brilliant, skipping one grade in school and completing four years of college in three.

"I see you ordered the rosé. It's very popular," Carmen said, taking the chair across from Elle.

"It's great. This place is adorable. So many new businesses in town. I haven't explored much, but I saw a bookstore/coffeeshop and some boutiques when I drove in. You've done well, Madam Mayor." She raised her glass in salute.

After earning her MBA, Carmen moved back to Perry and worked with businesses across the region. She worked her magic with local businesses and the entire community, organizing events and fundraisers. Eight years ago she was elected as Perry's mayor, a role she'd maintained unopposed since.

"I am loving these photos." Elle pointed to one of Janet taken at the Village Rose.

"Mathew took them." Carmen's eyes grew starry at the mention of her husband.

It still seemed unreal that the sweet and studious Carmen married the clownish Mathew Fischer, the same boy who had once run through a pep rally dressed in wings and bumble bee boxers over a black unitard. Like chocolate covered bacon they were an odd pairing, but they worked. Despite keeping Herrera as her surname, she burst with pride to be married to Mathew Fischer.

"Can I get you something, Madam Mayor?" Todd shouted from the bar.

"Rosé and the cheese board for the table. Thank you, Todd." She turned back to Elle. "The cheese board is so good. All local cheeses and meats."

"Remember how we'd drink Welch's grape juice out of your mom's fancy glasses with cheddar cheese, Ritz crackers, and Doritos? We thought we were so classy."

"We were very classy teenagers. We watched PBS." Carmen preened a bit, until interrupted by Todd bringing her wine to the table.

"Here's to classy girls, who grew up to be badass broads." They clinked their glasses.

"You look great. How are you?"

"I'm good. Work is good." Elle shrugged.

"I know you're good, but how are you, really?" Carmen leaned close, placing her hand on Elle's.

"I hate that you know me so well." Elle blew out a pent-up breath. "I'm not going to lie; it is weird being here. Like there are memories around every corner. Maybe it's been too long or not long enough. I feel like a snow globe toggling between being shook and sitting still. It's just..." Elle searched for the right word.

"Weird."

"Weird," she agreed.

"Can I address the Mommy Dearest elephant in the room? Will you be seeing her? How are you handling this?"

"Uncle Pete brokered a deal. He's like Switzerland. We will remain on opposite sides of the room, for the wedding and for Pete's birthday. She has been instructed to not cross the no-fly zone, to stay the fuck away from me."

"Ooh, you said fuck." Carmen lowered her voice as she uttered the vulgarity. "You mean business."

The fidgety crossing and uncrossing of Elle's legs was a poor attempt to self-soothe. Conversations about her mom were so much easier to have when the threatening thunderstorm of seeing her didn't loom. It wasn't just the guarantee of seeing her at Tobey's wedding and Uncle Pete's birthday but that each time she left the Little Red Barn, she played Mama Russian Roulette.

"Yes, I do," Elle said, her tone slick as ice.

Carmen squeezed Elle's wrist. "I know she hurt you, and I'll never understand how you feel. But is there any part of you that misses her?"

"Colin Firth." It came out almost as a croak.

It was their safe word. Beth had come up with it after seeing *Bridget Jones' Diary*. It was the signal that someone didn't want to talk about something. No questions would be asked, they'd simply repeat the safe word and change the subject.

"Colin Firth," Carmen sighed.

Elle offered a grateful smile.

"What are you wearing for Tobey and Jerome's wedding? If your social media and this outfit are any indication, you will be the best dressed. It's so funny to think that the girl who lived in hoodies and sneakers wears dresses and heels."

"I even wear sexy lacy panties these days." A prideful smile formed as Carmen's eyes widened with mortification.

Elle startled at the masculine clearing of a throat behind her, confirming Carmen's "clutched pearls" face was not *at* Elle but *for* Elle. She said a silent prayer that Clayton's gray eyes wouldn't meet hers as she turned around. Although maybe she wanted him to know about her sexy underwear.

Oh no! Turning, she did not find Clayton. Rather, Noah Wilson stood, hands in the pockets of his well-fitting jeans, bemusement glinting in his blue eyes. A smirking Mathew Fischer beside him.

Elle's pulse thrummed at the sight of Noah. A red T-shirt stretched over a broad chest. Its short sleeves showed off his defined biceps and forearms.

God, what is it about forearms that gets me going?

Noah slipped into the seat beside her. "Eleanor, it's been a long time. How are you?"

Light revulsion churned in Elle's belly at the use of her birth name. To so many in Perry she was still Eleanor. Even to her family.

"I've been good. How about you?" she asked nonchalantly, trying to avoid Carmen's "OMG!" gaze.

"Todd, can we get the usual?" Noah called to the bartender.

"Oh, did you order—"

"The cheeseboard? Of course," Carmen interrupted her husband with a sweet smile.

"Such a boss!" Mathew fist pumped the air.

Noah tapped his fingers on the table. "Mathew mentioned that you're in town for a while."

"Remember Elle is Coach Coates's niece. She's in town for Tobey's wedding and Pete's fiftieth birthday," Carmen explained.

"I heard you're staying at Clayton's." The corner of Noah's mouth curled almost in accusation.

"I'm not staying *at* Clayton's. Like, I'm not in his guest room but renting the Little Red Barn."

"I'd bet he'd let you if you asked. Just that kind of guy… Always ready to help."

Elle's lips pursed at Mathew's words. She wasn't sure why Clayton doing something for her out of pure kindness instead of because of her caused a twinge in her chest. Open kindness shouldn't be frowned at, but she was frowning.

That was who Clayton was, a nice man that helped others. The running invitations were just an extension of his do-gooder nature. The thought deflating something in Elle's chest.

"What have you been up to, Noah?" Elle sipped her wine.

"Oh, bossman here owns this place," Todd snarked, placing the cheeseboard and two glasses of red wine on the table.

"Bossman?" Noah's eyebrow quirked. "You never call me Noah. It's Wilson or some sort of nickname."

"Save it for my performance review. Yell if you need anything." Todd sauntered away.

"You own this place?"

"Yup."

"It's amazing. The vibe, the wine, and the cheese board." Elle gestured around the space with a piece of gouda.

"Yeah. I can't take credit. I've had a lot of support."

"Don't be so modest. This is your baby. Noah is Perry's very own Mark Cuban, only minus the billions, basketball team, and TV show." Mathew paused, with a pained look on his face.

Elle had no doubt that his sweet-smiled wife had kicked him underneath the table.

Undeterred, he continued, "He owns this place and the bakery. He's also opening a brewery."

"You are kind of a big deal." Elle's smile widened.

"*Hardly.*"

Elle nudged Noah with her shoulder. "Nothing wrong with celebrating your accomplishments. It doesn't mean you don't acknowledge the help from your team. They wouldn't help you if you weren't worth it."

"Elle's accomplished too. She's an executive with Sloan-Whitney. They have hospitals and clinics across the country." In an uncharacteristic move Carmen bragged.

They're trying to Cupid us! Elle's eyes narrowed, noticing Mathew mouth *nice* to his wife.

"Your turn to take a bow." Noah winked.

Elle replied with a quick head bow.

Shortly after nine, the humid summer air their only companion, Elle strolled with Noah down the empty street. Teenaged Elle would have died, flattened by hormones exploding, from being alone with him. An ease settled inside her at his proximity.

"I'm just here. You really don't need to walk me." She pointed to her car down the street.

"It's not a problem." He placed a protective hand on her lower back, guiding her to the crosswalk. "So, what should I call you? I heard Mathew and Carmen call you Elle."

"Elle. Most people here still call me Eleanor, but my friends call me Elle."

"Elle it is."

The streetlight highlighted Noah's defined features, the dusting of dark stubble accentuated his strong jawline and reassuring warm eyes. A dimple still punctuated his smile. Noah Wilson was the quintessential leading man from any romcom.

Not handsome enough to tempt me. Mr. Darcy's words about Lizzie Bennet whispered in her ears. Unlike Mr. Darcy, who was lying to himself and everyone else about his feelings for Lizzie, this was Elle's truth. The smile and eyes that ignited a flutter in her belly did not belong to Noah Wilson. Not anymore.

"Goodnight, friend." Her words were a simple declaration.

NINE

"There is nothing I would not do for those that are really my friends. I have no notion of loving people by halves, it is not in my nature."
~Jane Austen, *Northanger Abbey*

The humidity broke with a clap of thunder at a little after four a.m. Though the storm did not jolt her awake. She'd slept on-and-off most of the night. Instead of trying to lull herself back to sleep with a book, she lay listening to the gentle hum of the air conditioner and increasing volume of approaching thunder. Rain was rare in Long Beach. It was a luxury to listen to the tap-tap of fat drops on the roof.

Pulling the soft cotton sheets up so they were snug around her body, she counted between claps and flashes to assess the storm's distance. A voice in her head, eerily similar to her dad's told her that nothing could get her if she kept her blankets tight around her.

How wrong he'd been.

Elle kicked the memory away with the sheets. Dull gray

light of a rainy sunrise filtered into the room. Rain was fore-cast for the entire day. There would be no run with Clayton, just a solo yoga session in the living room. Should she text him? Would he want to do yoga? This was all new and scary. Opening her contacts, she selected *Fitz's Human* and messaged him.

Elle: Good morning. Looks like yoga is forecasted for today.

She added a frowny face emoji.

An hour later, as Elle lay in corpse pose on her mat in the living room turned makeshift yoga studio, a gentle knock came at the door. *Had Uncle Pete come to inspect the state of the roof to ensure it wasn't leaking?* She laughed at herself, rising and walking to the door.

"Good morning." Clayton stood beneath an umbrella with a perturbed Fitz tucked under his arm.

"Morning?" Her head tilted.

"You look confused."

"I am. It's raining."

"Like cats and dogs." His gaze drifted up and then back to Fitz.

"Is that veterinarian humor?" she chuckled.

He smirked.

"Did you get my text?" She leaned against the wet door frame, the cool slickness refreshing against her sweaty skin.

"Yes, but I believe there was a post-workout Fitz playdate included in your Airbnb package." Clayton set Fitz on the porch, the pug puffing out an annoyed snort.

His gaze dropped to his four-legged companion and then back to Elle. The warm gray of Clayton's eyes matched the morning's sky with breaks of sunshine forcing itself through.

Her lips tugged up. "I'll make tea."

Elle sat cross legged on the floor, her back against the green couch, sipping peppermint tea. Clayton sat beside her, his long legs stretched out.

"Does he ever stop being entertaining?" Elle asked, listening to the sounds of Fitz's snoring, his little legs moving as if trotting along in his dreams.

"Fitz is endlessly distracting. The distraction and chewed sneakers are worth the price of admission, though." Pure unabashed love radiated from Clayton as he glanced at the pug.

"I hope he doesn't have a taste for high heels."

"Hasn't eaten any of mine yet," Clayton joked, a mischievous glint in his eyes.

"Ooh, we may have to go shoe shopping sometime," Elle said, cheekily.

He chuckled. "I don't know how you walk in heels. Nat used to con Evan and me into playing dress up. That girl had us wrapped around her finger. I don't know how anyone walks in those things." His lips curled with the mention of his sister.

"That explains so much."

Clayton's eyebrow quirked.

"In day camp, we asked the kids to draw a picture of their family. I don't know why I remember this, but Natalie's picture had what I thought were three little girls in dresses. Now, I realize two of those girls were Evan and you."

"Was there glitter?" His chest rumbled with soft laughter.

"Over everything."

A wistful expression covered his face. "The lengths we'd go to make her happy."

"How far?"

"One time, she'd found glitter eyeshadow leftover from Halloween, I guess, and smeared it all over my face. I looked like a deranged clown," he groaned. "Evan found us and threatened to take a picture. By the time he found a camera with film, I'd cleaned up. Thank god we grew up before cell phone cameras were a thing. He teased me for being a pushover, but he was Nat's next makeover."

Elle joined in his laughter. "I would have loved having a big brother, I think. Uncle Pete is fourteen years older than me and can be like a big brother. Although, I think it's different when you're closer in age and grow up in the same house. He had already moved out by the time we moved in with my grandparents."

Oh, god, just shut up. Elle drank the last of the now luke-warm tea to stop her rambling. She seemed to have no filter when speaking to Clayton, like pulling open the curtains to show him inside her house, the clothes strewn on the floor, dirty dishes, and unmade bed.

Clayton nodded. "But an uncle is more of a grown up. A big brother is going through it with you."

"I just would have wanted someone to be in it with me." She was losing the battle to keep her voice from cracking.

Clayton scooted closer, placing his hand in hers just as she had done the morning of their first run. The gentle squeeze of his fingers communicated the same words she spoke the day before. Her heart and logic fist-fought, the heart wanting to speak and logic wanting the words to remain tucked within. For so long, it had been up to her to carry her own burdens, her own sadness. The pads of his thumb coaxed her to speak or maybe she just wanted them to coax her.

"How much do you know?" she murmured.

"Some."

Steadying her voice, she focused on a wooden framed photograph of baby goats on the wall. "It's no secret my dad left. We didn't know it at the time, but he was messing around with a nurse at St. Luke's where he worked. Of course, he didn't mention any of that in the note he left for us. He just left and mom fell apart. I don't know what your parents told you…"

Clayton's mouth opened but closed just as quick, as if he wanted to say something but thought better of it.

Elle studied her kneecaps, continuing, "She tried to kill herself and I found her. Of course, she told your dad and everyone else it was an accident, but I knew the truth. I found her, and the note addressed to Dad." Elle gritted her teeth. Just like his note was to Mom, not one goodbye to her. *Is that what hurts the most?*

Clayton clasped her hand as she continued to explain.

After her mom came back from the mental health facility two weeks later, there were promises that it would all be different. Mom would find someone to make it all better, to make them a family again. At twelve, Elle wanted to believe her mom, but her stomach had pinched with nauseous doubt. It was difficult to trust her mother's frowning lips and vacant eyes that seemed to look beyond Elle, rather than at her.

"Sorry." Elle whispered, fearing anything louder would dislodge that lump in her chest and break the dam on her emotions. The sorry was for so much. For his quiet patience sharing her sadness, when he didn't have to. For her twelve-year-old self who wasn't asked to give up childish things but rather had those things ripped away.

Clayton scratched Fitz's belly. "You asked me what my parents told me. It was a Wednesday. I don't know why I remember that." He shook his head. "I was sitting in the kitchen doing homework and Nat and Evan were in the living room playing. My folks came home, and mom just stared at me for a long time making me feel like I'd done something wrong. She asked if I knew you." He placed her hand in his lap, absently massaging it, the hard lump in her throat dissolved with each slow circle across her skin. "When I told her I did, she looked at me with this expression that at the time I couldn't place, but now I know as admiration. She said you were the most beautifully strong-hearted young woman she had ever met."

"Wow." Her whispered response was breathy.

The day Mom had been admitted, Mrs. Owens had pinned her with a questioning stare when Elle defied the request for her to remain in the waiting room while Aunt Janet ushered her dazed mom into the clinic exam room. It *had* been a Wednesday.

"I knew of you before that day, but never really noticed you 'til then. After that all I could do was notice you." His admission drew her surprised gaze to his face. He tipped up his chin. "Mom was right, you were...are strong. Not to sound like a self-help book but being strong doesn't mean doing it alone or holding it all in. You said you wanted someone to be in it with you. I.... I think I'd like to do that for you. With you."

Elle's breathing sped up. *He's just that type of guy.* Mathew's words from the previous night slowed her pulse.

"You are a good big brother. I hope Natalie doesn't mind if I borrow you." Elle sighed, eyes closed, head lying on his shoulder. It was kindness, nothing more. Just another friend, like Noah.

"Of course."

"He's like the best therapy. You should charge." she said, raising her head to lift and cradle Fitz in her arms.

"No charge."

"Thank you." That faint aroma of citrus filled her senses, cleansing away the lingering sadness. Once more her head found his shoulder and his arm draped around her as they settled into each other.

TEN

"I may have lost my heart, but not my self-control."
~Jane Austen, *Emma*

"I don't know how many times I have to remind Wanda from accounting that my pronouns our they/them." Braedon took their black rimmed glasses off, placing them atop their head before pinching the bridge of their nose.

Elle frowned. Most people at Sloan-Whitney were respectful of preferred pronouns but there were still some that required a repeat lesson in etiquette.

"I'll speak with the head of accounting," she offered, twisting the blinds closed to combat the glare from the late afternoon sun that obscured Braedon's face on her laptop screen. She'd spent the afternoon working with them via video call.

"Already handled. They'll be sending Wanda to a two-day HR training." They waved a dismissive hand. "Also, did I mishear you earlier? Are you going to the VFW? That's a real thing? Not just something in cheesy small town romance novels?"

"It's real."

"Go figure." Braedon's forehead wrinkled. "Aren't VFW's a private club for Veterans?"

"I have a guy."

"*A VFW guy?*"

"Is there any other?"

They threw their hands up. "I can't with you right now!"

"*Jealous?*"

"How does one get a VFW guy?" Braedon tapped their chin.

"It's not as fancy as it sounds. Anyone can be a member of the VFW."

Elle shifted in the chair, trying to loosen her tight muscles. She may not survive a month working in a chair that was closer to an antique torture device than the comfy ergonomic chair at her desk back in L.A. How had Jane Austen written five novels in a chair like this?

"I'm still going to tell people you have a VFW guy. It makes you sound mysterious." Braedon motioned at the screen. "Found a great deal online for an ergonomic chair. Want me to have it delivered?"

"I do, but I should probably make sure it's okay with the owner."

"I already spoke with Dr. Owens, and he's signed off."

"You what? How?"

They gave her an "are you new here?" look. Of course, They'd spoken to Clayton. Braedon was the best assistant.

"I Veronica Mars'd who the owner was and found his contact info. I spoke with him earlier today and explained that I had concerns about debilitating back injuries from that chair. I might have dangled a potential lawsuit to make him see the light."

"You did not!"

"Nah. I explained who I was and that I was concerned

for your comfort. He shared the concern and said he'd go purchase a chair for you and asked me for recommendations. He was very nice and had a 'hot guy' voice." A salacious grin stretched across their face.

Elle rolled her eyes.

"I told him that I would speak with the boss, AKA you, before any course of action was decided."

"I appreciate your proactive thoroughness. Let me talk to Clayton and I'll let you know about the chair."

"Clayton? I see from the blush on your cheeks he has a face that matches that 'hot guy' voice."

"Back to work." She wagged her finger.

Around six, Elle ended her workday and changed to head to the VFW. Smoothing her sleek low ponytail and throwing on a denim jacket over her mint-green sundress, she stepped into the cool evening. Yesterday's thunderstorm had popped the humidity bubble that had engulfed Perry for the first few days of her trip.

The cooler weather had been perfect for this morning's run with Clayton at the Silver Lake Outlet Trail. After their run, they grabbed to-go breakfast at Cassie's Corner Café. Sitting at the table in the Little Red Barn, Elle spooned up her yogurt parfait, while Clayton ate his breakfast burrito. Comfortable silence and laughter over Fitz's blatant begging for food flowed between them.

Smiling at the memory, Elle pulled into the VFW's parking lot. The red trimmed brown building stood on Washington Street, behind Daryl's Pizzeria. The fragrance of pizza elicited memories of slices with friends, schooling Tobey at pinball, and Uncle Pete raising a glass of Pepsi in celebration of one of her Academic Bowl wins.

Memories flooded her senses as she walked into the VFW. The coo of her mom's voice coaxing her to smile for photos with Santa, the smell of fish fry dinners, and the feel of dad's rough hands twirling her across the dance floor during Uncle Pete's wedding. The VFW banquet room had been the epicenter of so many milestones for her first eighteen years of life.

One of the last big events she'd had here was her high school graduation party. Blue and yellow balloons, an ode to the school's colors, tied to chairs and tables lined with streamers had filled the banquet room. It wasn't the intimate pizza party at Daryl's with her family and her two best friends that she wanted, but her mom had pushed. Well, Jamie, her mom's boyfriend at the time, insisted saying what Elle wanted was boring. If it was between Jamie or Elle, her mom picked Jamie… *Every time.*

"Eleanor!" Uncle Pete called, his big hands waving.

Elle slipped into the bar's seating area. High-top tables surrounded the two dartboards, providing the perfect view of tonight's action.

"Hope you haven't eaten. We ordered a bunch of wings," he said.

"Don't you own a pair of jeans? That sundress is a little fancy for VFW darts," Janet, who was dressed in jeans and a floral top, tutted.

"No such thing as too fancy for the VFW," Elle quipped.

"Eleanor! You're here," Jerome's deep voice boomed as he picked her up in a swinging hug.

The relentless affection was the love language of each member of her little family. There were hugs, kisses, squeezes, and full-body clenches with every greeting, goodbye, and in-between moments. Elle tried to melt into them, fighting her natural impulse to pull away.

"Bear! We talked about this, stop manhandling people," Tobey scolded, but replaced his fiancé's arms with his own, drawing Elle close to his firm chest.

"I'll manhandle you later," he said with a suggestive wink.

"Not 'til you're married," Pete and Janet warned in unison.

"You look so fancy, Lady Eleanor," Jerome said, ignoring his parents-to-be and twisting his finger for her to twirl.

Shrugging, she complied catching an "I told you so" look from Janet as she spun. "Not as fancy as you. Is that a team shirt?" she awed at the navy *Team Paw Patrol* T-shirt featuring a dog and cat with backwards baseball caps. "Tobey, where's your team shirt?" She pointed at Tobey's plain T-shirt.

"Dad and I just wear black shirts. It's our vibe, we're not so in your face." Tobey flicked the end of Jerome's nose. "We are channeling our inner Johnny Cash. We're Team Walk the Line."

"I want team shirts, but this one won't sign off," Pete grumbled, tussling Tobey's hair as if he was still a little boy instead of a grown-ass man.

"Team T-shirts just distracts from our can't lose strategy." Tobey smirked.

"What's that?"

"Hit the bull's-eye," Tobey and Pete hooted jointly. Their over-the-top high five causing everyone else to roll their eyes.

"It's the same strategy Churchill had in WWII. Don't lose," Janet snarked.

"Nice historical burn, mom." Jerome fist bumped Janet, whose eyes brimmed with tears.

"Is it the first time he's called her mom?" Elle turned to her cousin and uncle, who were shaking their heads. "Yep, we're going to need a lot of tissues for this wedding. She's going to be in a puddle on Saturday."

"Just like the Wicked Witch of Western New York that she is," Jerome teased, placing a kiss atop Janet's head.

"The moment is over." Janet pushed him away.

"Do they do this a lot?" Elle asked, her eyebrow cocked.

"Yep." The tiny group laughed in unison.

"I'm going to need a drink to handle you people and beer makes me bloat, so I'm going to grab something at the bar."

"They don't have Dom Pérignon here, Ms. Fancy No-Pants," Janet bellowed as Elle headed toward the bar.

Zigzagging between the mix of tables and patrons, Elle approached the well-used bar. A blue Dutch door separated the long counter from the banquet room that held so many memories from Elle's youth. A yellow glow of hanging lamps lit the room with a sense of comfortable casualness reminiscent of a pair of well-worn jeans.

The last time she had been here was a week after her twenty-first birthday. Uncle Pete bought Viet and her their first legal drink here.

"What can I get you, honey?" The backwards cap-wearing bartender drawled.

"Can I get a Ketel One and soda?"

"We don't have Ketel One."

"Oh, how about Tito's?"

"Sweetheart, this is a VFW." The bartender smirked.

"Vodka soda with whatever you have, please." Noticing the pitcher of beer at their table was getting low, she thought a refresher would be needed to fuel Janet's cheers and the guys' aim. Just like her uncle, she was always anticipating her people's needs. "Can I also get a pitcher of Genny Lite? Thank you. What's your name?"

"It's Laney. You?"

"It's Eleanor." She winced. "Uh…Elle, I mean. Sorry.

Legally my name is Eleanor, but I go by Elle." She bit her lip to stop her runaway blurting.

"Nice to meet you Eleanor uh Elle," Laney sassed, placing the drink in front of Elle. Then she filled a pitcher with foamy beer.

"Thank you. How much do I owe you?" Elle asked, digging her wallet out of her purse.

"No worries, it's on him." Laney shot a glance behind Elle.

She turned to find a sly smile, gray eyes, and a Team Paw Patrol T-shirt hugging a muscular chest. "Clayton." A far-too-big smile invaded her face.

"Elle." His was equally large.

"I didn't see you when I came in."

"Bathroom." His voice dipped low, somehow making the word "bathroom" sound sexy. Inching closer, he caged her between his strong arms and the bar. "Let me carry this." His hot breath kissed below her ear as he spoke.

Clayton straightened, stepping back with the pitcher in one hand and her drink in the other. His gaze was pinned on her, the air between them sizzled.

Calm yourself, Elle!

"I can carry things," she protested, scrunching her face at the lackluster retort, she took her drink from his hand.

"I know... Just sharing the load."

Her heart *thump-thumped* at the flirtatious nature of his tone. "So, you're the other half of Team Paw Patrol?"

"Will you be cheering for us?" he asked, his mouth curled into a playful grin.

"I'm Team Walk the Line."

"What would Fitz say?"

"I'll just give him belly rubs. I hear it's very effective." Her voice was breathy. The ghost of Marilyn Monroe was in possession of her again. Leaning into it, she gazed over the brim of her plastic cup and batted her lashes, trying to appear sexy and aloof despite the urge to blanche at the sour taste of what was, no doubt, moonshine.

"Extremely effective." The deep timbre of his voice vibrated across her body.

They were flirting. She knew this. Men just being nice didn't have hungry eyes that devoured a woman as if she were the last piece of cake. Clayton looked at her like she was covered in frosting.

"Doc, you want to settle now or after?" Laney's voice popped their flirty bubble.

She was in the middle of the VFW, ten feet away from her family, eye fucking Clayton. Molten heat flamed in her face. What was this man doing to her?

"After." He cleared his throat, a light pink dusting his cheeks.

At least, Elle wasn't alone in uncontrollable blushes. He had promised to be in it with her, and it appeared he was taking that promise to heart. Even when it came to eye fucking at the VFW.

"Well, you know where I'll be," Laney quipped, turning to help another patron.

"So, I heard you had the distinct pleasure of speaking with my assistant, Braedon." Elle said, regaining non-eye fucking footing.

"Twice." He held up two fingers for emphasis. "Braedon called again as I was parking here to tell me that they had conferred with Ms. Davidson and was awaiting a final decision and that they'd follow up with me on Monday upon your return to the office on the status of said decision."

Elle placed a hand over her eyes. *Oh, Braedon.* "They're an amazing assistant. Maybe a little overzealous at times, but the best."

"I think I need a Braedon," he mused.

Warmth fizzed in Elle at both the impressed expression that covered Clayton's features and with his use of Braedon's preferred pronouns. In meeting new people, Braedon always introduced themself with their preferred pronouns. There'd be no HR training for Clayton.

She beamed. "Everybody needs a Braedon."

"How do you think they'd feel about running a small town veterinarian clinic?"

"I will fight you in the streets!" She poked his very firm chest and lost her train of thought over the images of burying her face against that chest. *Calm your loins, Elle!*

"Consider me warned."

"We should get back to the table. You have a dart game to lose," Elle teased with a sassy bump of his shoulder with hers.

"Oof, you wound me." His hand covered his heart.

Shaking her head, she stepped around him, threading through the crowded bar. Falling in step, Clayton's hand found the small of her back, guiding her to their table. Heat rippled from where his hand was pressed, traveling up her spine and reverberating everywhere. Reaching the table, his hand remained fixed until she sat in the chair beside Janet. He stayed close, just a step behind her. The heat radiating from his body to hers warmed her in an unfamiliar sensation of belonging, like they wore matching team shirts. It was foreign but not unwelcome.

"Owens!" Both Elle and Clayton looked to see Noah strolling their way.

"Wilson." The two men greeted each other with the standard male back slapping hug.

"Elle." Noah bent, hugging her.

"I di... didn't know you two knew... were..." Clayton stuttered.

Elle fought the urge to grab his hand that rested on the

back of her chair and twine their fingers. To squeeze away whatever had tripped up his words, letting him know they were in it together. That would be too brazen. Leaning back, she allowed her ponytail to drape over his arm, the silky tendrils kissing his skin.

"I had drinks with Elle on Tuesday at the Wine Down," Noah said.

"Correction. I was having drinks with Carmen when Mathew and you crashed."

"Clayton!" Jerome waved dart filled hands to get his attention.

"I should go."

"Good luck," she murmured, touching his arm causing him to turn and mouth *thank you* before joining Jerome.

"Yeah, I should get over there. I'm playing with my dad. I'll see you ladies Saturday." Noah strolled away.

Aunt Janet elbowed Elle. "Either would be a good choice."

"Excuse me?"

"They're both good looking, successful, good looking, nice, good looking, single—"

"And live in Perry," Elle interrupted Janet, who was counting their attributes on each finger.

"Pish-posh, logistics. Did I mention good looking?"

Janet was the Perry version of Willa or maybe Willa was the Long Beach version of Janet; both were obsessed with Elle's love life. The term love life was probably too generous for Elle's romantic interludes, as that's all they were. There were brief moments of non-starters or quickly fizzled out relationships.

There had been a time when she daydreamed about romantic picnics with Noah in the park, when she'd been open to the idea of love. Open, but knowing that the frizzy-haired, glasses wearing, and heavyset girl wasn't the heroine of anyone's love story, not even her own.

It wasn't until she moved to Los Angeles for grad school with Viet that she learned that may not be entirely true. Leaving the emotional baggage in Perry, Elle felt it was time to lose her physical baggage. She'd started keeping a food log, making healthier choices. Just a slow walk on the treadmill, but after a few months that slow walk became a jog, then a sprint. In one semester, Elle had lost thirty pounds.

More confident, she'd attended a party with Viet wearing a red V-neck top that he'd picked out. The fabric had hung in a way that flattered Elle's transforming body. Drinking white wine out of a red solo cup, Elle had flirted for the first time with Devon, a first year law student. Walking arm-in-arm with Viet to their small apartment near campus, she'd lamented giving Devon her number and said if he asked her out, she'd say no.

Viet had rolled his eyes, telling her that there had been many men who'd wanted to date her, even before the weight loss, but she'd pushed them all away. With a frown she'd protested, but when Devon called two days later, she'd turned him down.

"I'm just saying they are both worth turning the bedroom TV off for," Janet said, winking and pointing a chicken wing at Elle before biting into it.

"Oh, I'm sure Uncle Pete would *love* to hear that."

"Honey, I always turn the TV off with your uncle." She puckered her lips suggestively.

"I lost my appetite." Elle dropped the wing she'd been about to bite onto the plate.

After darts, as she pulled into the Little Red Barn's driveway. A happy fizz in her belly from the night of endless affection from her people and those stolen glances with Clayton.

When was the last time her chest fluttered from the flirty quirk of someone's lips?

Smiling, she jumped out of the car and into the darkness outside. Her vision drawn by the distant white glow of the farmhouse's front porch light where Clayton stood, back turned to her, unlocking his door. Before entering, he pivoted and faced her. Was there enough moonlight for him to see her leaning against the car door watching him? Could he make out the rise and fall of her chest? Could he see how she nibbled her lower lip, biting off the urge to invite herself into his home?

She watched as he looked into the dark where she stood. He waved. With a shaky smile, she waved back making out his lips mouthing *Goodnight.*

"Goodnight," she whispered into the dark before turning to go inside.

ELEVEN

"Where the heart is really attached, I know very well how little one can be pleased with the attention of anyone else."
~Jane Austen, *Northanger Abbey*

C an't wait to see you all on Saturday! ~Love, Aunt Amanda.

An uneasy tremor hissed through Elle as she stared at the message from her mom on Tobey and Jerome's wedding page's message board. The phone slipped from her fingers, clattering onto the floor. Gasping for breath, she gripped the edge of the sink.

"You're fine," she panted, her self-soothing words were empty promises.

Like a prisoner on death row her time drew near. The easiness she'd been lulled into over the last few days with Clayton, family, and old friends extinguished. In twenty-four hours, she'd be in the same space with her mom.

"Breathe," she commanded herself, picking up her phone.

As administrator of the page, she had the power to make

the message go away but didn't have the power to make her mom go away. Taking in two reassuring breaths, she clicked *Delete* and then, *Yes* after the site asked her for confirmation of the action. She was sure. *So, fucking sure.*

"You're okay," she crooned in a self-soothing manner, hands shaking as she gathered her hair into a ponytail.

A knock sounded on the front door. She tossed the hairbrush aside and went to answer.

"Goo…" Clayton's greeting halted, his eyes studying her.

Elle tilted her eyes to avoid his concerned gaze. But his strong arms enfolded her into a protective embrace. Her body trembled with unshed tears that she refused to release.

He brushed an escaped tendril behind her ear. "We can stay here. I can listen. We can talk. We can run. You decide. Either way, I'm here. I'm with you."

He's with me. Enveloped in the steadying embrace of his promise, she debated allowing her anguish to come out with this man, who was so willing to catch her if she fell.

"Let's run," she said instead, not yet ready to be caught.

"Uncle!" she declared an hour later, collapsing onto the ground.

"I may die," Clayton groaned, falling beside her on the grass.

"It's a good place for a grave," Elle puffed, running her fingers in the crisp blades of grass. Long Beach's grass was brittle and coarse, but this felt decadent against her slick skin. "I think I've missed grass." Her head twisted toward Clayton.

They laid close enough to almost touch but far enough away to miss the heat of his presence. If only she'd let herself reach those few inches.

His mouth quirked. "They don't have grass in California?"

"Not like this. It's so silky."

"All this time I thought you brought ladies flowers. I could have saved so much money by just bringing them grass," he joked.

"Clearly you've been dating the wrong women."

"Clearly." A lopsided grin stretched across his face and her belly flipped.

How was this patient, kind, and thoughtful man divorced? *Not to mention good looking.* Elle's heart fluttered as Aunt Janet's words scampered into her thoughts.

"I shouldn't ask, but I'm curious." She gnawed her lip. "Your divorce…What happened?"

"You can ask me anything. Nothing much to tell. I was married and now I'm not."

"What was she like?" Elle asked, letting her curiosity and his permission lead her.

"Marianne and I met in Veterinarian school at Cornell. We were in the same study group. She was from Pittsburgh and lives there now. She preferred cats to dogs."

"Cats?" she guffawed.

"I know, a red flag," he chuckled. "We were friends, and then we dated. I loved her but not in the way you're supposed to."

"How were you supposed to love her?"

"Like Darcy loved Lizzie." A thoughtful smile curled his lips.

No further explanation was needed. Darcy and Lizzie's love hadn't been instant, even though the seeds were planted from their first meeting. It wasn't swoony; although, the story made many readers swoon. Darcy didn't recite poetry, bring flowers, or make cheesy romantic gestures. His was a quiet and enduring love of Lizzie, even when there appeared to be no hope that she returned the affection.

"You may read too many novels." She winked.

"Says the woman in two book clubs," he teased, tossing plucked grass at her.

"Hey! One of them is a professional book club so we only read nonfiction." She ripped a few blades of grass free and tossed them at him in playful indignation. Elle bit her lip, but allowed the question rattling inside her to come out. "If you knew she wasn't your Lizzie, why did you marry her?"

"Evan had died, and my mom was so sad. I think I just wanted to see her smile again. At the time, I didn't realize why I was doing it. We had been dating a few years and I thought..." He struggled upright and stared into his lap, refusing to meet her glance.

"When did you realize?"

He shrugged. "Marianne and I didn't fight. We just existed, doing the things couples do...getting married... buying a house. We were living in Ithaca at the time, and Noah had moved back here, so he'd drive up to see me from time to time. He saw it before I was willing to see it and told me I didn't love her."

"Wow."

"It wasn't anything about Marianne. He liked her. I liked her. Still do. We'll text every few months to check in. I worried about divorcing her but not about her. I knew she'd be fine, but I worried about what my parents would think. I ha...ha...had..." He closed his eyes tightly as if hiding, not from his stumbling words but from what they meant. "I didn't want to fail them. A few months later, we separated. I moved here. I moved in with Noah until the divorce was final and the house was sold. When I took over the clinic and then bought the farmhouse, Noah was with me every step of the way."

"I'm glad you have Noah. He's a good man."

"He's the better man."

He's not you. Those three words tapped against her closed mouth trying to get out, but she wouldn't let them.

"You're both good men," she said instead, reaching to squeeze his hand.

"You're pretty good yourself."

"I don't feel pretty good right now," she said playfully. "I mean here you are showing me your granny panties and—"

"Granny panties?" he laughingly interrupted.

"You know the stuff you don't put out there for everyone to see. Your granny panties."

"So, how do we rectify the granny panty situation?" Playfulness sparked in his eyes.

"I think it's only fair for you to ask me anything as well." Repositioning herself cross-legged, back straight, she braced for his question.

"Anything?" He drew out each syllable.

Elle looked at the sly glint in his eyes for a moment before nodding yes. Anxiety pulsed through her, but she'd meet his vulnerability with hers. There was so much he could ask. So much she wasn't ready to say about her mom, about herself but she'd take Viet's advice and be open.

"Do you want to go shopping for a desk chair Sunday afternoon?"

She burst out in relieved giggles. "You can ask me anything, and that's the best you can come up with?"

"There are no boundaries to anything. Plus, you need a better chair, and it is a good investment for the Little Red Barn to have a chair that won't hobble future guests. We could go Sunday after the post-wedding brunch. Braedon sent me some chair options and several locations in Buffalo where they can be purchased."

"I'm surprised they didn't send you a map to each store." Hearing his quick snort, she shook her head, knowing they'd indeed done just that. "I would happily accompany you to purchase a chair, but I am buying the chair and dinner after."

"But it's for my establishment."

"Because of my butt."

"But I'll be keeping the chair." He stood up, brushing grass off his backside.

"Consider me an investor, then."

"Deal." He put out his hand for her, lifting her to her feet.

"Deal," she replied with a grin.

"It's a date."

Had she just agreed to go on a date with Clayton? *Yep.*

TWELVE

"Life seems but a quick succession of busy nothings."
~Jane Austen, *Mansfield Park*

Bolstered by this morning's run with Clayton, Elle stopped at Daryl's Pizzeria on her way to Tobey and Jerome's house and picked up lunch. The rest of the day would be focused on wedding setup and the rehearsal dinner.

Pulling up to Tobey and Jerome's tree lined property, with its snatches of wildflowers and sloping hills, she smiled. Leafy trees danced in the breeze creating a romantic and whimsical setting perfect for a wedding or a production of *A Midsummer Night's Dream*.

"You are aware that I live alone and carry many bags at once from my car to my condo, right?" Elle grumbled as Uncle Pete rushed from the garage to help her with the bags of food.

"Don't remind me," he muttered.

"Does he do this to you too, or is it a girl thing?" She tipped her head to Tobey, who'd followed Pete out.

"It's worse when you live here." Tobey relieved her of a

carrier tray of drinks. "Lets himself in all the time to be sure we haven't left the toaster plugged in."

Elle laughed. "You should take away his key."

"Eleanor, this is Perry. We don't lock our doors. Wouldn't be neighborly," Pete scoffed, placing the bags of food on a table set up in the garage.

"You made sure I locked the door at the Little Red Barn!" she accused, hands on her hips.

"That's different; you're a girl." He cleared his throat. "Excuse me, a woman." His tone was self-congratulatory, as if calling her a woman instead of a girl made it less sexist.

"Never change, Uncle Pete." She pressed a soft kiss to his scruffy cheek. Despite the anxiety dully meandering within her, she was grateful to be here, to be with them.

"Aw, shucks." He kissed the top of her head and brought her in for a hug.

"Stop with the sap!" Tobey wagged a finger. "Eleanor you're my designated non-crier. Mom has cried three times already today, and it's barely noon. And don't get me started on *that* one."

"My baby is getting married," Pete mocked, chasing Tobey out of the garage with kissy-face noises.

"Oh good! You're here and finally wearing something appropriate. Nice shorts!" Janet burst into the garage from the house. She carried a broom, wielding it like a determined general leading troops into battle. "Okay folks! First, lunch. Then we work."

"Hello to you, too," Elle snarked with a playful expression.

"Boys, stop fooling around!" she chided Pete, who was either trying to hug or put his son in a headlock, maybe both.

They straightened at the "I mean business" tone of Janet's voice, each shifting blame to the other.

"Mom, did I hear you say lunch?" Jerome boomed, as he exited the house, a blue cap with *Groomy* in white block letters atop his thick black hair.

"Mom!" Janet sniffled, placing her hand over her heart.

"Jerome did it!" Elle pointed at the bewildered Jerome, his fiancé glowering at them both.

After several hours of arranging and rearranging the tables to Janet's exact specifications, Elle stood surveying what she prayed was the final configuration of the reception tent. Tobey and Jerome had left to pick Jerome's dad up at the airport.

Elle, Pete, and Janet stood in the center of a temporary wooden dance floor. Janet consulted her clipboard and mumbled to herself. They'd strung fairy lights throughout the large white tent. Crisp linen cloths covered the mixture of round and rectangular tables. Mason jars wrapped in white ribbon sat in anticipation of pink carnations. Tomorrow the flowers would be placed and the tea lights lit to complete the table decorations.

Soon, Pete and Janet headed inside to clean up for the rehearsal. Dinner would follow the dry run. Elle volunteered to wait for the bartending crew coming to set up for tomorrow's festivities. After, she'd head out to doll up for tonight's mini shindig.

Ten minutes later, Noah strolled into the tent followed by Todd. Elle had been texting with Willa and Viet, who were dying for Clayton updates.

"When you said you'd be at the wedding I assumed it was as a guest," Elle greeted Noah.

"Can't I be both guest and servant?" Noah teased with a lopsided grin.

"A man who wears many hats."

"And they all look good on Prince Charming here." Todd pinched Noah's cheeks.

"Prince Charming?" Noah groaned, his mouth open and brows lifted.

"If the crown fits." Todd flicked Noah's forehead.

"Ha!" Elle snorted. Yes, she snorted.

She was realizing that keeping her goofy and sometimes awkward self hidden was a losing battle, and she was fighting too many other battles with emotions and memories that wanted to come out. Losing this one in hopes of winning the more important one that she'd face the next day seemed a small concession.

"The bar can go over there." Elle directed them to set up the bar at the edge of the tent.

"I'll get Terry and Jasper from the truck. We'll bring everything over." Todd nodded and then smirked at Noah. "Don't worry Prince Charming, your minions got this. You go flirt."

"He's either the very best or the very worst employee," Elle mused as Todd sauntered away.

"He's actually my business partner."

Elle barked out a laugh. "Some partner."

"His constant verbal gut punches keep me from getting too full of myself." Shrugging, he scanned the space and let out an impressed whistle. "This place looks great."

"It's going to look even better tomorrow. So, are you the bartender tomorrow? Should I have complicated drink requests ready to stump you?"

"Nah. It will be Todd and Jasper. This is our first time bartending an event, so I just wanted to make sure setup went okay. We'll have wine from the Wine Down and some of the beers from the brewery," he explained, tapping the top of the chair and pulling it out for her to sit. He dropped onto the one across from her. "Not to be too nosey, but I noticed last night your family still calls you Eleanor. Have you asked them to call you Elle?"

"No." She shook her head.

To them, she would always be Eleanor. Asking them to use her preferred name bubbled the worry inside her. Like somehow being Eleanor to them and Elle to everyone outside of Perry kept the two worlds separate. Kept her separate. Even though, she allowed Carmen and Mathew to call her Elle... And asked Noah and Clayton to call her Elle. Somehow that seemed different, less risky.

"So, they don't know to call you Elle, then." Knowledge shimmered in his stare, like a secret he held of a truth she didn't want to yet share.

Noah Wilson was far more perceptive than she and others believed. That charming smile hid a deep well of understanding.

"So, you've been running with Clayton I hear."

"He's told you about our runs?" Her tone reminiscent of a teen asking a friend if the boy they like talked about them in PE.

"He's mentioned them."

Her cheeks heated. "Clayton showed me some safe running trails. Keeps me off the roads."

"Makes sense. He wouldn't want you running on the roads."

The solemn expression on Noah's face provoked a wave of realization to crash into Elle. "Is that how Evan died?"

Noah nodded. "He was hit by a semi-truck while jogging. When Nat called, I jumped on the first flight. I had just been discharged from the Marines and was living in San Diego. Clayton was working in Ithaca." He scrubbed a hand through his hair. "I think Clayton blames himself a little for not being here. I know"—he raised a hand to stop her protest—"he shouldn't, but you know Clayton. He has this drive to take care of the people he loves. He's like a golden retriever, loyal and protective."

Words always failed her in moments like this. She had a sprinkling of memories of Clayton from high school. A few of the effervescent Natalie from day camp. But only one of Evan. Two years younger, with an easy smile, swinging Elle across a square-dancing circle in PE. Anyone could see that Evan was a happy kid.

Noah sighed. "It was hard for him, Nat… the whole family."

The desire to wrap her arms around Clayton filled her. Hugs were a temporary balm, she knew that, but the urge filled her.

"Thank you for being there for him." She reached across, taking his hand in hers. "I'm glad he has you."

"I'm glad he has you," Noah said, his voice hopeful.

Does he have me? The thought stole Elle's breath.

After rehearsal, the crew headed to the Sea Serpent, a nautical-themed restaurant on the lake. The guys had opted for casual cocktails and small bites served in the lounge on the restaurant's first floor.

"Lady Eleanor." Jerome greeted her with a bow, followed by a bear hug.

Despite the strangle hold, she scanned the room. Pure magic, with lit candles and greenery. The burnt orange and purple of the setting sun streamed in through large windows overlooking the lake.

"Lord Jerome." She backed out of his embrace and dropped into a small curtsy.

"Looking lovely as always, milady." He affected a British accent. "Let me get a gander at this outfit." He let his gaze flow over the simple yet sophisticated lavender maxi-dress she'd decided to wear.

"Stop objectifying me. I'm not a piece of meat, sir."

"I'm aware you are a very smart and talented woman. I will ask you about your thoughts on Brexit and climate change after I ogle you in this getup."

"The only person you should be ogling is over there." She tilted her head toward Tobey, who stood with his back to them, near the small buffet table.

"Oh, I plan to do that for the rest of my life." A spark twinkled in his brown eyes as he admired his fiancé across the room.

"I am so glad he found you."

"Not as glad as I am that I found him."

"Stop! Tobey has me on strict no crying duty for the next twenty-four hours." She elbowed him. "Hey, I have something for you all. Where're all the parents and Clayton?" Elle looked around the room.

"Clayton is around somewhere. Mom and dad are upstairs with my dad talking to the manager about the post-wedding brunch. They should be back shortly. Here, let me take that. How rude am I? Don't tell my soon-to-be father-in-law."

Jerome took the six small shiny gold gift bags, and one bottle-shaped bag she'd clutched and placed them on a high-top table. The smaller gift bags contained a single flute with the still chilled bottle of champagne in the larger one, a celebratory token before tomorrow's festivities for the wedding party.

Clayton strolled in, stealing Elle's breath in his camel-colored slacks and a pale blue button up with sleeves rolled to his elbows. *Good god.* In the last six days, she had only seen him wear workout clothes, T-shirts, jeans, and shorts. Casual Clayton was handsome, but dressed up Clayton was knee-wobbling gorgeous.

He surveyed the room, as if looking for someone. When those piercing eyes caught her gaze, he paused, seeming to drink her up like she was the last sips of nourishing water in the middle of the desert. A lazy smile lit his face, making heat crawl up her torso. He walked, no—sauntered toward her with the grace of a prowling wolf.

"Hey," he murmured when he reached her side.

"Hey," she said breathlessly.

"Well, hello Jerome," Jerome joked with a slight grumble. They ignored him.

"Thank you." Clayton's eyes glimmered.

"For what?" She bit her lip.

"Lunch."

"They weren't supposed to say anything." Her cheeks flamed.

When she picked up lunch at Daryl's, she'd ordered several pizzas and buckets of wings to be delivered to the clinic for Clayton and the staff. She asked Big D, the pizzeria's owner, to keep the lunchtime benefactor anonymous.

"They didn't." He smirked.

"How did you know it was me?"

"I knew." He stepped close, his citrus scent almost caressed against her skin. "You look beautiful by the way."

"You too, but handsome." Hopefully nobody heard the loud drumming in her chest.

"Oh, Jerome, you look dapper in your green shirt. It brings out the chocolate in your eyes," Jerome quipped. "Why thank you for noticing."

Clayton rolled his eyes as Jerome went on having a conversation with himself.

"This will be lovely." Janet's voice filled the room as she walked in with Pete and Jerome's dad.

"Good, you're here. Lady Eleanor has something for us."

"It's just something small, but I wanted to give it to you all tonight before everyone arrived."

"This is awesome!" Tobey beamed, holding the flute in his hand, turning it to examine the engraved script proclaiming *House Coates-Evans* beneath a silhouette of a black lab.

Each flute had been handcrafted by a local business. She'd had one made for each parent, groom, and their best men.

"I love it!" Tobey pulled Elle into a side hug, kissing her temple. "I love you, cuz."

"I love you, too." She snuggled a little deeper into his side.

"Oh!" Janet squeaked, placing a hand over her mouth to stop her next sob fit.

"It was her!" Jerome pointed his flute accusingly at Elle.

"I come prepared. This will help." Elle pulled out the bottle of booze for a toast.

"Lady Eleanor, you do the honors," Jerome commanded, filling each glass.

"May winter never come." She raised her glass in a nod to their favorite television program, *Game of Thrones*. "But if it does, may the love between you keep you warm and away from white walkers."

THIRTEEN

"I have the highest respect for your nerves, they are my old friends."
~Jane Austen, *Pride and Prejudice*

Two hours of sleep, that's all Elle got last night. Excited happiness for Jerome and Tobey, laced with dread about seeing her mother. Like sunset, it was inevitable. Today she would see her mom.

Thank god for the distraction of being tasked to entertain Janet until the wedding. Elle had scheduled them for mani/pedis at a spa in Batavia, a small city about twenty minutes away. The agenda of nails, a short lunch at a little café, and hair salon ensured they'd be back to the house with two hours to spare to finish making themselves fabulous for the day.

"This is so nice," Janet purred with pleasure as the technician massaged her short legs.

"Agreed." Elle sighed, her muscles relaxing with the technician's soothing strokes.

"Not just the massage. That's nice, though." Janet looked

down with an appreciative smile at the tech working on her legs. "It's nice to get some one-on-one time with you. We never get alone time."

Elle blinked. It had been years since they had any kind of solo girl time. Most of her time with Janet included Pete and Tobey. Her weekly calls were with Pete, not Janet. When Janet came to Long Beach, it was with Pete.

"You're right. I'm sorry," Elle said, a long sigh slinking through her.

"Honey, no." Janet threaded her newly pink gel manicured hand in Elle's. "I'm not using my Jedi-mom mind tricks to make you feel bad. I'm just saying how nice this is."

"It is." Her lips curled in agreement.

"I guess what I'm saying is, I'd like to have one-on-one time with you more often. Like maybe our own video chats. I know I annoy you with my constant interruptions during your weekly chats with your uncle, but I just want you to know that I'm there for you." Elle started to protest but Janet forged on. "I know you don't need us to be there. I think I know that better than your uncle. I was there to see you go from little girl to woman in an instant. I was there." She choked back tears.

"I know you were there. I called you." Elle whispered. The memory scalded over her. *That* day, with her mom limp under the blankets, Elle's fingers had trembled as she'd dialed Aunt Janet.

"You can be so strong, so independent. You always have been. I remember being at Pete's football games in high school with your grandparents. You were always there, cheering loudly. You were like three or four and had to pee. I offered to take you, but you insisted you were big enough to go by yourself. I walked about a foot behind you just in case you needed me. All the way to the bathroom, you never looked back, not once."

"I don't remember that."

"You were so little but so determined to do it on your own. You still are."

"I overheard you tell Clayton during the barbecue that you worry about me."

"I do. Tobey will come to us when he needs us. You rarely did, and that has gotten more and more rare over the years. I worry because if we don't know if you need us, how can we help? How can we be there, and will you let us?"

"But you are. You're still a foot behind me every step of the way. Even if I don't turn around, I know." Elle turned to her weeping aunt.

"And we always will be. I know Pete and I aren't your dad and mom. I keep my thoughts to myself about your mother because she's Pete's sister. Your dad, however, is a dick."

"Ha!" She barked out a laugh.

"I don't know entirely what happened with your mom, and I don't expect you to tell me, but I know you have your reasons for staying away for so long. I may needle you about a few things…" At the sight of Elle's raised eyebrow, she relented. "Ok, many things, but not that. Whatever your reasons, I just want you to know that even though we aren't your parents, we love you like you are our own."

A large lump formed in Elle's throat, strangling her response. "I love you, Janet," she whispered.

"I love you, Eleanor."

Eleanor? A wince contorted her face. Sitting beside Janet, who asked Elle to let her in fully, there were no more excuses to not ask. To not pull the people she claimed to love a little closer.

"Janet, can you call me Elle? That's what my friends call me."

"Of course, Elle."

"Tobey is going to be so pissed at me." Elle pulled a

package of tissues out of her purse, handing them to Janet. "No more crying. Let's talk about something happy."

"Let's talk about boys." Janet said, blowing her nose loudly. "Have you decided which guy, yet? They're both cute, but I'm Team Clayton."

Elle shook with laughter. *Only Aunt Janet.*

FOURTEEN

"Time will explain."
~Jane Austen, *Persuasion*

Tobey's getting married…*And I might see her.* Elation and anxiety spun through Elle as she sat in the front row clasping Aunt Janet's hand. The officiant stepped beneath the birch arbor. Taking a deep breath, Elle joined as guests twisted to the back as music heralded the wedding party. Clenching her jaw, she rallied herself for emotional impact, but there was no sight of Mom. Like seeking a beacon in the dark, her gaze was pulled to Clayton strolling toward the chairs in a suit identical to Uncle Pete's. But he filled it in a way that sparked every one of her nerve-endings to life.

Pete strode from the opposite side and the two men met at the start of the grassy aisle to begin their walk to the altar. Clayton's stare tethered to Elle as he moved closer. Passing the first row, he winked at her causing her belly to swoop. He took up his position on one side but didn't shift his eyes away from her. His intent gaze on her sent happiness fizzing within her.

Guests *oohed* as Lt. Scout, dressed in full police uniform, trotted down the aisle, stopping to sit next to Pete. With a lift of his hands, the officiant motioned for everyone to stand while from opposite sides of the lawn, Tobey and Jerome glided toward each other with the biggest smiles on their faces. Elle tried to focus on them and not scan the backs of heads for familiar blonde curls. As they reached the chairs, Jerome and Tobey intertwined hands and continued to the altar together.

"Dear family, friends, and the rest of you folks they had to invite." The officiant paused for laughter with an impish grin. "We are here to join two hearts together, to witness the love of Tobey Coates and Jerome Evans."

In less than the blink of an eye, the happy couple were pronounced married while their guests applauded.

As the wedding party posed for pictures, Elle followed the other guests to the tent for drinks before dinner. Quickly locating Carmen and Mathew standing in line at the bar, she joined them.

"You look so pretty," Carmen gushed, taking Elle's hands to inspect her. "Like a mermaid."

The comparison was spot on. Her auburn hair was styled in loose waves. A silver starfish necklace and matching earrings accompanied a strapless tea length lavender dress that shimmered in the sunlight.

"And I didn't even have to sell my voice to a sea witch."

"The night's young." Noah joked, joining their group.

Carmen, Mathew, and Noah were at Elle's table, located near the bar and far away from where her mother's assigned seat was. In addition, Meghan, the third partner at the vet clinic, and her wife Karla joined them.

"Alright folks, let's hear it for one of the best men, Clayton Owens," the DJ hooted, ushering in the best man toast portion of the reception.

"Here's our guy." Noah elbowed Elle.

Our guy?

Clayton gripped the microphone. "Evening." Those gray eyes scanned the guests seated under the tent, lit on Elle, and remained there for a beat. He cleared his throat and began his toast. "Speaking words isn't my forte but reading them is. One of my favorite authors wrote that happiness in marriage is entirely by chance."

Elle beamed. The *Pride and Prejudice* reference created a moment just between Clayton and her in this ocean of people.

He continued, "But Jerome and Tobey, you are a sure bet. Thank you, not just for letting me stand up with you today but for reminding me that love is everything and when I find my everything, I plan to hold on to it, just like you two. Congratulations!"

The air practically sizzled between them. Elle placed her hand on her heart hoping nobody else could hear its loud drumbeat.

The sun had set, and after the wedding feast was cleared away, fairy lights illuminated the tent with a romantic glow. Carmen and Mathew had moved onto the dance floor for the first of what Elle knew would be many dances. Noah headed to the bar to check on Todd. Elle sat alone reading texts from Willa and Viet demanding pictures of her hot farmer in his wedding suit.

"Elle."

She looked up to find Clayton, hands in his pockets and a flirtatious grin on his face.

"I liked your toast. It was the perfect Austen fanboy moment."

"Can I buy you a free drink." He gestured to the bar with his head.

"Ok," Elle agreed, ignoring her full glass of rosé on the table.

As they walked to the bar, his palm pressed against her lower back. Heat flooded every inch of her body at his touch.

"Clayton! You look so handsome in your suit." A silver-haired woman turned from the bar her arms spread. It had been eighteen years since Elle had last seen Mrs. Owens, but she knew her thanks to the pair of soft gray eyes identical to her son's.

"Thanks, Mom." He blushed. "You remember Elle Davidson?"

"Elle…" Mrs. Owens searched, her eyes growing wide with recognition. "Eleanor!"

"Mrs. Owens. It's nice to see you again."

"What a beauty you grew up to be. I'm not surprised. I must find Chris. He'd love to say hello." She held Elle's hands.

"Where is Dad?"

"He's in the restroom. Old age, small bladder."

"TMI, Mom." Clayton shook his head.

"Here you go, Mrs. Owens." Todd placed a beer alongside a glass of red wine on the bar.

"Thank you. Let me get these back to our table," she said.

"Mom, do you want me to carry those?" Clayton asked, looking at Elle with apologetic eyes.

"I wouldn't want you to desert Elle."

"Oh, I'm fine. I helped set this joint up, so I won't get lost." Elle brushed it off with a wave.

"Thank you, Elle. I haven't seen him all week. I'll have him back to you shortly." Mrs. Owens held her drinks out to Clayton.

"It was nice seeing you, Mrs. Owens."

"I'll see you later." He shrugged.

"Clayton, come back and buy me that free drink later?"

With a big smile, he tipped up his chin before spinning to catch up with his mom.

"Eleanor, you still want that free drink?" Todd teased.

Eleanor? There'd been a familiarity about Todd at the Wine Down earlier that week, but she couldn't put her finger on it. The use of Eleanor, when he'd heard her referred to as Elle by Carmen and Noah made her flip through the pages of her mental photo album.

"Todd Krueger!" she gaped.

"The one and only." He bowed.

Todd was two years younger than Elle, but had been in band with her. The brass section had been made up of all boys and Elle. The shy, pint-size Todd was so different from the cocksure tall man in front of her.

"I wasn't sure you'd remember me."

"I do. You were in the Kiss Our Brass section."

A pleased smile swept his face at the mention of their band section motto. "You know you put that in my year-book. It reminded me What Would Eleanor Do, when I got picked on for being scrawny. Just ignore the fuckers."

Affection curled her lips. "Todd, call me Elle. It's what my friends call me."

They fist bumped in band geek solidarity.

"Alright, here's that extra case" Noah slipped behind the bar with a case of beer, his jacket now gone, and sleeves rolled to his elbows.

Elle started to move away. "I'm going to put this on the table and then go dance with Carmen. I'll see you both later."

"Elle, save me a dance," Noah shouted from behind the bar.

"Hey Elle, you're too good for Prince Charming over here. Tell him to kiss your brass," Todd teased and slapped a wet towel against Noah's forearm.

Noah flinched. "Dude! Really?"

"Save it for my performance review," Todd snarked.

Oh, Todd. Shaking with laughter, Elle walked away.

As the DJ played pop hits, she let the music take over her body, shimmying her hips, tossing her arms, and hooting with laughter as she danced with Noah, Carmen, and Mathew.

Between finding her own version of the dance beat, her gaze flicked to the head table, where Clayton sat talking to Jerome's father. She hadn't seen Clayton after he left to carry his mother's drinks to her table. There was still the matter of that free drink he owed her.

"Let's slow this down." The DJ's deep voice came over the mic.

"Yay!" Carmen cheered, her arms wrapped around Mathew's neck, his hands at her waist. She nuzzled into his neck at the first notes of "Perfect" by Ed Sheeran started.

Couples paired, singles shuffled off, and others held hands while walking to the dance floor. Elle started to walk back to her table when Noah stepped in her way.

"How about that dance?" A dimple punctuated his charming smile.

Elle tilted her head, peeking around Noah, to where Clayton stood in front of his table, his gaze fixed on the dance floor. The tiny paw prints tattooed on his right forearm were visible thanks to the absence of his jacket and his rolled-up sleeves.

Shifting her stare back to Noah, she grinned. "Sorry. It's saved for someone else."

He glanced at Clayton and then back to her. "It's about time. Go get our guy." He kissed her cheek and walked away.

Elle strode toward Clayton, whose grin got bigger with each step closer. He closed the distance between them. As they reached each other, she took his hand and led him onto the dance floor. Just as she had seen Carmen do with Mathew, she encircled Clayton's nape.

Clayton rested his hands at her waist as they swayed, their gazes intertwined. "I didn't get a chance to tell you how beautiful you always look in purple," he whispered, pulling her closer.

Elle nestled her face against his collarbone. "I didn't get to tell you how handsome you look in this suit."

"I thought you were going to dance with Noah." He swallowed hard.

"You thought wrong."

Chin rested atop her head, his arms banded around her. It wasn't the first time his chin had been there. It found its way there, when his strong teenaged arms caught her body as she almost fell from the bleachers at that Winter Ball so long ago. In his arms, snug under his chin, she was safe. Then and now.

"You always smell like Thanksgiving."

"Like turkey and stuffing?" Her giggle was muffled against his chest.

"Like vanilla and pumpkin. I can't smell it without thinking of you." He inhaled deep.

"Now let's get this party going again. I think it's getting hot in here." The DJ hyped as Nelly bounced from the speakers.

Elle raised her head. Clayton still held her, pressed against him, staring at her. The beat of the new song interrupted, and they realized at almost the same time their position was no longer fitting. Elle slipped her hands from his neck to her sides as he stepped back a few inches, but his hands remained on her waist.

"Elle…" he started.

"Clayton!" A grinning Jerome yelled as he hurried to them.

"What's up?" He dropped his hands but kept his focus on Elle.

"Lady Elle." Jerome gave her a courtly bow.

Elle? A quiet laugh fell out of her. Clearly Aunt Janet had set up the bat signal to call her Elle.

"Sorry to steal Clayton, but I need my best man for a bit."

"I was about to take a break anyway." Elle patted Jerome's arm and then strode off the dance floor.

"Elle!"

She pivoted at Clayton's voice.

"When I'm done with this, can I buy you that free drink?" Hands in pocket, he flashed a lopsided grin.

"You better." She winked, turning to sashay away. It was a little sassy, but a lady likes a man's gaze on her backside sometimes. Especially the *right* man.

She went back to the table, scooped up her silver clutch, and ducked out of the tent to what Uncle Pete had dubbed the fancy crappers.

Pete had been obsessed with these impressive portable restrooms. For weeks he'd blathered on about them during their weekly calls. Taking in the row of stalls, piped in music, the fresh floral scent, and a basket overflowing with an array of fancy toiletries, Elle got it.

"These are fancy." Helping herself to one of the luxurious hand soaps, she smiled. "*Tres chic.*"

Humming along with Jan Arden, she washed her hands. Her eyes raised at the *creak* of the door opening. A pair of familiar blue eyes and darkened blonde curls filled the mirror in front of her.

Elle's breath grew ragged, and her pulse sped as if coming face-to-face with a shark in the deep.

A firm line was fixed on her mother's face; her gaze stony. Tiny wrinkles lined the corner of her eyes. Sadness still swam in their depths but was shaded with something different. *Remorse?*

Sucking in deep breaths, Elle spun to confront her past. There she was, not a phantom, not a memory, and not an image in the mirror, but her mother in the flesh. That ball of dread she'd fought all day inflated.

No words. No smile. No reaching hands. Mom just shrugged and walked into a stall. The lock sliding into place knocked the wind out of Elle with its indifference.

With her hands still damp, Elle clutched her handbag and retreated outside. The celebratory sounds of the wedding behind her were trumped by her shallow gasps. Going back wasn't an option, because she was there. *Mom is fucking here.*

The last few hours of clinked glasses, swaying hips, stolen glances with Clayton, were a mere distraction lulling her into false safety.

"Elle," Clayton rasped, his hands holding her trembling shoulders, eyes clouded with concern.

When did Clayton come? She blinked.

"Take me home." she croaked as he tucked her against his chest.

Ten minutes later, parked in front of the Little Red Barn, Elle slumped against Clayton's shoulder. The emotions drizzled; her tears screamed for release. She rubbed a hand over her tight chest as if the mere act would erase the locked away feelings.

"When Evan died," Clayton broke the silence, "It was hard for me to talk about it and, at times, it still is. Noah reminded me I'd made him talk about what happened during his second tour in Iraq and that it helped. So, when I need to talk, I talk. When I can't, I don't." In a soothing caress, his fingers moved from her hair to her arms. "I'm not telling you what to do, just saying if you need to talk, I'm here. I'm in it with you."

She lifted her gaze to capture his, seeking his strength as cracks formed in the well-constructed dam holding everything in. *Let it break.*

She sat up, pulling out of his hold, and scooted over a few inches, her eyes focused on the past. "The last time I saw my mom was winter break my freshman year of college. We didn't spend much time together because she was either working or with Jamie, her boyfriend." Her voice broke. She shook her head and carried on. "Jamie taunted me about my weight saying I had a pretty face, if only I'd lose fifty pounds, I'd be attractive. But he made Mom happy, so I said nothing."

Clayton's fingers threaded in hers, anchoring them together.

"It was the last week of break... Mom was working late. Jamie was there, drinking, waiting for her. We were in the living room watching TV. He was in the chair, and I was on the couch. Then he was beside me. He asked me if someone had popped my cherry yet...fucking crude. Jamie said big girls shouldn't be choosey as he started touching my leg. Then he kissed me. I tried to get away... I tried to fight..."

It's strange what details of that night she remembered. The scratch of grandma's afghan beneath her bare behind. She'd tossed it in the garbage bin after. The mug of hot chocolate that had spilled on the coffee table after he'd pushed her down. She'd wiped the mess up with her torn pajama pants after. The taste of bourbon from his forced kisses. She wouldn't know what that taste was until her first year of grad school, when Viet dated a guy from Kentucky who brought some from back home. After she tried it, she spit it in the sink.

"After, he rolled off, he told me I should be grateful that someone like him took my virginity. Then he walked out of the room."

Heavy silence reigned in the pickup. Elle focused on the white trim and large window of the Little Red Barn. A safe corner in Perry. Along with the man sitting beside her. Clayton is the first person in eighteen years she'd told what had happened that cold January night.

"Did you report it?" Clayton whispered.

"No. It doesn't matter now. Jamie died in a drunk driving accident two years later. I guess Karma got him."

"What happened when your mom came home from work?"

"I don't know. I wasn't there. I left and stayed with my friend Viet for the remainder of the break. I never told Pete what happened. It wasn't until I got back to school that I told someone." Her voice quaked.

"Your mom?"

"She didn't believe me. Kept saying he wouldn't do that. She chose him over me. It would never be me. I was not enough," she croaked.

Crack. Crack. The sound of her heart breaking filled her senses.

"When I saw her tonight, I thought she'd say something. I was wrong. She didn't say a damn thing, just shrugged and walked into the stall."

Crack. Crack. Crack.

"I will never be enough!" The dam holding back her emotions broke. Her body heaved with deep wracking sobs.

Clamping his hands on her face, he guided her gaze to his. Desperation glistened and tears dripped from his stormy eyes. "You are enough. You are everything. You hear me Elle? You are enn…enn…enn…enough." He gulped in air as he stuttered. "You are ev…ev…ev…everything." Soothing lips brushed against her forehead before pulling her weeping and quivering body into his strong arms, telling her it was safe to fall because he was there to catch her.

FIFTEEN

"If I loved you less, I might be able to talk about it more."
~Jane Austen, *Emma*

E lle woke with a vague recollection of Clayton's strong arms carrying her up the stairs to the sleeping loft. He'd tucked her in and sat beside her, stroking her hair as she fell asleep. *Had he really pressed his lips to her forehead and whispered,* "I'm here, you rest?" *Or was that a dream?*

Still in her dress from the wedding, Elle sat up. Tiny cracks of light slipped through gaps in the closed blinds. She wasn't sure what time it was or how long she had slept. What she knew was that she had slept. No nightmares, haunting memories, or racing thoughts interrupting her slumber.

Grabbing her phone from the bed stand, she checked the time. "8:05 a.m.?" she murmured in disbelief. It had been years since she'd slept this late or this soundly.

When I need to talk, I talk. Clayton's words answered her questioning thoughts. Finally, she had chosen to talk instead of run.

The dread that had coursed her veins was gone. All that was left was a tiny ache in her chest.

She noticed several missed messages.

Carmen had messaged at ten p.m., asking Elle where she was and if Elle wanted her to snag a piece of cake. She responded with an apology and a made-up excuse for leaving early. On the group thread with Viet and Willa there were more texts, asking for updates on hot farmer, if mommy not-so-dearest made an appearance, and how Elle was doing. It was just after five a.m., in California, but she messaged that she was okay and would reach out later. The last message, sent just before midnight, was from Clayton.

Fitz's Human: I didn't want to leave you. I'm on the couch downstairs.

Elle had spilled all her ugly truths last night, but he held her tight and whispered that she was enough, she was everything.

Pushing the blankets off, she found her slippers and shoved her feet into them.

Where the sleeping loft was dark with only slivers of light, downstairs was bathed in sunshine. Clayton curled on the too-small-for him couch, a green checkered pillow on his face.

Enveloped by the warmth of his presence, she tiptoed to the bathroom. There she pulled her hair into a messy bun, washed away her dried tears, and brushed her teeth before heading back to the living room.

"Good morning," Clayton said, his voice a little hoarse and stifled beneath the pillow.

"Why do you have a pillow on your face?"

"To shield my eyes." He cleared his throat. "I wasn't sure if you'd see my text and come down not dressed. I didn't want you to think I was trying to sneak a peek."

"You may remove your shield. I am fully clothed." A silent laugh curled her lips.

Removing the pillow, he lifted his head to look at her.

"You didn't need to stay. That can't have been comfortable."

"I know, but I wanted to." He stretched.

The white button-up shirt from the wedding was thrown over the desk chair, leaving him wearing just his trousers and undershirt like a hero from an old movie. A cell phone and keys lay on the end table beside the couch, his dress shoes tucked under it to keep anyone from tripping. His thoughtfulness jellied her knees.

"What about Fitz? Was he home by himself?" A twinge of concern in her voice.

"With my parents." He swung his body into a seated position facing her. "Whenever I'm gone for long periods of time, he goes to visit them. My mother spoils him and loves to remind me it's because he's the only grandbaby she has."

"Thank you for staying and everything else," Elle said, fidgeting with her hands.

"How did you sleep?"

She fixed her gaze on the space beside Clayton occupied only by that pillow. She wanted to kick that pillow off the sofa and take its place next to him.

"Better than I have in years," she said. Would she have slept even better next to him in the bed? She brushed the errant thought away, focusing on her feet. "Did you put my slippers by the bed?"

"Yes."

"And closed the loft blinds?"

"Yes."

"Wow, maybe I should show you my ugly granny panties more often. Such service." The snarky comment was a veiled attempt to hide the overexposed feeling wrapping around her.

"There's nothing ugly about you. Ugly things happened to you, but everything about you is beautiful. Here." He motioned to his face. "And especially here." He placed his hand on his heart.

"Where it counts." She ducked her head, the rawness of last night making her feel overexposed.

"You have the most generous heart despite people repeatedly trying to break it. What I see is a thoughtful woman… smart as hell, funny, adorably goofy at times, beautiful, and so strong. I've always seen you," he said, his eyes not looking at her but *into* her as he spoke.

Her heart thumped as their stares melded as one. *I've always seen you.*

Like fog clearing, realization slammed into her. He'd watched her reading during his high school football practices and had been so curious to know what had such an impact on her facial expressions, he'd started reading the same books.

You are everything. His words in the truck. His toast at the wedding about how when he found his everything, he'd hold on to it.

Really didn't notice you 'til then. After that all I could do was notice you. His words as they sat pressed up against the couch on that rainy day.

Her eyes widened. "Why did you come look for me?"

"To buy you the free drink, when I—"

"No, not last night. The night of the Winter Ball when you saved me from falling off the bleachers." Her pulse quickened with certainty.

"I had finally gotten the nerve to ask you to dance."

"Were you scared of what your friends would say?" She kept her tone light, as if the answer didn't have the power to devastate her.

"No," he said, his gaze steady. "I was scared of what you would say."

"But you were you"—she pointed at him and then to herself with a frown—"and I was me."

"Exactly." He rose, determination darkened his eyes. "Our favorite books are our favorite, not because of pretty covers but because of what's written inside, and you are a goddamn masterpiece."

The air crackled like a coming storm. Anticipation prickled beneath Elle's skin.

"Are you going to kiss me?" Breath shallow, she stepped toward him.

"Do you want me to kiss you?" he rasped, moving closer, hands clenched at his sides.

"Yes." She closed the space between them.

He cupped her face and lowered his mouth to hers. It wasn't sweet and tentative like a boy's first kiss but ravenous, as if the only thing that could appease his hunger was her.

Sliding his hands to her waist, he pulled her tight against him.

A small moan escaped her as his tongue coaxed her lips open, taking the kiss deeper into the sweet release of this moment. Every nerve-ending exploded like her own internal fireworks show. His kiss, his touch, ignited something deep within her. Something she thought had been lost.

Lifting her hands to his shoulders she pressed harder into the firm angles of his chest. He moved backward as she pushed forward, their steps a faultless dance.

He captured her lower lip, and bit softly. The luscious pain released a whimper of need from her. The back of his muscular legs hit the couch and they separated, staring at each other. His raised eyebrow a silent dare. With a teasing smile, she pushed Clayton to a seated position. His grin was a delightful mix of playful and wicked as she straddled his lap.

A throaty grunt escaped him at their newfound closeness, followed by a groan as her mouth met his, her lips leading. And he followed her lead, move for move. With a rumble of pleasure his tongue tangled with hers.

"Clayton," she panted.

He ceased his kisses, his gray eyes hungry but patient.

Elle rested her hands over his, guiding them to the dress hem and helped him raise the fabric until it bunched at her waist.

Clayton's eyes flicked to her bare legs. His gaze, desirous and questioning, returned to hers.

With a nod, she mouthed *yes*.

This is where she wanted to be. With him. The ghosts of her past were not welcomed here. On this couch it was just them.

He trailed languid kisses from her lips to below her ear, over her flushed cheek to her chin and down the long column of her throat to the collarbone and back up. With a sly smile, he moved back to her cheek, and his kiss turned chaste. As Elle let out a frustrated noise, he chuckled before licking her throat. The delicious rasp of his tongue made her back arch.

More! Deep within, a switch flipped, and her movements turned feverish and frantic. Her hips writhed against his lower belly as he continued to suck at the base of her throat. The touch of his hands scorched her already heated skin.

"Touch me, please," she pleaded breathlessly.

"Where do you want me to touch you?" His voice a low rumble.

Raising her hips, she guided his fingers to her core shielded by a thin layer of lacy underwear, already damp with need. Grazing his fingers under the fabric, he pushed it aside.

The smooth pads of his fingers slipped through her slick folds. "Hmmm...so wet." The vibration of his deep voice intensifying her need. "Do I do this to you?"

"Yes," she hissed with the first slow stroke of her clit.

The heat of his gaze moved like a wave across her body as his finger stroked and rubbed and flicked. Hips grinding, she rode his hand, her nails digging into his shoulders. A pleasurable pressure built, readying to rip through her.

She widened her legs and he pushed a second finger inside her body, while continuing to massage her sensitive nub with his thumb. The pressure climbed until he slipped another finger inside her, catapulting her over the edge.

"Clayton," she whined, her body shuddering.

"Elle," he rasped and swallowed her moans with a deep kiss.

"That was nice." Panting, she caressed his cheek.

"Oh, I can do better than nice." A devilish glint sparked in his eyes. Just as his lips met her skin, an alarm chimed.

"What?" Elle blinked, confused and a little mortified. The alarm sounded like church bells. The worshipping they had done this Sunday morning was certainly not church appropriate.

"Ugh," he groaned and buried his head against her neck. "My alarm. I set it last night to ensure we had time to get ready for the post-wedding brunch." His long arms grabbing the phone and turning off the alarm.

"For what?"

"The brunch for your cousin and Jerome, remember?"

"Oh, yeah." Her tone was a little dazed. "Brunch. Sorry, orgasm brain." She pointed to her head and then to her satiated smile.

"I noticed." He kissed below the shell of her ear.

"You're very good at that."

He arched a cocky eyebrow.

"Noticing." She aimed a playful swat at his bicep.

The swat resulted in him kissing her. Maybe she'd swat him more.

"So, you put me to bed last night, closed the blinds, made sure my slippers were by the bed, and set the alarm so we wouldn't be late for the post-wedding brunch?" She pecked his lips after listing each thing he had done.

"Yup."

"And gave me an orgasm?"

"Yup."

"You may be the perfect man."

His mouth curved into a smirking grin. "I can cook too."

"Oh god, you *are* perfect." A whiney laugh fell out of her.

"We should get ready," he murmured, licking her throat, causing her to throw her head back with a "mmmm."

"Oh, yes. Right now," she whispered, rubbing herself against his impressive arousal hidden beneath those slacks.

"Yup. Right now." He sucked on her throat.

Their lingering kisses lasted until the ten-minute backup alarm broke them apart.

SIXTEEN

"Oh! I am delighted with this book. I should like to spend my whole life in reading it."
~Jane Austen, *Northanger Abbey*

"We need to get this out of our system here, because there will be none of this in front of my aunt and uncle," Elle warned with a cheeky tone in between more Clayton kisses after they'd pulled into the parking lot of the Sea Serpent for brunch.

"I waited this long to kiss you; I can make it two hours." He rested his forehead against hers.

"Ok, let's go," she said, backing away from him, turning for the door handle.

But Clayton had other thoughts, pulling her back into his arms he thoroughly kissed her.

Her brain was still reeling as he said, "Ok, now we can go."

They were five minutes late. Elle jogged inside while Clayton waited in the parked truck to come in a few minutes after. This was all too new to expose to the flurry of questions, raised eyebrows, and searching glances of her family. In the end, keeping their status quiet gave them time to figure it out.

"Interesting, you're both late," Tobey observed, elbowing his husband.

Damn his cop spidey sense.

"Yeah." Jerome quirked an accusing brow. "Come to think of it, you both disappeared early from the wedding."

"I was sick," Elle blurted.

"Oh, Lady Elle, no." The sweet natured Jerome was easily distracted from sussing what was happening between Clayton and Elle.

"How are you feeling?" Tobey narrowed his eyes, less convinced.

"Much better. I just overindulged on that mac and cheese. Clayton ran into me when I said I wasn't feeling well and offered to drive me back, since I had ridden with your mom," she explained, then bit her tongue to keep from spewing unnecessary details.

"Mmhmm." Tobey's tone said he wasn't convinced.

"Oh man, thanks for taking care of my cousin-in-law." An appreciative Jerome slapped Clayton's back.

"Anytime," Clayton said with a mischievous glance her way.

Heat flushed her cheeks with the knowledge of where his mind had gone about how he took care of her.

The brunch was less formal than the wedding. Baskets of fresh pastries, pitchers of mimosas, fruit, meat, and cheese platters, tea pots, and coffee carafes sat at each table. Elle sat with Meghan and her wife Karla.

Between stolen glances with Clayton seated across the room, Elle learned that Jerome and Meghan had been in the same class at Cornell, a few years behind Clayton. After meeting Clayton during a clinical rotation where he worked in Ithaca, they'd developed a friendship. When Clayton invited them to become his partners and expand the clinic, they'd both jumped right in.

After brunch, and a good hour of chatting and schmoozing, Clayton appeared next to Elle, enveloping her senses in a citrus-scented haze. Heat invaded her cheeks and led to Jerome asking if she was okay.

"Too much tea," she insisted and patted her flushed cheeks.

Jerome tilted his head to one side. "I didn't know tea could do that."

"It doesn't," Tobey mumbled, his narrowed gaze locked on Elle.

"You drink coffee. I drink tea. Therefore, I am the expert." She flicked his nose.

Pete strolled over, a small, reusable Buffalo Bills grocery bag in his hand. "We should all get going. They need to get ready to reopen to the public in an hour."

"Thanks, Dad Number Two—"

Pete smiled at the term of endearment from his new son-in-law.

"—We still need to pack before tonight's flight."

"You haven't packed?" Elle pasted her hands over her heart.

"Easy, Elle, do you need your smelling salts?" Pete teased.

Her heart squeezed with the sound of her preferred name. Leave it to Janet to make sure that in a little under twenty-four hours the entire family knew to call her Elle.

"I'm sure someone here will catch her if she faints," Tobey snarked, his blue eyes dropped on Clayton.

"I think any of us would catch her if she fell." Pete nudged his son.

All four men nodded in unison.

"And she'd catch us if we fell," he added.

A sense of belonging ensconced Elle eliciting a large smile. These men. They were good and they were hers.

Pete handed her the reusable grocery bag. "Just a few slices of wedding cake, since you had left before the cake was cut."

Wrapping her arms around his waist, she gave a thankful squeeze. She knew he probably suspected why she'd left early. The tightrope he had to walk between his sister and his niece was, no doubt, difficult.

"That was the longest two hours of my life," Clayton almost whined, pulling her into a small space between the restaurant's brick wall and a tall hedge when she stepped outside. Pressing her against the wall with his body, he placed impatient kisses.

She giggled…actually giggled, but she gave zero fucks.

"I'm telling you Jerome…" Tobey's voice came from the other side of the hedge.

Elle pushed on Clayton's chest, and he led her further down the hedgerow, cloaking them in its leafy secrecy.

"…something is going on there," Tobey continued.

"Would that be so bad?" Jerome replied.

"He's great. She's amazing. I just…" Tobey stopped speaking,

Elle stretched her neck to try to hear better.

"You worry too much. They're adults. Both sexy, single adults," Jerome teased in a sultry voice.

Tobey grumbled something Elle couldn't make out as car doors slammed and an engine charged to life.

After a few minutes, they checked that the coast was clear and ran to Clayton's truck to drive to Buffalo for their chair buying date. Once there, they bought two chairs. Correction. Elle bought one for the Little Red Barn, and Clayton got one for the farmhouse. Clayton, who had a Post-It note fetish, bought Elle a packet of purple ones.

Clayton suggested hitting the Anchor Bar for dinner. As she sat across from him, a basket of wings between them, she wasn't entirely sure if this was a date. To Elle it felt like a date, and it was the best date she had ever had. The flow of the conversation and the fun facts of life he shared helped her to know more and more about this man.

"So, is this our first date?" She bit into a drumstick.

"Well, yes and no. No, because in many ways I feel like I've been dating you since our first run. Yes, I never said they were dates aloud 'til I asked you to join me today. I may not be doing this dating thing right."

"You're doing it right," she said, trying to ignore the little flutter in her chest.

"For the record, so are you."

"I'm very unpracticed."

"I know you said there weren't any gentlemen callers currently..."

She snorted.

He continued, undeterred "...but have you had...a... any...oh, boy...serious relationships?" he asked, forehead wrinkled.

"After it... uh, Jamie happened, I didn't date for a long time. Not until my first year at Sloan-Whitney. Javi was a surgical resident I had a very brief thing with. Not serious. He was sweet, but I wasn't ready. Other than him, nobody beyond a few dates."

"I haven't dated anyone since Marianne."

"Did you date before her?"

"A few girls. I dated and had one girlfriend in undergrad but nothing too serious. I'm not a big serial dater." Barbecue sauce coated his fingers as he bit into a wing.

Elle squashed an urge to lick his fingers clean. "Yeah, I don't remember you ever dating in high school."

"There was only one girl I wanted to date in high school,

and I missed my chance." His intense gaze pinned her in place.

Those eyes had such a power over her. Was it possible that what she'd seen as judgement in his eyes in high school was not for her but for himself? For the things he couldn't say when he was in her presence? How had her vision been so impaired to not see him before now? She assumed boys like him wouldn't want girls like her, when he'd wanted her all along but had been too afraid that she wouldn't want him in return.

"We didn't miss our chance. It was just waiting for us to get here. We're here now," she murmured, leaning across the table to press her lips against his mouth, coated with the barbecue sauce's tangy sweetness.

A large grin bloomed across his face.

"Clayton, can I take a picture of you?"

"I'd rather take a picture *with* you," he countered, wiping his hands.

"Ok." She wiped her hands and opened the camera app on her phone and selected the selfie mode, as she started to crouch next to him, Clayton pulled her onto his lap.

Grabbing the phone with his left hand, he held her close with his right hand on her stomach, as their heads pressed together.

"Much better. At the count of three say, wings. One… two…three…wings!"

He snapped several selfies. Right before he snapped the last one, he turned his head and placed a small kiss to her cheek.

She couldn't stop smiling as she reviewed the pics and sent the first selfie of her on his lap, heads close, and giant unabashed grins, to Viet and Willa with the message, *My hot farmer*, finally appeasing their demands.

SEVENTEEN

"I must learn to be content with being happier than I deserve."
~Jane Austen, *Pride and Prejudice*

"Your proposed expansion plan is interesting," mused Malcolm Sloan, Elle's boss.

They were on a last-minute video call to discuss her proposal to fund their foundation's rural clinics by offering specialty care telehealth services at primary care clinics in affluent areas. The strategy would increase profits, which in turn would be used to pay for clinics in underserved communities.

This initiative was important to Elle, who'd grown up in an underserved community. Accessible healthcare shouldn't be a luxury for the rich.

Malcolm slapped his hands gleefully. "I want to include this as one of the key objectives for our annual presentation to the board and I'd like you to present it with me. When are you back again?"

On screen, Elle appeared cool and collected, but beneath the Little Red Barn's desk her slipper-clad feet did a jig.

"I'm physically back in the office September eleventh."

"Perfect. The board meets on the twenty-first. Plenty of time to go over a few things. Very good work, Elle."

"Thank you." She looked at Braedon, who sat quietly grinning on the screen. Braedon was in all her meetings, as her assistant and to prepare them for the day they jumped to their next career step. "I also want to recognize my team. They were integral in the research for this plan."

"Of course. Nice work, Braedon."

"It's Ms. Davidson's vision,' Braedon said.

"Elle, your people love you. I hear the same thing from your regional directors when I'm visiting our sites. Nice leadership." His eyes darted off screen as if being flagged. "Ok, I'm off. Braedon, get all the travel info for Elle from my assistant. This year's board meeting will be in Chicago after the ribbon cutting for our new Oncology Unit. Elle, I'd like you to attend that with me, as well." With a wave, he popped off the screen.

For a moment, they were both silent before Braedon snapped their fingers. "Totally bad-ass, boss!"

Elle barely contained her excitement. Not only would she be presenting to the board, but with the meeting being in Chicago she'd have an excuse to see Beth. Elle had worked for Sloan-Whitney since she'd graduated with her Masters, and in all that time, she couldn't remember a single National Director presenting to the board.

Picking up her cell, she texted the good news to Clayton, and his response was instant.

Fitz's Human: You are such a boss! Let's celebrate with dinner Tuesday. I'll cook.
Elle: A date?
Fitz's Human: For the record, anytime we're together it's a date.

Elle squealed, then slapped a hand over her mouth. Far too undignified for a thirty-six-year-old woman with a very important job. Tuesday couldn't come soon enough.

Thank god she was going to get some one-on-one time with Uncle Pete tonight to distract her. He was coming over to help her put together the new desk chair.

Pete arrived twenty minutes after she logged off for the day.

After they'd assembled the chair, Elle made tea and served some of the leftover wedding cake.

"Tea and cake. I feel like the King of England," Pete jested, taking a large bite.

"Take a sip of the tea after each bite. It complements the flavor of the cake nicely." She demonstrated this, taking a sip of the still steaming tea after her first bite of the lemon chiffon delicacy.

"Oh, that is good." Pete moaned with pleasure. "You have a tea convert but only with cake."

"Thank you for saving me some."

"Of course." Pete's lips trembled as if debating whether he should speak.

Her right brow ticked up. "What?"

Pete hissed out a long breath before saying, "You left the wedding early. I saw you dancing with Doc, then you were gone. Then he was."

"It wasn't like that. I ran into him as I was coming out of the bathroom, and he saw I wasn't feeling well and offered to take me home."

"Yes, but you didn't tell me."

"You were busy. I didn't want to bother—"

"You didn't text me," he interrupted, hurt shaded the blue of his eyes. "That's not like you to not let me know where you are."

"I should have sent a text. I'm sorry you worried," she apologized.

He shrugged. "When I went looking for you, I ran into Jerome's dad. He said when he was walking to the bathroom, he saw you leave with Doc. I knew you were safe with him. I didn't know why you left. Was it your mom? Did she approach you? Did she try to talk to you?"

Tightness spread in her chest and crawled up her throat. "No."

He reached out one hand. "What did she do? Please tell me."

"She came into the bathroom while I was there. She just shrugged and walked into a stall."

"What?"

"She saw me but went into a stall like I wasn't her daughter. Like I was someone she was indifferent to. Someone not worth it."

"We asked her not to approach or speak to you."

"I know," she gritted through clenched teeth. "This was the one time she gave me what I asked for, so I shouldn't complain or be upset."

She wasn't angry at Pete but at herself for being disappointed that her mother didn't prove her wrong. The woman was selfish and would always choose herself over her daughter.

"I don't know all of what happened between the two of you. You just stopped speaking to her and then slowly stopped coming home."

The sadness in his eyes sliced Elle's heart. *I've done this. I've hurt him.*

"Pete, I am sorry. I know that I've made this hard on you. I know that I—"

"No." His interruption was firm, but gentle. "You haven't done anything. You're the kid. If it was Tobey and me or you and me…" he croaked. "…I would never listen to anyone who told me not to approach or speak to you. I would never shrug and close a door on you."

"I know you wouldn't." A slight wobble shook her voice.

"I was jealous of her because she got you." Pete frowned. "I remember standing in front of the glass watching you in the hospital nursery the day you were born. Everyone else was in the room, visiting your mom and dad. I was there watching you. I swore you could tell I was there, when I put my hand on the window telling you I was your Uncle Pete, and you better get used to me because I'd always watch over you."

Elle drew a shaky breath. "And you have."

"I think if I had been watching closer, if I had done a better job…I would have seen what was happening. I worry that you stayed away for so long not just because of your mom failing you but also me failing you."

"Pete."

He shook his head. "I worry that I put too much on you. You've always been so grown up, so independent. I keep thinking about when your dad left and how I told you your mom needed you. Then when your mom came back from the hospital, I sent you back with her. I sent you back every fucking time." He slammed a hand on the table, and she flinched.

She'd never seen Pete this angry, not at anyone and not at himself.

"She was my mom. You were just doing what you thought was best." She laid a reassuring hand upon his larger fist.

"You were hers, not mine. That's what I kept saying. Each time I sent you back. Each time I dropped you off from a school event she didn't make it to. Each time I grabbed you for dinner because she was out. I saw the disappointed coolness of acceptance in your eyes that this was just how it was." He blew out a harsh breath. "Each time I told myself to keep you, but I didn't... I was wrong."

Her heart both broke and swelled. This man had been so much to her. Her rock. Yet, he felt lacking, just as she had.

"I am yours," she affirmed, standing and walking to him and wrapping her arms around him.

He wasn't just Uncle Pete; he was her dad. Dads aren't made by blood but by the big and small things a man did out of love. Pete was the man who'd wiped tears that accompanied skinned knees. A man who'd taught her to ride a bike without training wheels, holding on 'til she screamed "Let go."

Here sat the man who put together this chair and unknowingly was helping put her back together. Pete always had, and always would, love her like a father.

"I am yours," she repeated and added, "I love you, Dad."

"I love you, kiddo," he sniffled, placing his hand on her head gently stroking the soft strands.

He is hers and she is his. They are enough.

EIGHTEEN

"She had been forced into prudence in her youth, she learned romance as she grew older: the natural sequel of an unnatural beginning."
~ Jane Austen, *Persuasion*

No more running! Certainty pinged through Elle's veins as Clayton parked at Letchworth State Park. She asked if they could skip the run and do something different. It wasn't her plan, but as she surveyed the forest's edge at the end of the parking lot, she knew she wanted to change their morning routine. She wanted to change how she handled moments like what happened with Pete. The urge was still there to hold it in, letting the thoughts meander until they were packed away in keyless lock boxes but dulled with her resolve.

It felt right to do it here. Letchworth was one of her favorite places as a kid. She had memories from this place for each changing season. It was the perfect place to make a change. To do something different.

Perhaps her favorite spots in the park were the sets of

three waterfalls along the Genesee River that flowed through the center of the park. A set of one hundred weathered stone steps led up a steep climb along the falls.

Clayton laced their fingers together as they took the first step. They were the only ones in the pre-dawn park. Clayton's gaze flipped between the well-traveled steps watching for ruts and debris that dotted the path and at Elle, as she shared what happened with Pete the night before. She confessed her fear of changing her and her mom in Pete's eyes if she told him the real reason she stayed away so long. She'd missed so much by staying away from Perry.

"This is *part* of your story. It's not your entire story. You decide which chapters and paragraphs to share. No matter what you decide, you are still my favorite book." His warm, earnest eyes held her gaze as he lowered his head to kiss her.

"Thank you." She smiled, placing her forehead against his, breathing in his tantalizing scent.

"Keep going?" He gestured to the *No Trespassing* sign stapled to the tree.

They had reached the top of the stairs, but there was so much further to go. She knew his question wasn't just about their walk.

"Absolutely." Taking his hand in hers again, they continued.

There had always been *No Trespassing* signs on so many doors within her heart. Things she wouldn't say, wouldn't let herself feel, or let others feel for her. It was time to knock those signs down and let people in and herself out.

Clayton lifted her up onto the plateau at the top. They walked along the old wooden and steel tracks toward the bridge. Rust-covered iron rails lined each side, providing a thin protective line between tracks and the river one-hundred feet below.

Elle exhaled with admiration, as she reached the center of

the bridge, stepping close to the iron rails and looking out at the lush trees sprinkled along both sides of the gorge. "This is amazing."

"I'll never get tired of this view," Clayton said, his arms wrapped around her waist, resting his chin on the top of her head.

Eyes closed, she melted into his embrace. "When's the last time you were here?"

"I come up here every June tenth… Evan's birthday. We used to come to the park a lot as kids and when we got older, we'd hike the trails. He died two months shy of his twenty-fifth birthday. That first year, we didn't know whether to celebrate him or not. It was tough for us all. Mom stayed in bed all day, crying. Dad just stayed in his office. Nat bought a cake and took it to Evan's grave. I came here. Being in this spot I felt like I was with him."

"Do you have a favorite memory of him?"

"So many memories. Evan could walk into a room of strangers and within five minutes be their new best friend. I'm typically the guy hanging in the corner, waiting for a stranger to approach me or for someone I know to walk into the room," he said self-deprecatingly.

Elle twisted to face him, wrapping her arms around his nape, their gazes mingling. "Not everyone is an Evan, but more importantly, not everyone is a Clayton." She lifted on her toes, nuzzling her nose against his.

A goofy grin tugged at the corners of his lips. "You're a little cheesy," he teased, pulling her up into his arms.

Elle squeaked, her long legs wrapping around his hips. "Like Muenster," she declared, as Clayton clutched her behind, holding her tight. "Are you grabbing my butt?"

"Just want to make sure you're secure."

"Clearly, butt grabbing is only a safety measure."

"Clearly," he murmured, his mouth inches from hers.

Those damn butterflies somersaulted as he captured her mouth in his. It was sweet and slow. As they broke their kiss, Elle's fingers traced where her lips had been. This kiss was playful yet grateful. Each kiss with him felt like the first time, because each one was different.

"Thank you for listening and sharing Evan with me."

He placed her back on her feet, keeping her pressed to his warm chest.

"Thank you for everything." she sighed with gratitude.

"Even the butt grabbing?" He grinned.

"Especially that." Elle said, her tone saucy.

With a hip check, she sauntered off the bridge, her hips swaying a little more than usual. Reaching the end of the bridge, she peeked over her shoulder and shot him a flirty wink. Clayton stood with both laughter and heat in those gray eyes that followed each movement of her body.

The rest of the day was standard workfare, minus all the moments she spent thinking of Clayton. Logic cautioned her that this was not a sound course of action. They lived on opposite sides of the country. His life was here, and hers there.

But no man had ever unsettled her in such a delicious way, causing her to feel both upside-down and right where she should be. She wasn't acting like her normal businesslike self, but she never felt more like herself than when she was with Clayton.

Blowing out a hot breath, Elle pushed her laptop away, she picked up her phone and sent a message to the group text, asking her friends if they were up for a lunch time video chat.

"Elle's Bells!" Willa cheered, her caramel-colored hair bouncing as her outstretched arms mimicked a clenching hug.

"Elle. I just told my assistant to push my next meeting,

so you've got me for a full…" Viet looked down at his watch. "…twenty-five minutes."

"Oh Viet, you didn't need to do that." Elle sighed.

"First, I don't do anything I don't want to do. Well, except visit my husband's racist grandmother." Viet wrinkled his nose.

Elle snickered.

"Anyways, Elle's Bells you seldom…wait, you *never* want to process things, so I'm shocked we're here, in the best way of course!" Willa's warm smile filled Elle's screen.

"So, how are you?" Viet asked, his dark eyes warm and comforting like a perfect cup of tea.

Elle sat in quiet hesitation, wondering if she should really answer that question and if so, what she would say. "I am a smoothie of feelings."

"What are some of the ingredients in that smoothie?" Willa asked.

"Angry. Disappointed. Guilty…alive…happy."

"Let's unpack those," Willa said, her voice less friend-like and more Dr. Willa Andrews. Perhaps taking this call from her office made it easier for Willa to slip into psychologist mode instead of remaining her normal bubbly self.

Elle puffed out her cheeks. "Angry and disappointed in my mom *and* myself. I saw her at the wedding in the bathroom. We didn't engage. At all."

"Oh, Elle. I'm so sorry," Viet consoled.

"It's fine."

"You mentioned anger and disappointment with her and yourself." Willa's tone was curious.

"I think deep down I wanted her to apologize. When she didn't, I was disappointed in myself for having that hope. That hope that she missed me as much as…" Elle stopped when her voice quivered. "I was angry with her for taking that hope away, again. She is who she is. I just need to remind myself of that and let go of that delusion."

"It's not delusional to want your mom in your life. It's normal," Willa soothed.

"Maybe for you or Viet."

A twinge of shame reared up. Snapping at Willa wasn't helpful. Both Viet and Willa had wonderful mothers whom they were close to. Elle had witnessed the loveliness of Willa's relationship with her mom, Gloria, and Viet's with his mom, Anh.

"Elle…" Willa stopped when Viet's shook his head.

Elle looked at Willa's remorseful face.

"Sorry, Wills," Elle apologized. "I shouldn't have snapped at you. You're just trying to help."

"No need to apologize. You weren't snapping at me, but at her. My Elle's Bells deserves to have what we have. I wish we could give that to you."

"Grieving my relationship with my mom is like being on a hamster wheel. It's never-ending and pointless. But I don't want it to stop me from appreciating other relationships. I stayed away too long, and Pete thought it might be a little bit about him. I think keeping her at a distance kept a lot of people away as well. I just… I don't seem know how to completely open my doors." Elle's voice cracked.

Willa made a small cooing noise. "You do it one door at a time, one lock at a time."

"Remember doors are meant to both open and close. We choose who we open them for and who gets them slammed in their face," Viet said, causing Elle to grin.

"I love you, both."

"We love you." They grinned in unison.

"So, can we talk about the banana in that smoothie?" Willa asked, a glint of naughtiness in her big brown eyes. Dr.

Andrews had tapped out for girlfriend Willa to come out to play.

"By banana, we mean hot farmer's dick." Viet winked.

"Yes, please. Has he plowed your field yet?"

"Baled your hay?" Viet added.

"Herded your cows?"

"Shucked your corn?"

"Stop!" Elle laughed, throwing her hands in the air. "I don't even think those are actual euphemisms!"

"You've got to give us something. My imagination has been in overdrive since you sent that pic." Willa begged.

"I don't think I want to know what you are imagining Clayton and me doing."

"It involves a tractor…" Willa fanned herself with a manila folder.

"I will give you this; He is an excellent kisser, and we have a date tonight." Elle's head jolted backward at Viet and Willa's joint hoots and whistles.

NINETEEN

"Anne hoped she had outlived the age of blushing, but the age of emotion she certainly had not."
~Jane Austen, *Persuasion*

There was debate on what number tonight's date with Clayton was. It was either date nine if Clayton was counting, or date two if she was. Either way, as she pulled on a denim jacket over her flirty red dress, she was excited. It was a departure from her signature purple, but tonight she wanted to be the woman who wore a red dress on a date with a *very* attractive man.

Despite the fact he was cooking at his place, he'd insisted on picking her up like a real date.

"Hey." Elle flung the door open at the first knock.

"Wow," he breathed out. "You're stunning."

Elle's face erupted in a giant smile. "You look pretty stunning yourself." Biting her lower lip, her gaze roamed over Clayton's muscular body. His blue jeans and fitted button up plaid shirt hugged him in all the ways she wanted to. Elle wanted to run her fingers through his freshly cut sandy blond hair, the sides shorter than they'd been this morning.

With an almost bashful smile, he slipped his fingers in hers, they were a perfect fit. Hands linked they strolled to the farmhouse.

The clack of nails against hardwood floors greeted them when they walked into the farmhouse. Fitz bounded up to Elle in the small foyer. Crouching, she massaged his velvety ears and got a smack of his tongue on her face in return.

"I see the maître d' at this restaurant is very affectionate," she giggled.

"He'll also help with any leftovers."

"Full service."

She rose and slipped off her sandals. Clayton placed his big shoes next to her smaller ones.

"So, you can either come help me in the kitchen or go snoop around the house."

"Oh, snoop please." Elle imagined her grin was reminiscent of a five-year-old's on Christmas morning. "Any rules or forbidden zones?"

"Nope."

Elle wrapped her arms around his neck in an excited hug.

His lips quirked up. "I'll come collect you when the food is ready or, if you get bored, I'm in there." He gestured to the large entry to the right of the front door.

Peeking around Clayton, Elle spied a large, open kitchen and dining area.

With a squeeze of her waist and gentle press of his lips, he slipped away.

Curiosity buzzed in her bloodstream as she wandered. Passing a set of steps leading upstairs and a narrow hallway that ran toward open French doors, she shuffled into the living room. A navy sectional couch sat across from a large flatscreen suspended over the fireplace. She could picture

Clayton with his feet kicked up on the coffee table binging a cooking show or reading a book from one of the oak bookshelves on either side of the fireplace. She traced the well-loved book spines that lined the shelves. Each book organized by genre. He had an entire row of Austen.

Swoon.

A copy of *Wicked and the Wallflower* by Sarah MacLean lay on the circular coffee table. Elle skimmed the back cover, eyebrows raised at the historical romance's description. Keeping it in her hand, she headed down a narrow hallway.

The French-style doors at the hallway's end opened to his study. More books sat on two bookshelves flanking a cushy leather chair. Envy swept over her at the plush pillow-top window seat overlooking the treelined backyard. As a kid, she'd push two chairs together against the large window in the dining room, and pretend it was a real window seat.

"Hey." Clayton leaned against the door frame, his mouth curved into a grin.

"How much extra to use this window seat during my stay?" She nestled into the cushy window seat.

"No charge. I can give you a key, so you can come over here anytime."

"A key isn't nec—"

He raised a hand, shaking off her protest.

"Well, thank you."

"Dinner is ready." He held out his hand.

Still holding the book in her left hand, she took his hand with her right, allowing him to lead her to the kitchen.

Two settings of blue stone plates, silverware, cloth napkins, glasses of water, and stemless wineglasses sat on the oak table. Most people would have sat the plates across from each other, but Clayton placed them side-by-side. A bowl of fresh salad, grilled chicken breasts, grilled parmesan-encrusted asparagus spears, and a bottle of Riesling sat on the table. The herby aroma of the chicken flooded Elle's nostrils. The room was lit with the soft light of candles in the center of the table and the orangey glow of the setting sun.

Conversation over dinner included a spirited discussion of favorite recipes. Both were amateur chefs in the kitchen with a healthy obsession with cooking shows.

After her last bite of the tasty chicken, she decided to tease Clayton about the historical romance she'd found. Kind of like the chicken, it was juicy reading.

He smirked as she displayed the book. "Book club."

"The book club you're in with *your* mom and Noah's?" she teased. "You realize this book screams heaving bosoms and randy dukes, right?"

"Nothing wrong with a heaving bosom or two." He winked.

The first rule of book club, he explained, was when it's your month to select the book, nobody complains, they just read. Noah's mom was a huge fan of historical romances, so Clayton had a shelf in the bedroom filled with books about feisty women and the rogues who loved them. Discussing the "sexy bits" with his mom had thoroughly traumatized him.

"I haven't read a historical romance before," she admitted, studying the book's cover which featured a curvy, sexy brunette in a pink dress.

"We could read it together."

"Okay. I noticed the bookshop on Main Street. I could stop there tomorrow. How late are they open?"

"Nah." He took the book from her hand. "We can read it together."

"Like reading aloud to each other?"

"Our own adult version of story time." He winced. "That sounded far dirtier than I meant it."

"I wouldn't mind a little dirty." With a bat of her lashes, she pointed her fork at him.

Grinning, he ate the small piece of asparagus at the end of her fork.

Damn. Her vagina clenched.

"Noted." He speared his last piece of asparagus and held it out.

She took it.

"When was the last time you had a…little dirty?"

"Sex?" She blurted almost spitting out her bite.

"Yes." He cleared his throat.

"Ten years ago. It was fine, but I… I wasn't ready then."

"I haven't had sex since Marianne, and that was at least a year before we separated," he said as he started clearing their empty plates.

Elle rose to help. "You weren't ready either?" She turned on the sink and squirted in dish soap, lemon-scented steam rising from the hot water and bubbles.

"Nope. I'm not the casual kind of guy, remember?"

"I'm not a casual kind of girl."

"I know." He stared at her.

A beat passed, their gazes caught and held. He saw her, and she saw him. It was both exhilarating and terrifying. Like the time she'd gone zip-lining with Willa in Catalina. Weightless, she dangled twenty feet in the air but felt secure in the anchored sensation of being tethered to the safety line.

"So, you can help, or you can go explore. There's a whole second floor and basement."

"I should probably help you clean."

He kissed her cheek. "Go snoop. I'll find you after I take Fitz out."

While he had his arms elbow deep in sudsy water, she glided out of the room. Choosing the second floor, she glanced at family photos dotting the wall leading upstairs.

There were three doors in the upper hallway. The first was a guest room, decorated in simple shades of gray, with a single picture of Letchworth in the fall. The next door opened into a bathroom with the smallest counter space. That would never do for all her hair products. At the end of the hall stood the last closed door. It was Clayton's bedroom.

Entering the dark room, she hit the switch turning on the overhead light and two small wall sconces. Two large windows were draped in navy-blue curtains, flanking a king-sized bed. The matching navy blankets were soft under her touch as her fingers skated along the neatly made bed. More bookshelves, including the promised row of books filled with feisty historical heroines, lined the walls. A barn-style door separated the bedroom from the bathroom.

Her gaze drifted to the closet door on the other side of the room, and she squealed. *The hat!* On the drive to Buffalo, Clayton had mentioned a cowboy hat that he'd worn to a Garth Brooks concert with Noah as teens, which he still owned. Swinging open the door and switching on the closet light, she observed his organization. Shoes neat on racks at the bottom, clothes hung by type. On the top shelf sat several rows of baseball caps. That's where she found the black cowboy hat. Rising on her toes, she reached for the hat and slid it to the edge of the shelf. It tumbled into her chest. Laughing, she placed it on her head, turning to check herself out in the long mirror that hung on the wall across from the closet door.

"You look good, cowgirl," Clayton drawled in a twangy accent, leaning against the door frame.

"I bet you'd look better," she said.

Sauntering to her, he reached for the hat. Skimming her fingers with his, he took the hat and settled it on his own head. The brim obscured his eyes just enough to leave anyone looking at him puzzled at the story hidden within.

"I think I need you to answer the door wearing that hat, jeans, and nothing else."

With the rise of his lips, Elle knew that she'd said that aloud. *Perhaps don't speak all your thoughts.*

"Noted," he said, those gray eyes smoldering. His chest bumped hers as he returned the hat to its spot.

Heat from his body lapped against her skin.

He settled his hands on her waist. "Any other discoveries?"

"Do you make your bed every day?" Her breathy voice kept cadence with the thump of her heart.

"Yup."

Oh, god. He's perfect.

"I think we should muss it up," she purred.

"Are you sure?" His throat bobbed.

In response, she lifted to her toes, placing her lips against his.

Pulling inches away from her, he whispered, "I want you so much, but I don't have protection. I tried to buy condoms, but they have them in the same aisle as the lady products and I ran into your aunt. I pretended I'd gone down the wrong aisle until she left and when I attempted to sneak back over, my mom walked into the store."

"Small towns." She rolled her eyes.

"I know." He looked sorrowful.

Elle thought for a moment before speaking. "I'm on birth control to regulate my periods." *Period? Really?* She closed her eyes in embarrassment, but then opened them with certainty. "It's been years since I had sex and I was tested after the last time. I see my doctor annually. I'm safe."

His eyes were soft and sincere. "I'm safe."

"Ok." She wrapped her arms around his neck.

"Are you sure?" he asked again, his mouth scant inches from hers.

"Yes!" She sloshed an eager breath.

"We can stop at any time." The heat from his breath was a ghost of a kiss on her.

"Kiss me already," she almost growled.

With that, he sealed his mouth to hers. Strong hands splayed across her arching back taking their kiss deeper, and his exploring tongue danced with hers. Elle threaded her hands into his hair, tugging him closer. A small whimper left her lips as his hands gripped her backside. The firmness of his body pressed hard against her softness.

He moved her backward until she was against the door frame, then lifted her, settling her legs around his waist. The giggles returned but were soon replaced by a soft moan as his rigidness rubbed against her. The friction of the layers of satin panties and his jeans sparked a deep need.

"Bed. Now," she gasped.

Clenched firmly against his body he carried her to the bed then set her on her feet in front of it. With his eyes tethered to her, she slid her denim jacket off and let it fall to the floor. He found the zipper of her red dress and lowered it. The soft fabric fell down her curves, pooling at her feet. Arching her brow, she unclasped her bra dropping it on the pile of clothes at their feet. Holding his gaze, she tugged her underwear off. Stepping away from the pile of clothes at her feet, she stood naked in front of him.

"Say something," she whispered resisting the urge to cover herself with her arms.

"I'm afraid if I do, I'll wake up from this dream," he rasped.

"Your turn." She bit her lip, both amused and eager.

Clayton's swift fingers unbuttoned his shirt, letting it drop behind him. Before the shirt hit the ground, he had pulled his white undershirt over his head and tossed it aside. With a sexy glint, he undid his belt, then stepped out of his jeans and kicked them to the side.

His muscular body clad only in black boxer briefs was a work of art. The planes of his sculpted chest rising and falling with his deep breaths. The proof that he truly liked what he saw tented the fabric. Maintaining their locked stare, he dragged off his underwear.

Wow. She swept an appreciative gaze up his impressive length. A twinge of need contracting in her pelvic muscles.

"Come here," she ordered.

Crossing the distance in two steps, his arms pulled her in close. His mouth demanded, while his hands explored. Elle teased her fingers up and down his spine reveling in the clenching of his back muscles. The wet heat of his mouth traced down her throat to her collarbone. A pleasurable groan escaped as his teeth grazed one nipple then drew the tip deep for a sharp nip followed by a soothing suck.

Elle's back arched as he repeated the action on her other breast. The liquid heat between her thighs surged as he raised her right leg to his hip. Holding her in place he lowered one hand between them, his fingers finding her throbbing clit.

His capable fingers moved in a slow circular fashion. Tingles raced through her, taunting her with promised release. Gripping his shoulders, she melted into his increased pressure against her. Sweet sensation built with each flick, swirl, and press of his finger until she panted his name as she came.

Hungry and wanting more, she slipped out of Clayton's hold, pushing him onto the bed. Like a prowling lioness, she crawled over him. Positioning him at her entrance, her eyes locked with his as she sank onto him. His guttural moan of satisfaction filled the room as he was sheathed in her, inch by slow inch.

The brief pinching sensation morphed to a decadent full-ness as her body stretched to accommodate his girth. Placing her hands on his at her hips, she squeezed as they moved in a gentle rhythmic pace.

"You feel so good." His whisper was hoarse.

She moved her hands to his chest and braced herself as their movements became more frantic. She lowered her chest to his, an angle that reached deeper and sent shockwaves of ecstasy through her. The pleasurable waves inched closer, hazing her vision.

Clayton's fingertips bit into her hips, then he moved a hand between them, pressing just where she wanted him.

"Clayton!" she screamed with release. Her thighs trembled and she pressed her mouth against his neck to stifle her cries.

"Don't hold back. I want to hear you," he growled, thrusting up into her, drawing out her orgasm and driving to his own.

Riding out her climax, she whimpered with each pleasurable aftershock.

"Fuck!" he gritted out as his release claimed him.

Spent, she collapsed on his chest, and Clayton wrapped his arms tight around her back, his fingertips tracing lines on her ribs. Elle remained on top with Clayton still inside of her, panting against his neck and pressing a palm to his cheek.

"That was nice," she panted as she wiggled her hips and patted the side of his face.

The rumble of his laughter vibrated through them. His laugh really was her favorite song.

TWENTY

"Mr. Knightley, if I have not spoken, it is because I am afraid I will awaken myself from this dream."
~Jane Austen, *Emma*

C hurch bells stirred Elle from a luxurious slumber. Clayton grumbled, rolling away from her to turn off the alarm on his phone. Rolling back to her, he snuggled Elle close, one arm wrapped firmly around her waist.

"Good morning." She flipped onto her back, remaining happily caged in his arms.

"Morning," he said, his sleep-drunk voice low and deep. "How did you sleep?"

"Fantastic. You?"

"Better than I deserve."

"You deserve a lot." She placed a hand on his cheek, her chest filled with emotion.

"So do you." He captured her lower lip.

The fluttering in Elle's chest settled in her belly and turned nervous. Unspoken words, a needed conversation, waltzed between them.

"I don't want to ruin this." Her voice was soft.

"Hey." Clayton combed his fingers into the tendrils of her sleep-mussed hair.

"This moment… I leave in a few weeks. I don't know what will happen then. This could just be a moment for us or…" She stopped, searching his eyes.

"More." His stare was intense and hopeful.

She squashed the potential promise building inside her. "I don't have a plan, which is weird for me."

His fingers slipped from her hair and traced the line of her lips.

"What I do know is that I like you…a lot. I'd like to keep seeing you, but I don't know what tomorrow looks like for us. I want to live in the today with you…but I understand that is not fair to you and if you want to dial this ba—"

The hungry press of his lips stole her words.

He shifted away. "If losing my brother has taught me anything, it's that we're not promised tomorrow. Elle, I would rather have one single moment with you than a life-time with anyone else."

Her breath caught at his words. "Did you just paraphrase Julia Roberts from *Steel Magnolias*?" she grinned.

Humor was always her go-to for uncomfortable moments. It was hard for her to put herself out there, to ask for something she wanted. Elle had never experienced a moment where she wanted someone to care for her so much that they chose her. He chose her. No guarantee. Just his declaration that it was Elle, nobody else.

"Perhaps," he said, with a playful lilt.

"I mean… it's no Austen."

"True. Ms. Austen would say…" He licked at the seam of her lips. "What are men to rocks and mountains?"

"*Pride and Prejudice*," she giggled.

He coaxed her mouth open for a deep kiss before

running his tongue down her neck. "If I could but know his heart, everything could become easier." His tongue flicked her collarbone.

"*Sense and Sensibility*." A flush of desire surged between her thighs.

"Very good, Ms. Davidson," he said, lifting the hem of her T-shirt up. A slow hot flick of his tongue grazed one pebbled nipple, then the other. "There could have been no two hearts so open, no tastes so similar, no feeling so in unison."

"*Persuasion*," she moaned, as he rolled her nipple with his slick tongue.

Her fingers threaded through his hair as he licked over to the second breast repeating his tantalizing action. Her breath shallowed as he pressed kisses in a firm line down her stomach, lingering with a soft kiss on her belly button. He cupped one of her breasts before moving farther down until his head was between her legs. His sharp inhale, and the soft touch of his lips made her stomach clench and pleasure sigh through her.

Elle pressed her hand flat against the smooth sheets, grounding herself to this moment. This was the first time anyone had gone down on her. This was so intimate, her sex open and bare to him. Heat swept up her chest and face as her heart raced with the unexpected need tumbling within.

"Oh! I am delighted with this book! I should like to spend my whole life reading it."

His words made her heart pulsate not just with the anticipated pleasure but with what he was saying. She was his favorite book, and he had no intention of putting her on the shelf.

"*Northanger Abbey*," she gasped as he lathed his tongue through her folds.

Her fingers grasped the sheets finding purchase as he

took her to the edge. The rhythmic pressure of his seeking mouth and licking tongue and the sudden dip of his fingers inside her body urged a release from both the building tension between her legs and the fears of what would come next.

Thank you, Miss Austen.

TWENTY-ONE

"Do not be in a hurry, the right man will come at last."
~Jane Austen, *Pride and Prejudice*

W ho would have guessed Elle Davidson would be excited to go to the VFW? Wrapping up her workday early, she had enough time to change, freshen up, and get to the VFW by seven. With Clayton and Pete debuting as a one-night-only team, she wanted to be there for every second of it. Pulling on her favorite pair of skinny dark blue jeans and a flowy red tank, she felt sexy but not too sexy. She was going to the VFW to watch her uncle play darts, after all. The jeans screamed "Take me off!" while the top more subtly suggested "Take me to dinner first." Although, she doubted she'd make Clayton take her to dinner before helping her out of these jeans.

After clasping on her starfish pendant and tugging a brush through her long hair, she grabbed a cardigan and headed out. The VFW parking lot was almost filled. Elle had to park around back, away from the main entrance.

"Hey, Laney!" Elle waved, walking over to the bar as she entered the VFW.

"Hey, Eleanor... Elle." Laney said.

Guess that's sticking.

"Do you know if Pete and Janet have ordered anything yet?" Elle asked.

"Nope, but I know they're here. I saw Janet come in about ten minutes ago."

"Great. Can I order a pitcher of Genny Lite, and an order of mild and an order of hot wings?" Elle paused, her face drawn into a hopeful expression. "Do you have Ketel One yet?"

"Still a VFW." Laney rolled her eyes, filling a pitcher.

"A girl can dream. Vodka soda with whatever moonshine you have." Elle took the handle of the pitcher as Laney pushed it toward her.

"I'll bring the wings over when they're out." Laney smiled, handing Elle her drink.

"How much, Laney?"

"It's on him," she gestured to someone behind Elle.

Elle spun to find her favorite gray eyes looking at her. An unabashed grin accentuated Clayton's strong jaw line.

"Hey, Laney." He tipped his head toward Laney without breaking eye contact with Elle. "Elle."

"Clayton." Heat inched up her neck to her cheeks. It had been twelve hours since she last saw him, and they had texted on and off most of the day. Yet, her body reacted as if it had been days. The *thump, thump* of her heart drowned out the raucous laughter of the men at the corner of the bar.

"You look..." His darkening eyes raked over her. "... nice." His lips said nice, but his stare said something else entirely.

"Thanks." She licked her lips, staring at his mouth.

"I thought you'd like some help..." His voice was buttery

as he bent close to her ear, his arm reaching around her to the bar. The warmth of his breath planted a phantom kiss below her ear as he spoke. "…with carrying all this." Clayton's tone was flirtatious as he straightened, holding the pitcher of beer.

Elle gulped her drink, her throat suddenly dry.

"Nobody is in the banquet room if you two need to be alone," Laney snarked from behind Elle.

Elle laughed nervously, turning. "Oh Laney, you're funny."

"Suuuuree. I'll bring those wings out in a bit. Have fun, you two." Laney moved down to the large group of men at the end of the bar.

"You need to stop that." Elle hissed with a laugh, pointing at Clayton.

"Stop what?" His eyes smoldered.

"That!" She motioned to his eyes.

"Well, you need to stop that." He wagged his finger at her.

"What?"

"Being you. It's utterly irresistible." He winked, placing his hand on her lower back, guiding her away from the bar.

"I'm serious." She warned, the crimson of her cheeks no doubt matching the color of her top.

"Me too." He smiled, a glint of mischief in his eyes. "Don't worry. I'll be good, starting now."

"Thank you." She bit her lower lip. "If you're good now, you can be naughty later."

"Noted." he murmured, the pads of his fingers massaging her lower back.

"Elle!" Pete greeted, hugging her as they arrived at their table.

"Look at you in jeans!" Janet fawned, turning her around to inspect. "Who knew you had a nice little booty."

"Janet!" Elle swatted away Janet's hands.

"Pete, we're still good with Walk the Dog as our name, right?" Clayton shifted talk away from Elle's butt.

In the thrall of her hormones since seeing Clayton tonight, Elle hadn't looked closely at what both men were wearing. Pete wore a black T-shirt with large white block lettering spelling out *GrandPAW* over a white silhouette of a lab. Clayton's white T-shirt featured a sleeping Fitz, of course, with the words *Pug Daddy* hovering above the image.

Team Walk the Dog played in one of the first matches. They played Let It Wine, comprised of Noah and Todd. Team Walk the Dog won that match.

The night proceeded with match after match filled with good natured ribbing. When the guys weren't playing, they joined Elle and Janet at the table, munching on wings and sipping their beer.

"Elle, beer?" Todd asked, as he appeared with a fresh pitcher for the table.

"Sorry, I don't like beer," she scrunched her nose.

Todd placed his hand on his heart and let out an exaggerated gasp, "She says to the brewmaster!"

Talk turned to Noah and Todd's soon-to-open brewery. The new place, located just off Main Street around the corner from the Village Rose, would open in May once renovations were finished.

"I bet I can change your mind on beer." Todd winked at Elle before motioning to Noah. "We should do a tasting."

"Yes! At my house. What are you all doing tomorrow night?" Noah said.

"Pete and I have a date. He's taking me to the drive-in." Janet grinned.

"To neck?" Elle teased.

"*Maybe.*"

"Gross. Why did I say that?" Elle groaned.

"Elle, you free?" Todd asked, his eyes expectant.

"I'm supposed to meet up with Carmen."

"Just bring her."

"Umm…alright." Elle said.

"Clayton, you in?"

Clayton shrugged and Elle nodded. Guess they were going to a beer tasting.

"I'll make a cheeseboard," Elle offered.

"Hey whiners, you're up!" someone shouted from the darts area.

"Let's go." Todd tugged Noah away.

"I love Todd for him." Elle sighed gleefully, motioning to Noah, now in a headlock by Todd.

"He's the only person who flusters Noah." Clayton said, sipping from Elle's drink like it was the most natural thing in the world. "Oh, you need a fresh drink. Want something?" He scrunched his nose.

"Better make it an iced tea. I'm driving."

"I'll grab it." He squeezed her shoulder.

Elle's gaze lingered on his back as he retreated. Or rather on how his jeans hung on his hips until snapping fingers flashed in front of her.

"What's going on there?" Aunt Janet probed.

"He's getting me an iced tea," Elle said coyly.

"Is that a euphemism?"

"Janet!" *Distract her.* "Hey, I have news. I have to fly to Boston on Wednesday for a work thing. I need to buy a dress. Do you want to go shopping on Monday? I'm taking the day off. My assistant found an adorable boutique in Williamsville that I'd like to check out. We could do lunch after."

"Hell yes!" Janet squealed.

They finalized details as the last match of the night began. The Charles Brothers, who had won every Thursday for the last six years, stood against Team Walk the Dog. The air thick as everyone inched closer to the dart boards.

Clayton stepped to the line holding his yellow dart. Tiny beads of sweat dotted Pete's brow, undermining his confident stare. Elle gave Clayton a reassuring thumbs up as he lined up his shot.

Everyone held their breath as Clayton lifted his arm and let his dart fly.

"Bull's-eye!" Noah yelled, jumping in the air to chest bump Todd.

Everyone cheered, Pete swung Clayton in the air like a rag doll.

Janet bellowed at Pete to put Doc down before he hurt his back. "You're almost 50!" she jeered.

Placing Clayton down, Pete ran over to his wife, scooping her up for a big sloppy kiss.

Elle watched Clayton, who shook hands with the other team.

As Clayton turned to walk away from the Charles Brothers, he stopped and locked eyes with her. Grinning from ten feet away the sea of congratulating spectators faded away.

Jump! Elle's heart sucker punched her logic and took control. Without thinking, she ran toward Clayton and leapt into his waiting arms. Clayton dipped his head and kissed her hard. In that moment everything and everyone else dissolved. It was just them.

"I knew it!" Janet's shrill voice jolted Elle back to reality.

Elle wiggled free of Clayton's arms and faced her aunt. Clayton threaded his arms around her waist. Janet's features toggled between "I knew it" and gushing. Pete stood, arms crossed, with an expression that Elle couldn't read.

"Him?" Pete gestured to Clayton but kept his stare on Elle.

"Yes." Elle leaned against Clayton for support.

Pete's blue eyes flicked between them.

"Son…" Pete cleared his throat, placing a firm hand on Clayton's shoulder. "…The family will be having dinner Monday to welcome Tobey and Jerome back home. I hope you can be there."

"Of course."

"Great. I can show you my gun collection." Pete's stare featured a slightly menacing glint. "Alright kiddo, we're heading home. I love you." He kissed Elle's forehead and she pushed into his chest, his arms tugging her close.

"He's a good man. Just like you."

"To me, nobody will ever be good enough. Although, I know he'll come close." Pete whispered back, clenching her tight. "Make sure she gets home safely."

"Yes, sir."

"Oh man, I thought Coach was going to kick your ass." Todd chuckled, once Pete and Janet were out of earshot.

"Nah." Noah waved Todd off. "Elle will protect him."

Later, hands clasped, they walked to her rental. The dark parking lot was nearly deserted. The only illumination a single flood light hanging on the side of the VFW several feet away from her parked car.

As Clayton traced her lips with his soft fingers, he said, "Did Braedon get your travel booked?"

"Yeah. I fly out of Buffalo at seven a.m. Wednesday and fly back Thursday early."

"Is the dinner something you'd take a date to?" he asked, his fingers slipping into the loops of her jeans.

"If it was back in L.A., I'd probably drag Willa or Viet."

"So, dates are allowed?"

"Yes." Her voice was thready as the pads of his fingers dragged up her torso over the thin fabric of her top.

"Do you want a date?"

Her body was heating from his touch and questions. "It's in Boston."

"Do you want a date?" he repeated, his fingers moving torturously slow up her throat.

"I'm only gone for twenty-four hours."

"Do you want a date?" His fingers inched up her face to her hairline, combing through her smooth strands.

"It's too much to ask."

"Answer my question."

"Clayton." she sighed.

"Ask for what you want." he said, eyes determined.

Something tight filled her chest. To just ask for what she wanted was huge for her. Asking left her vulnerable to being crushed by a "no". If she didn't ask, she couldn't be crushed by his response. This man stood in front of her demanding for her to ask, to say what *she* wanted.

"Will you fly to Boston with me for a day to wear something pink at a boring fundraiser with me?" Her voice cracked a little.

"Of course."

"But it's such an imposition—"

He stopped her with a kiss.

Lifting his head, he cupped her face. "Nothing's an imposition when you care about someone. And I care about you Elle, very much."

Her smile trembled as much as the butterflies in her belly.

"Will you stay with me tonight?" Clayton asked.

"Well, as you are a dead man walking, I should."

"I think I know what I'd like for my last meal." He nipped at her bottom lip.

"We should probably get home then."

Clayton kissed her slowly, his hands moving to her waist.

"Yes." he murmured, dragging his mouth to her throat. "I thought your yoga pants were killing me, but these jeans are annihilating my self-control. I fought pulling you into the banquet room all night."

"And what would happen in that room?"

"I'd start here." He kissed below her ear. "Then here." He licked her throat.

He dropped his hands to grip Elle's butt and lifted her. She wrapped her thighs around his hips. A small moan escaped as Clayton ground against her. The friction of the denim layers between them heated her core like a pan of water just starting to boil.

"Seriously, if you two need a room I can unlock the door for you." Laney's mocking voice shattered their lust-filled bubble.

Clayton released Elle's legs, allowing her to slide to her feet while remaining pressed against her either to keep her shielded or to hide his erection. Elle buried her blazing face in his neck. Had she just gotten caught making out in the VFW parking lot? *Sure did.*

"Thanks. I think we'll head home." Clayton cleared his throat.

"Good night…Sleep tight," she taunted suggestively as she walked away.

Elle burst out in horrified laughter, grabbing at her stomach. "If she tells anyone and my uncle finds out…"

"All the more reason for us to hurry home. I've got a final meal to devour."

TWENTY-TWO

"Every moment has its pleasures and its hopes."
~Jane Austen, *Mansfield Park*

The news was out! By ten-thirty, Elle's phone pinged with incoming messages.

Beth had sent a group text.

Beth: CJ OWENS!? YOU'RE DATING CJ Owens???

Carmen: YAY!

Elle: Beth, you live in Chicago. How do you know this?

Beth: My Mom. Everyone knows the pastor's wife has the BEST gossip.

Elle: He's Clayton now, not CJ, and yes, I am seeing him.

Beth: So, I guess you aren't Charlotte Lucas, after all.

Carmen: Lizzie!!!!

Elle had never been the Lizzie Bennet of her story, always playing the tried-and-true best friend, the wise one with witty comments and sage advice that seemed to come from no actual experience. This was an undiscovered continent for Elle to explore…the leading lady of her own story.

Taking the rest of the day off, Elle drove to Noah's bakery, the Farmer's Wife, picking up a variety of treats and headed to Clayton's vet practice. The clinic was located on the edge of the village.

Meghan, Clayton and Jerome's partner, greeted her with a smile as she walked through the front door. "Elle!"

Elle placed two large boxes of cupcakes on the counter. Needless to say, she was a hit with the staff, who referred to her as "Mrs. Doc." Upon hearing that, the tug-of-war between tensing muscles and spreading warmth left her head spinning.

Clayton was with a patient, so Meghan led her down a narrow hall, past bathrooms, and several storage closets to an alcove with three office doors. A picture of Fitz hung outside one of the doors. The small office walls featured exposed brick and little else. Pulling the pad of purple Post-Its Clayton bought her out of her purse, she scribbled a quick note tacking it on the inside lid of the cinnamon roll box, setting it on the desk beside the laptop.

As Elle walked to her car, her phone pinged with Clayton's response to her flirty Post-It.

Fitz's Human: Something sweet for me to devour other than you, eh?
Elle: To quench your appetite until tonight.
Fitz's Human: Impossible.

In the mirror, Elle could see the full-faced smile plastered on her face. The entire experience with his staff had been warm and welcoming, like she was family.

On her way back to the Little Red Barn she stopped for a tea from Cow Tales, the town's book and coffeeshop. She'd also picked up supplies for the cheeseboard and a few bottles of wine to take to Noah's house. As she stowed a couple of gifts she'd bought, she lounged on the couch, bare feet swaying, getting lost in the romance of Anne Elliot and Captain Wentworth.

Her reading pleasure was interrupted by a knock.

"Ma'am." Clayton drawled, tipping the brim of his black cowboy hat, standing shirtless in jeans that hung low on his cut physique. A black T-shirt dangled from one of his hands.

Elle licked her lips and dragged him inside. Shutting the door, she pressed him against it and lowered to her knees in front of him. Clayton's breath caught, as she opened the top button of his jeans and unzipped them. Pulling down his jeans and underwear, she released him. She grasped him, peering up through hooded lashes, to see his throat bob.

"Elle," Clayton moaned, as she licked up his length. His guttural "Fuck" and the thud of his head hitting the back of the door was all the encouragement she needed.

Sated and cleaned up, they stood in the kitchen preparing the cheese board to head to Noah's. Confidence bloomed in Elle as she hip-checked Clayton, who stood next to her slicing cheese. The sleeveless creamy white dress, her loose waves allowing the purple of the newly purchased lilac earrings to stand out against auburn strands, making her feel like the heroine from a summer romance.

"You wear this a lot. Does it mean something?" he asked, rubbing the starfish pendant hanging a few inches below her collarbone.

"It does." Her lips tugged up with the memory. "Viet's mother, Anh, told me this story once. An old man is on a beach watching a young girl throwing starfish into the sea. He asks her what she's doing. She explains that it's low tide and if they don't get thrown back into the water, they'll die. As he looks down the miles and miles of beach filled with hundreds of starfish, he says you won't save them all. You won't make a difference. She picks up a starfish and tosses it into the ocean telling the old man that she made a difference for that one."

Clayton traced the edges of her starfish pendant as if imprinting it to memory. "I like that. It's how I feel about my practice. Saving the world one pet at a time."

Noah lived in his childhood home buying the blue Victorian from his parents when they decided to downsize. Their small party gathered in Noah's mancave. It was an actual mancave complete with a large bar, oversize leather couch, and framed Wheaties boxes with Doug Flutie and Jim Kelly, posters of Buffalo Sabres players, and team photos featuring he and Clayton in football, basketball, and track uniforms.

"Elle and Clayton!" Carmen squealed, her arms in the air, an amused Mathew standing nearby.

"Who needs a drink?" Todd smirked from behind the bar, lining up small beer tasting glasses. "Our mission, if you choose to accept it, and you will, is to help find Elle a beer she likes."

The first beer he served was a blonde ale called Sunrise at Letchworth. It was smoother than Elle had imagined but wasn't something she'd have more than one of. The next was called The Yellow Jacket named for the school's mascot and featured a tinging bite courtesy of added jalapeño. *No thank you!*

Next up was the Farmer's Wife's Cookie, a stout with a

nutmeg and vanilla that tasted like liquid dessert, but its richness wouldn't allow her to drink more than a few sips. They sampled an IPA called the Mayor, an ode to Carmen. Elle confessed to liking the real Carmen better than the beer. Todd slid the next one in front of her. The sour brew was called The Detention Slip. Todd pointed out that he doubted Elle would like it but wanted her to try all standing menu items. Carmen and Elle laughed as they toasted to finally getting detention. *Terrible!*

"I saved this one for last. I know this is going to be the one you want over and over again." Todd's mouth curved up with confidence, pouring a smooth amber liquid into fresh, tasting glasses.

"Best for last." Noah winked.

Elle sniffed the creamy liquid before raising the small glass in a toast to their brew master. "Kiss my brass!"

Noah watched Elle's face as she sipped. Flavor cascaded along her tastebuds.

"That's the winner," she declared and took another sip. "Todd, that is really good. I could have that every day."

"I told you!" Noah said, his grin cheeky as he high-fived Todd.

Carmen buried her face in her hands, trying to conceal her loud giggles. Mathew looked away, hiding his smirk. Even Clayton chuckled.

Elle's forehead wrinkled. "What's so funny?"

Todd turned the bottle he had poured from, revealing the label. "This one is called the Doc Owens."

Realization reddened Elle's face knowing full well the "Doc" on the label was not Clayton's father. She buried her face against Clayton's chest as the entire group erupted in raucous laughter.

"The beer is smooth, just like my guy," Noah bragged, raising his glass.

"To Doc!" Everyone shouted, raising their glasses to Clayton in salute.

Todd poured more beer and the cheese board was emptied of its contents. The best of the late 90's played in the background. Elle finished a second full glass of Doc Owens as her Doc Owens's arm twined around her.

With an "I'll be back," Clayton slipped away to call his sister, who was flying in the next morning for their mom's sixty-second birthday.

"I've got a treat for you all," Todd announced. "It's called Surviving Christmas, and we'll have it and the pumpkin ale in our sample packs for the holidays. See if you can taste the different flavors. I age it in a special barrel." He poured samples for Mathew, Carmen, and Elle.

She sniffed and the aroma assaulted her nostrils. Every muscle grew rigid, and a chill slithered down her spine making the air feel like a cold January night instead of the heat of August. The scent of bourbon flooded her senses and her hands trembled as she placed the glass down. She splayed her fingers on the bar's smooth surface, trying to anchor her in the now and not slip to the past.

That smell. Closing her eyes, the softness of her dress suddenly transformed into the scratchy fabric of her grandma's afghan. Mathew's laugh morphed into a sneering voice saying, "*You're lucky it was me.*" The faint aroma of chocolate in the beer transformed to sticky, spilled hot chocolate.

Gripping the edge of the bar, she sucked in a hard breath. *I'm safe. I'm in Noah's basement and not on that couch.*

"Elle." Noah's voice was hushed as his warm hand covered hers.

She flinched. *It's Noah, not Jamie.*

Noah's eyes were bright with concern. "I almost forgot you asked where the bathroom was. Guys, we'll be back," he said, like nothing was happening and everything was okay.

But it wasn't. *Fucking bourbon.* All it took was one tiny sniff to drag her to the past.

Gently, Noah took Elle by the arm, and guided her nonchalantly up the stairs. "I got you, you're safe," he whispered so only she could hear.

Blinking as if waking from a long sleep, Elle found herself in an unfamiliar room, atop a plush armchair. Noah knelt in front of her, patience and worry drawn on his features.

Elle's breath settled, and her eyes focused. Her tense muscles released, and she felt as if all the air whooshed out of her. She inhaled sharply and realized where she was and what had happened. It had been so long since that had happened, since Jamie crept into a happy moment like an unwelcome dinner guest.

"I'm sorry. Did everyone notice?" She steadied her breathing.

"No. Everyone was focused on something stupid Mathew was doing," Noah assured her.

Elle exhaled shakily, thankful for Mathew's goofball antics. "But you noticed?"

"Only because I know that look… I have PTSD from my time in the Marines," he said.

Elle closed her eyes, trying not to picture what horror Noah might have seen or heard during his two tours in Iraq. Better than most, she understood how trauma affected people.

"I used to love fires in our firepit. My family did them every Sunday, even in the winter. But after… we don't anymore. I can see images on the news and watch war movies, but when that burning smell comes up…it clobbers me."

"Bourbon does it for me."

"Shit. Todd ages that brew in a bourbon barrel. I saw the

dazed look in your eyes when you smelled it, I knew something was wrong."

"Did he tell you?" Her whispered question held an unspoken hope that Clayton hadn't said anything.

"Clayton? He'd never utter a word unless you told him it was okay." His look was earnest. "I don't know what happened, but I do understand triggers. I've had some great counselors at the VA. The triggers and the memories never go away, but you get better at dealing with them. Good friends and a sturdy shoulder to lean on help."

"Thanks for…" She knew she didn't have the words to express the depth of her appreciation.

Behind Noah's charming smile hid a deep well of intuition, patience, and kindness. On the surface, he appeared the handsome entrepreneur always ready with an unbridled smile, flirty wink, and perfect words. It was easy to overlook his watchful eyes that saw so much more than others. He was exactly who she thought he was in high school and so much more.

"Just standing in for him." Noah said, tipping his head to the door.

Elle twisted in the chair. Clayton stood in the doorway worry etched on his face.

"I'll leave you two." Noah squeezed Elle's hand, then rose, and moved toward Clayton.

"Noah…"

He stopped, looking over his shoulder, his blue eyes warm like a tropical sea.

"…Thank you."

"Anytime." He smiled.

"What happened?" Clayton murmured, walking to the chair and kneeling in front of Elle, who wrapped her arms around him.

"Todd served this beer made in a bourbon barrel. That night Jamie had been drinking…"

"Bourbon." He finished her sentence, tightening his arms protectively, as if Jamie was in the room.

In a way he was. The alcohol's aroma summoned Jamie's ghost, which sank into her like a razor toothed crocodile.

"I just froze. Noah noticed."

"When I went back you and Noah were gone."

"Why'd you come to find me?"

"Call it intuition. Something told me I had to find you."

"You always find me when I need you, don't you?" Elle tilted her face to him.

"I try." He pressed a tender kiss to her forehead.

There was no trying; he just did. His presence was a warm blanket to wrap herself in. He'd always catch her if she fell.

"I think I'm ready to go back down." She squared her shoulders.

"Are you sure? We can leave if you want." He released her and straightened to his full height.

"No. I can't let him continue to control me."

For years, she had relinquished so much control to Jamie and her mom. *No more.*

"Plus, I have my support human." Elle laced her fingers through his.

"Always." He lifted her hand to his lips and kissed her knuckles.

As the night ended, they paused next to his pickup.

"I have two questions," he said.

"I have two answers," she teased.

"My mom's birthday dinner is on Sunday. Will you go with me?"

"Of course." They'd be flying to Boston for her, she could

come to dinner to celebrate his mom, a woman she liked. "What's your second question?" Her tone flirty.

"Will you stay with me for the rest of your trip?"

Her throat went dry. "What?"

"Stay with me every night while you're still here. It makes sense to move your things over to the farmhouse. You've stayed there every night since Tuesday. Or we can keep things as they are, and I'll ask you to stay with me daily. I just… I…" He let out a steadying breath. "I just want you with me."

Elle's pulse quickened with each word. They'd be living together. It would be temporary, like going on vacation with someone, but he wasn't on vacation. This was his home, his life. Although she had known him as a girl, until two weeks ago when they'd reignited a friendship, he'd never been anything but CJ.

Now, he was Clayton, a man she was falling for. A man who was worth taking a leap for.

The pace of her heart roared. With a long intake of reassuring air and eyes wide, she jumped. "Yes."

TWENTY-THREE

"I am the happiest creature in the world. Perhaps other people have said so before, but not one with such justice."
~Jane Austen, *Pride and Prejudice*

It was too late to pack up her things tonight, so they decided to do that tomorrow. After a stop at the Little Red Barn to get Elle's overnight bag, they walked into the farmhouse.

"I want to show you something." Clayton slipped Elle's overnight bag off her shoulder and placed it beside the stairs.

Taking his warm hand, Elle let him lead her into the kitchen. "This is when I find out you are the Dexter of Perry, isn't it?" Elle teased, standing in front of the basement door.

"I only chop up people who leave their dogs out in the rain."

"Completely justified."

"Start walking," he laughed, pressing his chest against her back, and reaching in front of her to open the door and turn on the light.

Elle walked down the stairs and discovered his version of

a mancave. Like upstairs, there were hardwood floors. A small bar made of light wood and three matching high-back stools sat in the front of the room. A plush sectional couch, the color of a Christmas tree, drew Elle, and she sank into pillowy cushiness that hugged her body. Adjusting to sink deeper, she admired the cream-colored walls bedecked with photos of Letchworth in every season.

"You have a mancave!"

Clayton crossed his arms, eyes crinkled in amusement. "It's not a mancave, it's a finished basement."

"This is a mancave. Look at that TV. We are so watching *Sense and Sensibility* on that." She exclaimed, pointing to the extra-large flatscreen TV hung opposite the couch.

"Can you watch *Sense and Sensibility* in mancaves?" he mused.

"If the man in the mancave reads Austen. Hey, what's that?" She pointed to a door in the corner.

"Go find out," he winked.

"If there are dead bodies in here, I'll be most displeased."

As she stepped through the door, she squealed. Clayton had a home gym with a weight bench, a series of dumbbells in different weights and, she gasped, a treadmill. In Long Beach, she'd converted her guest room into a combination office and exercise room, but this was impressive.

"You should have led with this. I would have agreed to stay with you *much* sooner."

"Well, I had to make sure you didn't just want me for my home gym." He leaned against the door frame, his eyes following her as she explored.

"This is a perk." She looked up with a flirtatious timbre to her voice. "Although, I only want you for your body…and Fitz."

"My body, eh?" His voice lowered as he inched closer.

"And Fitz." She took two steps closer to him.

"Mostly my body, though." His brows arched as he closed the distance between them.

"Mostly Fitz." She winked, hip checking him as she walked past. "It's a close race, but I could be convinced," she purred.

Looking at him over her shoulder, she unzipped her dress. The garment floated to the ground, pooling at her feet. With a seductive glance over her shoulder, she swayed out of the room. She'd made it halfway to the couch when strong hands came around her waist, tucking her flush against a firm chest.

"How can I…" Clayton ran his hands up her waist to her breasts, pinching her tightening nipples through the lacy fabric of her bra. "…tip the scales?"

She let out a soft moan as he pushed the cups of her bra down, freeing her aching breasts. Goosebumps bloomed across her body with the heat of his mouth dragging down her neck. As he pinched and rolled her nipples, she rubbed her backside against his growing arousal. One hand continued teasing the taut peaks while his other crawled down her stomach, slipping beneath satin panties. She bucked into his stroking fingers.

"Clayton," she whimpered, as he increased the pressure on her aroused nipple and clit.

"Tell me what you want," he rasped.

"You," she gasped.

"Hmmm…I know that." He nibbled her earlobe. "Be specific."

A swell of lusty empowerment exploded within her. This man ignited her in all the best ways. She was not the same woman she'd been when she returned to Perry fourteen days ago. Who was this Elle Davidson?

The real fucking Elle. She twisted out of Clayton's hold, placing her hands on his chest.

"Take off your clothes and get on the couch," she commanded.

With a grunt, Clayton ripped his T-shirt over his head. He worked fast to unbuckle his belt and then tugged off his jeans and red boxer briefs, leaving on his socks. Elle dragged her glance away from his swelling erection and wagged her finger as she gestured to his socks. A quiet chuckle slipped from his lips as he removed them and tossed them onto a haphazard pile of clothes on the floor.

Satisfied, Elle stripped off her bra and panties and tossed them atop Clayton's discarded clothing. She gestured to the couch again and Clayton sat, his thighs splayed in an invitation.

Straddling Clayton, she sank onto his rigid length, satisfying a needy pulse between her thighs. She rocked her hips in a slow rhythm. His fingers bit into her waist, like a plea to go faster.–Ignoring his desperation, she continued in a slow taunting pace. The tightening of his hands on her ass telegraphed the restraint he was exercising.

"Elle," he begged, as she rocked harder.

He moved one hand between their bodies and massaged her clit. Undeniable pressure swelled in her. Their ragged breaths crested like a wave as Clayton lifted his hips off the couch, thrusting deep within her.

She clasped his face, imprisoning his gaze. "I want you on top."

He cupped her face in return, pressing his forehead to hers. "Are you su—"

She interrupted him with a kiss and a nod.

Clayton laid Elle on the couch and lowered himself between her thighs. He propped himself on his elbows, keeping his chest off hers, then eased into her. She moaned, and he paused, tense and holding back. Cupping his cheeks, she nodded and then rocked against him.

"Keep your eyes on me, baby," he murmured when her gaze began to drift.

She snapped her eyes back to his and he moved deeper. She wrapped her legs around his hips as their passionate rocking gained momentum. The darkening gray of his eyes intensified the pleasure coursing within her.

"Clayton," she cried, her eyes rolling to the ceiling as the waves of pleasure almost drowned her.

"You are so fu...fu...fucking beautiful," he stuttered, chasing his own pleasure.

That familiar pressure built again with his praise and vigorous thrusts. The pressure between her legs erupted.

"Oh...god!" she whined, her legs quivering.

"Fuck," he grunted as he shuddered inside her.

Clayton's gaze wove with hers, his eyes fading from hungry to peacefully sated. Her body still trembled. Self-doubt and fear had slipped away, replaced by the knowledge that this man had her. Being unapologetically uncontrolled around him was safe. She could let go with him in a way she'd never been able to before. One tear leaked from the corner of her eye.

"Are you okay?" he asked, swiping his thumb under the tear.

She tightened her hold on him, keeping him in place. "That isn't sadness or fear. It's trust." In him, and in herself.

TWENTY-FOUR

"It isn't what we say or think that defines us, but what we do."
~Jane Austen, *Sense and Sensibility*

Elle's back was cool thanks to the emptiness on Clayton's side of the bed. Rubbing her eyes, she tried to focus, the room lit by the gray light peeking through the blinds.

Fully dressed, Clayton stood beside her bedstand, a Post-It pad in hand, writing something.

"What time is it?" she whispered, trying not to wake the sleeping pug in her arms.

"Hey," Clayton said, slipping the Post-It pad in his back pocket before crouching beside the bed. "It's six-thirty."

"I didn't hear the alarm."

"I woke up before it. You were sleeping so soundly, I turned it off so you could get more rest." He smiled, combing his fingers through her sleep-rumbled hair.

"You're sweet to me."

"You're cute when you're sleepy."

"You're cute all the time." She yawned.

"Come on, Fitz." He tried coaxing the snoring pug awake.

Fitz burrowed against Elle's chest.

"I can keep him, if you'd like," she offered.

"I don't know if I have much of a say." He chuckled and lifted his brows. "Are you sure? He's a good boy but can be a handful."

"You're a handful," she smiled.

Clayton's laugh was low and sent a wave of happy pleasure through her. He pressed a quick kiss to her cheek. "I know you have lunch with Janet. He's good here, but if you want to take him to Cassie's, she has a few tables outside on Saturdays during the farmers market. I can text to have her hold a table if you'd like."

"Yes, please."

"I'll see you two tonight." He pressed his lips to her forehead, then headed out the door.

Fitz sat shotgun as Elle drove to downtown Perry to meet Aunt Janet. She smiled for the entire drive. Who wouldn't with a grinning pug in the front seat?

Clayton had requested a table on the edge of the sidewalk, where she could watch folks wandering to the farmers market. Fitz had made himself at home on her lap, and Aunt Janet sat across from her. A blue and gold striped umbrella rose from the center of the table, emblazoned with *Cassie's Corner Café*.

"If you're taking his dog to lunch with me, this is serious." Janet folded her hands on top of the table and leaned toward Elle.

Elle took mercy on her aunt, giving her some details but not all. That they reconnected during the barbecue, and that the next day Clayton offered to be her running partner. A bit of an odd feeling came over Elle as she shared their relationship details with her aunt. She'd never chatted about romantic interests with a mother-type figure before.

"Here you go." A soft female voice said placing Elle's grilled pear chicken salad and Janet's tuna melt and fries on the table. "I'm sorry for the wait. We got slammed and your server was packing up a large to-go order."

"Oh, it's totally fine. We didn't wait that long." Elle looked up and her eyes widened in recognition. Summer Michaels, childhood bestie turned teenaged tormentor had delivered her meal.

The Summer that stood in front of her was so different from what Elle remembered. She'd let her once blonde hair return to its original chestnut tone, which was now tied back in a ponytail. The fashionable plaid skirts and fitted blouses of their teen years were replaced by worn sneakers, khaki shorts, and a white T-shirt under a black apron. The venomous teenager had been replaced by a frazzled and soft woman, watchful eyes glancing to the other tables.

"Hey, Summer. How're your folks?" Janet asked.

"They're good."

"Do you remember my niece? You two were inseparable as little girls."

"Eleanor?" Summer's tone was a mix of happy and regretful. "Gosh, I heard you were in town."

"Elle is visiting us for a few weeks from California."

"That's great you could stay so long. I heard you were an executive for a hospital out there. Must be hard to get that amount of time off."

Aunt Janet beamed. "Not *a* hospital."

Elle cleared her throat, cutting off Janet's attempted bragging, "I'm with Sloan-Whitney at their national headquarters." She didn't add that she was their youngest and first female senior executive in the company's fifty-two-year history, that hundreds of staff ultimately reported up to her, and that she was traveling this coming week to represent Sloan-Whitney at a breast cancer fundraiser. Did she want to brag? Well, yeah. Summer had been Elle's Caroline Bingley after all, but she'd been a friend before…

"That's great." Summer said.

"Thanks. Summer, I love that you went back to your chestnut hair. It was always really pretty on you. I used to be envious of your hair when we were little." Elle smiled, channeling her inner Jane Bennet.

The woman standing in front of her was so different than the girl who had once tossed cruel jabs. Brown eyes that used to assess and dismiss with a glance, now shifted and turned down. While still pretty, Summer looked beat down, like the years since she was the Caroline Bingley of their story had stomped away her spirit.

"That's sweet of you." Summer blushed, touching the end of her ponytail. "I should get back in there. Do you need anything else?"

"No, thanks."

Summer hurried away, stopping at the door into the restaurant and flashing a tentative smile back at Elle.

"You're a good girl." Janet patted Elle's hand. "You make me so proud to call you mine."

"If you cry, I will not let you go shopping with me on Monday," Elle warned.

Janet promptly chucked her napkin at her.

After lunch, while Janet waited outside with Fitz, Elle ran into a little boutique to pick up a gift for Mrs. Owens' birthday, a small box styled like a hope chest and an assortment of flower-themed earrings. She purchased an extra pair of earrings for Natalie. It wasn't necessary to get a gift for Clayton's entire family, but the sparkling rose teardrop earrings would likely be coveted by the glitter-prone Natalie.

While paying for her purchases, a framed photograph of the train trellis over the Letchworth gorge caught Elle's eye. Had it really been just five days since she'd stood there with Clayton? It felt like a lifetime. She bought the photo to give to Clayton, not Sunday but someday.

Two hours later, Pete watched baseball from his seat on the floor, because Lt. Scout and Fitz had commandeered the couch. Both dogs were snoring. Elle snapped a picture texting Tobey, Jerome, and Clayton. There had been a group thread with the four of them since Thursday, when Janet alerted her sons that their best man was "banging" Elle. She actually put that in the text. Tobey sent a screenshot of her text to Clayton and Elle with many, many question marks.

"So, these need to bake for thirty minutes," Janet directed as Elle put the pan of Magic Bars, Dr. Owen's favorite, in the oven.

The front of Pete and Janet's house had a panoramic view allowing approaching vehicles from the road to easily be spotted. A red Prius eased along the lane. The lighthearted family atmosphere shifted to tense as Janet and Pete's gazes met. A look of fearful recognition passed between them.

"Be right back," Pete said, smile tight as he struggled up from the floor.

Lt. Scout and Fitz lifted their heads.

"Stay, boys," he commanded as he shuffled outside.

Five minutes later, Pete returned, reporting the driver was lost. The man was a terrible liar. The person driving the red Prius wasn't lost. It was her mom.

With a sigh, Pete suggested they walk the dogs. As a kid, Elle would ride bikes with Tobey down the tree-lined lane.

Might as well get this over with. "So, she has a red Prius," Elle said.

"Yes." Pete's face was pinched. "I think it's Pastor Danny's influence."

"Pastor Danny?" Elle's eyebrows raised.

"Her boyfriend."

"She's dating a preacher?" Elle's gasped, then gaped. Both reactions seemed appropriate.

"Yep." Pete made a sour face. "Sorry. We didn't know she was stopping by."

"It's okay," Elle said, watching Fitz mark his territory on a third tree. "So, was she coming back? Is that why you took me for a walk?"

"Yeah. She had some photo albums that Janet needs for my birthday."

"Will Pastor Danny be with her at your party?" Elle asked.

"Yes. He's a nice man."

Elle rolled her eyes. Was her mom capable of finding a nice man? There were nice men, Elle knew. The proof lay with the men surrounding her, like Pete, Clayton, Tobey, Jerome, Noah, and Viet. Such a list of wonderful men.

"I wish it wasn't like this between you two." Pete's voice was small. Too small for a man of his size and with such a big heart.

Elle wished it wasn't like this, but it was. What would life be like if she could have had lunch with her mom and shared her budding romance with Clayton instead of with her aunt? Some moments were made to be shared between mothers and daughters. Her chest tightened with sadness that it wasn't to be for her.

Pete and Janet deserved to know that their interference was for a reason. That she wasn't behaving like a toddler having a tantrum.

The unspoken truth lodged in her throat. "Pete…" Elle faltered. She couldn't just spit out the truth and steal his sister from him. If he knew, he'd choose Elle. The knowledge, a tonic that she couldn't drink. She sighed, "Can I get your help with something?"

"Always, kiddo."

The parts of the unassembled chair Clayton had bought on Sunday for himself were strewn on the floor of Clayton's office. She'd drafted Pete to put it together. As she guided him through the house, Pete asked how much time she had spent at the farmhouse but then raised his hand, saying, "Wait, don't answer that."

As Pete put together the chair, Elle ran over to the Little Red Barn telling him she had to answer some work emails. Best to keep her moving into the farmhouse a secret. After Pete left, she'd bring her stuff over. By half-past six, Pete had finished the chair and was ready to head home. As she walked Pete to his SUV, he let out a long breath and asked her to let him help move her suitcases over to the farmhouse.

"How do you know?" she gaped.

"This was a giveaway." Pete lifted up one of Clayton's Post-It love notes welcoming her to staying at the farmhouse. He heaved a concerned sigh, "Are you happy?"

"Blissfully," Elle said without thinking. And she was. Unaccustomed happiness had bubbled through her since Clayton had crossed that field of goats. "I like him a lot."

"I do too. He's a good man." He wrapped an arm around her shoulders, pulling her close. "I'm still going to show him my gun collection, though."

They both laughed.

"Poor Clayton. I am so not worth it." She shook her head.

"You are worth everything," he chided with a warm smile. "I have a feeling that man would walk through fire for you."

"Do you plan on being the fire?" she teased.

"Nah, I think you've had enough fire in your life." He placed his lips to her temple.

Elle swallowed hard. *If only you knew.*

"I am happy though, that you found someone you feel is worthy of you. I know your aunt has needled you a lot about dating. I knew you wouldn't waste your time on the Mr. Almosts out there. There's a reason why he was one of Tobey and Jerome's best men, because he's the best man…best man for you."

"That means a lot coming from the other best man… Don't scare him off, though. I really like him."

"As long as he keeps you blissfully happy, he's okay in my book. I just never want to hear the details of how he's making you blissfully happy."

After Pete left, the rest of the evening was quiet as she unpacked. Clayton had made space in the closet, a section of empty hangers waited for her, and the top drawer of the dresser featured a yellow Post-It proclaiming, *Elle's Drawer.*

After some light cleaning, dinner, and laundry, she settled with Fitz on her reading seat. Losing herself with Captain Wentworth and Anne Elliot she drifted into the angsty love story waiting for her own leading man to come home.

"I like this view." His deep voice called her away from the book.

She glanced up to find him leaning against the door frame. Had door frames always been sexy, or was that just a consequence of proximity to Clayton?

"Hey." She grinned.

"I like when you do that."

"Do what?"

"You smile with your whole face." He waved his hand in front of his face. "You have all these different smiles for different things. You have so many, but that one…that's my favorite."

"It's my 'Clayton' smile."

"Yeah," he murmured. Deep lines of exhaustion were etched on his face as he approached the window seat.

Elle scooted up, allowing him to move in behind her. "Did you have fun?" she asked, as his arms snaked around her waist.

"I did. Mom was so happy." He nuzzled her neck. "They can't wait for you to come to dinner tomorrow."

"I'm glad she enjoyed her birthday outing. I got your mom and sister gifts for tomorrow. Janet helped me make Magic Bars for your dad."

"I see you've been busy." He gestured to the assembled chair.

"Pete helped…um… He also helped me move my things over. So…"

"He's going to show me his gun collection," Clayton chuckled. Tiredness chugged through his tone like a car about to run out of gas.

"You're so tired. You have been taking care of everyone today." She twisted her head to look at him. "Let me take care of you. Let's go to bed and I can read to you until you fall asleep."

"Elle, I am…" He paused, cupping her face, his eyes tired but adoring. "…so ha…ha…ha…happy you are here," he stuttered.

"When Pete found out I was moving my stuff over here, he asked me if I was happy." She stroked his cheek. "I told him blissfully."

He pressed his forehead to hers. "There's that smile again."

TWENTY-FIVE

"I could easily forgive his pride, if he had not mortified mine."
~Jane Austen, *Pride and Prejudice*

E lle had never been inside Clayton's childhood home, a two-story Victorian around the corner from Noah's house and the village park. A cobblestone path led to an oversize porch with two white rocking chairs, a white wicker table with a potted plant between them. Elle clung to Clayton's hand as Fitz skipped up the stairs. He dropped to his haunches on a blue welcome mat and gave a small *woof.* A large oval shaped window with vines and leaves etched into the glass made the door opaque.

Elle hesitated on the top step and gnawed her lower lip.

"Hey." Clayton stroked his thumb under her mouth. "Don't be nervous."

"Easy for you to say. You're not meeting *your* parents."

"True, but I know for a fact they don't have a gun collection like your uncle," he teased. "Also, you're not meeting them. They know you and already adore you."

"Elle!" Natalie threw open the front door and dragged Elle close for a hug.

"Natalie." Elle laughed, allowing the sprite-like Natalie to tug her into the house.

Clayton and Fitz followed.

"Please, call me Nat. I'm so happy you are here!" she gushed, yanking Elle in tight again.

"Natalie, show some decorum. Poor Elle, let her in," Mrs. Owens' melodic voice called from the living room where she sat beside a woman with gray-streaked brunette hair and ocean blue eyes. Elle knew she could only be Mrs. Wilson, Noah's mom.

"This is for you," Elle said, handing the small glittery gold gift bag to Nat. "This is for your mom. Is there a table for gifts or should I just give it to her?"

"Mom, Elle brought presents!" Nat announced.

"Happy Birthday, Mrs. Owens." Elle handed her the gift bag.

"Oh!" Mrs. Owens placed a hand on her heart. "You didn't need to bring me a gift."

"She also baked Magic Bars for dad. Is he in the kitchen?" Clayton asked, holding up the container of sweets.

The two women eyed Elle as if appraising her like a prize cow being shown at the county fair. Though the comparison wasn't flattering, Elle hoped for a blue ribbon.

"Should I open it now or wait?" Mrs. Owens asked already removing the tissue paper.

"I hope you like it." Elle focused on the other woman. "Mrs. Wilson, it's nice to meet you."

"Maura, look!" Mrs. Owens held up the small jewelry box.

"Oh, Heidi, isn't that the one you wanted from the shop in town?" Maura leaned in, examining the small box.

"Elle, how did you know? Every time I go in there, they are sold out of these." Her fingers danced along the smooth edges of the box, eyes wide as she opened it, finding the four pairs of earrings. "Oh, sweetie."

"I remembered you always wore earrings, and I wanted something for you to put them in. I just found the box and thought it looked like something you'd like." Elle fiddled with her starfish necklace.

Clayton looped his arm around her middle, and when she looked at him, gratitude sketched his features.

"Those are adorable. We need to go shopping together. Ooh, sparkles." Nat said admiring the rose tear-drop earrings in her mother's hand.

"Open yours, Nat." Clayton grinned, his head tipping to his sister.

Nat dug into her gift bag. "A matching pair! So cute… Seriously, how did he score you? You're too good for him."

"I've been asking myself that too." He squeezed her tight.

How did I get so lucky? Clayton was the book she wanted to read over and over again. Beneath its handsome cover were paragraphs of thoughtfulness, sweetness, kindness, laughter, patience, trust, and all the best words to lose herself within his pages.

"It's because you're wonderful," Elle whispered.

"Oh, I like her, Heidi." Maura elbowed a smiling Heidi. "I wish Noah could find someone," she sighed.

Clayton kissed Elle's cheek and changed the subject. "Is Dad in the kitchen? Is Noah here?" he asked, turning to his mom.

"Your dad is in the kitchen with Scott. Noah will be here in a bit."

"Ok, we can take these into him," Clayton said, starting to lead Elle out of the room.

"Oh, no you don't," a grinning Nat scolded, pulling Elle

back to her. "I want to give her a tour and show her all your embarrassing photos."

With a resigned smile, Clayton headed toward the kitchen. Clasping Elle's hand, Nat tugged her along with a childlike energy that did not match her twenty-seven years. They passed a portrait gallery filled with snapshots of family moments as they climbed the stairs.

"Ta-da!" Nat threw open a door at the end of the hall.

Clayton's room was like a time capsule. A full-size bed draped in a green plaid comforter. Classics, action adventure, and animal science books filled two bookcases flanking a small desk.

On the bedstand was a small lamp with a white shade and a copy of Clayton's senior yearbook. Flipping it open to a page bookmarked by a ticket stub she found a picture from that Winter Ball her Junior year, his Senior year. In the front of the picture a teenaged Noah swayed with some girl but in the background, Elle sat in the bleachers, her eyes fixed forward. Beside her Clayton sat looking at her, while she looked at everyone else.

Even then he saw me.

"I haven't looked at this in forever." Nat sat beside Elle, flipping through the glossy pages. "I had such a crush on Noah when I was a little girl. I used to flip to all the pictures of him. I was such a dork."

"I crushed on Noah in high school too."

"But you don't have a crush on him anymore?" Her tone was playful yet protective.

"I'm crushing hard on your brother, and only your brother."

"Good. You make him happy. Keep it up."

Nat finished her guided tour. The experience was reminiscent of Lizzie's walk around Pemberley, seeing the little things that made Darcy who he was. Elle was seeing the things that had formed Clayton into the wonderful man he was, and she tumbled further into feelings for him.

Noah called them in from the deck for dinner. Clayton's mom's favorite holiday was Thanksgiving, so every year for her birthday they did a mini version of a traditional feast. Sliced roasted turkey breast, bowls of honey-glazed carrots and red mashed potatoes, platters of roasted squash, corn-bread dressing, and dinner rolls covered the table. The savory scent of the dishes enticed Elle. It would be a struggle finding the balance of being a good guest and not overindulging.

After an introduction to Noah's dad, Scott, and a very formal handshake reunion with Dr. Owens, Elle sat between Clayton and Nat, their parents sat at the opposite heads of the table. Noah across from Nat, beside his parents.

"Eleanor, I forgot to thank you for the Magic Bars. Very thoughtful," Dr. Owens said between bites of cornbread dressing.

"Honey, she goes by Elle," Heidi corrected with a warm smile.

"It's okay." Elle looked back and forth between them. "I only hope they are half as good as your turkey."

"Thank you." His blue eyes sparkled with pride.

"My aunt says to hold on to a man who can cook. No wonder you two have been married for so long." Elle said and then winced wondering if it was an appropriate thing to say. The whoosh of laughter from Clayton's mom eased her fear.

"You know, Chris taught Clayton to cook. He's quite good, just like his father." She winked at her son.

"I know." Elle blushed.

Lively conversation crisscrossed the table. Clayton, his mom, and Maura discussed book club. Both women gushed when Clayton shared that he and Elle were reading that month's book together. Noah and Nat went back and forth, teasing each other about her bad cooking and his obsession with puppy videos. Clayton's dad sat quietly as Scott went on about all the things he was doing now that he was retired.

"You must be excited that Nat will be done with her residency next May," Scott said, forking up a bite of carrots.

"We're very proud." Heidi grinned at her daughter.

"You'll finally be able to retire, thanks to Nat," Scott said.

Clayton gripped his fork tight, jaw clenched.

"Medical school can be a lot. It's not for everyone." Dr. Owens' gaze flitted between both his children.

"Some people choose different paths," Heidi said, her tone sweet on the surface but the narrowed eyes aimed at her husband held an undercurrent of indignation.

Elle's gaze was fixed on Clayton's right forearm, the fingers of his left hand traced the outline of the paw print tattoo. As if each caress of inked skin anchored him to the path he'd chosen.

His path. The right path.

Looking up, Elle cleared her throat. "I work with some of the best doctors in the country. I'm amazed by anyone that goes into the medical field helping others just like Dr. Owens, Nat, and Clayton. It takes a certain kind of person to give so much of themselves to heal others."

"Clayton didn't go to medical school," Dr. Owens cleared his throat and stared at his son.

"He's a doctor, though. He cares for his patients, just like Nat or you. Some may argue that in a town with more cows than people vet trumps human doctor." Her hazel eyes narrowed into not quite a glare, but glare-adjacent at Dr. Owens. *Not to mention he's qualified to care for multiple species, not just homo sapiens.* The thought danced in her head, but she bit her lip to hold it inside.

Forks paused halfway to mouths, eyes widened, smiles tightened, and hands clenched napkins. A strange tension engulfed the table with her words. Clayton's hand left Elle's lap. An icy shiver ripped through her body at the loss of his touch.

Dr. Owens lips were drawn in a firm line, his stare fixed on Elle.

"Who wants coffee and pie?" Heidi interrupted the silent standoff between Elle and her husband. A bit of desperation quavered in her voice as she changed the topic.

After helping with cleanup, Elle left the family downstairs and sought the safety of the closed bathroom door before releasing the bubbling over anger. *How fucking dare he not see his son?* Her blood boiled. She'd take back every nice thing she'd said about Dr. Owens and his stupid bow ties over the years. Clayton wasn't a man to be found lacking; he was the man all men should be measured against. Sure, not everyone could go to medical school, but nobody could be Clayton with his quiet thoughtfulness, patience, kind heart, musical laughter, loving strength, and so many other attributes that she adored and could spend weeks listing.

Splashing cold water against her face, she washed away the lingering irritation. With a long exhale, she opened the door, finding Clayton standing there, his face unreadable.

"Elle, I…" He stopped, sucking back the words he might have planned to say. Cupping her face, he pressed the softest kiss on her mouth. Pulling back, his fingers outlined her lips. "Come with me," he whispered, taking her hand.

Clayton led her down the hall to his room. Once behind his childhood bedroom door, he pulled her into his arms and captured her lips. "Thank you," he said, his voice hoarse.

"You don't have to thank me." She breathed in deep his citrus scent. "What was that about down there with your dad?"

"I was always supposed to be the next Dr. Owens at the clinic. Since my great-grandpa, the first son has always been Dr. Owens. When I went to undergrad declaring pre-med my major, I did it to please my dad. My heart wasn't in it, though. When I told him I was going to go to Veterinarian school instead of medical school I could see the disappointment in his eyes. I'd failed him."

"The only failure is his in not seeing you. Not knowing your heart," she said, her tone firm but soft. "I see you. I see who you are…who you've always been."

"I know he loves me. Someone can still love you and be disappointed in you."

"He's the disappointment." She gripped his face forcing his stare to hers. "You hear me, Clayton. You are a goddamn masterpiece." She used his words to her.

"Elle, I…"

She halted his words with a consuming kiss. Hoping each press of her lips branded him with the truth that he was everything even if his father didn't see it. Even if his vision was clouded, not seeing himself the way she saw him.

A lopsided grin spread on his face. "I used to have very naughty fantasies about you in here."

"Yeah?"

"Yup." He trailed his hands to her waist, bending to kiss her.

"Too bad your parents are downstairs."

"That may have been one of my fantasies."

Her right eyebrow arched.

Amusement sparked in his eyes. "Just up here with you trying to be quiet, so we didn't get caught." Clayton's steamy gaze jumped between the bed and her, causing Elle's breath to hitch.

She considered pulling him atop her on the bed, allowing his hands to roam under her dress, covering her with a hungry mouth. Their careful ears listening for the sound of footsteps while she unbuckled him, slipping hands beneath boxer briefs. The stolen moments of pleasure, knowing that any moment the unlocked door could open, and they could be caught.

A tingle in her lady bits accompanied her X-rated thoughts.

"When we get home." Her response was breathless and wanting.

Home? It was like a foreign word, yet it slipped from her tongue so sweetly.

TWENTY-SIX

"Silly things do cease to be silly if they are done by sensible people in an impudent way."
~Jane Austen, *Emma*

"Still a chance to pull out." Elle warned, as Clayton parked at her aunt and uncle's house.

Twenty-four hours later and they were at another family dinner. Elle's family was gathering for an Aloha-themed dinner to welcome Tobey and Jerome back from their Hawaiian honeymoon. Clayton was invited…well more like *told* or silently threatened by Uncle Pete to attend. He was a good sport, though, rocking an obnoxious yellow Hawaiian shirt that complimented Elle's green palm printed strapless maxi dress. Even Fitz was dressed for a party in a tropical-patterned top, curtesy of his Aunt Nat.

"No chance," he chuckled, turning off the ignition before leaning over to capture her lips with his.

Jumping out of the truck, Elle grabbed the bottle of wine she'd brought. Scooping Fitz up, Clayton placed him on the gravel driveway, grasping the pug's blue leash. Rounding the front of the truck, Elle clasped Clayton's left hand.

Uncle Pete, Tobey, and Jerome stood stone-faced, hands behind their backs. Clayton's steps faltered, glancing between the three men and Elle. Individually, the three men weren't intimidating. However, with their features unreadable, their large frames were a bit menacing. Uncle Pete stood on the porch, Tobey on the next step down, and Jerome another step below, just above the stone walkway. Pete towered over everyone like a general riding a massive white stallion.

"Son…" Pete rasped ominously. "I'm sorry to do this, but you need to understand how important Elle is to us. If you hurt her, you will face us."

Clayton nodded, clenching Elle's hand. "I'd expect nothing less."

"This is a little over-the-top." Elle shook her head.

"What are your intentions?" Tobey's question was less inquiring and more accusative.

"Seriously?!" Elle blustered, wielding the bottle of wine in the air. "Intentions? Is this Victorian England? Does he need to ask permission to court me?"

"I do like the idea of that." Pete grinned.

Elle rolled her eyes.

"Lady Elle, we must defend your honor," Jerome proclaimed, his smirking face betraying the not seriousness of the situation.

"Men, take out your weapons." Pete called, hoisting up a yellow and red Super Soaker from behind his back, aiming it at Clayton and Elle.

Jerome pulled a neon green water gun from his back, posing like the opening credits of a James Bond film as Tobey revealed his own Nerf water gun. With devious smiles, each man pointed their weapon at Clayton.

"Sorry man, you're a friend… But she's family," Jerome said, playfully apologetic.

Elle's chest tugged at that.

"At the count of three," Pete bellowed, his finger settling on the trigger.

Clayton stepped in front of Elle. "Take Fitz. Behind me," he commanded, handing the pug's leash to Elle.

As Pete counted off, Clayton put his arms out, guarding Elle and Fitz. Elle crouched behind Clayton's back to brace for the water's impact.

"Fire!"

The first spray cut through the distance between the four men. The echoing slap of the water hitting Clayton's chest and face and Fitz's barks filled Elle's ears. Crouched behind him, she struggled to stay on her haunches as deep belly laughs rioted through her. Clayton was such a good sport to play along.

"Sorry son, we needed you to understand what consequences there'd be," Pete chuckled, as the water siege subsided.

"You three," Elle lovingly chided, as she stepped from behind Clayton, holding a wiggling Fitz.

Water drizzled down Clayton's face onto his shirt. Elle frowned at his drenched upper half until she saw the bemused expression on his face. Butterflies bounced in her belly at his sweet indulgence of Uncle Pete, Tobey, and Jerome. The four men who, during the post-wedding brunch, declared they'd catch her if she fell, reissuing that promise in the silliest of ways. The three doing battle with their water pistols, while Clayton acted as her human shield. In the ridiculousness was a deep sincerity that made Elle want to kiss all four.

"Sorry, we had to mess with you," Pete said as he handed a towel to Clayton. "Truthfully, if I didn't already know what a good man you are, her choosing you would be proof enough. I'm happy for the two of you." He smiled, placing an approving hand on Clayton's shoulder.

"What on earth?" Janet shrilled, stepping through the front door onto the porch. "What have you done?"

"Initiated Clayton into the family," Pete smirked.

Janet tossed her hands up and then stormed back inside.

"Oh, mom's mad," Jerome gulped as he started walking up the stairs toward the front door.

"Yeah, but we'll blame it on Dad," Tobey snarked.

"I'm sorry," Elle winced. "They can be a little much."

"You have to be a little much when there's so much at stake."

Those words flipped like a gymnast in her belly. What was at stake? His heart? Hers? Them? Perhaps, everything.

"I may swoon," she jested.

"I'll catch you, so swoon away." His lips met hers.

TWENTY-SEVEN

"It is very often nothing but our own vanity that deceives us."
~Jane Austen, *Pride and Prejudice*

Elle still hated flying; however, it was less of a horrible experience with Clayton. When he caught her fidgeting after they boarded, Clayton laced their fingers and held tight for the entire flight.

They arrived at the hotel around nine-thirty a.m., giving Elle a very short window before she needed to meet Malcolm and Dr. Holton in the lobby. While she was checking in, Clayton told her he'd be right back and slipped away. Elle nodded, not looking up from the paperwork. She was distracted by the self-doubt crowding her belly. She had to be here. It was work. But Clayton did not. A seed of fear wanted to blossom telling her this was the last time she'd see him. That any minute he'd be gone. It was irrational. It was unnecessary. It was obnoxious. But it was present. Like a tiny pebble in one's shoe that won't be shaken loose.

"Elle." Malcolm's deep baritone cut through Elle's dismal thoughts.

"Malcolm," she said, a little surprised, looking up from the check-in desk and turning to face him.

A perfectly tailored black suit hugged Malcolm's tall and lean frame. With his leading man worthy good looks, he was a fantasy come true. Willa had fanned herself the first time she'd met him at a benefit she'd attended with Elle three years ago, referring to him as "hot boss".

"Where are my manners?" he chided, his green eyes moving to her suitcase. "Let me help you with that."

"Oh—"

"I've got it," Clayton's voice was warm but firm as he stepped beside Elle, placing his hand possessively on her lower back.

Elle stiffened as Clayton's hand flexed against her back. Was he jealous? *No.* She shook off that thought.

"You must be Elle's plus one. Malcolm Sloan."

"Clayton Owens." He took Malcom's hand. "You're Elle's boss. Nice to meet you. She has spoken very highly of you."

"We are very fond of her. Elle, when my assistant said you were bringing a plus one, I assumed it would be that delightful friend of yours, Dr. Andrews." Malcolm had met Willa several times at various Sloan-Whitney events.

"Clayton lives in my hometown…Shorter flight for him than Willa. He offered to accompany me. It's a short flight." Did she just repeat herself? Why is she sputtering? "He's a veterinarian. His sister is doing her residency here, so this is a good excuse for him to visit her." Elle pulled at the end of her ponytail, using the smooth strands to ground her.

"Quite the opposite, I assure you. I used my sister as an excuse to escort Elle tonight." Clayton assured, his calming fingers stroking her lower back.

Soothing warmth seeped through the blue silk blouse she wore.

"Smooth." Malcolm winked at Clayton. "I should let you get to your room. Are you still good to meet soon, or do you need more time?" he asked, turning to Elle.

"No, I'm ready. I'm just going to run my bag up and I'll be back," Elle said.

"Perfect. We'll be over there." Malcolm pointed to a cluster of sofas to the far left of the reception desk surrounded by giant potted palms. "A vet, eh? Well, Doc you'll be a hit at our table. I have two chocolate labs, Jack and Diane, and Dr. Holton and his husband have cats."

They walked quietly to the elevator, Clayton carrying his duffle over his shoulder and pulling Elle's luggage, despite her insistence she could take her own.

The downtown Boston hotel was fancy adjacent. White marble floors led to a bank of elevators. Their room was on the fourteenth floor. Elle's black heels sunk into the sumptuous green carpet as she stepped into their room. The room had an old world meets new motif with throwback antique-looking furniture and minimalist wall decor.

"The room is nice." Elle placed her laptop bag and purse on the bed as she surveyed the space.

Clayton deposited his duffle on the wingback chair tucked in the corner. The silence didn't feel like the companionable one they could fall so easily into. A twinge of something festered in the unspoken between them.

Wringing her hands, she made idle small talk to fill the silence. "The Wi-Fi password is written on the key envelope. I'll leave it on the table for you. They have room service if you want to order anything. Just charge it to the room. There is a pool and a gym. Braedon said there's a park two blocks away if you'd prefer that. There's also a restaurant."

God, she was being inelegant about this. Like a stealthy emotional ninja, her self-doubt slunk in. All the sacrifices Clayton had made in order to accompany her, and its rippling effect on others slammed into her like a bus. Elle suspected Clayton was thinking the same thing and asking himself "Why?" as he looked at her.

"You're spinning a bit."

"Sorry. I think it hit me when we got here…This was too much to ask of you," she said.

"Elle." Those eyes pinned her. "I need you to understand, I am here because I want to be here."

"I'm being silly. You get to see Nat, this is great—"

"Stop." Exasperation punctuated his sigh. Placing his hands on her shoulders, he said, "Yes, I get to see Nat, but that's not why I am here. You are never an excuse; you are the reason."

"I'm sorry." She swallowed a newly formed lump in her throat.

"Tell me what's going on in that beautiful brain of yours?"

"I…" She sucked in a steadying breath. "…I am so confident when it comes to work. I am a fucking rockstar and I refuse to humble myself to fit anyone's image of a woman. I can slay everyone else's dragons without fear of getting burnt, but when it's me…just me…just Elle, I feel not enough… not worth it."

"Oh, baby…" He pressed his sad smile against her forehead. "There is no such thing as just Elle. I wish you could see yourself through my eyes."

There was no reason to doubt Clayton. His behavior was evidence of his desire to be there, to be with her. This was all about her inadequacies. Was she so broken that she couldn't allow his affection to penetrate the bricks of fear and self-doubt that layered the still intact, but crumbling, wall around her heart?

"I like when you call me baby." A small smile budded.

"Me too." He ran soothing strokes down her back.

Elle could feel the gentle thumping of his heart as she pressed against his chest, letting the citrus scent invade her nostrils. Its freshness and the heat of his body were a soothing balm. She needed to remember this. He was there for her. She was precious to him. She needed to hold that like an amulet, warding off the ghosts that howled that she was unworthy.

TWENTY-EIGHT

"To be fond of dancing was a certain step to falling in love."
~Jane Austen, *Pride and Prejudice*

After a long afternoon of meetings and site visits, Elle reentered the lobby and found herself riding up in the elevator with Malcolm.

"You did great today," Malcolm said, as the elevator dinged for her floor. "When we were at the clinic earlier today, their director pulled me aside to say how excited they are about this Tele-Cardiology pilot you spoke with her about. I didn't know you would be pitching anything."

"Well, I was prepared if the opportunity arose," Elle replied as she stepped off the elevator. She turned to Malcolm, who wore an unsurprised smile on his face.

"I've noticed that the opportunity always seems to arise when you are in the picture." He nodded. "See you tonight."

As the mirrored doors closed, Elle did a victory dance. She needed to carry this confidence with her for the rest of the day. No doubt the hotel's camera caught every sashay of her happy hips, but who cared.

The TV hummed in the room as Elle entered. Slipping her shoes off at the door, the faint sound of the shower greeted her. Scanning the room, she noticed a yellow Post-It beside a bottle of water and bag of nuts. Warmth spread through her at his careful handwriting saying, *Elle's snack*.

With a mischievous grin, Elle disrobed, leaving her clothes in a heap on the carpet. Creeping into the bathroom, tendrils of steam danced around her.

God bless glass showers! Clayton's backside was framed in the door of the shower, his face raised under the spraying water. Licking her lips, she watched the soapy foam glide down his muscular back, dripping to his ass. The muscles flexed as he lathered shampoo through his sandy hair. Elle's breath shallowed, thinking of those massaging fingers exploring her body. As he washed away the shampoo, Elle slid the door open.

"Elle." A smile filled his voice, as he continued to stand with his back to her. "You're early."

"Indeed," she sassed, running her finger up his spine, feeling his pleasure shiver against her. "Turn around."

"Elle." He repeated her name with a lopsided grin, as he turned facing her. The water licked every taut inch of his torso.

"Let me take care of you," she murmured, running her fingers along the small trail of hair from his belly button leading down.

Eyes locked with his, she lowered to her knees. Her hands caressed up his strong legs, cupping his ass, eliciting a breathy laugh from him. Her lips pressed against Clayton's inner thighs as she moved up to his swelling length. His needy moans, ragged breath, rocking hips, and gentle tugs on her hair signaled his enjoyable undoing.

Later, Elle stood in front of the bathroom mirror, swiping a soft pink lip stain over her lips, the final touch to her outfit.

Her hair hung in loose wavy tendrils past her bare shoulders. Pink pearls, a gift from Tobey from his Hawaiian honeymoon, rested at her collarbone, a slightly lighter shade than the rosy satin dress she wore. Elle's hands glided down the smooth fabric, admiring how it hugged each curve creating a sexy and sophisticated silhouette.

Aunt Janet was spot on about this dress! Maybe she'd have to go shopping with her aunt more often.

Pushing into her strappy silver kitten heels, she turned a few times in the bathroom mirror before taking a selfie to send to Viet and Willa.

Reveling in the surging confidence, she stashed her phone in her silver clutch, and joined Clayton in the other room.

"I'm ready."

"You are stunning." A big smile filled his face.

"You look pretty *wow* yourself." She stepped closer to him, waggling her brows.

The black suit he wore molded over his muscular figure. He wore the pink tie she'd bought him on her shopping trip with Aunt Janet.

"I have something for you," he said, pulling a small black box out of his pocket.

"Clayton." Elle bit her lower lip, as she opened the box revealing a thin silver bangle engraved with starfish. "This is beautiful."

"After lunch, Nat took me to that dog bakery the two of you had been apparently texting about, to pick up the dog cookies you wanted to bring back for Fitz," he said, bemused. "The cashier had one like this and said she got it in a shop down the street. I knew you were going to wear the pearls, but I wanted you to also have your starfish tonight to remind you of how many you have helped to get back into the sea and how many more you will." Clayton slid the bangle onto Elle's right wrist, kissing her hand like the hero from an Austen novel.

"I love it." Pressing up to her toes, she placed her grateful smile against his admiring one.

Clayton was a hit with the Sloan-Whitney crew. Over cocktails, he and Malcolm had bonded over the importance of animal rescue. Malcolm had shared pictures of Jack and Diane, the chocolate lab pair he'd adopted from a shelter and named for the John Mellencamp song.

"I know this pug," Malcolm chuckled, as Clayton showed him a picture of Fitz. "He attended our director's meeting yesterday. I didn't realize he was yours. The way Elle fawned over him during our meeting yesterday, I assumed he was hers."

"I didn't fawn," Elle laughingly protested.

"Oh, she fawns," Clayton's smile curled with teasing appreciation. "I went to a dog bakery today specializing in organic dog treats to pick up treats for Fitz. Apparently, Elle had researched dog bakeries and texted my sister to help secure the treats."

"Well, I promised Fitz a treat."

"I don't know if he needs more treats. He seems a little pudgy," Malcom chuckled.

"Don't body shame our dog!" Elle *tsked* with a laugh. *Our dog?* Realization wagged its finger at her. "I mean Clayton's dog," she corrected, tightening her grip around her wineglass.

Clayton's fingers located at the small of her back massaged slowly. "Fitz isn't ours, we're his."

The words and his stroking fingers easing the threatened tension of muscles in her body.

Before dinner, Elle excused herself to the ladies' room.

"Oh shoot." A tall woman with long black hair grimaced in the mirror, as Elle washed her hands.

"Are you okay?" Elle asked, watching the woman dab at her hot pink taffeta dress.

"I dribbled some wine on my dress. At least it's white."

"I got you." Elle opened her clutch pulling out a stain removing pen. Elle always kept a few essentials in her clutch just in case something happened, a stain-removing pen, Band-Aids, breath mints, Tylenol, and a tampon. The essentials.

"Bless you! I have to give a speech in ten minutes, and I didn't want to be thinking about this the entire time."

"I once got a run in my pantyhose before a grad school presentation. I took them off and tossed them in the trash rather than deal with knowing there was a run in them."

"Men never think of these things. I once had a male colleague that presented with his shirt misbuttoned, and nobody said anything. A week later, I had the tiniest smudge of toothpaste on my blouse and three people commented on it after a meeting."

"At least they knew you brush your teeth," Elle quipped.

The woman tossed her chin up with laughter and then outstretched her hand. "Magda Parsons." The Geneva Breast Cancer Foundation's Chief Executive Officer known for her no nonsense management-style was the last person that Elle expected to be fretting over a stain.

"Elle Davidson."

"Sloan-Whitney." Magda wore an impressed expression.

Ah, so Magda knew who she was.

"I read that piece in the *LA Times* about the Mobile Mammography program in Arizona and New Mexico. Very impressive outcomes through increased routine screening in rural communities."

Elle preened a bit. "Thank you. I'm very proud of that program. We're partnering with Indian Health to support Indigenous Communities as well. I'd like to expand it to other rural areas across the country," Elle said, pulling out her phone. "I know you need to get out there for your speech, but if you're open, I'd love to set a time to speak to you. I read an article in the *New Yorker* about your desire to move your foundation toward service provision, as well as retaining the research you fund."

"You know what..." Magda said, placing her hands on her hips. "...I'm the boss. This is my fundraiser. They can wait an extra ten minutes. Give me your pitch."

Elle glided back to her table with a massive smile on her lips and a meeting with Magda on Monday to discuss a potential partnership between the Geneva Breast Cancer Foundation and Sloan-Whitney. *Yes, boss bitch!*

"You look happy," Clayton commented as she sat at the table.

"I am." She leaned and kissed him, not caring that her boss sat a foot away.

At the end of the night, Elle and Clayton walked, hands clasped along the red and gold carpeted hall leading to the elevators. Music waltzed into the long corridor from the large ballroom. Streams of blue and white light from the ballroom crisscrossed the ceiling outside its entrance. Clayton halted mid-step, his eyes drifting to the open doors of the ballroom, causing Elle to stop short. The first bars of "Perfect" by Ed Sheeran played.

With a grin, Clayton turned to Elle. "Our song." It had been the song they'd danced to at the wedding.

Ours? Her smile couldn't get bigger. Maybe she'd let herself swim in the waters of "Ours" even if only in the shallow end.

"Dance with me?" Clayton asked, holding her hand against his heart.

"Here?" Elle's eyes swept the hallway lined with an assortment of red sofas, chairs, and potted plants.

"Yes." He placed his hands on her waist, pulling her in close.

"Ok," she whispered.

Wrapping her arms around his nape, she moved in tandem with him, their eyes tethered. The small wall sconces bathed them in soft light.

The gentle thump of her heart accompanied Clayton's husky voice as he sang. Each word, each lyric, seemed a secret message from his heart to hers. Closing her eyes, she drowned in the moment. The entire world faded away. In that moment, despite the self-doubts and flaws or, maybe, because of them, Elle felt perfect.

TWENTY-NINE

"It's such a happiness when good people get together."
~Jane Austen, *Emma*

As the plane touched down at the Buffalo-Niagara Airport, Elle's phone pinged with an incoming message from Braedon, who was just checking in, despite it being only six a.m., in California.

Beside her, Clayton was also checking his phone as they taxied to the gate, his free hand casually caressing her arm. Earlier that morning as they lay in bed, their naked limbs tangled, he felt like hers. The question remained, was she his? She wasn't questioning him wanting to be with her. That was clear, but that was the here and now. Belonging to one another was something entirely different, it spoke of a tomorrow. All the tomorrows, not just the todays.

Long distance worked, but only if someone was willing to leave their life. Elle couldn't imagine uprooting Clayton, taking him from his corner of the world to inhabit hers. Clayton didn't just live in Perry; he was its heartbeat. She'd never ask him to give that up or take him away from everyone who depended on him. He may be hers, but not hers to take.

Elle slipped her phone into the pocket of her denim jacket as Clayton stepped into the aisle to pull down their luggage. Since she wasn't working, she dressed more casually for the flight, wearing a pair of skinny black capris, a purple halter, denim jacket, and black flip flops. Clayton was in clinic dress, wearing a pair of tan slacks and a blue button up, his sleeves rolled up. *Tease.*

The plan was to drive to the farmhouse and drop Elle and their luggage off before he went to the clinic. She volunteered to unpack, toss the laundry in, and pick up Fitz at Clayton's parents' house.

The Owens Family Clinic was open six days a week. Tuesdays and Thursdays they had extended lunch breaks, but stayed open until seven p.m. It allowed the staff time to run errands and decompress on the longer days. It also gave Dr. Owens time to visit any patients admitted to the county hospital in Warsaw or the area nursing homes.

Clayton headed to the clinic soon after they arrived back at the farmhouse. Elle unpacked and tossed their dirty clothes into the wash. While putting things away, she looked at the picture she had bought him the previous week. She still hadn't given it to him. Running her fingers over the starfish bangle he gave her in Boston, she wondered when the right time would be to give it to him. A *just because* gift was always nice, but this felt more special. The picture of the train trellis over the gorge signified something important for each of them. It needed an important occasion to be given. When the moment arrived, she'd know.

She walked up the path to the Owens' yellow Victorian, a box of cookies from the Farmer's Wife in her hand. Climbing the steps, a tall shadow appeared through the leaf-engraved window of the front door. Elle braced herself. Likely it would be a brief interaction, like a prisoner exchange between feuding nations.

Cookies for my dog. Wait…*Clayton's dog.* Double Wait… *We're Fitz's.*

The door opened, revealing Dr. Owens in a yellow short-sleeve shirt with an evergreen bow tie. They had an awkward stare-down until Elle broke the standoff.

"I brought cookies." She held up the pink pastry box.

"Thank you. Come in," he said, stepping aside to let her enter. "Heidi had to run an errand, so I volunteered to hang with Fitz until you arrived." It felt strange to hear the bow tie-wearing Dr. Owens use the phrase "hang with."

"Oh." Elle looked around for Fitz.

"He's napping on the couch in the TV room. We were watching a program." The corners of his mouth lifted into almost a bashful grin.

"A program?" She arched a brow at Dr. Owens' flip flop between new and old school vernacular.

"Yes." He chuckled. "*Grey's Anatomy.* It's a guilty pleasure of mine. Heidi got me into it a few years ago."

"It's a good show. My best friend Viet and I have watch parties." To think Dr. Owens was into the sexy and melodramatic antics of the doctors of Seattle Grace. "Who's your favorite?"

"Dr. Torres, I like her feistiness. You actually remind me of her, although I suspect there is a little bit of Bailey in you too."

"Wow, you really are a fan."

"Do you have time for a cup of tea?" Dr. Owens asked as he accepted the cookies. "I remember from Sunday that you prefer tea over coffee. Me too."

Elle followed him to the kitchen then took a seat at the small breakfast nook overlooking the backyard. The parted emerald curtains allowed the midday sun to light the room.

As he prepared the tea and Elle plated a few cookies, they talked more about their shared love of *Grey's Anatomy*. It was surreal to chat about something so mundane in the same kitchen where his disappointment had oozed just a few days earlier. Part of Elle wanted to apologize for Sunday, not for standing up for Clayton. Dr. Owens had always seemed a steadying presence to her, but Elle didn't think he offered the same stalwart support to his son. Elle wrinkled her nose, thinking about holding Clayton as he shared the complicated relationship with his dad.

"Something wrong with the tea?" Dr. Owens inquired, his eyes dropping to Elle's displeased face. They sat opposite each other at the breakfast table, a pot of English Breakfast tea and plate of cookies between them.

"No. It's fine," she assured.

He broke off a piece of a molasses cookie, dunking it in his tea. "How was the trip to Boston? Natalie texted a picture of her and Clayton at lunch. That was nice he went with you."

"He's a good man," she said, her tone soft, but firm.

"Yes, he is…I suspect though, it was more than just being nice. He seems very fond of you."

"I'm very fond of him too."

The quiet standoff reared again. Both looked at each other over the tiny porcelain hummingbird teacups.

"Natalie mentioned his clinic has doubled their clients in the last year. Is that true?" he asked, placing his cup on the saucer.

"Yes, they are in the process of looking for another doctor to join the practice."

"Impressive."

"You should tell that to your son," Elle's hazel eyes locked with his.

Dr. Owens pursed his lips, his wide eyes meeting her

narrowed ones. Fitz click-clacked into the room interrupting their stare down.

"Excuse me," she said, moving over to have her usual chatty greeting with Fitz.

His curly tail moved furiously as she massaged his velvety ears, asking him how his time with his grandparents had been. Out of the corner of her eyes, she tracked Dr. Owens' expression soften as he watched Fitz press his stocky body into Elle's petting.

Dr. Owens' frown curled into a small smile. "Fitz is quite fond of you, as well."

"The feeling is entirely mutual." Elle straightened and brushed some stray hairs off her capris.

After washing her hands at the kitchen sink, she sat back down with Dr. Owens. The silence was a momentary reprieve. An unspoken challenge sat between them, waiting. Should she press?

I've failed him. Clayton's confession whispered in her mind.

No baby, he failed you. She squared her shoulders. "You know, you should stop by the clinic one Friday afternoon or during one of your long lunch days."

"I wouldn't want to…" he trailed off, looking around the kitchen as if the words could be found somewhere in the cabinets.

"I assure you, all that would happen is your son would feel his father was proud of him."

Dr. Owens eyes widened.

Elle considered how to proceed through this minefield. In many ways she was threatening to blow up her relationship with Clayton or his with his dad with any misstep in this conversation. It was risky but the pull to fix this, to slay that dragon for him, overpowered any trepidation.

"It's like when we were kids, and your parents would

come to open house at school. We'd get all excited to show you our desk, locker, and whatever project was being displayed. The last time my uncle came to visit, I took him on a tour of the Sloan-Whitney building and showed him my office. It sounds silly but just having him there…it just made me feel like he was proud of me. Even if he doesn't always understand what I do, just the fact that he asks means so much to me."

She had a deep, secret desire, one she didn't share even with herself, to have her mom see who she'd become. To take her mom around the Sloan-Whitney offices. Pride glinting in her mom's blue eyes as she snapped too many pictures of Elle in her office and shared embarrassing childhood stories. If only she had any of the memories of those moments an adult child rolls their eyes at as their parent mortifies them with too much pride, too much love.

It was too late for Elle, but not for Clayton and his dad. There's still hope for them. They are not broken. He still loved his son. He just needed to get past the expectation holding him back from fully embracing the amazing man his son is. For him to understand that Clayton exceeded the generational Owens' first son expectations. That he is so much more.

That he is everything.

"I love my son," Dr. Owens whispered.

"I know, and he loves you. We can love someone but sometimes forget how to show that we're proud of them. We respect them. They are worthy." Elle's voice cracked. In many ways, this conversation was one she wished someone had with her mom long before that January night. If only someone had battled for Elle before, waking her mom up to what she stood to lose: her daughter.

"You really care about my son." Dr. Owens' eyes warmed as he studied Elle.

"So much." she croaked, the depth of her feelings for Clayton both heavy and light in her chest.

"Thank you." He reached across the table, taking her hand. "You are definitely a Dr. Torres."

"Well, I am feisty, Dr. Owens."

"Call me, Chris. That's what my friends call me."

THIRTY

"In vain have I struggled. It will not do. My feelings will not be repressed. You must allow me to tell you how ardently I admire and love you."
~Jane Austen, *Pride and Prejudice*

"Is this normal?" Forehead creased, Elle handed the shampoo to Clayton, the shower's spray licking down his muscular body.

After this morning's run, they'd barely made it past the foyer before she pounced on him. Like breadcrumbs their clothes were strewn along the path leading to the bathroom.

"Washing hair?" he chuckled and squirted the coconut scented liquid onto his hands before massaging it into Elle's head.

"No. The sex. We have *a lot* of sex."

"Are you complaining?"

"No! It's good sex…*really* good." She laughed at the proud grin on his face. "We just have a lot of sex. Is this normal? Like was this how it was with you and…"

"Other women?" His right eyebrow quirked.

She winced. "I'm not fishing for compliments…. I just don't know if this is normal. Are we normal?"

"No." He shook his head. "I can honestly say this is not normal for me. I've never been like this with anyone else."

"I know this will *not* surprise you, but it's never been like this for me with anyone else either." Her mouth tipped into a coy smile.

This man both unlocked and consumed her. And she didn't mind one bit. With him she was flirty, sassy, sultry, vulnerable, and more Elle Davidson than she had ever been.

"I've never wanted anyone like I want you." Her eyes met his.

It was far more than sex. The intimacy between them was something she had never experienced with anyone else. Elle wanted to devour it all. His laughter. His pain. His heart. His body. She wanted not just their yesterday and today, but tomorrow…all the tomorrows.

"I know," he murmured, running his finger along her lips. "I've never wanted anyone the way I want you."

The reverent way his hand caressed her cheek reinforced that his want wasn't just about the sex either. A soft longing in his gaze telegraphed that he had the same burning desires that rattled unspoken within Elle.

What if she asked for his tomorrows? What would that look like? She couldn't ask him to leave with her and she wouldn't stay.

She finished her shower silently, and then stood in front of the bathroom mirror, wrapped in a towel, drying her hair. Clayton appeared in the mirror's reflection dressed for work, the sleeves of his green striped shirt rolled up.

"Have a good day, baby." He pressed his lips to hers, as though they were an old married couple.

Elle turned back to the mirror, Clayton's image lingered there, watching her, his throat bobbing as if he had something else to say. Their eyes danced with each other in the mirror.

"I like not being normal with you," Clayton murmured.

"I like not being normal with you, too." Elle's heart spoke first, not letting her logic clamp its hand around her mouth, nagging her that she didn't get to keep him.

As Clayton disappeared, his footsteps growing faint, Elle let out a shaky breath. It was Friday. Tomorrow would start her last week here, her last week with him.

Elle knew they needed to have this conversation. She had put it off too long.

If this was just them playing house until next week, she was okay with that. She would be okay with as much of Clayton as she could have until she left Perry…until she left him.

THIRTY-ONE

"When I fall in love, it will be forever."
~Jane Austen, *Sense and Sensibility*

E lle walked quietly through Hope Cemetery. The baby blue sky was clear, not a cloud to mar its brightness.

Somberly, she strolled on the cobblestone path looping through the graves, a bouquet of pink roses picked by Aunt Janet in her right hand. The area she sought was toward the back of the cemetery in the middle of a row of other long gone loved ones. Some kind soul had positioned a stone bench across from her grandparents' final resting places. A perfect spot for the living to visit the dead.

"Hi grandpa." Elle smiled sadly as she placed her hand on his smooth gravestone.

She'd been so little when he'd passed that she'd never grieved him like she mourned her grandma. Grandpa seemed like a wispy, cloudy memory, but grandma was her sun; warm, nourishing but sometimes able to burn. Walking carefully around his marker to avoid stepping on his actual grave, she crouched placing the pink roses at the foot of her grandma's gravestone beside another arrangement of pink tulips, a gift from Uncle Pete, she was sure.

"Happy birthday, Grandma. It's Elle…Eleanor."

Grandma had only ever known Eleanor.

"I know it's been a long time. I'm sorry. I don't know if mom ever visits you, but we're not talking." Elle's voice cracked. "I don't want to talk about that, though. I'm doing good, Grandma. I have a career that helps a lot of people." She traced a finger over the starfish bangle she'd worn since Clayton clasped it on her wrist. "I live in California. Remember my friend, Viet? I told you about him last time I was here. He's still my best friend and I have another one, Willa. You'd like her. She really embodies 'let me be me.' I have a…" she trailed off, her gaze pulled to the moss-covered brick wall surrounding the cemetery.

They were so similar to the walls around her heart that kept the living out, and the dead in. Had she been a ghost merely haunting this world instead of truly living in it? Sucking in the late summer air, its freshness filled her lungs, reminding her of the reinvigorating citrus scent of her Clayton.

My Clayton. My boyfriend. My everything. My love.

She exhaled, finally naming that feeling inside her. The feeling she refused to see, that she fought. It had been slow and quiet, but she'd fallen in love with Clayton. Each moment with him was a step to this realization. His off-key voice singing to her as they slow danced in the hallway outside the ballroom. Their first run together, neither seeming to want to let go of each other's hand. It started even further back when beside her in Spanish class he murmured his apology for their interaction at that Winter Ball. Had she known even then that she loved him?

She refocused on the headstone, a tender smile curving her lips. "I have a boyfriend. It's Dr. Owens' son. His name is

Clayton and I love him so much." An errant tear rolled down her cheek. "You used to say boys don't like fat girls. Well, he liked me when I was fat. I just didn't like me for a very long time. I think even now. I think you're part of the reason why. I know you meant well, but you sometimes left me feeling like I was unlovable."

People can love you and hurt you at the same time. They only have that power because you love them. It was something Willa had once said.

She sighed. "You hurt me, but I still love you. I still miss you…" Elle bent down to place a gentle kiss on the engraved *Grandmother* on the gravestone. "…I forgive you."

Forgiveness takes the power away from the words that bound her, allowing her to try to be free.

Wiping her eyes, she sat back on her heels. Her cell phone pinged with an incoming text. Slipping her mobile out of her dress pocket, a tiny thrill swept through her at the message from Clayton.

Fitz's Human: How are you?
Elle: I'm visiting my grandma for her birthday.
Fitz's Human: Are you at the cemetery? I'm taking a lunch break. I could come by if you want me.

It was nice how he asked "want" and not "need."

Elle: I appreciate that, but I'm just about to leave. How's your day?
Fitz's Human: Good but it will be better at 5:15 p.m.
Elle: Why?
Fitz's Human: That's when we come home to you.

Home? Pulse ticked up, she ran her thumb over his words

and the selfie he's sent of him and Fitz in his office. "My boys," she whispered.

> **Elle: Remember, I'm going to Daryl's with Tobey and Pete for dinner. I'm meeting them at 5 p.m.**

She let out a loud snort at a second selfie of Clayton and Fitz, pouting. Although, it was Fitz's normal face.

> **Elle: I'll bring you a few slices of mushroom pizza that you can have after we work up an appetite by not being normal together.**
> **Fitz's Human: I like not being normal with you.**

With a salacious smile that felt inappropriate for a cemetery, Elle made her way, through the rows of sun-soaked gravestones, towards the entrance. The residue of sadness from her interaction with her dead grandma fell away with each step. Reaching the cobblestone path that looped through the cemetery's center, she spotted a small figure bent down at a grave. They were the only visitors in this solemn place. The figure was at the second marker from the path's edge. As Elle's eyes fixated on the dark blonde curls, her stomach knotted.

Mom... Who is she visiting?

Elle squinted at the back of the stone her mother crouched at. Wordlessly her mother rose and faced her. Reminiscent of gunslingers in a bad western movie, their stares squared off in a showdown between mother and daughter. Who will speak first? Who will walk away first?

With a deep breath, Elle's steps resumed.

"Eleanor." Her mom's voice was soft.

She'd intended to walk on by, but her feet stopped, despite her will to keep walking.

Mom's smile was shy. "You look good."

"Excuse me?" Elle snarled.

It had been almost eighteen years since the woman who'd given her life had failed her. The last words her mom spoke to her before today was, "He wouldn't do that. He loves me."

This greeting felt too insignificant to be the first words she heard from her mom's lips after nearly two decades of silence. Fiery indignation ignited in Elle. What did she expect? What did she hope for? *An apology?*

"I…" Her mom lowered her gaze to the ground.

Words are hard.

A flicker of something, hope or guilt, propelled Elle toward her mom until her eyes fell on the name engraved on the marker. *Jamie Leicester.*

Bile rose like a snake, choking and viscous. Bending over, she heaved, the acidic anger burning her throat as she vomited.

"Eleanor," her mom soothed, wrapping thin arms around her shoulders.

"Get off!" Elle screamed and shoved her mother away.

Her mom stumbled to the ground. "Eleanor—"

"I am not *fucking* Eleanor. I am Elle," she bit out, wiping the sick from her mouth before facing her mother, who remained sprawled on the ground, her blue eyes welling with tears. Elle wiped her mouth again. "Are you visiting *him*?"

"El…"

"Are you visiting him?" she hissed.

"Yes, but—"

Elle cut the woman off with a flash of her hands and let an angry laugh escape. "You still choose everyone over me. I have been here for three weeks, and you have not tried once to see me. You've never reached out."

"But your uncle said—"

"You're *my* mother. Although that's a joke, isn't it? You

haven't been a mother for a very long time. You were too consumed with being a fucking wife. You completely forgot you were a mother. You forgot about me! You weren't being a mom when you tried to kill yourself, leaving a note saying you didn't want to be alone. You weren't alone. I was there. I. Was. There!" She drew a harsh breath. "You weren't a mother when you kept choosing man after man over me. Men that emotionally abused me with cruel names and comments. A man who raped me."

She practically gagged on the word. She'd never said out loud. Rape. That's what Jamie had done. He'd raped her. She always referred to it as "What Jamie did" or "That January night." All the flowery language that hid the truth of his brutal attack and the impact on her. And it wasn't just him. But her mother's refusal to protect her, the bigger betrayal.

Her mom's lips quivered. "Honey…I…"

"He raped me." Elle slammed her fist against her chest. "He raped me, and you did nothing."

"What?"

Elle spun at the pained deep baritone voice from behind her.

Tobey stood, his face drawn with heart-wrenching disbelief.

"Tobey." she gasped, falling to her knees in a heap of convulsing sobs.

"Eleanor," her mom bent and reached for Elle.

"No!" Tobey growled, blocking Elle's mother's approach. Flinging his arms around Elle, he pressed her shaking form into his steady chest. "Leave."

"Tobey."

"Aunt Amanda, just leave," he demanded.

"Tobey—"

"Fucking leave!" The venom in his voice was mismatched with the tenderness his arms provided Elle.

Retreating footsteps grew distant as Tobey held her. "I'm here."

Elle buried her face against his chest. Heavy, guttural sobs quaked through her.

She didn't want him to see her like this, to see her broken.

"I'm here. I'm here," he soothed as if a mantra, warding off any ill that threatened.

Time is a funny thing. The sweetest moments can feel like seconds and the most painful, hours. Elle wasn't sure how long she remained slumped in Tobey's arms, but he never moved, remaining on his knees, his arms tight around her.

"I'm sorry." Elle finally sat up, brushing lingering tears off her face.

"Why are you sorry?"

"I don't know."

"Elle, what happened?"

"Are you asking as my cousin or as Officer Coates?" she sniffed.

"Trooper Coates," he corrected reflexively. He winced as he realized what he had said, but with a reassuring squeeze of his hands he relaxed. "Your cousin. Always."

Her ugly truths, long unspoken, tripped on her lips. "I… I was visiting Grandma." Elle motioned to the pink carnations Tobey had discarded, an offering for their grandma. "When I was leaving, I spotted Mom here. Then I saw who she was visiting." Each syllable twisted angrily in the breeze,

"Who was she visiting?"

"Do you remember Jamie?"

"Yeah. He was a dick," Tobey grumbled.

"You thought so?" Elle raised an eyebrow.

"The things he'd say to you and the way he looked at you. I didn't like him. I didn't trust him." Tobey stopped speaking, looking between Jamie's gravestone and Elle, an angry red flashing into his face. "Was it him?"

She swallowed hard. "During winter break my freshman year, Jamie raped me."

Tobey's hand hovered over hers, as if trying to figure out if he should touch her or not. Elle held her breath until his warm palm rested on her. She closed her eyes in relief.

"I've only told two other people this. Well, now three." Mom still didn't believe her, so she shouldn't count.

"Your mom and…"

"Clayton."

"Clayton?"

"I told him the night of your wedding, after running into Mom. I had a bit of a break down, and he was there."

"He's a good man."

"The best." Her lips tugged up.

"Your mom?"

"I told her a few weeks after it happened, but she just kept saying that he wouldn't do that and repeating that he loved her."

"What the fuck?" Storm clouds darkened his blue eyes.

"She always chose them, her men, over me."

"If my dad knew, he'd be furious with her."

"Please don't tell him. He can't know," she begged.

"Elle, this is your story; you choose who to share it with."

"No. It's not my story!" Elle screamed, gesturing to her heart. "It's part, but it's not all. I'm so much more than this. I'm so much more than all of it."

This had defined her for so long. All of it. The abandonment, the emotional neglect, the mocking cruel jabs, the prodding to be better somehow, and the rape had wrapped their gnarled fingers around her, holding her in place as their sharp teeth attempted to devour all that was good about

Eleanor. But as Elle, she'd discovered she was a phoenix rising from the ashes of who she'd been.

"You're right." He squeezed her hand. "You always are."

"Well, I am one of your favorite people." Her statement sounded more like a question as she peered back at his softening features.

"I think you're my favorite, actually." He leaned in and looped his arm around her shoulder, pressing her into his side. "Just don't tell Jerome."

"Your secret is safe with me."

"I'm not going to say anything to dad, and I won't push you, but if you told him, he'd understand. He loves you."

"I know and I love him, that's why I can't…why I won't tell him."

"I don't understand."

"First, what would it do to him to know he wasn't there to protect me? There was nothing he could have done, but you know he'll blame himself. Second, he lost his parents. I don't want to be the reason he loses his sister."

"Third, you don't want to take him away from her." Tobey said, his voice resigned. "You're still taking care of her, even though she never took care of you."

"Are you Oprah-ing me?" Elle snarked, lightly elbowing his ribs.

"You get a car! You get a car! You get a car! Gayle! Steadman!" Tobey's Oprah impression was truly horrific.

"Never do that again." She chuckled. "Ugh, I am a mess." She sat up, surveying her rumpled dress. She was certain her face was splotchy and eyes rimmed in red.

"Let me take you to the farmhouse. You can clean up and then I have a surefire solution to turn that frown upside down." Tobey suggested, standing up and putting out his hand for Elle to take.

Forty-five minutes later, face washed, and clothes

changed, Elle bounced on her feet excitedly like a squealing teenaged girl at a Taylor Swift concert. Tobey said he was taking her to the barber to pick up Lt. Scout from his monthly haircut, but this wasn't an ordinary barber. Paws of Perry-dise was the premier, and only, dog groomer in Perry. The peanut butter cookie scented puppy salon featured bone-shaped dog beds for its clientele to lounge in between mani/pedis, trims, sudsy baths, teeth cleaning, and massages. It rivaled a human spa.

"Stop it!" Elle gushed, as a recently groomed Lt. Scout pranced into the room wearing a lavender bow tie.

"Damn right, he's a sexy beast. All the Coates men are." Tobey puffed out his chest.

"Aw, you're a sexy beast." Elle stood up, pinching her cousin's cheeks.

"How was dinner?" Clayton asked as Elle walked into the farmhouse carrying her leftovers and a small mushroom pizza for him.

"Really good. How was your day?"

"My dad showed up at the clinic this afternoon." Clayton grinned boyishly, taking the bags and pizza box from her.

"Really?" Her lips curled up.

"He showed up mid-afternoon. I gave him a short tour and introduced him to the staff. He even asked to stay and watch me work. He stayed for the rest of the day."

"*Really?*"

"Yeah. When we were closing, he asked if he could take me for ice cream."

"Really?" She may need to learn a new word, but joy was stealing all her other words.

"We used to go for ice cream when I was a kid and did well on a test or scored in a football game."

"So, a celebratory *I'm proud of you* ice cream?" Elle's voice was sweetly reassuring.

"Yeah," he said, his smile reaching his eyes.

"Baby, that's great." She wove her arms around his torso, leaning into his strong chest to listen to the steady beat of his happy heart.

"How was seeing your grandma?" he murmured.

"A lot." She looked up at him. "I want to tell you, but it's a lot."

"I have a proposal. How about we go upstairs and be not normal together, then we can have a snack and talk."

"Counter proposal." Elle bit her lip. "Let's be not normal together, have a snack, take Fitz for a walk, burn off said snack with more not being normal, and then talk."

"Deal." He traced his fingers along her lips.

How did she fall in love with the boy whose eyes she once thought judgy but the man whose grey gaze she wanted to submerge herself in? She loved this man deeply, but she wouldn't tell him. What would come of it? How could she stay here where too many ghosts lurked? How could she ask him to leave? They needed to talk about tomorrow, the metaphoric one hurtling toward them. But she didn't want to discuss that today. Today they would be "not normal."

Yet later, limbs twisted together on the couch, those words tapped on her lips, but remained unspoken.

I love you, Clayton.

THIRTY-TWO

"But people themselves alter so much, that there is something new to be observed in them forever."
~Jane Austen, *Pride and Prejudice*

E lle leaned against a low bookcase separating the children's section with the rest of Cow Tale, the village's only bookstore. Each week, Mathew hosted story time. To the delight of the pint-size attendees, he acted out the characters' voices, used props, and sometimes dressed up like the characters. This week, Fitz sat in his lap, grinning crookedly at the attentive listeners. The plump pug had been recruited as a prop for this week's story about a Clifford the Big Red Dog-sized pug named Franklin.

"He's so good at this," Elle whispered to Noah as Mathew concluded the story to the beaming smiles and happy claps of the children surrounding him.

"He is," agreed Noah, who was there to pass out cookies and coupons from his bakery, the Farmer's Wife.

"Though, Fitz is the real star." She pointed at the wiggly

pug being adored by entranced children. With Clayton at the clinic, Elle had volunteered to bring Fitz.

"Agreed." Noah broke a sugar cookie and offered Elle half.

Between cookie bites, they settled into a companionable silence. Somehow over the three weeks Noah went from the boy she'd daydreamed about to the man she called friend.

Twisting at a sudden crash, she looked beyond the woman picking up a book and landed on a little boy. His curious face pressed against the glass. Big brown eyes peered through the window. A doting hand sat upon his shoulder. Hair the same chestnut shade as his tumbled over a woman's face as she bent, whispering into his ear, eliciting the eruption of an oversize grin on his small face.

"I'll be right back," Elle said to Noah and headed to the door.

She stepped outside to the sidewalk. "Summer." Elle greeted her old frenemy.

Summer Michaels stood next to the little boy clad in a Jets sweatshirt and shorts. The late summer almost autumn mid-morning air was cool.

"Eleanor." Summer's hand remained protective on the little boy.

"Who's this?"

"This is Liam, my son." Pride sparkled in her chocolate eyes, the same as her sons, as she looked down at Liam, his eyes fixed on Fitz through the window.

"Hi, Liam."

"Hello. Nice to meet you. I am Liam." He introduced himself as if reading a script and extended his hand.

"Hello. I'm Elle." She shook Liam's outstretched small hand.

Looking up at his mom for reassurance, she nodded and smiled at him. Those little eyes turned back to Mathew who danced between the bookshelves lining the store's aisles, a barking Fitz in his arms.

"He loves dogs," Summer explained.

"They're the best, especially Fitz."

"He's a pug." Liam's stare remained locked to the window. "Just like Otis."

"He watched *Milo and Otis* with my dad. He's now obsessed with pugs. Well, with all dogs, really. He's been reading books about dogs and learning lots of facts about them." Summer said with a "proud mama bear" quirk of her lips.

"Liam, would you like to meet Fitz?"

"Yes, but…" Liam trailed off, a frown pulling at his mouth.

"It's okay, baby. We can see Fitz from here." Summer squeezed Liam's shoulder again.

Elle's eyes flicked to Noah inside and mouthed for him to *grab Fitz and come out*.

"Here's Fitz!" Noah announced when he emerged a minute later.

A bright grin exploded on Liam's face as Noah joined them, holding a wiggling Fitz.

"Hi. I'm Noah and this is Fitz." He crouched, holding Fitz close to the open-mouthed boy.

"Can I?" Liam's hopeful eyes peered up at Summer.

She smiled. "Of course, baby."

"Hi Fitz. Nice to meet you. I am Liam." His tiny fingers skated along Fitz's silky fur.

A contented moan purred out of the pug.

As if remembering his manners, Liam looked at Noah. "Hi Noah. Nice to meet you. I am Liam."

Noah shook his hand.

A short while later, Elle sat next to Summer on a bench as Liam skipped down the street with Noah and Fitz.

Summer had explained that her eight-year-old son was on the Autism Spectrum, which made large group events challenging.

"We've tried to join story hour in the past, but the level of noise in a bookstore and coffee shop proved too distracting for him," Summer told her. "Sometimes too much distraction triggers a meltdown. The stimulation of loud noises and crowds can overpower Liam's ability to be present in the experience."

They'd come early today because Liam had seen Fitz's picture in the advertisement for the event, but it was still too much for him. So, they watched from outside. A sharp tug jerked Elle's heart. So often, she'd spent much of her life looking in from the outside.

"He's eight, but he reads at a sixth-grade level. You could call him a voracious reader," Summer chuckled. "I bring him to the library three times a week."

"Liam's a reader like you were." Elle offered, a wistfulness curving her lips up.

Summer grinned. "Oh, my goodness we were fanatics about *The Babysitters Club* and *Sweet Valley* books."

"Until I moved on to Austen."

"I just checked *Pride and Prejudice* out from the library."

Elle tipped her head. "Have you read it before?"

"No. I kind of lost that love of reading for a while. In the last year, I started getting back into it because of Liam. The classics section is right across the hall from the children's and Young Adult reading rooms in the basement of the library. I hang out in that section and that way I'm close to Liam while he's in the children's room. I want to give him a little independence. You know, not hover. But I want to be close, just in case he needs me," Summer said, her eyes following Noah and Liam who were about three blocks down the street.

"What part are you at?" Elle warmed to the conversation, and the chance to discuss her favorite parts of the novel.

"Jane is sick at Mr. Bingley's and Lizzie has come to visit her. Can we talk about Caroline Bingley? She's the worst."

Elle nearly spit out the sip of tea she'd just taken.

Summer raised an eyebrow. "What?"

Elle's cheeks heated. "In high school, Carmen, Beth, and I played a game where we would assign characters from different Austen novels to our classmates."

"Let me guess; I was Caroline?"

Elle nodded.

"Makes sense." Summer's brows drew together. "I was pretty terrible in high school. Especially to you."

Elle merely nodded again.

"I'm really sorry. I wish I had some excuse like in the movies where we find out the bully has a reason for being a jerk and we realize they are just hurt. You know hurt people hurt people." Summer punctuated her point with a jab at her own chest. "I was just an asshole. I got into high school and made friends with some of the 'cool' kids. They picked on you, so I did too. I was so focused on making them like me that I lost a true friend."

"Wanting to belong can be catnip for us. I can understand wanting to be accepted."

"Yeah, but you never compromised who you were. You were still you…" She paused; her mouth opened as if trying to think of what to say. "…still Eleanor."

"I go by Elle now."

A thoughtful grin etched Summer's face. "Elle. It fits you."

"You're not Caroline Bingley anymore," Elle said, placing her hand on Summer's.

"Thank you. Now, my job is to keep the Caroline Bingley's of the world away from Liam." A hint of a 'don't mess with my cub' glint lit her eyes.

"Can I ask where Liam's dad is?"

"He's not in the picture." Her smile tightened in a firm line. "It's better that way."

Elle nodded. She suspected there was more to that story, but she'd wait until Summer was ready to share. They all had unshared chapters of their stories. Elle understood that better than anyone.

Liam skipped over; hand clasped with Noah's. "Mom, look what Fitz can do."

"What, baby?"

"Here you go." Noah handed Liam a small piece of peanut butter cookie.

"Fitz, sit!" Liam commanded, holding the cookie up.

Fitz's wiggly butt plopped onto the sidewalk.

"Fitz, shake!" Liam held out his palm and Fitz tapped it with his front right paw.

Liam gave Fitz the treat and a scratch of his ears for good measure.

"Very cool," Summer praised Fitz and Liam.

"I taught him everything he knows." Noah winked.

"Mom, Noah owns the bakery. He said I could have a cookie. Is that okay?" Liam asked.

"Hope I didn't overstep. The free ones I brought are gone, so I texted Diana at the bakery and said if my new friend Liam stops by to give him his favorite cookie on me." He looked between mother and son.

"Noah, that's very kind of you. I will totally pay for—"

He held up his hand, stopping Summer's offer. "It's a treat for my friend here. How often do I get to look like a baller in Perry?" Noah insisted, his blue eyes warm like a tropical sea.

"What's a baller?" Liam asked, his face scrunched.

"It's someone really cool that everyone wants to be around," Summer explained.

"Oh, like Fitz!" Liam declared cheerily.

"Yep." All three adults laughed as Liam fawned over Fitz.

"I am so sorry for how I was to you," Summer whispered, as she hugged Elle goodbye.

Elle murmured back, "I know. That's not you anymore."

"You're a good egg, Davidson." Noah looped his arm around her shoulder as Summer and Liam moved down the street.

"She's not who she used to be."

She'd seen glimpses of her old friend and hated the way the feeling of lost time rushed over her. She'd missed Summer, the old, pre-high school Summer, and was grateful for the reconnection with her. There wasn't much time left in her stay in Perry, and it felt like she had a lot of time to make up for.

"Are any of us?" Noah said, a deep breath accompanying his words.

How true that is. Elle studied him. So much of the boy she'd crushed on in high school was still in the man that stood beside her, but he was so much more. Kindness and thoughtfulness were wrapped in this handsome package. Behind his charming smirks was a perceptiveness that most people didn't realize was there.

A perceptiveness that led him to play matchmaker. Clayton had told her how Noah encouraged him to go for it with Elle after she'd returned.

"When you said it was about time at the wedding when I turned you down, so I could dance with Clayton, you weren't just talking about now were you?" She arched her right eyebrow.

A bashful smile quirked on Noah's lips. "I've long suspected how Clayton felt about you. He wasn't as subtle as he thought he was when he'd stare at you all the time in high school."

It was strange to think that a man like Noah, who pushed his friends to chase the women they liked, was single. On paper and in person, Noah was rather perfect. Even if he wasn't Elle's perfect, she knew he was for someone.

"You know she's pretty cute." She hip-checked him, her stare following Summer and Liam as they walked into the bakery down the street.

"Oh my god, you sound like my mother," he groaned.

"How dare you!" she said in mock dismay. "Seriously, though. How and why are you single? You're good looking. You're successful. You're nice."

Somehow Aunt Janet had possessed her. Elle was not responsible for the words coming out of her mouth. It was Janet, totally Janet.

"I am waiting for the right woman." He shrugged.

"I can understand that."

"Because you waited?"

She nodded.

"Until Clayton."

"Until Clayton." She smirked.

"Speaking of Clayton…" He let out a heavy breath. "You leave next week. Have you two talked about it? About what happens, then?"

Saying nothing, she looked away.

He sloshed a hard breath. "I don't want to pop the bubble you two are in. I'm Team Clayton and Elle all the way, but you two should talk about what happens when you head back to California." He placed his hand on her shoulder and squeezed. "There doesn't have to be an expiration date." His soft voice almost mocked with its promise of what couldn't be…or could it?

THIRTY-THREE

"Always resignation and acceptance. Always prudence and honour and duty. Elinor, where is your heart?"
~Jane Austen, *Sense and Sensibility*

T*his time next week, I'll be gone.* The thought pulsed a continuous ache in Elle's chest. Each slap of her sneakers against the Greenway's well-run path punctuated the knowledge that goodbye was coming. That this time next week, she'd not run with Clayton beside her.

All the *if onlys* mockingly danced inside her. If only she could flip the calendar back, to get a do-over of these weeks. If only she could freeze time, then she would have frozen the moment Clayton first kissed her. If only she could have pressed pause last night as Clayton asked if she was warm enough as he held her in his arms at the drive-in.

Even now, if she could stretch this run out for a few more minutes, a few more miles, she would. Anything to not say the words choking her.

"That was good." Clayton sucked in a deep breath as they

reached the pickup. "I am thinking omelets when we get home."

Elle just nodded.

Clayton studied her and his smile faltered. "You're quiet."

"It's Sunday," she croaked. "This time next week, I'll be gone."

Clayton opened his mouth but shut it quickly, his face pinched.

"I'm mucking this up." She scrubbed her hands down her face. "Clayton, I told you that I didn't have a plan, but I did. Not about us, but about me. The plan was always to go back."

"I thought you were ha…ha…happy here…with your family, our friends… You told Pete I make you blissfully happy."

That ache twinged in her heart. "You do, but I don't belong here. This isn't home. This isn't my life. It's—"

"Just your vacation."

His words gut-punched her.

"I think I realized it in Boston."

Is that what she'd been doing with him? It wasn't her life, but it didn't feel temporary like the fanciful vacation romances Willa had. Even if the time with Clayton was brief, what she felt for him was engraved permanently on her heart.

This place was home for Clayton. After his marriage ended, he could have gone anywhere, but he came here. To his family. To his friends. To his home. This was his shelter in the storm. Perry had only ever been her storm, not her refuge.

A quiet clap of thunder broke the heavy silence between them. The sky grew dark gray, the same as Clayton's eyes, with the impending storm.

"We should go." Clayton cleared his throat and motioned to the pickup.

The cab of the truck was stifling with thick heaviness as they drove back to the farmhouse. Fat raindrops tapped angrily against the windows. The rain dulled to a mist as they arrived at the farmhouse. Entering, Clayton grabbed the leash to take Fitz for a walk.

Elle offered to join, but he said, "No, you go take a shower."

Once he'd left, Elle slid to the floor and pressed her back against the farmhouse's door. Head buried into her bent knees, she let the tears flow. Each salty sting punctuated the truth roaring inside her. *I hurt him. He deserves better. I don't belong here.*

"Stop! You're not this girl." She swiped at her face and stood up.

With a deep inhale, she pushed the emotions down and made her way to the bedroom. She pulled out her suitcases from the closet and placed them on the bed. Normally packing was a more thought-out process, but she just pulled things out of drawers and off hangers, tossing them in.

"What are you doing?" Clayton's pinched greeting startled her.

She'd been so lost in thought she hadn't heard him enter the room. "Packing."

His forehead creased. "Why? You don't leave for another six days."

"I'm moving back to the Little Red Ba—"

"No," he interrupted sharply.

"It makes sense. There's no reason to drag out the inevitable."

"In…in…in—" he sucked in a breath. "—inevitable?"

"I'm leaving," she huffed, flinging a T-shirt onto the pile of clothes in her suitcase.

"Not for another six days," he repeated, his steely gaze fixed on her.

"It doesn't matter." Realizing she'd accidentally packed his Team Paw Patrol T-shirt, she yanked it up and handed it to him. "This is yours."

He shook his head and refused to take it. "It does matter."

"Clayton." She held it out. "Just take the fucking shirt… please." Her voice cracked.

"No." He reached for her.

But she stepped back.

"Why are you doing this?"

"I've already been so unfair to you. Like you said, I'm on vacation. I'm the one who's crashed into your life and in six days I get on a plane."

"I know. You were always going to get on that plane."

"I'm sorry." The back of her throat burned.

"No." This time when he reached for her, she didn't pull away. "I di…di…didn't mean it like that. I me…me…meant we always knew you were leaving. We both went into this kn…kno…knowing that."

"I am leaving, but it doesn't have to be like before. I'm not like before. I'll come back. I'll visit."

"I know." He stroked her cheek.

"I don't know what it looks like, but I want you in my life. That I know."

His hands gripped her biceps. "I want you in my life too."

"I don't want to give you false hope, though. My home is there. Yours is here."

"Your home…is there." He said each word carefully as if they were a hot ember threatening to burn him.

"Yes." She sighed. "I… I want to do what's fair for you."

"Let me worry about what's fair to me. I don't know what it looks like either, but I want you in my life too." He closed his eyes. As they reopened, sharp intensity filled his gaze. "Stay with me…until you go. I told you I would rather a mo…mo…moment with you than a lifetime without you. If all I have is a moment or some future stolen ones, I'll take it."

"Clayton—"

"P…P…Please," he implored.

She couldn't deny him or herself. It would break her to say goodbye, but to be separated by the little pond between the farmhouse and Little Red Barn for the remainder of her time would destroy her. To be so close and not touch or be touched by him was a harsher punishment than having a whole country between them. The remaining tiny sliver of time with Clayton was better than none.

She nodded.

"Promise me something?"

Promises were scary. So many had been made and broken to Elle through the years, so she was careful to only make ones she could keep.

She swallowed thickly. "What?"

"Let's not live this week like there's a t…t…t…ticking clock. You will get on that plane the day after Pete's party. Until then, can we go back to just being us? Please?" His thumbs stroked along her bare arms.

"Ok."

"Ok." He pressed his forehead to hers.

"Do you always knock at your parents' door?" Elle asked, as Clayton and she walked up the steps of the Owens' yellow Victorian, Fitz trotting in front of them.

"Yes," he said, shifting the tinfoil covered carrot cake she'd baked to knock.

"Why? You told me that Noah and you never knock on

each other's doors. Why do you knock on your parents' door, then?"

"Two years ago, I didn't knock and caught my mom and dad kissing in the kitchen."

Her face scrunched. "Well, that doesn't seem so bad."

"It wouldn't have been if they had their clothes on." He shuddered.

"Oh my god!" She barked with laughter. "Oh baby, I am sorry. Were they completely naked?"

"Well, Dad had his bow tie on."

"What?" Elle stood dumbstruck, as the front door opened.

"Kids! You didn't need to knock," Heidi welcomed them with a grin. "Chris, they are here."

"Coming! Just fixing my bow tie."

Elle bit back a snicker as Clayton placed a hand over his mouth.

They sat in the formal dining room eating grilled lemon pepper tilapia, aged white cheddar and chive mashed cauliflower, tomatoes and cucumber salad, and garlic biscuits. Chris was a master in the kitchen.

"Your dad tells me he came by the clinic on Friday." Heidi gushed, a big smile popping. "I was a little jealous when your dad said he got to come into the exam room to watch you work. I've only had a tour."

"You're very good with your patients." Chris' warm smile broadened.

A similar smile lit Clayton's face. "Thank you."

Elle's heart swelled.

"I was really impressed by the way you got that pit bull to sit calmly as you gave vaccinations. You may need to teach me your Jedi mind tricks so I can use them on my patients."

Elle gasped. "Are you a *Star Wars* nerd, Chris?"

"Huge!" He beamed, but then his smile dimmed. "I

should have come to your clinic sooner, son. I'm sorry I didn't."

"It's okay." Clayton glanced at his plate.

"No, it's not okay, but it will be." He clasped Clayton's shoulder.

Elle fought the urge to do a fist pump in the air.

Clayton and Elle offered to clean up before coffee, tea, and cake. Elle rinsed dishes as Clayton stacked them in the dishwasher.

Chris hummed "Chasing Cars" by Snow Patrol. Quietly, Elle pulled her cell phone out of her dress pocket, brought the song up and hit play.

"I know this one!" Heidi crooned and shimmied her arms a little.

Clayton playfully nudged Elle's hip as his mom swayed in the middle of the kitchen. With the swagger of a ballroom dancer, Chris took his wife in his arms, making her giggle like a schoolgirl.

Elle's heart tripped, witnessing these two affectionately slow dance in their kitchen as if nobody was watching. The love spiraled around them with every turn, dip, and twist like a private romantic play staged just for them.

"Dance with me." Clayton's whisper caressed the shell of her ear.

"Always." She took his hand.

Clayton spun her around the kitchen, joining his parents.

His out-of-key voice sang along softly, pulling her in before twirling her back out.

Elle's smile was too big for her face as they swayed, and he sang. He didn't sing every line but certain ones, as if trying to tell her something through the lyrics. Like a secret only for them. In that moment, she forgot the world, forgot the pain she anticipated from leaving Clayton, and settled in to just being in the moment of the last days of her vacation.

THIRTY-FOUR

"I have not wanted syllables when actions have spoken so plainly."
~Jane Austen, *Sense and Sensibility*

Labor Day was the first holiday she'd spent in Perry in fourteen years. More importantly, it was the start of the "Week of Pete," as she and Tobey dubbed the various birthday-themed shenanigans planned for the week that included individualized dates planned by Janet, Tobey, Jerome, and Elle.

Despite being a holiday, Elle had to take a business call regarding the mobile mammography initiative partnership she'd pitched to Magda at the fundraiser in Boston. With early detection lives could be saved. Lives like her grandma's.

By the time she disconnected the call, she was soaring with a sense of accomplishment. The program was shaping up nicely and the call had gone exceptionally well, solidifying the non-profit and healthcare company's partnership to expand services in underserved rural communities. The thumbs up emoji text from Malcolm was the cherry on what was already a sundae of a day.

When Elle finished with her meeting, she FaceTimed Clayton. "You're a fucking rock star," he praised while elbow deep in puppies at the shelter where he volunteered.

"Look at them!" Elle squealed as Clayton held the phone toward the yelping puppy pile that had been dropped anonymously at the shelter.

"They are pretty rambunctious." Clayton chuckled as a brown and white puppy leapt at its siblings then flopped to the newspaper covered floor.

"What about that little nugget over there?"

A patch of brown covered the right eye of the smallest puppy, and ink blot-shaped brown patches littered its torso. The puppy sat quietly, more a spectator than a member of the little orphaned family.

Elle was drawn to that outsider puppy.

"This one?" Clayton asked, crouching down allowing the camera to come close to the puppy's face.

"Yes." Smiling, she pressed her face to the phone as if pressing her nose to the pup's. "Hello there."

"This is the sister." He massaged her ears.

"She's not playing. Is she okay?"

"Yeah. She's healthy."

"Are they not letting her play?" A furrow creased her brow. "Hello, lovely girl. Are your brothers being obnoxious?" she cooed to the puppy.

"No, she's just watching over them. The staff say she's sweet and friendly, as you can see." As if on cue, she licked Clayton's fingers. "She's just protective of her brothers... keeping an eye on them."

Elle could hear the smile in his voice, even though all she could see was his hand caressing delicate fur. She knew how great those same fingers felt as they stroked her.

"Like Lizzie Bennet always looking out for her sisters. Maybe we should call her Lizzie."

"You know, she needs a good home." Clayton winked, turning the camera to himself as he sat on the ground.

"I work and travel a lot."

"Malcolm has dogs." Clayton countered.

"Yes, but he's married so he has someone that can help."

"Noted." Clayton grinned, as the puppy climbed into his lap and nuzzled his chest. "You know unmarried people can have pets."

"Noted," Elle mimicked his response.

She had thought about it in the past. There were times she walked by adoption fairs outside pet stores or lost herself down adoption website rabbit holes debating with herself whether to commit. There was always an excuse not to.

I work too much.

I travel too much.

I am alone.

They deserve a real home.

The strongest reason she hadn't ever said "Yes" was the home piece. Everyone deserved a home and Elle had so recently forged her own home in Long Beach.

"I won't push but you love dogs. You're also really good with them," Clayton said.

"How is that not pushing?" Elle cocked her brow.

"If I was pushing, I'd do this." Clayton pressed the camera close to Lizzie's face and pitched his voice high. "Please be my mommy, Elle. I'd be such a good girl. I could keep your always cold feet warm. I could lay on your lap as you read to me. I could eat burnt bacon with you."

"Stop!" she barked, the giggles rumbling through her. "Your emotional terrorism will not work with me."

"Sorry, Lizzie I tried." Clayton pouted, pressing a kiss to the puppy's cheek.

Elle bit her lower lip, suddenly thinking of Summer Michaels and her little boy. The precocious Liam would adore all these puppies.

"You have your 'I have an idea' smile."

"Remember how I told you about Summer's little boy, Liam?"

"Yes."

"If Summer is okay with it, would you be open for Liam to come to the clinic and spend time with you to learn more about being a veterinarian?"

"Of course." Clayton's quick response didn't surprise her.

"You have your 'Elle' smile."

"Yeah." He sighed. "Moments like this just remind me why your heart is one of my top three favorite things about you."

"But my butt is your number one," she said cheekily.

"It is a fantastic ass."

"Clayton, there are impressionable ears present." Elle gasped in mock dismay, referring to the yelping puppies in the background.

After her video chat with Clayton, Elle raced to pick Uncle Pete up for their memory lane inspired solo birthday outing.

"We're heading toward Niagara Falls." Pete rubbed his hands together, attempting to guess where she was taking him. "We're not going to the casino, are we?"

"When have we gone to a casino together?"

"True, that would be more your aunt."

"She does love the slots."

"Oh, my slotty woman," Pete deadpanned.

"I'm so torn by that joke." Elle fought a laugh at the word play but also, was mortified by his very bad dad and a little sexist joke.

"That was gold!" Pete said, his blue eyes twinkling with

pleasure. "What could be in Niagara Falls?" He tapped his index finger on his chin.

Elle's lips curled at his pretend perplexment of their destination. There were few options of where and what they'd be doing in Niagara Falls that would be worthy of a fiftieth birthday week date.

In seventh grade, Elle had missed a field trip to the Niagara Falls Aquarium. Her dad had already left, and her mom was in the psychiatric unit, she had no legal guardian to sign the permission slip.

Elle wasn't sure how or when Pete found out she'd been denied the trip on a technicality, but one Monday morning in May, Elle had been called to the school office. A grinning Pete had come for her to take her for a dental appointment. Only there was no dental appointment. Climbing into his truck, Pete had pulled out the unsigned permission slip for the aquarium field trip, telling her to come to him whenever she needed anything. "Anything," he'd repeated hitting every syllable.

The dentist appointment was just a clever ruse to take her out of school. Pete took her to the Maid of the Mist, where their raincoat-clad forms were dosed in the cool waters of the Niagara Falls as the tour's boat ventured close the falls' base. It had been a good day. *A great day.*

Now, as she pulled into the parking lot for the Maid of the Mist, Pete shouted, "I knew it!!"

His words that long ago day came back to her. *I'm always here for you, no matter what.*

"Thank you." Elle sighed, gratitude filling her up. She was thanking him for all those times when he had, in fact, been there for her and all the times yet to come when she knew he'd be there.

Pete's forehead wrinkled. "Aren't I supposed to be thanking you?"

"No." Elle shook her head. "I appreciate you so much. I don't know if I say it enough but thank you for everything."

"You show me in so many ways. I'm a lucky uncle."

"I feel like the lucky one."

"Let's agree, we're both pretty damn lucky."

"I don't want to only see you on video chats or every couple of years when you fly to Long Beach. I don't want to go another fourteen years without coming back." Elle inhaled a steadying breath. "I'm going to come back more often, at least one proper trip a year and maybe some quick stopovers when I fly to New York City for work."

"I'd like that."

"Maybe I can come back for Christmas?" Elle asked, playing with her starfish bracelet.

She wasn't sure whose permission she sought, her uncle's or her own. It had been so long since she'd spent a holiday in Perry. Labor Day wasn't one generally marked for homecomings, but here she was. Even her last few years at UB, when she lived only an hour away, she'd come back to Pete and Janet's just a handful of times. The already complicated holidays with her mom's influx of rotating boyfriends became more strained after she broke with her mom. It was hard to relax into Pete and Janet's cozy Christmas cottage, like something out of a Hallmark movie, when Elle kept looking over her shoulder for the lurking specter of her mom.

She could do this. She could come back for visits and holidays and survive. Only days away from leaving, she recognized how far she'd come.

"You never have to ask." Pete took her hand. "Our door is always open. You're my favorite niece."

"I'm your only niece." Her lips tugged up, sweetly sarcastic.

"My one and only." His smile large.

THIRTY-FIVE

*"Know your own happiness. You want nothing but patience – or
give it a more fascinating name, call it hope."*
~Jane Austen, *Sense and Sensibility*

A wicked grin grew wider on Elle's face with each
rhythmic tap of fat raindrops against the pane of the
farmhouse windows. She looked over to Clayton asleep
beside her on his stomach, his left-hand lay over her in a
claiming gesture, as his head faced his side of the bed. *His
side. My side.* The heat of his body next to her pulsed every
wanton need awake.

Giddy anticipation jigged through her limbs as she lay in
the still dark room listening to the rain and quiet hum of
Clayton, or maybe Fitz's, snores. Pulse racing, she waited for
the chime of his church bells that had served as her alarm for
the last few weeks. As her eyes adjusted to the dark, she
studied Clayton's outlined form sleeping next to her. The
navy comforter draped over his middle revealing the ridges of
his muscular back. Her fingers itched to slink up his
spine. Desire pooled in her core, spreading through her.

Clayton's alarm screeched and he let out a muffled groan then searched blindly for his phone on the bedstand. With a grumble, he turned it off, then flipped toward Elle.

"Good Mo...oof." Clayton's good morning was interrupted by Elle pushing him to his back as she landed on top of him like a jungle cat.

Not a sweet little tabby but a ravenous panther. Straddling him, she crashed her mouth against his.

"Well, hello." His raspy sleep-worn voice chuckled.

"It's raining....so..." She drew the *Team Paw Patrol* shirt over her head, flinging it somewhere in the room.

"So, you want to macramé?"

"No." Elle placed his hands on her aching breasts.

"Oh, you want to play chess?" His tease was a deep rumble as he rolled her hardening nipples with the pads of his fingers.

Her pelvic muscles tightened with want. "No." With a sly smile, Elle took his hands and moved them to cup her backside.

"Oh, you want to make pancakes?" His brow cocked as he squeezed her ass.

"No." Elle sighed, falling back on the bed, taking Clayton with her, his hard body settling between her open legs.

"I think you'll have to tell me what you want, because I'm really at a loss here." He smirked, rubbing the growing arousal beneath his black boxer briefs against her naked core.

"I want you." Need crept up her body with each delicious movement of his erection against her.

"What do you want me to do?" He kissed her throat.

She bit her lower lip in carnal consideration, although she knew what she wanted him to do in exquisite detail. Those images flooded her dreams all night. Clayton's roaming tongue trailing down her body, teasing licks down her center until feverishly devouring her. Her fingers threading through his short hair as he brought her to the edge and back over and over again. Nails digging into his shoulder as he inched inside of her, taunting her with the promise of even more pleasure before sinking fully into her.

"Be specific." His hoarse murmur in her ear rippled through her entire body like a cresting wave.

"I want you to go down on me and then fuck me until I scream your name."

"Good girl," he growled before sealing his mouth to hers.

With a grunt of her name, Clayton collapsed atop of Elle. His orgasm shuddering through both of them.

"That…was…nice." Elle's voice was breathless and body limp with sated contentment.

"I do like…" He stopped, gulping needed air. "…when you ask for what you want." He kissed her before pulling himself out of her and rolling onto his back.

Elle frowned at the loss of fullness. A blend of satisfying connection and instant grief at the end of sex with Clayton consumed her. Her body was deliciously sore and wrung out from but once their physical connection was broken, it craved that fullness to come back.

She wondered if it was normal to be so blissfully contented and longing in the same moment. Clayton's tender strokes along her spine telegraphed that he felt the same way. After sex, he always held her tight, like a precious gift that he was afraid he'd misplace or lose. At first, she thought it may be his wanting to reassure her after all she had shared with him about the assault, but she noticed how his entire body relaxed with her touch just as hers did with his.

"Is that your kink?" Elle inquired, wrapping her leg over

him in almost a claiming gesture. At least for the next few days, he was hers.

"My kink?" he said bemused.

"The thing you are into...you know, sexually?" She waved to their naked bodies as if he needed an image of "sexually."

"Do you have a kink?" He traced her lips with the tip of his index finger.

She blushed. "I felt like I was into almost getting caught until we actually got caught by Jerome."

He'd surprised them in Clayton's office at lunchtime yesterday. Elle had, also uncharacteristically, been straddling a *very* enthusiastic Clayton's lap. His shirt unbuttoned and her sweater tossed somewhere.

What was this man doing to her? *All the right things.*

"You didn't have to work with him the rest of the day. The not-so-subtle comments he made." A wincing laugh covered his features.

"Such as?"

"Patting my back each time he saw me at the reception area and saying, 'Hope it's not a *hard* day for you, big guy.' He did this so often that staff started to ask me if I was okay."

She buried her face in his neck, trying to stifle the guffaw. It didn't work.

"I'm sorry." She pulled back with a pitying smile. "Well, if it's any consolation, I think Jerome has cured me of that kink."

"We'll see." Devilish defiance played in his challenging tone.

"Anyway, back to your kink. Do you like it when I tell you what I want?"

"I do." He swiped along her jawline. "It's very sexy."

"You find it sexy to be told what to do?" she teased.

"Not like that. I'm not into being dominated." His forehead creased. "I don't know if it's a kink, but to have you say what you want is very attractive."

"Sounds like a kink to me."

"No, not kink," he insisted. "It is sexy, though, but it's more...it's important."

Her brows knitted. "Important?"

"Of course. What you want is important to me because I..." he paused, his eyes cast to the ceiling. "Um...because you are important to me, and I want to know what you want. You bite your lip when you're considering something you want to say. So often what you are thinking stays here." He tapped her forehead. "As much of a turn on as it is to watch you bite this lip...." He grinned, brushing her bottom lip. "...it's far sexier to have the words come. You don't always say what you want, what you're thinking."

Elle bit her lower lip in contemplative frustration, then stopped after realizing she was doing exactly what he had just said. Part of her was indignant at his presumption that she wasn't her own advocate, but she knew he was right. It was just like the afternoon in Boston when he told her he wished she saw herself through his eyes.

It was refreshing and a little perplexing that he always seemed to know her pages, her paragraphs of truth. She was his favorite book, after all. How often had she let the unspoken simmer within her instead of allowing those words to escape her lips?

"I know that for a long time your wants sat on the back burner second to what your mom wanted. You talk about me always taking care of everyone else, but you don't see how you do the same thing. There's a drive in you to protect your people, to make sure they have what you feel they need.... what you feel they want. Even if they don't ask you to slay their dragons, you do. I just want you to be your own warrior. To kindly have a 'Come to Jesus' chat with yourself like you did with my dad."

Elle's face burned from the realization that Chris had told Clayton about their conversation when she not-so-subtly implied that he needed to show his son that he was proud of him by taking an active interest in Clayton's career.

"Did your dad really call it a 'Come to Jesus' talk?" She cringed.

"He said you were sweetly persuasive."

"When did he say that?"

"Last night at dinner."

Clayton had met his dad for dinner prior to joining Elle at the Wine Down with their friends to celebrate Carmen and Mathew's baby adoption announcement. He'd been so happy when she walked through the door that she simply lost herself in his joy not asking for details about his dinner.

"We had a long talk about a lot of things. Things that we both kept locked away from one another."

"I didn't mean to overstep. I wanted to help…to take care of you the way you take care of me and everyone else."

"I know," he murmured.

"Viet says I have a habit of blurting out things or acting without considering what someone truly wants."

She closed her eyes, assigning the term "carelessly thoughtful" to herself. So blinded by wanting to help that she sometimes missed the entire picture. Not stopping to consider if what she'd deemed best was truly what someone wanted. How different she and Clayton are with this, him all patience, her all sword.

"I am really sorry. You trusted me with your feelings about your dad and I betrayed that." A hard lump in her throat made the words wobble.

"I'm not upset. From how my dad described the conversation, you didn't betray me. You never said to him, 'Hey, your son says you're being a dick," His reassuring grin coaxed a small, relieved smile to her face. "You want to take care of your people and I love being one of your people."

Love? She'd not let herself get lost in that thought.

"Sometimes we have to push the people we care about to ask for what they want. I am not mad, but maybe next time, use your sword to push me into asking for what I want... what I need instead."

"Ok," she croaked.

He kissed her. "No regrets. Yes, you maybe went about it differently, but in the end, it forced me and my dad to talk about things we hadn't. To face what our relationship had become...to restart from an honest place. For me to see how it wasn't just me."

"What?"

"There's more than one person in a relationship, so both play a part in its growing or withering. I didn't realize that after I told my parents that I wasn't going to go to medical school, that I stopped talking to my dad about school...or about anything important to me. I *thought* I was his great disappointment and that shaped our relationship. The reason Evan and my dad talked all the time was because Evan shared with my dad what he was doing. Same thing with Nat. It wasn't that I was a great disappointment compared to my siblings, it was that they invited Dad into their lives. I hadn't because I just assumed he wasn't interested. For him, he felt rejected. Like I didn't want his input. Like I didn't want... him. Neither of us talked about it and just went on with this wall between us, based on very wrong assumptions of how the other felt."

"Wow." It was the silliest response to Clayton's confession, but it was all she could muster.

"I know." He kissed her forehead. "I can't be angry with you for what you did because it broke that wall down. There are times we overstep for the people we care about, and you did a little, but I'm thankful you did. If you hadn't, I don't think my dad and I would have had the talk we had last night."

"I'm glad you two talked. I am sorry, though." Her earnest eyes tethered to his appreciative stare.

"Make me a promise." His command was gentle and sweet.

"What?"

"I know you mean well, but next time, talk to me before you have a conversation that I should be having. I'm glad you did it, but next time talk to me before you pick up your sword. Also, be your own dragon slayer. Fight for yourself the way you fight for everyone else. Ask for what you want."

"That's two things. You said *A* promise." A teasing smile quirked.

Despite the playful smirk, thoughtfulness shaded his gray eyes. "Well, then two."

"I'll try." She agreed, her voice a whispered promise.

It was the second time he had asked her to promise him something this week. This one felt harder than pretending the days that ticked away weren't doing so. Elle wasn't sure if it was the second or third of her promises that felt harder. The second promise empty because after Saturday, would she have the opportunity to keep it? She would be gone. As much as she wanted to keep Clayton in her life, she knew she couldn't. After Saturday, the best thing for Clayton would be to forget Elle. It would hurt, but she would need to use her sword to sever her hold on him, allowing him to find his true "Lizzie." That future woman would be the keeper of his heart and he, the protector of hers.

The third promise pressed hard against Elle's chest. At work she spoke up. She commanded. She demanded. She was a "boss bitch." The professional wants within her slipped so easily from her lips. In her personal life, they were merely phantoms of the unsaid, bitten away before being allowed to come out of her mouth.

Long before her dad's abandonment and mother's falling apart, Elle had been groomed to keep her wants to herself. So much of her early life was defined by "No, Eleanor," "Quiet, Eleanor, the grownups are talking," or "Be a good girl, Eleanor." These messages along with so many others made up so much of who Elle became. The commands given to her at six cemented the foundation of who she was at thirty-six.

"When do you have to be at the clinic?" She bit her lower lip.

"I'm on farm rotations today and my first appointment isn't until later." A knowing smile etched his features.

"Could we go to Cassie's Corner Café for breakfast?" It was a small ask but it was an ask.

There were only a few more days for these small asks with Clayton. Only a few more days to share her tiny wants, leaving the big wants unspoken. The biggest of all, "Let me keep you. Let's stay "us." Some wants are too big. Some asks too much.

"Yes, but first…" He kissed down the column of her throat. "…I'm hungry for something else."

Elle giggled, tilting her head giving him greater access to his target.

THIRTY-SIX

"I have the highest respect for your nerves. They are my old friends."
~Jane Austen, *Pride and Prejudice*

Misty rain clung to children in backpacks and umbrellas walking down Main Street, heading to the first day of school. Perry's downtown buzzed with people as businesses opened for the day. From their perch in a front booth of Cassie's Corner Café, its floor to ceiling windows overlooking Main Street, Clayton and Elle had a front row seat to the waking up of downtown.

"Hopefully they beat the attendance bell." Clayton's head tilted at two teenaged boys racing down the street, a little girl skipping behind them with a pink umbrella. The slightly taller boy turned to scoop up the little girl, then rushed off with her on his back.

"They're cutting it close," Elle said, shaking her head.

"I was never late for school. You?" Clayton asked. "Never mind." He laughed, taking in her "Have we met?" face.

"Do you want kids?" she blurted.

"I'm open to it with the right person, but it has to be a mutual decision," he replied, stirring his coffee before taking a sip. "You?"

"I don't know." She peered at the tiny pockets of sun breaking through the gray sky like beacons of hope. "Although, I suppose not knowing is an answer."

"I suppose." Clayton's face was thoughtful.

"You're open to it?" she pressed.

He nodded, as her eyes flicked from the world outside to the world sitting across from her holding a black ink spot patterned white mug in his hand as he gazed back.

"You'd be a good dad," Elle offered.

He reached for her hand, their fingers threading together. "You'd be a good mom, if you wanted it."

The word mom souring in her ears. How could she be a good mom? She'd had a terrible example. Elle slipped her fingers free of his, grabbing her cup of tea with a small smile.

The exterior door opened, admitting a small breeze.

"Amanda!" A newcomer had entered the café to a loud greeting from the crew of retirees in the back.

Elle's eyes locked on her mom's familiar frame. The bright rainbow-striped sweater she wore was a colorful vortex, drawing all gazes to her in the café's sea of black and white décor.

"Where's Pastor Dan?" An older woman with bluish-gray hair asked, wrapping her arms around Elle's mom.

"He's on his way," Amanda said warmly, her back turned to where Elle and Clayton sat.

The sight of her mom's back was a fitting punch to Elle's gut, a reminder of the importance, or rather Elle's unimportance to her mom.

Turning to take a seat and finally facing the booths along the front windows, her mother's blue eyes grew wide as she spotted Elle staring back. Their gazes stood in a fierce tug-of-war from across the room. Elle knew the tight "nothing's wrong" smile painted on her mom's face was reflected in her own. The chattering voices of her mom's companions were muffled by the pounding of Elle's heart.

"Baby, look at me." Clayton squeezed her hand, drawing her attention back to him. "Tell me what you want."

Elle looked into the pleading gray of Clayton's eyes. *What do I want?* Such an easy question with so many complicated answers. She wanted so much. For her mother to walk across the room and say, "I'm sorry." But sorry wouldn't fix any of this. It never had in the past. How many empty apologies had spilled out of her mother's lips after another disappointment? The stream of broken promises babbled through Elle like a brook of lies.

"Elle." He slipped into the booth beside her and wrapped his arm around her. "I got you."

She just nodded at him, knowing he had her.

"Aren't you two adorable." Cassie's sarcastically sweet voice filtered into Elle's ears as she placed their food on the table. "Anything else?"

"Cassie, I'm so sorry to do this. Could we get to-go boxes and the check? We forgot about an errand we need to run before work," Clayton apologized.

"No problem." She scooped the plates up. "I'll go ahead and wrap this up for you. Give me five minutes and meet me at the counter."

"I'm sorry." Elle's whisper was pained.

The apology was for Cassie for their abrupt departure, for Clayton for ruining their breakfast date, and for herself for not being strong. She made these promises to herself, but each time her mom appeared, her resolve crumbled.

I'm not a baby. She was a grown-ass woman who commanded respect at work. She was a dragon slayer who burned down the foes of her loved ones. She was a jungle cat pouncing on her man and demanding all her itches get scratched. She was all these things and also a scared lonely girl who wanted the love of the first person who'd held her, her mom. The person who was supposed to love her but didn't.

Clayton stiffened and tightened his arm around her protectively.

"Hi." Her mom's voice was hesitant.

Clayton's tall frame hid the face of the voice entering the safety of Elle's corner of the little café, but she could picture her mom standing in front of their booth, her nervous hands picking at a cuticle.

"Eleanor…"

"I'm sorry. I don't think this is the right place or time, Amanda. We were just leaving," Clayton said, pulling Elle out of the booth to leave, his hands anchoring her to him.

"I'm sorry," her mother croaked. "I'm really sorry."

It's what Elle wanted, an apology. *For what, though?* For interrupting their breakfast with her presence? For visiting Jamie's grave, when she hadn't attempted to reach out to her daughter in eighteen years? Who knew what she was apologizing for. Certainly not Elle.

"It's too late," Elle said, her face set in stern lines.

"Eleanor, it's never too late for forgiveness," her mother pleaded.

"What do you want forgiveness for? Be specific," Elle demanded, a quiet fury in her voice.

Her mom's mouth opened, closing quickly. An unspoken questioning glinted in her mom's eyes. She said nothing, just stared at her daughter.

"If you don't know or can't say it, you can't be forgiven. This is goodbye. We're done."

Her mom flinched as if Elle had smacked her. In many ways, her steely glare did just that.

"Clayton, I'd like to leave." Elle's tone was firm and final.

"Of course." He pressed a tender kiss against her temple, the gesture reassuring and grounding. "Do you want to wait in the pickup while I pay or come with me?"

"Truck."

"Okay." He nodded. Then kissed her forehead again before digging his keys out of his pocket. "Here."

The chicken wing keychain she'd bought him at the Anchor Bar on their first official date was an obnoxiously welcomed sight in this tense tableau of a final goodbye between a mother who'd stopped caring and the daughter who could no longer risk her heart waiting for an apology.

"I'll be right there, baby." Clayton stroked a gentle fingertip on her cheek, then kept himself between Elle and her mom as they walked toward the door.

"Eleanor…"

Elle stopped for a moment, just a moment, closing her eyes and reminding herself that she's heard her mom's song before and the tune always ended the same, with Elle's heart broken.

"…I am so sorry."

With a resigned shrug, Elle opened the door to leave.

"Please, stop." Clayton addressed Amanda as Elle walked out the door.

"Who are you to her?"

Elle heard her mom weepily ask.

"I'm the man who—"

The slam of the café door behind her interrupted the exchange between Clayton and her mom.

Unlocking the pickup, Elle crawled in, shutting the door behind her. Slipping onto the front seat of Clayton's pickup felt like a hug, it wrapped around her almost like arms keeping her safe. Elle finally pointed that sword at herself, fighting back the feelings of loss and grief the encounter with her mother had evoked. She was done letting them impact her.

The driver's side door creaked open, and Clayton climbed in.

His fingers combed through her hair, stroking as he said, "Talk to me."

Elle sat up straighter. "She never says what she's sorry for. I doubt she even knows. Her apologies were just to placate me. It was about her not wanting to be alone. I was just there, not because she loved me, but because she didn't want to be alone. I was a filler."

"You're nobody's filler." Clayton's jaw clenched.

"Well, I was." Elle exhaled.

"I'm sorry, baby." He pushed a stray strand of her auburn hair behind her ear. "You're leaving work early today to meet Tobey, right?"

She nodded.

"I shouldn't ask but take the rest of the day and come with me today."

"To the farms?"

"Yes."

"Moo." It was a silly response, but it made him laugh.

"*Moo?*"

She smirked. "It's cow for 'yes.' What kind of vet doesn't speak cow?"

THIRTY-SEVEN

"Her heart did whisper for he had done it for her."
~Jane Austen, *Pride and Prejudice*

T he end of a workday hadn't ever been so satisfying as they had over the last few weeks in Perry. In Long Beach, logging off and leaving the Sloan-Whitney offices meant fighting traffic for an hour only to log back on, reading more emails and reports from home. Here, when the day was over it was over. As the screen dimmed on the laptop when she shut it off, she'd moved into time with friends, family, and Clayton.

"Hey." An almost wicked smirk spread on Clayton's face, as he walked down the steps of the farmhouse to her. "You and those jeans." He wrapped his arms around her, cupping her ass through the painted-on skinny jeans she wore.

She squeaked when he pinched.

"I can't tell if these jeans will motivate me or distract me tonight."

"If you're good tonight, I'll let you take them off me," she purred.

"What will you let me do if I'm bad?" His low voice rumbled through her, making all her lady bits clench.

"Why, Doc Owens, are you flirting with me?"

"Oh baby, I think we are *way* past flirting." He nipped her lips.

The warmth of his hand on her lower back as he guided them through the crowded VFW toward their usual table caused a starry-eyed smile to bloom on Elle's face. Clayton's hands had been on every single part of her body, but still the feel of his protective palm on her back made her feel like the Hope Diamond. There was no doubt that her uncle, aunt, and Tobey loved her. That she was important to them, but with Clayton it was different. Something she couldn't explain, but the sensation cascaded within her.

"Lady Elle!" Jerome's bulky arms scooped Elle up in a hug, then turning to Clayton. "Sir Clayton."

"King Jerome." Clayton bowed.

"Kids," Pete drawled, walking over.

"Where's my handsome husband?" Jerome's gaze darted around the room.

"He's helping Janet lug a few things into the banquet room for tomorrow. I was told I'm not allowed to help, because it's birthday stuff."

It seemed fitting that Pete's fiftieth birthday party would be held in the VFW banquet room. This place had played a pivotal role in this family's life. Uncle Pete had played darts here for years with his dad, then his wife, and now his son. Janet and Pete's wedding reception had been held in this very room. Both Elle and Tobey had graduation parties here.

"Hey, Clayton, why don't we see if Mom needs more help?" Jerome suggested, placing his hand on Clayton's shoulder.

Clayton nodded at Jerome before placing a kiss on Elle's cheek. "Be right back."

"I'll go order drinks and wings. The usual, everyone?" Elle peered at her trio of men, who all grinned in agreement.

Breaking away, Elle made her way to the crowded bar. As usual, Laney was behind the counter directing customers with the grace and ease of a sassy orchestra conductor.

"Eleanor…Elle… the usual?" Laney asked with an upward tilt of her backwards-cap-wearing head.

"Yes. Do you have Ketel One?" Elle teased with a sardonic smile knowing what the response would be.

"Still a VFW, darlin'." Laney's impish smirked taunted as she leaned onto the bar.

Elle joined Laney leaning against the smooth bar surface. "A girl can hope."

"Sweetheart, the VFW is where hope comes to die." Laney jested, yanking a bottle of vodka from the mirrored shelf behind the bar.

As Laney stirred the drink, Elle took in the sea of boisterous smiles, teasing grins, and jovial faces. Hope did not come here to die. It lived here. In every crevice.

"I wouldn't agree with that," Elle countered.

"You haven't worked here for five years." Laney shrugged and placed Elle's drink in front of her before reaching for a clear pitcher from below the bar.

"Laney stop, you love it here!" An elderly man in a Vietnam Veteran hat hollered warmly. "If you didn't, you'd take Noah Wilson up on his offer. I've seen him try to poach you on five different occasions to work at that fancy bar of his."

"Lloyd, if I went to work for Noah Wilson, who would cut you off and call your wife to pick up your sorry ass after too many Labatts?" Laney pointed at the older man with her right hand as she slid the now full pitcher of beer over to Elle.

It was clear to Elle that Laney's sassy and snarky retorts were a total act. The warm glow in her green eyes as she bantered with the regulars and newcomers spoke of a woman who loved what she did. Although she and Todd together behind the Wine Down bar would be an endless barrage of sarcastic spunk for Noah.

"How much do I owe you?" Elle set the drink and pitcher on the worn bar and moved to pull out her wallet.

"Oh, I think that *very* handsome man behind you plans on paying." Laney clucked her tongue.

Elle rolled her eyes, knowing it was either Clayton or her uncle but suspected the "very" in Laney's statement spoke of Clayton. Elle wasn't the only person not immune to the penetrating gray eyes, cut body, and thoughtful smile of Clayton Owens. With a shake of her head, she turned.

"Hey, gorgeous." Viet's handsome face beamed at her.

"Oh my god!" Elle shrieked, throwing her arms around her friend and startling a few of the bar patrons. "You're here!"

"I know!" He agreed with a deep laugh, as they jumped up and down like giddy kids.

"How are you here?" Elle stepped back, blinking at him.

"Well, there are these things called planes," he quipped.

Elle lightly punched his arm in response to his sarcasm.

"I missed Tobey's wedding. I couldn't miss Pete's birthday. They're family, just like you are."

Elle brushed the happy tears from her eyes.

"Are you crying?" he gaped.

"I seem to do that more these days. These are happy, though."

"I missed you." He tugged her in, squeezing her tight.

"Uncle Pete is going to lose his mind that you are here."

"Oh, he knows. He and Clayton helped orchestrate this surprise." Viet gestured over to where Elle's family and Clayton stood at their usual table, wearing giant grins while watching her reunion with Viet. "Your man DM'd me last week and worked this all out. I guess you've told him a lot about me, and he felt it was important I was here…and I agreed."

"What about work?"

He waved his hands like a king dismissing his subjects. "I can afford to take a few days. After getting Clayton's message, it made me remember what is important to me. You are my people. I really should have been here sooner for you."

"You were here for me. You always have been." Elle clenched his hands and pulled him in for another hug.

Even when Viet had not been physically there, he had been a constant presence in her life. He had always been, since their first meeting as college freshmen. He was one of her people, and always would be. Viet was a steadying force in her life. An unyielding source of patience and, at times, pushing love for her.

"And you have always been there for me." Sincerity swam in Viet's warm eyes. "Oh! I have another surprise for you."

"Elle's Bells!" Willa's voice boomed as she ran from behind a group of Navy veterans. She darted toward Elle, almost tackling her in a joyful hug.

"I can't." Elle sniffled, the happy tears overwhelming her.

"Girl, you lied to me." Willa chastised. "The other hot farmer picked us up at the airport. You said that hot farmers were a myth, but the Greek god that picked us up is even better than the pictures you sent. Oh my god, I want to have his babies."

"What? Who?"

"Him!" Moaning as if taking the first lick of ice cream, Willa gestured to Noah, who stood with his hands in his pockets, talking to Clayton. "That man is the living breathing embodiment of every sexual fantasy I have ever had. The things I would do to him."

"Please keep those things to yourself," Elle warned.

"Too late. I may have to represent her in a forthcoming sexual harassment suit." Viet looped his arm around Elle's shoulders.

"What?" Willa batted her eyes. "I made a simple offer to bear his children. Plus, I didn't see him protest."

"Willa, please don't," Elle begged with a laugh.

"What if I get written consent for some extra saucy flirting?"

"Poor Noah." Elle waved her hands in the air toward Noah, whose blue eyes floated between Clayton and their little threesome. A flirty grin tugged at his lips as he peered at them. Elle suspected the smile wasn't for Viet nor her.

"You mean the future Mr. Andrews," Willa purred, twining a long strand of her caramel-colored hair around her finger.

"The future Mr. Andrews?" Elle choked back a laugh.

"Oh, he's going to take *my* name after he has all my babies."

"Have we told him this yet?"

"She sure has." Viet shook his head.

"Stop clutching your metaphorical pearls, Viet. I wasn't *that* bad." Willa's glare glinted with playfulness.

"Hey!" Pete shouted from across the room. "Stop hogging Viet!"

"My public awaits." Viet announced, grabbing the

pitcher of beer in his left hand and looping his right arm in Elle's.

"So does my future baby daddy." Willa grabbed Elle's drink with her right hand and looped her left arm in Elle's.

"I love you both so much." Elle gushed, walking arm and arm with her two best friends toward her favorite people.

THIRTY-EIGHT

"Do not let the behavior of others destroy your inner peace."
~Jane Austen, *Sense and Sensibility*

By the time the impromptu party broke up, it was after midnight. Noah escorted Willa to the Little Red Barn, and Clayton had excused himself to get ready for bed. Elle showed Viet to the guest room.

"I still can't believe you're here," she sighed, lounging on the bed with Viet.

"I think it's more unbelievable that *you* are here," Viet said as he stroked between Fitz's ears.

"You were the one to convince me to come back home."

"I'm not talking about here in Perry. I'm talking about you shacking up with Clayton."

"I'm not shacking up."

Viet made a "whatever" face.

Elle mumbled, "I'm just staying here."

"I believe that's the definition of shacking up." Viet's teasing smile lit up the dim room.

"What do you think of Clayton?"

"I like him."

"I do too."

"I think you *more* than like him." He lifted his brow as he looked at her.

Elle's eyes turned away from Viet's perceptive stare, looking on to the framed photo of Letchworth hanging above the dresser. The canopy of vibrant green trees hanging over the weathered wooden bridge, a gentle stream dotted with fallen leaves below. It was easier to focus on that than answering her friend's assessing stare.

"Have you told him?"

The words "I love him" didn't need to slip from her lips. He read it in her face and the shift of her gaze that she hadn't told Clayton, yet. God, he knew her so well.

"Elle." His tone was reproachful.

"I can't."

"You can't or you won't?"

Shifting away from Viet, her eyes flicked to the creamy white wall on the other side of the room. How easy it was for him to look the picture of comfort as he quietly pushed her into discomfort. Viet was nothing but patient with her, and with most people, but the man could push when needed. It's what made him a good attorney and an even better friend. Where Elle would run in waving her sword, Viet strategized. His pushing was never without thought.

Once Elle had stopped returning to Perry, Viet had never nudged, never spoke of nor forced the issue. Never pointed out the holidays, or birthdays, or anniversaries she'd chosen to miss. There'd never been a case made to go back until this summer.

Elle twisted her body toward her friend. "For fourteen years you never pushed me to come back. Why now?"

"Well…" He sat up straighter in the bed. "…first, I think you would have really regretted missing Tobey's wedding and

Pete's birthday, but especially Tobey's wedding. For weeks after his graduation from high school and then the Trooper Academy, you had this guilty expression. You texted or called him incessantly and sent him gifts. I've had a front row seat to the 'Elle Davidson Guilt Fest'. You weren't ready to come back, but you felt awful each time you said no or made an excuse to stay when you should have gone." He patted her knee. "I didn't want you to have those regrets anymore. I didn't want you to have my regrets." Viet's voice cracked.

Elle crawled closer, pressing her shoulder to his, reminding him she was there. He didn't need to elaborate. She knew his regrets as much as he knew hers. His dad died of a heart attack when Viet was fourteen. The first day of summer each year, they would go fishing. That year, Viet had bowed out of the annual tradition so he could go to the mall with his friends. It was no big deal. They could always go the following weekend. Like every teenager, he assumed there was a never-ending supply of time. His dad died the next day, leaving Viet with a profound sense of *what if?*

"Second…" Viet continued, clearing his throat. "…I think I knew it was time, because I knew you were finally ready."

"How did you know?" She blinked.

"You seldom talk about Perry. Once Tobey's wedding invite came, you started reminiscing more about here. I think you've spoken more about home in the last six months than in the last six years. We don't wax lyrically about things we don't miss."

"I didn't wax lyrically!" she guffawed.

"Eleanor Marie Davidson, if I had to hear one more time about how none of the pizza places in Long Beach compare to your sainted Daryl's, the loveliness of Letchworth in the fall, or your aunt and uncle's house, I was going to staple your mouth shut."

"Had I really been talking about home so much?"

"Yes. Willa will confirm. That's why we ambushed you at happy hour that night."

She gasped. "I had no idea."

"It was almost like a nervous tick that you couldn't help. You'd slip tidbits about Perry in with the most random connections. Like Willa wore this orange blouse to brunch and you went on for ten minutes about how it reminded you of the color of leaves in the fall. Then you started talking about collecting leaves at Letchworth for your grandma. It was then that Willa and I knew you were ready and that you needed to go back."

"Wow."

"Well, I am your best friend. So is Willa…but I'm the best of the best." He smirked. "Elle, we've known each other since we were eighteen. I know I have my older sisters, but you're my *real* sister. We know each other better than anyone else in this world. You know things about me that even my husband doesn't know. You knew when to drag me into that jewelry store to finally buy that ring to propose to Ryan. Just like I knew it was time for you to come home, and how I know that you are in love with Clayton." He looped his arm around her, pulling her close.

"I leave…" Her eyes flicked to the old-fashioned metal alarm clock on the bed stand. It was after one in the morning. It was now Friday. "…tomorrow."

"You know there are these things called planes where couples can fly to see each other and phones where they can talk to each other."

Elle elbowed his ribs, annoyed with her friend's sassy logic.

"Seriously, long distance works. Look at Ryan and me." Viet gestured to himself.

"It works if somebody moves. His home is here." Elle

motioned around the room. "Mine is there" She pointed out the window.

"I'm pretty sure that window is east-facing and last time I checked, California was west," he teased.

"I can't stay here, and he can't come. Clayton and I talked about it on Sunday. It's not fair to drag something on that won't happen, at least not in the way he deserves." Her voice wobbled but was decisive.

"What about what *you* deserve?" Viet took her hand, his thumb skating across her knuckles.

"I think it's late and we've both had too much to drink to have this conversation," Elle said with finality in her tone.

She didn't want to discuss this, to lay out her defense for her decisions. Not now. There would be time to rehash this over future happy hours with Viet. No doubt he'd bide his time until he pounced on her reasons, dissecting them like a lion with his prey. For the remainder of her time here, she just wanted to exist in her bubble of happiness, surrounded by everyone she loved and not thinking about the day after tomorrow when she'd wake up in her lavender sheets in her condo overlooking the ocean on the other side of the country. Away from Clayton.

"Alright. I'll let you off the hook tonight but only if you take me to Daryl's tomorrow for lunch. You've talked about it so much in the last six months that I've been craving it. Truthfully, it may be the only reason I said yes when Clayton messaged me." Playful resignation curled his lips up.

"Deal." Elle kissed Viet's cheek before scooting off the bed. "Come on, Fitz." She called to the stocky sleeping pug who made no movement.

"I think he's staying with me." A smug expression brightened Viet's face as he looked down at Fitz curled in a tiny ball beside him.

"Traitor." She scowled at Fitz's wrinkled face.

"Aww sorry, Elle, you know everybody likes me best."

Running water and the buzz of Clayton's electric toothbrush floated from the attached bathroom as Elle walked into the bedroom. Surveying the room, the bed was already set for them. Two fresh bottles of water sat on the bedstands on their respective sides. On Clayton's side, his phone was plugged in. A folded red T-shirt sat on the end of the bed. Unfolding it, Elle smiled at the white cursive lettering proclaiming *It's a Puggin' Good Day* with an image of a happy round-belly pug. She knew he had laid it out for her. Despite her array of adorable PJs that she brought with her to Perry, she had taken to wearing one of Clayton's shirts each night.

Everything was as it was each night, except no Fitz. A tiny sting of jealousy pricked her, that on her second to last time sleeping here, Fitz wouldn't lay atop her feet. Tomorrow, well actually today, would be her last full day here.

Nope. Nope. Nope. Not going to think about it.

Elle inhaled a steadying breath, allowing it to fill her with thoughts of what remained, rather than what would soon be lost. She was here now and needed to just live in the moment. The bathroom door was cracked open, and she peeked in almost like a voyeur, drinking Clayton in as if the first quenching taste of water after a long run. Readied for bed, he stood at the sink in a pair of red boxer briefs.

God, he's gorgeous.

Elle's gaze swept over Clayton's form. The gray of his eyes pierced her soul even within the mirror's reflection. Tiny crinkles kissed the edges of his eyes. The cut of his muscles flexed with the slow movement of his arm as he brushed his teeth. The paw print tattoo scampered up his right forearm, telling a story she was privileged to know about a man that chose to forge his own path despite one already being mapped out for him. Clayton's entire being was served up as a physical representation for the many reasons she loved him. His toned arms strong, caring, and protecting. Seductive lips, kissable, teasing, and sweet, but above all the portal for him to speak all the words that had captured her heart. That broad chest perfect for holding her but even more perfect for holding his kind, thoughtful heart. Those versatile strong hands that made her melt at their touch, wiped away her tears, clasped her hands, caressed her cheeks, and supported her.

I love you so much. Elle stared as the familiar *thump-thump* of her heart pounded.

"You're staring at me like I'm the last piece of pizza." Clayton grinned, setting aside his toothbrush, and then wiping his mouth.

"Sausage." She licked her lips.

"Is that a euphemism or are you hungry?" He turned and faced her, the muscles in his exposed back reflected in the mirror, giving Elle a full-circle view of his vigorous physique.

"Are you aware of how unbelievably beautiful you are?" Elle whispered. "I mean, look at you."

"I'd rather look at you." A devilish glint sparked in his eyes as they roved languidly down her body, as if taking a slow Sunday stroll in the park.

"You like looking, eh?" With a bite of her lower lip, she slipped her sweater off, dropping it to the floor. "I should give you more to look at. You know, keep it interesting." She unclasped her pink strapless bra, letting it join her sweater. She felt brazen and a little wanton, but she could excuse it. She only had a few more hours with Clayton. A few more hours to touch and be touched.

Desire darkened his eyes, as Elle skated her fingers down her bare torso to the button of her jeans.

"Stop." His dark eyes bored through her. "You said if I was good, I got to take those off."

"I did." Elle's voice dripped with warm honey.

"Was I good?" He stepped closer. "Or was I bad?" The rumble of his low voice tingled through her.

"You were *very* good." She almost purred.

"You know we have a guest." He cocked his head, his features drawn into a devious expression. "Do you think you can be quiet?"

Biting her lip, she nodded, and gasped as he popped the button of her jeans.

THIRTY-NINE

"Surprises are foolish things."
~Jane Austen, *Emma*

S treaks of sunlight nudged Elle awake. Well, half awake. Her brain wasn't fully firing yet, but she had a dim notion that she was no longer dreaming. Snuggling into the soft sheets, she blinkingly watched Clayton button a blue plaid shirt before rolling the cuffs up. *Those forearms.*

"Tease," Elle mumbled, her voice sleep drunk.

"You're supposed to be sleeping in." He chuckled, stepping away from the closet and shutting the door.

"But your forearms," she whined.

"Oh, 'Sleepy Elle' is back." He moved to her side of the bed. The mattress dipped as he sat.

"You love 'Sleepy Elle.'" Elle covered an extra-large yawn with the back of her hand.

"Yeah." He stared at her for several minutes, his fingers caressing her cheeks, eyes singing a yet unwritten song.

"She's your favorite Elle."

"They're all my favorite."

"Even Eleanor?"

"Yes." He pressed his lips to her forehead. "They're all you."

"You liked me before I liked me." She sighed, her sleepy brain taking full control of her mouth.

"You like you now, right?"

"Yeah." She exhaled. "I do."

"Good." His fingers skimmed across her lips. "I'm a big fan, so I'm glad you're joining the Elle fan club."

"Clayton…I have a secret. Wanna know?" she whispered.

"Sure." He bent closer.

"I'm in *your* fan club."

"Oh, my, Sleepy Elle." He kissed her softly.

"Oh, my, Awake Clayton."

"Have fun with your friends today, baby." He rose, turning to leave.

"I'm your baby…You too…Good day." She yawned around the words.

When Elle rolled downstairs around ten, she was surprised to find Noah in the kitchen with a box of pastries. She wasn't as surprised to find Willa at his side batting her eyes or Viet brewing a pot of tea. Over pastries, they made plans for sight-seeing at all of Perry's hot spots. There weren't many, but it was fun nonetheless. Good company made anywhere perfect.

A bit before five, Noah left them at the farmhouse to get ready for Pete's party. A bouquet of purple roses wrapped in the Village Rose's trademark rose-patterned paper sat on the porch. Elle slipped the card into her purse to read later knowing the flowers were from Clayton, but the card was, no doubt, a sassy note from Aunt Janet. She'd made a habit of writing a saucy note with the weekly flower delivery.

When they entered the house, Fitz immediately ran to Viet, who gathered the chubby pug in his arms, planting kisses all over his squishy face.

Clayton drove up to the farmhouse just as Elle was grabbing some things for girl time with Willa. The two would be getting ready together at the Little Red Barn.

Both Willa and Elle opted for softer looks. Willa's long caramel locks were arranged in loose curls around her face, the pair of lilac earrings Elle bought her poking out through the silky strands. The lilac contrasted perfectly with the sky-blue sheath dress she wore.

Elle wore the tea-length, jewel-tone purple dress she'd bought while shopping with Aunt Janet. Her hair hung in its natural waves. As she gazed into the mirror, putting in her matching lilac earrings, she smiled. *Purple.* It had always been her favorite color and the one Clayton thought she looked beautiful in.

Just before seven, the four drove over to the VFW. Clayton volunteered to drive Elle's rental as it had a backseat and four doors. As he held the front passenger door open for Elle, he leaned in and told her she was beautiful, stirring the butterflies in her belly. She traced the paw print tattoo exposed by his rolled-up sleeves cooing he was beautiful.

The banquet room in the VFW was a simple open space with burnt-orange walls and chocolate-brown trim. The room felt like fall every day of the year.

Aunt Janet's decoration goddess magic had transformed the space into, as the gold banner hung over the bar proclaimed, *Studio Fifty.* Shiny blue and gold fabric covered the burnt orange walls. A shimmer flooded the room from the reflection of multicolored fairy lights in a mirror ball suspended above the dance floor. Thin gold vines twined around circular tables draped in bright blue tablecloths.

A large DJ booth with a rainbow of strobe lights was pressed up against the far wall. The DJ adorned in a black top hat and Van Halen T-shirt stood behind a large sound panel like a king surveying his court.

Elle wove through the throngs of familiar and not-so-familiar faces to find the birthday boy.

"Lady Elle! Big Buddy! New Friends!" Jerome swaggered over, holding a bottle of Doc Owens beer.

"Where's the rest of the Coates clan?" Elle inquired as Jerome gave her one of his signature bear hugs.

"Tobey's at the bar." He cocked his head toward the bar along the far-left wall, surrounded by people getting drinks. "Mom's at the DJ booth and I haven't seen Second Dad yet."

"Attention!" The DJ's deep voice boomed in the mic, as the music trailed off to a quiet hum. "Everyone gird your loins; the man of the hour is here. Gather around the dance floor and welcome the man who ages like fine wine or stinky cheese…Pete Coates!"

The room erupted in clapping hoots, hollers, and whistles as "Hot Stuff" by Donna Summer played. Pete hustled onto the dance floor in a white disco suit *a la* John Travolta in *Saturday Night Fever*.

"Is he doing the lawnmower?" Viet gaped, as Pete pumped his arms up and down as if pulling the cord for an engine and then pushing it around the dance floor.

"Yup." Clayton and Jerome laughed in unison.

As Pete wiggled around the dance floor, he stopped and bellowed, "Looking for the Olivia Newton John to my John Travolta."

That was Aunt Janet's cue to saunter over to him with a sexy sashay of her hips. The two of them mirrored each other's dance moves. They rocked their hips, tapped their feet, and raised their arms to the cheers of everyone. Pete held his hand out and his wife placed hers in his, letting him spin her around the room.

"Your family really likes a choreographed dance number, don't they?" Clayton teased, threading his arms around Elle's waist, tucking her into his chest.

"Yup." Elle grinned.

As they stood watching, her gaze caught a pair of sad blue eyes across the room, looking past Pete and Janet and directly to her.

Mom. The historical dread and hurt of seeing her mother that normally crumbled Elle in its oppressive grip was absent. In its place was sadness, disappointment…and indifference. The power her mom held on her had slipped away after their encounter Wednesday morning.

Elle had told her mom that they were "done," and they were. At least, she was done.

"Wanna get a drink?" Clayton asked, the soothing glide of his hands over her midsection told Elle he hadn't missed her mom's stare.

Her face tipped up to him, their gazes mingling. "Are you finally going to buy me that free drink?"

"Sure am." He pressed grinning lips to hers.

The bar was still lively but had thinned since Pete and Janet had called folks to join them on the dance floor. Tobey leaned on the bar, sipping a Yellowjacket beer and talking to Noah. Elle and Tobey commiserated in mortification at the dance stylings of his mother and father… mostly his father. The moment Pete dropped it like it was hot had Tobey considering changing his name to Evans and fully dropping Coates all together. Elle nursed a Doc Owens beer alongside her actual Doc Owens and her cousin before joining Willa, Viet, and Jerome on the dance floor. Carmen and Mathew appeared shortly after, as if manifested with a single wish. Almost all of her people were in one place.

There was no rhyme or reason to the songs bumping through the banquet hall turned nightclub. When Elle hit the dance floor, ABBA played, then it flowed into New Kids on the Block, next DMX, followed by Taylor Swift. When the DJ spun the Spice Girls, Elle and Viet laughed through their made-up dance routine.

Willa and Elle dragged Noah and Clayton onto the floor to join them. By the last lines of the song, Elle was encircled with all her people; Clayton on her right, Pete on her left, and everyone else just a gaze away. On the edge of the dance floor stood Summer, bobbing her head with the music, smiling as she watched the swaying party goers. Elle raced over and pulled Summer to join them. The sensation of completion surged in her chest.

As the party bumped along, full of swinging hips, sipping lips, hugging arms, and laughing hearts, Elle snuck off the dance floor to help Aunt Janet check on the refreshment table.

"I think it's dessert time." Janet declared, as they surveyed the mostly empty snack trays.

Elle picked up two trays. "We should move these into the kitchen to consolidate onto one tray and put it back out with the cupcakes."

Janet picked up a couple trays and followed Elle to the kitchen.

Elle consolidated the remaining appetizers onto one tray as Aunt Janet recruited volunteers to bring other items into the kitchen and take the cupcakes out. Virginia and Summer's dad, who was Janet's cousin, along with some random man with black hair streaked with wisps of silver rotated in and out of the kitchen as Janet pulled out multiple cupcake trays filled with a kaleidoscope of colored frosting and flavors. The regular size fridge was like a clown car of cupcakes, they just kept multiplying.

"Elle, you almost done?" Janet asked, twisting to look over her shoulder as she stood holding the door as Virginia carried out the last of the cupcakes.

"Just about done." Elle bit her bottom lip in concentration as she organized the assortment of snack trays into one super one.

"Alright." Janet followed Virginia out of the kitchen.

As the door shut, the room quieted, a gentle hum and light vibration slinked in from the music in the other room.

"No more cupcakes?" A low masculine voice asked, a twinge of relieved astonishment lacing the words.

"Virginia and Janet just took the last tray of them out." Elle looked up from the tray she'd been working on.

It was the random man that had been helping them. Happy crinkles hugged the edges of his eyes. A sliver of green swam in his brown eyes like moss drifting atop a muddy pond. Despite the silver in his black hair, he had a youthful glow in his handsome face.

"There was a minute I thought about opening the fridge to make sure it wasn't like the wardrobe in *The Lion, The Witch and The Wardrobe* but instead of ending up in Narnia with Mr. Tumnus, it would take me to a land of never-ending cupcakes." He laughed, pointing to the fridge. "Well, just to be sure..." he opened the fridge door. "...*phew*! Normal fridge."

"I thought of it as a clown car fridge." Laughter lit her face.

"Good image." He placed his hands on the kitchen island's surface, his eyes gazing at the tray. "Nice work. I love the swirling patterns of functionality. Like you have every-thing that would go together...well... together."

"Thank you." Elle smiled, peering down at her tray. The circular parallel rows of corresponding food pleased her. It was both pretty and practical. "Thanks for helping with the cupcakes."

"To be of service is to love," he said, the green in his eyes seemed to sparkle, making Elle think of Santa. This man looked nothing like Santa with his tall broad form and face clean of any whiskers or even a whisper of stubble. But he had a cheerfully generous energy radiating from him as if any minute he'd pull out a big bag of presents.

"I like that. It sounds like something that would be stitched on a pillow."

"Fun fact, that's where I saw it. It was on a pillow at the house of one of my buddies from Fort Knox. His wife had made it. It just always stuck with me." His long fingers tapped against the metal counter, drumming the beat of the song vibrating from the other room.

"Pillows can be very profound."

"I've got some of my best advice from them," he said with a self-deprecating chuckle.

"Fort Knox? You were in the service?"

"Yep." He straightened as if his commanding officer had walked into the room. "I retired from the Army after twenty years. Now I work at the VA in Buffalo."

"Wow. You retired to work more? You must really enjoy being of service." Elle joked.

Smirking, he shrugged.

"Seriously though, that's great. I'm in healthcare too. What do you do at the VA?"

"I'm the Chief of Chaplain Service. I was an Army Chaplain and I've continued the work once I retired," he explained.

Elle's eyes grew wide. *Chaplain? Pastor?*

"Pastor Danny?" It was less of a question, more of an accusation.

"That's what they call me, but I prefer Daniel. I'm Daniel

Kwon." He extended his hand. "I'm not going to pretend to not know who you are or that you don't know who I am. It's an honor to meet you, Eleanor. Your mom has told me so much about you."

She hesitated but took his hand. The open kindness in his demeanor overtook the sting from the relationship with her mom and interactions with her mom's past boyfriends. Her hackles didn't rise in his presence. Her gut kicked back, waving its hands for her to proceed.

"I promise you I wasn't trying to ambush you. I was at the refreshment table when Janet appeared. When I saw you in here, I debated introducing myself. I didn't want you to feel cornered, but I wanted to meet you. Your mom has told me so many stories about her amazing daughter and when we've been with your aunt and uncle, they talk a lot about you. You've kind of become like a mythical being. I think I needed to talk to you to make sure you truly existed."

"Well...I'm real. Just an average woman." She turned, washing her hands in the sink after placing the last fried mushroom ball in the center of the second chance tray.

"Definitely not average."

"So, you've been with her for four years?" Elle said, her back to him as she allowed the lukewarm water to run over her soapy hands. She should politely excuse herself and rejoin her people in the other room instead of standing here talking to yet another one of her mom's doomed relationships. No doubt he'd leave soon, just like all the others.

She idly wondered how many boyfriends there had been between Jamie and Daniel. Her mother had never been okay with being alone, always in search of something to quell the loneliness that plagued her. Never realizing that she wasn't alone, she had Elle. She had herself.

"Yeah. We met at the nursing home where she works. I visit veterans living in the Assisted Living and Nursing

Homes across the area." His eyes grew wistful with memory. "During her breaks or after her shift, she'd read to some of the residents. I kept seeing her sitting in different rooms. After a month of just noticing her, I walked into one of my fellow veterans' rooms and found her sitting beside him reading aloud. I finally talked to her."

"What was she reading?"

It was a silly question, but the need to know nibbled at Elle. Her mom had never been a big reader. She wasn't sure where her love of books had come from. Reading had dominated her first friendship with Summer as little girls, then bonded her to Carmen and Beth in high school, and now fueled her love with Clayton.

"*Sense and Sensibility,*" he replied.

"What?" Elle whirled around, her wet hands dripping onto the brown and gold tile floor.

"Yeah. I hadn't read it. She said it was her daughter's copy. I guess you had left it behind." The cadence of his words was cautious. "Your mom reads that book at least three times a year. Our first conversation was about you. She talked about how smart you were and how your nose was always stuck in a book. She talked about how talented you were with your French horn. She talked about how kind, strong, smart, and beautiful you were. She always said 'were,' making me think you had died. It was always in the past tense."

"Well, I am very much alive, just not…." She stopped speaking, not knowing quite how to finish that sentence, so instead she wiped her hands on a paper towel.

"It took six months for her to agree to go out on a date with me."

Elle stared, dumbstruck at the idea of her mom, who was so quick to fall in love, waiting so long to go on a date with this attractive, accomplished, and, by all appearances and what Uncle Pete had said, nice man. The mother she grew up with would have only waited six seconds before agreeing to go on a date.

"I took her for coffee on our first date. It was the only thing she'd agree to. We talked for hours until the shop closed. We talked about you mostly. She told me you were alive and that she wasn't part of your life anymore. She said she'd lost that privilege."

"She gave it up," Elle snapped.

"It's a loss whether we give it up or it's taken away. We still grieve," he said, his tone tender. "I'm sorry. I know I'm overstepping. It's probably the soldier in me. I don't know when to give up a battle. I don't know everything, but I know she blames herself." Daniel raised his hands in surrender at Elle's glower. "As she should. I'm not going to make excuses for her or make her apologies to you. That's not my place. I just wanted... I don't know what I wanted. I was just helping with cupcakes and then you were here. I just wanted to meet you. I also wanted to check in on you."

"Why? You don't know me," Elle hissed, the fingers of her right hand traced her starfish pendant to ground herself.

"Your mom is worried about you after the last few times she saw you. She can't check on you directly. She can't talk to your uncle or aunt because she doesn't know what you've told them and doesn't want to betray you to them. Tobey isn't speaking to her right now so she can't ask him." He frowned. "She'll kill me for doing this, but when you really love someone, sometimes you overstep...So, here I am, overstepping. How are you doing, Eleanor?"

"You must really love her." Elle's ire leached out of her.

This man who'd never met her, who was dating her estranged mother, was in a kitchen asking her how she's doing. The weirdest part of it was the sincerity in each syllable. He truly wanted to know how she was. He truly cared. This man loved her mother so much that he was ready to risk the tension and potential wrath to have this conversation with Elle.

"I do. I want to marry her."

"She'll love that," she muttered.

"Well, she keeps turning me down." His smile was mournful.

"What? Why?" Elle's jaw went slack.

The key driver for her mother since her dad left was finding someone, anyone to fill that void in her heart. Boyfriend after boyfriend and date after date, Elle's mom searched for her Prince Charming. A man to sweep her off her feet, so she'd never be alone again.

None of her previous choices proved worthy of the role of being her mom's husband or Elle's stepdad. Daniel in his pink polo shirt with a tiny green alligator logo, tan slacks, Converse sneakers, and earnest stare looked the picture of a standup guy.

Daniel was a good guy. Uncle Pete had said so when they took Lt. Scout and Fitz on a walk a few weeks ago. He had never said that of any of her mother's other boyfriends.

"She lost the great love of her life," Daniel said sadly.

"My father?" Elle scoffed, then her heart sank in horrified realization. *Jamie?* The bile threatened to rise at that thought. Was Jamie her mom's great love?

His stare locked with hers. "No. You."

"You're mistaken. I was her consolation prize." Elle's arms wrapped around her middle in a steadying self-embrace.

"No child should ever feel that way…" He sighed. "That's why she blames herself. So many mistakes she made."

"Yet you want to marry her," Elle said incredulous.

"I do." He paused, looking around the room before focusing his gaze back on her. "I wouldn't want to be measured by the sum of my past mistakes, so I try not to do that to others. There's no expiration date on forgiveness, neither for ourselves, nor for others. As long as someone is truly sorry and changes. Apology without action is just manipulation. I think she's changed. I know I'm not a good judge as I have only had the pleasure of loving Amanda as she is now. You had the misfortune of knowing who she used to be. You deserved better. I'd like to believe she's better."

Elle's chest pinched as Daniel spoke. There were as many versions of her mother as there were of Elle. She had once been Eleanor, a stoically sad and lonely girl. Then she was an Elle who was walled off, holding others at arm's length. Even the select few she allowed to come close enough to touch the layers of brick around her heart were never actually granted entrance. Now, she was healing and taking down that wall. Two versions of her mother dance in her heart. The "smile like nobody is looking" mom with deep belly laughs and endless supply of hugs and kisses, who giggled with her as they read the police blotter. Then there is the mom after her dad left, broken and wanting, with a not quite real smile plastered on her face, whose sea of embraces for her daughter had dried up. Daniel spoke of this new version of her mother; one Elle did not know.

One she will never know. It's too risky for Elle's recently put back together heart, the once tattered pieces are still fusing back into place.

"Daniel, it's too late." Elle's voice was small.

"Is it? I think if it was, truly, you wouldn't have indulged my overstepping."

Elle shook her head.

"Ok, then. How are you?"

"I'm good." She replied, her trembling voice leveling. "I have good people in my life. You can tell her that. She doesn't need to worry about me."

"Ok." He tucked his hands in his pockets. "I am sorry. I really didn't mean to have this conversation. I was just helping with the cupcakes, but when God opens a door, you need to decide whether to walk through it or walk away. I clearly walked through."

"You sure did." Elle smiled at this very sweet, if a tad intrusive, man. "I'm glad she has you." And she really was.

FORTY

"But remember the pain of parting from friends will be felt by everybody at times, whatever be their education or state."
~Jane Austen, *Sense and Sensibility*

E lle couldn't sleep. Nightmares, roaming thoughts, and tossing and turning hadn't returned. Rather, the looming reality of waking up to pack the last of her things, say goodbye to so much. The farmhouse she'd called home over the last few weeks, her office in the Little Red Barn. To her family. To Fitz. To Perry. But most especially, to Clayton.

Some of those goodbyes, such as to her family, would just be a "See you soon." They deserved to have her there for the special occasions and holidays and she deserved to be with them.

Clayton, however, would be a Goodbye with a capital G. She had told him that it wouldn't be like before, that she'd be back. She told him she wanted him in her life. Those were promises she would break. He deserved his "Lizzie," his everything. His every day.

Once her suitcases were loaded in the rental car, she

would drive away, never to return to him. It would break her heart. She hated it, but she could put it back together. Hadn't the last thirty days shown her that?

All night she lay spooned with Clayton, his arms tight around her waist, as if not wanting to let go. Her head rested in his warm nook, listening to the rhythm of his breaths. Clayton fell in and out of sleep most of the night. His eyes remained closed but occasionally he tightened his arms, or sleepily pressed his lips to her neck or shoulder.

In the morning, when it was not quite daylight, Clayton's fingers trailed down her spine. He inhaled sharply but didn't speak. They lay blanketed in the quiet darkness, both awake but not yet ready to pierce the thick silence with words.

"Are you awake?" Clayton murmured, his voice hoarse.

"Yes."

"Did you sleep at all?"

In the darkness, Elle couldn't make out his expression but sensed the concerned knit of his brow as he looked at her.

"No." she said. "You?"

"Not really." He exhaled.

"I wonder what time it is." She started to move to turn toward her phone on the bed stand, but his arms held her tight.

"I'll check." He reached for his phone without removing his other arm from her waist. "It's five-thirty."

"Okay." She bit her bottom lip.

"What are you thinking?" He untucked her bottom lip with his finger.

"I know you have to work today and need more sleep…" She trailed off.

"But?" he coaxed gently.

"Can we go to the Greenway for a run?"

"Of course."

Orange nudged the black sky awake as they ran along the

trail. Nobody else was out yet. They ran silently, side-by-side for a while, in the crisp morning air.

As the orange and red glow of the rising sun pushed away the dark sky, Clayton slowed his pace to a gentle jog until he ceased completely, placing his hands on his hips and sucking in air. Wordlessly, Elle joined him, stretching her legs as he paced back and forth.

They hadn't spoken since Clayton had walked into the bedroom with his keys, asking if she was ready. The deafening tick of the clock counted down their last hours together, overpowering their ability to just be "us."

"Come here," Clayton whispered, holding his hand toward her.

Placing her hand in his, he clasped it, and led her up a sloping hill. Once there, he tucked her into his torso, her back pressed to his chest, as he rested his arms around her middle. Inhaling his scent of salty sweat and faint remainder of his citrus body wash, she mirrored his stare, looking toward the east at the waking sun. Its brightening beams were like outstretched arms, yawning awake to welcome the day. Sunsets are the end, the goodbye. Sunrises are the promise of today, the hello. This sunrise went against that. It was their goodbye.

"Last night, Janet asked me if you would be staying with me when you come home at Christmas," Clayton said, a quake in his voice.

"Clayton…" She didn't know what to say.

"You didn't tell me you were co…co…co…coming back for Christmas. We ha…ha…haven't di..di…di…discussed plans." He stumbled over the words.

Elle's heart wagged an accusing finger at her that she caused this. Clayton's childhood stutter reared when he was tired or emotional. Despite the lack of sleep, she knew his tripping words were all emotions.

"This is goodbye, isn't it?" Clayton's tone was flat.

"Yes." She breathed.

"You said you wa…wa…wanted me in your life."

Elle closed her eyes, feeling the prick of hot tears forming. She did want him in her life. That was true. That would never stop being true, but there were two lives. His and hers. There was no room for a third, "theirs."

"Yes, but I also said I didn't want to give you false hope." She pulled free of his hold and turned to face him. "It's not fair to either of us to drag this out. I know this hurts but it's what's best."

"Elle—"

"No!" She held up her hands.

A pained and shocked expression twisted his features.

She wanted to run to him, to wrap her arms around his neck and kiss his lips, soothing away the despair that swam in his gaze. *God, I want a do-over.* "Clayton, I am so grateful for the time we've spent together, but this has to end. I'm sorry."

"I…" He looked toward the line of trees along the trail.

"You are an extraordinary man and I know that you will find your Lizzie. But, I'm not her. I can't be," Elle said with a shaky resolve.

It hurt, but she needed to break her hold over him and free him to find the great love he truly deserved. Whoever she was, she would be blessed to be his "everything." Elle would hate her just a little but would be indebted to the woman for giving Clayton the future he deserved.

"I'll miss you." His exhale sounded defeated.

All she could do was nod. If the words that choked in her throat came out, she'd never be able to let him go and she needed to… For him.

The cab of Clayton's pickup was heavy with the dull ache of breaking hearts as they drove back to the farmhouse, neither speaking. The crunching gravel was the first sound to break the silence as they pulled up to the farmhouse. Clayton turned the truck off. Elle wasn't sure what to do, so she looked out the window. The sky was now a warm blue. Cheerful white clouds floated slowly across the sky, a sharp contrast to the dark somber clouds enveloping the truck.

Clayton cleared his throat, his eyes avoiding Elle's as they looked forward. "I'm going to go for a walk while you pack."

"Ok." She opened the door and got out. Keeping her eyes fixed on anything but Clayton, she headed into the farmhouse.

The house was still quiet. Viet and Fitz were likely still sleeping. The three of them wouldn't leave for the airport for a couple of hours. Their flight was at noon, but they were going to have a quick breakfast at Pete and Janet's to say goodbye. Tobey and Jerome would be there. Meghan had offered to cover the clinic, allowing both Clayton and Jerome to have breakfast with Elle before she left. However, Elle doubted Clayton would keep those plans. She didn't blame him. Although, she wondered. He was someone that kept promises he made.

Unlike you. It didn't feel like a promise at the time, but hadn't she said she wanted to have him in her life? Hadn't she agreed to his wanting to take any moment, even future stolen ones? Some promises need to be broken.

Upstairs, she slipped her running clothes off and folded them neatly into a small plastic bag filled with some dirty clothes to pack for the trip to Long Beach.

As she placed the plastic bag beside her open suitcase, she stopped, her gaze captured by the framed photo of the train trellis over the falls at Letchworth. She had bought it for Clayton weeks ago, but was waiting for the best time to give it to him. There hadn't been a right time, and now, there might never be.

A lump formed in her throat, threatening to strangle her with tears she refused to release. She peered at the photo, manifesting images of them in the scene as she stared. Elle pulled out a small gift bag and put the framed photo inside. Taking the purple Post-Its Clayton had bought her on their trip to Buffalo, she wrote *Thank you for everything, Clayton. ~Elle.* For a moment she hesitated, almost writing "Love, Elle," but knew that wouldn't be right. She placed the bag on his bed stand, beside his half-drunk bottle of water.

The tile was cool against her bare feet as she stepped into the shower. This would be the last time in this shower, and she was alone. She had never been lonely in the shower before. It was the strangest pang in her chest to feel that. Elle closed her eyes, letting the spray's hot force consume her.

"Elle." Clayton's voice was muffled through the closed shower door and beating drops of water.

She turned. The shower's fogged glass obscured the details of him, but in his fuzzy outline she could see the framed photo in his hands. He raised the photo, looking at it and then back to her before opening the shower door.

"When did you get this?"

"The Friday after the wedding. It made me think of you. I know how special the train trellis is for you and that you go there to be with Evan. I guess I just wanted you to have it, so that you could visit him anytime even if you couldn't be there." She left out the other reason she gave it to him. So he could have a piece of her, even if he wasn't aware.

The climb they made that day was so much more than just a walk. That night she would open her body to him, fully, but that morning under the canopy of lush green leaves as they climbed each stone step, she'd opened her heart to him entirely. This little piece of them would remain with him. He may not know it, but she did and that was good enough for Elle.

"If this is goodbye..." he said, placing the photo on the counter turning to face her. His grey eyes capturing her. "...I don't want my last me...me...me....memory of you to be the Greenway. I want it to be this. I wa...wa...want it to be to... to...to...touching you....ki...ki...kissing you. I wa...wa... wa...want it to be of us being us."

"Ok."

"Ok." he said, undressing. The normally devious lift of his lips was replaced with sorrowful want.

She should have said no. That would have been the kinder thing to do. She couldn't deny herself this last memory, which would painfully and sweetly idle in her heart.

His strong hands cupped her face as those eyes, shaded darker with sadness, drank her in. Those playful and ravenous kisses were replaced with savoring ones, as if she was the last drop of food he'd ever have. He took her lower lip, the one she bit so often, claiming it as his own. His hands explored her, their tender touch mapping every inch of her as if committing to memory her peaks, valleys, and paths so he would never forget how to traverse the terrain of her body.

Their eyes never left one another the entire time. The sex was an achingly slow, neither seeming to want the moment to end but the quickening of their breaths signaled that their bodies were coming to their climax, to their end. As they finished, Elle pressed against the tiled wall and Clayton holding her tight, she burrowed her head into his neck, allowing a few tears to sneak out.

"Thank you, for everything," he murmured, pressing his lips to her neck.

"Thank you for everything," Elle croaked.

Later Elle stood, Fitz in her arms, staring at the farmhouse as Clayton and Viet loaded the luggage in the trunk of her rental. Willa stood beside Elle, gently squeezing her shoulder. A *thunk* of the trunk closing and murmured "Nice meeting you. Safe travels" between Clayton and Viet made Elle squeeze Fitz just a little harder. Shoes crunched on gravel until those eyes that Elle could swim in for days were staring at her. There was a pat on her shoulder as Willa told her she'd wait in the car.

Elle swallowed the choking lump and with a final kiss to Fitz's head, handed him over. "Goodbye, Clayton."

He accepted the pug with a sad smile. "Goodbye, Elle."

She turned but stopped at the touch of his hand.

"I will miss you." Clayton placed a trembling kiss on her forehead.

With a matching sad smile, Elle pivoted and walked to her rental, got in, and drove away.

After a short drive in uncomfortable silence, they pulled into Janet and Pete's driveway.

"Lady Elle!" Jerome waved from the front porch as Elle stepped out of the car. "Viscount Viet and Queen Willa!" A reckless smile was sketched on his face as he jumped down the stairs. He swung Elle up in a bear hug.

The yellow cottage's living room was once again transformed into their celebratory dining room. A glass vase with purple carnations sat in the center of the temporary table, surrounded by tiny purple starfish shaped confetti thrown around the table. A large banner hung from the ceiling saying *See You Soon, Elle.*

Her heart stuttered at that message. It wasn't "Goodbye," it was "See You Soon." She had told her uncle that it wouldn't be like before. This time when she left Perry, she would come back. She'd come back home to them. This banner told her that they believed her.

Elle sat at the table between her uncle and cousin. Nobody asked about Clayton. There had been a hushed conversation between Viet and Tobey when they first arrived and some stolen glances between Pete and Viet as they sat. Elle had only told her friends that Clayton wouldn't be joining them for breakfast, leaving it at that.

Breakfast wasn't a sad event. There was lots of laughter, wistful chatter about Elle's trip, discussion of plans for Christmas, and asking what Elle would do when she got back home.

"I'll unpack," she said flatly, shifting in her seat.

"Nothing you're itching to do when you get back?" A quizzical frown pulled at the corner of Janet's lips.

She said nothing.

"Brunch." Willa interjected. "The brunch game in the LBC is tight. We go a few times a month."

"Yoga at the Bluff and running along the beach path," Viet added, squeezing her shoulder.

She wasn't sure if her friends filled in the blanks for her aunt or to remind Elle of what she enjoyed from her life there.

"All those things," Elle confirmed, then took a long drink of her tea, allowing the hot liquid to push that lump back down.

Later, as Elle washed her hands in the bathroom, she stared into the mirror. Her first day in Perry felt like three days in one. That day had dragged on and on.

Now, today felt like mere seconds. Walking down the hallway back to the living room, Pete stopped her and tucked her into a tight hug.

"Thank you for coming back, kiddo. I've loved having you here." He kissed her temple.

"I've loved being here." She coughed to hide the tremble in her voice. "Thanks for having me."

"You always have a place here." He placed her hand on top of his heart. "I love you, kiddo."

"I love you too, Uncle Pete." She looked up at him, catching the sad twinkle in his eye.

"I'm your only uncle." He smirked.

"My one and only." She rested her head on his shoulder as he embraced her.

Aunt Janet, of course, cried. Her eyes were already watery as she squeezed Elle, her petite frame packing an affectionate punch as she held tight.

Hoisting her purse onto her shoulder, she said goodbye to Jerome and Tobey. Then her gaze dropped to Pete and Janet, who stood on the porch. She'd lost her biological parents so long ago but standing in front of her were two people that had been, and were still, willing to fill that role. "Thank you. I love you both."

With watery smiles, they both mouthed *love you*.

"I'll miss you." Tobey looped his arms around Elle's shoulders, walking her to her rental car. Lt. Scout trotted beside them. "Who's going to help me manage those two in there?" He cocked his head toward the house where Pete and Janet shuffled back inside.

"You've got Jerome," she teased.

"Not the same," he chuckled, checking to make sure his husband was still on the porch talking to Viet. "He finds their antics delightful."

"I think you find it just as delightful." She winked.

"Yes, but I also have the good sense to be mortified when Dad drops it like it's hot. As do you."

"True, but we wouldn't change them."

"Never." he sighed happily. "We're lucky to be theirs."

"Yes, we are." Her heart squeezed. "I remember when you were a baby. Your mom and dad let me hold you. I was so little myself and couldn't believe they'd trust me with something so tiny....so precious. I held you tight, making sure I didn't drop or hurt you."

"I'm pretty sturdy." He tapped his flat stomach, wincing in the realization that this was one of his dad's mannerisms.

She smiled. "That you are."

"Text us when you land and when you get home," Tobey commanded in the same gentle tone Elle had heard through the years from his dad.

Our dad.

She saluted mockingly. "Will do, Officer Coates."

"That's State Trooper Coates." He nudged her side with his elbow.

FORTY-ONE

*"We live at home, quiet, confined, and our feelings prey
upon us."*
~Jane Austen, *Persuasion*

O n the flight, Viet and Willa chattered away while Elle
spent most of it looking out the window, something
she generally didn't do.

They weaved through the bustling LAX crowds toward
baggage claim. Ryan waited at the carousel, his arms open
and smiling large as he spotted them.

"I missed you, baby." Ryan cooed, as he pressed a gentle
kiss against Viet's forehead.

Elle stopped watching the happy reunion between her
friends. Viet was her ride or die, but Ryan had become a
friend in the years he dated and then married her best friend.
A swirl of emotions fizzed through Elle. Joy at her friends'
deep love for one another. Gratitude for Viet and Willa
flying to Perry to be with her over the last few days. Jealousy
that there wasn't a pair of loving arms for her to walk into at
baggage claim. Not just any arms, but Clayton's arms.

An hour later, Ryan dropped Willa in front of her apartment a few blocks away from Elle's and then drove Elle to her building. Viet jumped out of Ryan's silver SUV, offering to help Elle lug her bags upstairs and unpack before walking back to his place. Elle waved him off, saying she was beat and just wanted to take a shower.

It was a half-truth. She just wanted to be alone. That choking lump in her throat needed to be released, and she didn't want to do it with Viet there. He'd want to ease the pain and wipe away her tears. She didn't want to be comforted; she just wanted to feel the grief. So much of her life was spent tucking her feelings away. It was time to just let them out, but in the safety of her own condo with herself as the only witness to her sorrow.

Unlocking her door, she dragged her two suitcases in, setting them in the small hallway by the front door. Hanging her purse on the hook by the door and placing her laptop bag next to her suitcases, she slipped her sandals off and tucked her feet into the slippers she kept by the door. Ned, Willa's cousin who had been renting her condo while on a contract with a local hospital as a nurse, had moved out to stay with Willa for the last week of his time in Long Beach. He'd be leaving for Alaska next week.

Elle walked around her condo like a visitor to a museum, taking it all in. Ned had made sure that the place was clean. It looked just as it had before she left. Dull light, tinted in gray, came in through the large windows overlooking the ocean.

Wandering her condo, she surveyed each neatly organized closet, clean counter, the perfectly folded purple throw blanket hung over her gray couch, categorized bookshelves, and the picture of her with Pete, Janet, and Tobey at her college graduation that sat on her nightstand. That lonely picture would soon have company. One of the pictures she planned to add would be that picture of her and Clayton at the Anchor Bar. Seeing the photo each day would stab painfully but that ache would allow her to remember when she was an "us."

She pulled her suitcases into the bedroom to unpack and settle back into this place that used to be so beloved, but now was just a condo. Not the home she'd left as she'd flown away from Perry.

At the bottom of a stack of folded shirts was Clayton's *Team Paw Patrol* tee that she had worn the first night she slept over and so many nights after. Taking the soft blue shirt in her hand, she sat on the corner of her bed, tracing the T-shirt's white lettering. With each stroke of her finger, another tear fell. Clutching it to her chest, she released the rest of her tears, letting them rage like a long awaited and much needed rainstorm. The hot tears tumbled down her cheeks and onto the shirt, dampening it in her sadness. She hadn't put the shirt in her suitcase. Clayton must have. She's not sure when.

She pressed the shirt to her face and mumbled into the well-worn fabric, "Thank you for everything, Clayton."

She wept, pressing the shirt close to her heart. She had left a memento of "us" with him, and he had sent one with her. When Elle's dad left, she took all the mementos of when her mother, father, and she were a "Them," tossing them in the trash in the hopes it would erase the pain. It hadn't. This was a different kind of pain. That had been the pain of the left behind, the unchosen. This was the pain of the leaver, the chooser. She was more like her father than she'd believed possible. She had left. She had chosen her life here and his life there.

"Goodbye, Clayton." She folded the shirt and tucked it, and her heartbreak, into the bottom drawer.

FORTY-TWO

"Elizabeth had never been more at a lost to make her feelings appear what they were not. It was necessary to laugh, when she would rather have cried."
~Jane Austen, *Pride and Prejudice*

I t had been five days since Elle returned to Long Beach. Five days full of an aching heart each time she saw the color gray, making her think of Clayton's eyes, smelled the aroma of Braedon's afternoon snack of peeled orange, making her think of Clayton's citrus scent, or Malcolm asked her how Clayton was doing, making her think of…well Clayton.

The pang in her chest rattled as she met Willa and Viet for happy hour, although nothing felt happy to Elle. A bottle of rosé on the table greeted her as she slipped onto the tall stool across from her two friends, cautious smiles on their faces. Their stale conversation hovered around the unseasonably hot weather and work for their first glass of wine.

Almost done with their second round, Willa placed her half-filled glass down, and declared, "Okay, I'm pulling off the bandage."

"Wills…" Viet cautioned.

"Noah says Clayton is heartbroken. He's been miserable since you left."

Breath *whooshed* out of Elle like she'd been punched. She'd known Clayton would be hurt, but this was confirmation of it. Noah would only say something to try to help, to try to fix. It wouldn't be a throwaway comment like *how's the weather* or *how about them Yankees* or *by the way my lifelong bromance bestie is heartbroken.*

"You're talking to Noah?" Elle blinked.

"That's your takeaway on what I just said?" Willa scoffed. "Yes, we're friends. We've texted and we spoke last night, but we're not going down that rabbit hole. We're going down yours."

"I don't know if I like the analogy of going down Elle's hole." Viet quipped, lightening the tension.

"He said that?" Elle's fingers tightened on her wineglass. The cool smoothness of the glass soothing her jackhammering heart. The confirmed certainty of Clayton's sadness flayed her.

"I'm not telling you this to make you feel bad. I just don't understand why this is happening. Even before I met Clayton, I knew this was so different. You *never* like anyone I've set you up with." Willa shifted off the backless stool across from Elle, taking the one beside her. "When I saw the two of you together, I thought this is him. This is the man finally worthy of my friend's heart. I just don't understand why it needed to end. The way you two looked at each other was like there was nobody else in the world."

"Willa…" Viet's tone was firm. "Elle's life is here, and Clayton's is there. They talked about it and decided it was best not to drag it on."

"Did they decide or did *she*?"

"Elle? Did you ask Clayton what he wanted, or did you

just decide what was best for him and tell him?" Viet's assessing gaze pinned her.

"It's what's best for him." she whispered.

Willa pushed, "Did you ask him?"

"No," she admitted, her sad response almost drowned in the revery of the lively bar.

"First, I want you to remember I love you." Viet clasped her hand, calling her eyes to his. "Remember that as I say this, but what the actual fuck, Elle? You fight for your people, but sometimes you don't stop to ask them what they want. Just because it's what you feel is best doesn't mean it's right. You should have asked him. You should have given him a choice."

"I know. You've said this before." she blew out a heavy breath. "Clayton had asked me to talk to him before making decisions for him…for us."

Her heart splintered with the memory of being wrapped in Clayton's arms as he asked her to keep a promise that she broke days later.

Wasn't that proof enough that he deserved better?

"Why didn't you ask him? Were you scared that if you asked him to come with you or for you to stay that he'd say no?"

"Or were you scared he'd say yes?" Willa's left arm looped through Elle's.

The gentle touches of her friends anchored her to this moment, despite the desire to run away or deflect from their prodding. Was she scared that he wouldn't choose her or that if he did, he'd regret it? She felt like her mother's consolation prize all her life, something Mom was stuck with after her grandmother died and her dad left. So many of her people left, she felt like a stray cat on the edges of the property, tolerated but not brought into the house. As much as she understood with her brain that some of that holding people at a distance was self-induced, her heart still wobbled. Maybe it was true. That she was unworthy. The scars were so deep in her bones that they never seemed to heal or allow her to fully embrace the possibility of being chosen with no regrets.

"I've spent so much of my life feeling not quite enough. Feeling like an unwanted inhabitant of the Island of Misfit toys." Elle swallowed hard.

"Ok, first you are *not* a misfit toy." Willa said, authority lacing her words. "Second, even if you were, at the end of Rudolph, Santa rescues them all and takes them to homes with loving boys and girls, teaching us all that even misfit toys deserve happy endings. Deserve love."

"Thanks." Elle laughed under her breath.

"Third, as a licensed psychologist and your friend, but mostly as your friend, have you thought about talking to someone? I see my own therapist twice a month and find it painfully cathartic. I can make some recommendations if you'd like," Willa offered.

Elle looked at Viet for confirmation that this was a good idea. She knew it was. It was time for her to do the work. She had already laid the foundation over the last several weeks. It was time to build a house of healing on top of it. She knew this but wanted her friend's approval.

Viet nodded affirmatively at Elle.

"Thanks, Wills." Elle leaned her head against her friend's shoulder.

"Sorry I kind of pounced on you. I know I can be a little much." Willa apologized.

"You are a little much, but that's what we love about you. Any less and you wouldn't be our Willa," Elle said.

"And we're big fans of our Willa." Viet raised his glass.

FORTY-THREE

"Angry People are not always wise."
~Jane Austen, *Pride and Prejudice*

The Southern California Marine Layer lingered as Elle's sneakered feet slapped against the paved running path along the shoreline. Hints of the coming heat of the day thickening the air as she ran. So many conflicting emotions swirled within her, but she took the first steps to tamp them down. On Friday, she called a therapist and scheduled a virtual appointment for the following week. She'd still be in Chicago at the ribbon cutting for Sloan-Whitney's new Oncology Center and announcement for their partnership with the Geneva Foundation. She'd extended her stay there to visit Beth, adhering to her desire to hold closer the people she cared about. It also felt fitting having the appointment on neutral ground, a place that was not Perry or Long Beach.

As Elle slowed to a brisk walk, the beach path crowded

with people out enjoying their Saturday, she mulled over the last seven days and nights.

The mundane.

The extraordinary.

The in-between.

The one constant in the last seven days, the pain, hadn't gotten any easier. In fact, the torment of daily living without Clayton had gotten worse. Each morning, she awoke to a sharp twinge of grief in her chest, an ache in her fingers to pick up her phone and reach out, choking words in her throat that wanted to climb out. *I love you, be with me.*

What would a future with Clayton look like, though? Could it be here in Long Beach, him running alongside her, the two of them coming back to Fitz napping on the condo balcony, the sound of the ocean his lullaby? Could she ask Clayton to move thousands of miles away from his loved ones and start over in a new city?

Or was it back in Perry, getting caught making out at the Greenway after a jog? Coming home to Fitz who click clacked up the stairs behind them, as they ran to the shower? The ghosts of her past lingering around each corner?

Breath heaving, she stepped onto the grass, stretching before walking back toward her building. Exhausted and wrung out, she just wanted to go back to her condo, shower, make tea, and curl up on the couch. Maybe she'd skip being the only one in the office on a Saturday, and just take care of herself for the weekend, instead of working.

Head down and lost in thought, she approached the condo building.

"Eleanor." An unsure voice startled Elle as she reached the front door.

Her mother stood there, hands clenched and wearing a tight smile, staring at Elle with pleading eyes.

"What are you doing here? How did you find me?" Elle's mouth hung open.

"I stopped by Pete's this week to drop off a 'Thank You' card from Daniel and me for his party. When I was there, I saw an envelope on the counter with your name and address. When your uncle wasn't looking, I snapped a picture of it. I bought a ticket and flew out here. There isn't an intercom, so I've just been waiting," she explained.

"I can't decide if that is a complete violation or ingenious," Elle said, aghast and amazed that her mom would go to such lengths to find her. "So, you've been waiting out here just in case I appeared? How long?"

"Since yesterday. I sat here…" She pointed to a short red brick wall that flanked the front sidewalk leading to her building's front door. "…until midnight last night and then came back this morning."

Of course, they hadn't seen each other. Elle had entered and left through the garage on Friday with her car and left before sunrise this morning for her run. Her mom had been here the whole time and she'd had no idea. In the small town of Perry, this would not go unnoticed, but in Long Beach, people loitering on the streets of downtown was not something anyone batted an eye at.

"Why are you here?" Elle asked, crossing her arms over her chest. "I told you we were done."

"I know and I believed you. I told myself I had to accept what I had done, but then Daniel told me about your conversation, and I knew I needed to try." Tears glistened in her eyes. "You are not a consolation prize. I can't have you think that. If anyone was stuck with anyone, you were stuck with me. You got the short end of the stick."

"It felt like quite the opposite." Elle snapped, turning toward the door.

"I was a bad mother. You deserved so much better. You

still do," her mom called, making Elle stop in her tracks, but her back remained turned toward her mom.

This apology was unlike the hollow apologies of the past. Her mother had broken her promises of trying harder almost the same moment they had been spoken. Never did her mom say *what* she was sorry for.

"Even before your dad left and your grandma died, I don't think I was a good mother. Not the mother you needed. So often your dad, your uncle, or your grandma were who you looked to for comfort. They always knew what to say or do. I… I didn't. So often my mom told me I wasn't doing it right. She'd interject or push me aside, taking over."

"So, it's grandma's fault?" Elle twisted with a snarl.

"No." She raised her hands, taking two faltering steps toward Elle. "That's not an excuse. It's just…it's just what it was. When your grandma died and then your dad left, I felt like I wasn't enough for you. That I was who you were stuck with. I couldn't see through my own pain and grief for all I had lost to see what I had. There are times I think if you hadn't saved me that day, your life would have been so much better. You were so strong, when I should have been strong for you."

"I needed you," Elle croaked.

"I know and I failed you. I failed when I didn't get off the couch for weeks after your dad left. When I tried to kill myself. When I chose men over you. When Jamie raped you. I wasn't there." She took a timid step closer.

"When I told you what he did, why didn't you believe me?" Elle's wobbly voice grew more forceful.

"I did believe you. I was in shock." She held up a palm to halt Elle's protest. "Again, not an excuse. I kept thinking, why would he do that to my daughter? Why had I let another man into my life who'd hurt my child? Your dad hurt you when he left. I chose him. I don't think you really liked my other boyfriends, and when I think of how I laughed off the things they said, I'm ashamed of myself. I let them hurt you over and over again. Then I invited Jamie into our lives, and he raped you. That last phone call, after you hung up, I knew I'd said all the wrong things." She hung her head, her voice barely a whisper. "I didn't know how or what to say. I called back a few times, but I'd get your voicemail at your dorm, or your roommate would say you weren't there. Your uncle told me to give you space, so I did."

"Pete? Did you tell Pete what happened?" Elle cried, placing a steadying hand on her middle as air whooshed out of her. Had Pete known all this time.

"No." Her mom stepped closer, the warm scent of vanilla and lavender soothingly wafting from her.

Elle let out a relieved breath as she stood taller. "Why didn't you keep trying?"

"Because I'm weak. I was mortified about my actions and was scared. How could we come back from this? How could we come back from me? I was the monster under your bed."

The once extinguished hope within Elle seemed to flicker at the remorse in her mom's eyes. Fear of being alone had consumed her in the past when her mom apologized, but today regret, true regret, shaded her gaze. Not regret for what she lost, but for her actions, for realizing she was the monster.

"Why were you at Jamie's grave?" Elle swallowed hard, keeping the spark of hope buried deep, not allowing it to thaw her heart when it came to her mom. It was too soon.

"I hadn't intended to visit him. I was there visiting your grandma. A few years after we stopped speaking, I started visiting her on her birthday like you used to. Each year, I'd see a vase full of pink flowers and knew they were from you. I waited there all day just in case you came in person to try to talk to you. I had messed it up so badly at the wedding. I had promised your uncle that I wouldn't speak to you at the wedding. I didn't want to cause an issue for you, but I needed…wanted to talk to you."

Elle tightened her embrace around her chest in a reassuring hug.

Her mom continued, "When you came through the gate, I wandered around the cemetery trying to give you space. When you told me what Jamie did, I confronted him. He denied it, of course. I told him he was vile and then I slapped him. He slapped me back. Then he left. The next time I saw him was in a picture in the obituaries."

"Ok, but why were you at his grave?" Elle persisted, venom dripping from each word.

"To forgive him."

"Excuse me?" Elle roared with indignation.

"No, not for the rape." Her mom insisted firmly, grabbing Elle's arm and twisting her back around to face her. "Never for that. There's a special corner in hell with a hot poker that will be inserted where the sun doesn't shine for that piece of dog poop."

For some reason the use of "dog poop" made Elle want to laugh. Her mom had never been a big swearer. Every now and then, curse words would slip out, but they were rare.

"Dog poop? What would Pastor Danny say about such language?" Elle mocked with a slightly playful lilt to her tone.

"He knows I am far from perfect." Her mom relaxed her grip on Elle's shoulders but still maintained contact. "I was there to forgive Jamie because I blamed him for so long for losing you. He didn't cause that. I did. I was a terrible mother. I should have held your hand instead of you holding mine. To say I am sorry will never be enough. I'm sorry for everything I missed, all the events of your life. I can't ever get those back." She dropped her hand. "Even if things remain as they are, I just wanted you to know that I am to blame. Your heart is such a precious gift that I didn't take care of. You deserve so much more than me."

Tears stung Elle's eyes and her lower lip trembled.

This apology was raw, honest, and without a requested transaction. It was filled with hard truths from someone that had truly taken stock of their actions. It asked for nothing in return. Her mother didn't beg for absolution or a second chance, her only need was for Elle to know that she was blameless. Elle had always felt that if she'd somehow been different, somehow more, her mom would have chosen her. It was never Elle who wasn't enough, it was her mom that felt lacking.

Elle swiped at her eyes and invited her mom upstairs. They sat at the kitchen table with a pot of peppermint tea steeping. Elle's hands folded in her lap as they sat. Her mother gazed around the condo, taking in the details of Elle's life.

The silence between them was both awkward and contented. How long had it been since she sat at a table with her mom?

"Do you remember how I'd push the chairs up against the window in the dining room to create my own window seat for reading?" Elle asked, breaking the silence.

"To this day when I see big windows, I think about that." Her mom smiled. "The apartment I live in has a window seat. I rented it because of that. It makes me feel close to you."

"Apartment? What about Grandma's house?" Elle gaped.

"I couldn't stay there. It was too painful. I sold it ten years ago."

"Pete never said anything."

"I asked him not to. I felt bad doing it, but I knew it was what I needed to do. That house had too many memories. I couldn't keep walking through the front door each day facing them. I'm sorry. I should have let Pete tell you," Mom explained with remorseful eyes.

"I wish I had known…" Elle paused thinking of her childhood home.

What would she have done? When she left eighteen years ago, she never looked back. In the brief times she returned to Perry before moving to Los Angeles, she'd never driven past that house. Yes, there had been beautiful memories in that house, but it was haunted with the phantoms of so much pain that Elle didn't want to revisit. Pain tends to linger in the foundation of homes. Elle was happy to be rid of it and to know her mom no longer lived there. That house had ceased to be a home long ago.

"I'm glad it's gone. You deserve a fresh start." Elle reached for the pot and poured two cups of tea.

The lavender curtains stirred in the warm Santa Anna breeze from the open sliding door that led to the balcony. A mix of fresh mint from the tea and salty ocean air filled the room.

Mom grinned. "This place is lovely."

"Thank you."

"I won't pretend I haven't internet stalked you through the years. I've read articles about the work you've done with Sloan-Whitney. I'm so proud of you. I know your grandma would be too. She always said you were the smartest of us all and she was right."

Elle's heart squeezed with a happy sadness at that.

"I also look at your Instagram and the accounts of your friends in your pictures just in case they post something with you that you're not tagged in. I see you and Viet are still close. I remember you telling me about him. I'm sorry I never got to meet him."

Elle raised a teasing eyebrow. "If you weren't my mom, Instagram stalking me would be totally creepy."

Elle drank her tea, contemplating this. If she didn't want to be found, she could have made it more difficult. Had Elle left her Instagram public in a secret hope that her mom would look? As angry as Elle had been, she'd always hoped that one day her mother would reach out.

They may never have the mother/daughter relationship either of them wanted, but they could have something else, something in-between.

"I'm going to start seeing a therapist on Friday," Elle said.

"That's good." Her mom smiled with approval. "I've been seeing someone for the last twelve years."

"Really?"

"Yes. I had...well, I have a lot of work to do. It's hard, but it's good."

"I'd like to get a few months under my belt first, but would you be open to us finding a therapist to see together? Someone to help us work through things. Today has been a start, but we have so much work to do."

"Of course." Tears welled in her mom's eyes.

A silent beat passed, allowing them to breathe in the moment of first steps. Of new beginnings. They would never be what they were, but they could be something new. Something better.

"What about Clayton?" Her mom's quick change of subject was dizzying.

Elle's forehead furrowed. "What about Clayton?"

"Perry's a small town. I heard the talk about the two of you and saw you together. My track record with romance may be less than desirable, but I can spot two people deeply in love with one another. I had a front row seat to your aunt and uncle, after all. That man loves you and I think you love him too." A teasing quirk of a smile lifted her mom's lips.

"So, you've been reading *Sense and Sensibility*?" Elle blurted, trying to change the topic. It was too painful to talk about Clayton and even more strange to talk about him with her mom.

"You still do that." She wagged knowing brows at Elle.

"What?"

"Change the topic when you don't want to talk about something. You've done that since you were a little girl."

Elle sipped her tea.

Shaking her head, she answered the question about the Austen book. "Yes, I have read it many times. I found your copy after you left. It was the last book I remember seeing you read. I guess I thought if I read it, I'd feel like you were there. I don't know. Then the story resonated with me. Elinor was so strong, brave, and lovely. She took care of everyone, not asking for anything for herself and languishing in sorrow until she got her happy ending."

"A wedding?" Elle smirked.

Mom just rolled her eyes. "Then there was flighty Marianne with no care for anyone but herself, chasing love without thinking of the consequences until she finally learned her lesson and got her happy ending."

"Another marriage."

"Smartbutt," her mom chided with a chuckle.

Elle laughed in reply.

"Yes, to Colonel Brandon. Marianne and Elinor were sisters, but I saw us in them. You in Elinor, of course and me in Marianne. It shouldn't have been that way, but it was." Her mom's apologetic voice was soft.

Elle shifted in her seat. She had the same thought when she and Clayton had snuggled on the couch in his mancave watching the film version of the book. The parallels between the Dashwood Sisters' relationship and she and her mother were a little startling. Elle the Elinor taking care of their broken family and Mom the Marianne swayed by her fanciful desires.

"Maybe Daniel is your Colonel Brandon." Elle bit her lower lip, thinking of the unassuming but dragon slaying soldier turned chaplain. His quiet patience and steadfast love for her mom was so similar to Colonel Brandon's for Marianne.

"Maybe." Her mom sighed, then pursed her lips.

"What?" Elle coaxed.

"Maybe Clayton is your Mr. Ferris." Then she paused, squinting her eyes. "Or, perhaps, your Mr. Darcy."

If someone had told Elle even three hours ago, that she'd be sitting in her condo overlooking the Pacific, drinking tea and talking to her mom about Jane Austen, she wouldn't have believed it.

They sat for several more hours, each taking those first steps on the new path they would traverse together toward healing and forgiveness. Elle's walled-off heart poking through the new gaps in the crumbling wall.

The relationship with Clayton had started dismantling Elle's wall, brick by brick. Not just allowing those Elle loved in but herself out. The work would be hard, but she'd continue, allowing her to build a new relationship with her mom and with herself.

Placing her teacup down, her gaze fixed on her mom. "Mom, call me Elle. That's what my friends call me."

"Ok… Elle."

FORTY-FOUR

"I am the happiest creature in the world. Perhaps other people have said so before, but not one with such justice. I am happier even than Jane; she only smiles, I laugh."
~Jane Austen, *Pride and Prejudice*

A loud vibration hummed from Elle's purse as she stood in front of the mirror of her Chicago hotel, slipping in a pair of silver hoop earrings. She was putting the final touches on her Willa selected ensemble for her big presentations at Sloan-Whitney's Annual board meeting. It was her second day in Chicago. The first day spent attending the ribbon cutting and announcement of their partnership with Magda's foundation that would expand Elle's mobile mammography program. It had been a huge success.

Shuffling over to the chair, she scooped up her black hobo bag grabbing the phone and a tiny envelope clinging to it out. The envelope tumbled to the red carpet. Letting the call go to voicemail, her eyes locked on the tiny, embossed logo of the Village Rose stamped on the envelope's top right corner. It was the card from the last flower delivery from Clayton that arrived the day before she'd left.

She'd slipped the card into her purse assuming it was just another sassy message from Aunt Janet. Bending down, she lifted the card, tracing her fingers over the logo. Tapping the envelope with her finger, she considered just putting it back without opening it, but compulsion nibbled at her to know what Janet had written.

And what if it wasn't from Janet? What if Clayton had written the card for the last delivery? Carefully opening the envelope, she read the tiny card's smooth print. It wasn't Clayton's handwriting. It wasn't Janet's either.

You're worth the risk. ~Love, Uncle Pete

Elle's face scrunched in confusion as she stepped back to sit on the corner of the bed completely missing it and falling to the soft carpet on her butt. "Fuck." She picked herself back up and lowered to the bed, hitting the corner this time.

What risk? Was he saying she was worth Clayton taking a risk on for love? *What does this mean?* Her brain swirled as her eyes studied each letter as if they would somehow reveal their hidden truth like one of those mysterious eye photos that if you stare at long enough suddenly a boat appears.

Pointless! Standing up, she grabbed her cell, which managed to land safely on the bed and dialed Pete.

He answered on the third ring. "Hey, kiddo. I was just showing my foreman the article about your event yesterday. So proud of you."

"Thanks." She paused, soaking in his praise like a warm bubble bath before continuing. "What does 'You're worth the risk' mean?"

"Straight to business. I see you finally read the card. Let me get in my truck."

Elle could hear the pound of hammers, buzz of saws, and

loud gruff voices distinctive of a construction site. With the slam of a door the sounds grew muffled and distant.

"Ok. Can you hear me?" he asked.

"Yeah. What does it mean?" Elle tapped the toe of her shoe on the floor eagerly.

"Well, love is a risk."

"I know," she huffed, but then winced. "Sorry."

"It's fine."

"Are you saying that I was worth the risk for Clayton? If so, shouldn't the card go to him? Also, why is the card from you? Wait, did you send the flowers? No, Clayton acknowledged them when I thanked him. I'm confused," Elle sputtered not letting her uncle answer any of her questions. She paced back and forth from the door to the window. None of this made sense.

"Kiddo, take a breath." Laughter lilted in Pete's voice.

Elle dropped onto the bed, crossing and then recrossing her legs.

"First, the flowers were from Clayton. He had called them in on Tuesday. I was there seeing your aunt before heading back to the house to meet Tobey. She told me how she had been writing silly cards to you that accompanied the weekly flowers from Clayton. I asked her to let me write that week's note."

"But what does it mean?" she pushed, agitation growing as she struggled to understand his message.

"The message was for you, not Clayton. I think he already knows you're worth the risk. I don't think *you* know that you're worth the risk. They always say that before you can find someone worthy, you have to know you are worthy of being loved. During our 'Week of Pete' date...side note, can we get that trademarked?"

Elle let out an annoyed breath.

Pete chuckled. "Ok, we'll put a pin in that for later. Back

to you. When we drove back and talked about you coming home for the holidays, I asked you if you'd be staying with Clayton and you were evasive. When you don't want to talk about something, you clam up. You avoid, deflect, or flat-out refuse. I knew you didn't want to talk about where you were staying because you didn't want to talk to me about ending things with Clayton once you left town. If you ended things with Clayton because it wasn't right, that's one thing, but I don't think that's what's happening here."

"I just thought it was best to not drag things out." *At the time.* "His life is there and mine is…" The ache in her throat cut off her words.

"Where your life is and where his life is doesn't matter. What matters is what you want your life to be, and with whom. The rest is just geography."

Elle bit her lower lip taking in her uncle's words. She had been stuck in *what was*, rather than the possibility of *what could be*. With her fingers she traced the shape of paw prints across her black pants mimicking the matching prints on Clayton's right forearm. Each paw-print a symbol of charting his own path for the life he wanted.

"Bottom line, you need to decide what you want and go for it. It's one thing if you don't want Clayton or anyone. It's quite another thing if you think you're undeserving. It would break my heart if you spent anymore of your life feeling you weren't worth loving." His voice cracked. "You are worth the risk, so bet on yourself, kiddo. I know I always bet on you."

"Oh, Pete." She exhaled weepily.

"Knock it off, kiddo. It's too early for me to be crying in my truck at a construction site." He sniffled.

"Is there an appropriate time to cry in your truck at a construction site?" Elle asked, dashing stray tears from her eyes.

"After lunch. Always better to cry on a full stomach," he joked.

"Sound life advice from my favorite uncle."

"Your one and only." he quipped.

He'd been the first man who'd loved her. He was her North Star shining his love upon her as he helped her navigate life. Now, he was pushing her to fully love herself and chase her heart's desire. So many wants spun through her like hopeful cyclones twisting wildly with no clear path or destination, because she had never allowed them to take root. He was telling her not to just let them take root, but to allow herself to be swept up in them.

Later, as Elle sat in the small restaurant in the lobby, Malcolm going on about their successful board meeting, including both of Elle's proposals being approved, and next week's meeting with Magda to firm up details for their joint venture, Uncle Pete's words danced in Elle's heart. There had been so many subtle and overt messages through the years proving betting on herself was a risk to not take. Her caution...her fear... was the foundations of the wall constructed around her heart.

The one thing Elle wanted was to be chosen. To be enough for someone. In Clayton, she'd found a man that told her every day in so many ways that she was more than enough...she was everything. Someone had chosen her, but she hadn't chosen herself.

Elle wasn't imprisoned by her past, rather she had tied herself to it allowing it to control her. Not choosing Clayton, not choosing *them,* was not choosing herself.

With stunning clarity, she now knew what she wanted. A plan began formulating in her head, and as soon as Malcolm stopped talking and paid the bill, she'd put her plan into action.

"One more thing…" Malcolm said as he handed his card to the server. "I'm not sure if you heard the rumors but we're creating a Deputy Chief Operating Officer position at Sloan-Whitney. I'd like to offer you the position."

"Excuse me?" Elle's head jerked back, rudely ripped from the excitement of her plan.

"That's why I wanted to have lunch after the board meeting. You are perfect for the job. The bord agrees with me. It will mean a raise and increased responsibility and that includes a little bit more travel. You can also pick your own assistant. I'm sure you'd like to bring Braedon over. It would mean a salary increase for them, as well, as is fitting for the assistant to the second in command for Sloan-Whitney." Amusement sparked in Malcolm's eyes. "What do you say? Are you interested? If so, we can work out the details on Monday and then make a formal announcement at the end of the week."

"Umm…" Elle bit her lower lip.

What matters is what you want your life to be… her uncle's voice whispered inside her encouraging her to follow her heart.

Fifteen minutes later, Elle ran through the lobby, yanking her phone out. Good thing Braedon was on speed-dial. Her breath stuttered with each ring. The first, the second, and finally on the third they answered.

"Can you get my flight changed from Friday to today and instead of LAX to Buffalo? Or even Rochester? Hell, Syracuse. Just somewhere near home? I'll need a rental car, too," she blurted.

Phone pressed to her ear; Elle jogged briskly toward the bank of elevators. She pressed the *Up* button repeatedly.

She wouldn't call Clayton. This needed to be a face-to-face conversation. She was risking it all for the everything she wanted her life to be.

The display showed the elevator stuck on the fifteenth floor. *Come on! Work with me!*

"Is everything okay? There wasn't an emergency was there?" A spike of panic colored Braedon's tone.

"No, just something I really need to do. Can you help me? I'm almost to my room to pack up."

"Yeah, but are you sure? You have dinner with your friend Beth tonight. Maybe I could reschedule for the morning."

"Shit. Ugh…" Elle grumbled at the uncooperative elevator and Braedon's reminder. "…No. Beth will understand."

In fact, Beth might drive Elle to the airport cheering her on the whole way. It was Thursday and she wanted to walk up behind him at the VFW to surprise him, just as he'd done to her. It needed to be tonight. She had waited long enough.

"If you're sure…"

"Yes… Finally!" She groaned in relief as the elevator pinged open at the lobby.

"The elevator finally arrived?"

"Yeah." She slammed her finger against the button for her floor. "I may lose you."

"Yeah, so—"

As the doors shut, the line went silent. They could put people on the moon, have video chats with people in submarines, and invent hairspray that actually held all day but still no phone that would let you continue a call on an elevator.

Elle's fingers hit redial as the elevator reached the fifth floor, knowing the call would connect as soon as the doors slid open. Holding the phone close to her ear, she stepped onto the red and gold swirl carpet leading to her room, her feet suddenly immobilized as her eyes anchored to the large mirror hanging across from the bank of elevators decorated with a series of purple Post-Its spelling out a single word. *Hi.*

FORTY-FIVE

*"Where the heart is really attached, I know very well
how little one can be pleased with the attention
of anyone else."*
~Jane Austen, *Northanger Abbey*

Elle's heart thudded in her chest as she stood frozen in the elevator vestibule.

"Elle?" Braedon's voice cut in from the phone, the call finally connecting.

"Braedon…" Elle's hands trembled, her stare locked on the greeting made up of purple Post-Its. "…what did you do?" Hot tears fell from the corners of her eyes, blurring her vision.

"I take it that my delivery is there. I'm going to hang up now and not rebook your flight 'til you call me later. Also, I've cancelled all your meetings for the rest of the week and next week," they said smugly.

"Where is he?" She scanned the empty hall.

"Go to your room," they commanded.

"Thank you." she said, her voice a breathy whisper.

"You're welcome. Just remember who gave him your room number when you do my performance review. Well, unless this is a bad thing, then it was Deborah from HR and not me." They were still laughing as he disconnected.

"Everybody needs a Braedon." she said to the already quiet line, slipping her phone into her purse.

Inhaling deeply, hoping this wasn't a dream, that this was real, she turned the corner toward her room. A furry bullet barreled into her.

"Fitz!" she cried, falling to her knees in the middle of the hallway pressing her face against his, allowing a barrage of snorting yelps and wet kisses to greet her.

"He missed you." Clayton's deep voice wrapped around her like the coziest blanket.

Tilting her head up, she drank in his tall frame, leaning against her room door, a smile lighting his beloved face. With a final stroke of Fitz's coat, Elle bounded to her feet and ran to Clayton.

He caught her in his strong arms, possessing her mouth with a hungry passion.

"I missed him. I missed you," she gasped between kisses.

"I missed you." He clasped her face in his hands, his gray eyes studying her as if she wasn't quite real.

"I was just on the phone with Braedon to get me a flight home so I could see you. You know, a big romantic gesture. What are you doing here?" she said with tearful laughter, motioning to him.

"Big romantic gesture." He winked, a devilish grin on his lips.

"Clayton, I am so sorry. I never asked you what you wanted, and I broke my promise to you." She stepped back.

"Which promise?" he asked, closing the space between them that she had just created looping his arms around her waist.

"To talk to you before I made a decision for you and to say what I wanted. I made a decision for us that it was best we end because of something so trivial as where we live. That doesn't matter. That's logistics. We can figure it out. I should have asked you what you wanted and told you what I wanted. What do you want, Clayton?" Elle looked up at him with beseeching eyes.

"I want you, Elle Davidson. I love you. I think I've loved you since you called me an asshole at that school dance." He caressed her cheek. "I should have told you sooner. I told myself I was taking it slow for your benefit, but the truth is I was scared I'd lose you if I pushed too hard or moved too fast. I should have told you every day. When you left, I knew I had made a huge mistake letting you go. You didn't ask but I should have taken my own advice and told you what I wanted. I want you. Now and always, Elle. If that means Fitz and I move to Long Beach or wherever, all that matters is that my life is gray without you. You're the sun. You're the moon. You're my everything." He captured her with a slow almost reverent kiss.

"That's a good want." Elle grinned as they broke their kiss.

"What do you want?"

"So much."

"Be specific." His mischievous smile teased her.

"I want to be with you. I want you to read aloud to me every night in your bad British accent. I want Fitz to sleep on my feet. I want to adopt Lizzie because I think I'm supposed to be her human and Fitz needs a sibling. Plus, I don't want to be the only girl in the house. I want to redecorate the guest room because it needs more color." She laughed. "I want you to hold my hand when we fly on trips together. I want to cheer you on at VFW darts. I want weekly dinners with your parents and my family. I want to run with you. I want to be not normal with you. A lot." She nudged his hips suggestively.

"That's a lot of wants."

"There's lots more. I'm not nearly done with the things I want. *With you.* Above all I want you to know I love you, Clayton Owens. I love you so much. I love you. I love you." She raised to her tiptoes pressing kisses between each expression of her love for him.

He savored her mouth with his, Elle's body flush against his.

He lifted her in his strong arms and Elle's legs folded around him. Pressing her against the door, her fingers threading through his hair as they devoured each other. Whimpering moans escaped Elle as Clayton's tongue found hers and their middles rubbed together.

The sound of a throat clearing was the only thing that could have pulled them apart.

"There are rooms for things like this." An older man wearing a kind smile and pink cheeks said from in front of the door two down from Elle's.

"Sorry." Elle's face flamed, as Clayton gently set her on her feet.

Clayton smiled apologetically.

Swiping her keycard, Elle ushered Clayton and Fitz into her room. Following Clayton's wheeled suitcase, Elle shut the door and kicked off her shoes, running across the room leaping into Clayton's waiting arms. Resuming their kisses, lips finding one another, tongues tangling, hands caressing, and bodies coming together.

Effortlessly he carried her to the bed, lowering her onto the soft comforter. Like a prowling predator he crawled up the length of her body settling between her legs, taking her mouth again.

Goosebumps blossomed across her skin as Clayton's

nimble fingers unbuttoned her blouse. With less grace, she yanked his T-shirt over his head. Clayton trailed his mouth downward. Her back arched in pleasure as he nipped, sucked, and kissed her body. His hands sliding down her belly toward the button of her dress pants, unbuttoning them, and slipping his hands under the fabric, never breaking the seal between their lips.

She moaned as his lips left hers, then gasped as he nuzzled above the lace fabric of her panties.

"Clayton." She bucked into his touch.

"Elle." He almost purred her name, then stopped touching her, his jaw slack with disbelief. "Wait."

"What?" Her face puckered.

"VFW? Farmhouse? Are you moving to Perry? What about your job? I can't let you give up everything you're doing. Baby, I love you too much to let you sacrifice all you've worked for."

"Do you not want me to move to Perry?"

"I want you to do whatever you want. As long as it's with me. I just don't want you to give up anything. You've got me, I'm going wherever you go." He threaded his fingers through her hair, his eyes adoring and pleading.

"I'm giving up nothing. I'm getting everything. I was offered a promotion today and accepted with one condition. They let me work remotely three weeks a month. One week a month I'll fly back to Los Angeles. I'll stay with Viet or Willa. It lets me still have time with my people there and the rest of the month with my people back home. I get it all because I asked for what I want...because I chose me and I'm worth the risk." Pride and happiness swelled within her.

"And what you want is to come back to Perry?"

She caressed his cheek. "What I want is home and I finally found it...with you.."

He beamed. "And we know how sexy I find it when you

ask for what you want." The timbre of his voice was a low rumble.

She bit her lower lip.

Wickedness sparked in his eyes. "Tell me." He tugged her panties off before coasting kisses down her body.

"I want you to taste me until you have your fill."

"Impossible," he growled with a deep inhale of her sex.

"Oh…god…" she hissed with pleasure with the first flick of his tongue against her clit.

Every muscle in her body wound tighter as Clayton took her to the edge and back again. His slow licks, hard sucks, and teasing flicks ignited every nerve ending into raging bonfires until Elle thought she'd be consumed.

"Clayton!" Her legs seized around him.

He pressed his smirk against her trembling thigh. "That's my girl," he murmured, stroking his rough hands against her smooth skin.

"Inside me! Now!"

"Yes, ma'am," he drawled, straightening and taking off the remainder of his clothes.

Climbing back on to the bed, he prowled up her body with nipping kisses until he reached her mouth. The taste of her still on his lips as he took her mouth in a devouring kiss.

With a seductive smile, she pushed him onto his back and climbed on top, sinking onto his rigid length. The fullness ensconced her in a sensation of belonging. She to him. Him to her.

"I love you," she breathed.

He cupped her cheek. "I love you."

Gazes locked, Clayton's strong hands guided her hips in a deliciously slow movement on top of him. Their "not normal" behavior had never been *just sex.* There was a physical desire and need for each other, but it was so much more.

It had always been love, even before she admitted the words to herself and spoke them out loud.

They were a tangle of naked limbs as they lay, the cotton sheets twisted around them, talking. Elle told him everything she wanted to tell him since she'd left. His lips gently kissed away her cautiously relieved tears about her mom. Then they laughed at how she had two ambush-style grand gestures in one week. He told her he read the article about the ribbon cutting and the partnership announcement on the plane this morning. Elle wiggled happily as Clayton told her about the fourth veterinarian who would be joining the practice in December.

His fingers traced her starfish pendant as he told her about Liam coming to the clinic on Saturday and how Meghan got him a child-size lab coat with *Vet in Training* stitched on it.

"Jerome's been calling him 'fun size' Clayton." He grinned happily.

She teased him asking if Noah had intervened to push him to fly to Chicago and surprise her.

Winking he said, "Perhaps."

She grinned. Thankful for their friend.

"Oh, I brought something." He scooted out of bed, walking over to the large black suitcase in the corner.

Clayton tipped the case flat, unzipped, and dug around. Her face scrunched at how much he had packed. There were neat piles of clothes, a Ziplock bag with toys for Fitz, a plasticware container full of dog treats, a pair of running shoes, and a pair of dress shoes. When they went to Boston for the night, he'd only had a small overnight duffle.

"That's a big suitcase. When are you planning to fly back home?" she said perplexed.

"Well, I'm flying with you to Long Beach tomorrow and staying 'til next Sunday. Meghan and Jerome are covering for me." A boyish grin played on his face as he looked up at her, his hands blindly searching for whatever he was looking for.

That's why Braedon had canceled next week's meetings. Her big smile couldn't be contained.

"Found it." He straightened and turned back toward the bed. "We have a book to finish."

"Our book... Wait, didn't you have book club on Monday?"

"I didn't finish it." He lifted Fitz into Elle's arms. "It's our book. It didn't feel right finishing it without you."

The familiar flip of her belly and *thump-thump* of her heart hit simultaneously. Books are littered with stories of men that conquer lands, slay monsters, find treasure, build kingdoms, or discover new worlds, all for the women they love. Life is full of stories of men showing up with roses or jewelry to declare their love. All the fictional and the real stories were nothing compared to the knee-wobbling, swoon-inducing idea that Clayton, who adored books as much as Elle, wouldn't finish one because they had started it together and together, they would finish it.

"I love you." She sighed, feeling as if her heart may burst with how much love filled it for Clayton, and how much he had for her.

"I love you." He slipped in beside her, looping his left arm around her. "You ready?" It felt like he was asking less about the book and more about this journey they were embarking on, together. A life together.

"I'm ready."

EPILOGUE
TEN MONTHS (MANY BOOKS) LATER

"'til this moment I never knew myself."
~Jane Austen, *Pride and Prejudice*

They were the picture of Jane Austen fan girls as Clayton, in his navy *Pemberley* and Elle, in her purple *Obstinate Headstrong Girl* T-shirts walked through a row of Georgian houses in the city of Bath, England. Hands clasped they trotted along the cobblestone sidewalk approaching the Jane Austen Center.

At the Georgian-style house a man dressed like Mr. Bennet from *Pride and Prejudice* greeted them. "Good day, Sir and Madam." Mr. Bennet tipped his hat to them. "I believe Mrs. Bennet is expecting you inside."

"Thank you, sir." Elle curtsied, elbowing Clayton to bow.

They wandered through the Jane Austen Center looking at family portraits and artifacts and attended a lecture from Captain Wentworth about the Austen family history, which made Elle think of her mom. Captain Wentworth was her mom's dreamboat. Over the last ten months, they had made slow but healthy progress. In March, after several months of solo therapy, they started joint sessions with a therapist that Elle's had recommended. It wasn't a mother/daughter relationship, but it was something. They had joint sessions every two weeks, and on the off weeks they would have a lunch date. Much of the conversation was shallow at first but had started to deepen. Elle had even had Daniel and her mom to the farmhouse for dinner at the end of June.

After Captain Wentworth's lecture, they found themselves in a room in the bottom floor of the house with quill pens, ink, and paper sat atop Regency-era style writing desks. Visitors were encouraged to write notes, just as Jane Austen had. Elle pursed her lips dipping her quill in the black ink trying to write a note to Carmen on the slip of paper.

"This is really hard." Elle's brows wrinkled.

"That's what she said," Clayton chuckled.

"Ha!" She rolled her eyes. Clearly, he'd been hanging with Uncle Pete too much. "Seriously, how did she write so many novels with this?" She waved the quill over her head.

"Just takes practice," Clayton said, his voice steady and patient.

"That's what she said," she smirked, listening to his soft laugh. Ok, they'd both been spending too much time with Pete. "Look at this." She turned to face him holding up her chicken scratch that should read *Hi, Carmen!* but looked more like dueling zig-zag lines.

"You'll get it, baby." He turned his back toward her, facing his work on the desk.

Shrugging, she twisted and grabbed another piece of paper to try again.

"Ugh…maybe I'll scratch the framed letter idea. Thank god for computers, I could never write with these quills. I don't even like pens." She crumbled the paper and placed the quill back in the holder.

"Look at mine." Clayton said, slipping his piece of paper in front of her.

"Oh, I bet yours is…" Her mouth hung open in disbelief as her eyes locked on the smooth letters in black ink dancing across the slip of paper reading *Marry me.*

Grasping the paper Elle spun in her seat, almost falling off the wooden chair. Grabbing the back of the chair to steady herself, she straightened to see Clayton bent on one knee holding a purple velvet box.

She blinked. "Clayton?"

Marriage hadn't been discussed. Neither had *not* getting married. They had been together for almost a year, although, there was a bit of debate on that. Elle said it was since the day after the wedding when they had their first kiss, and Clayton said in his heart it was the day she lost that game of tug-of-war with the goat. They decided to claim both August 11 and August 19 as their days.

"Eleanor 'Elle' Davidson, I love you so much…" Clayton took her hand with his left hand keeping the box in his right. The tiny paw print tattoo on his forearm seemed to walk toward the ring-box and her. "…and I want to spend the rest of my life showing you how much I love you. Will you marry me?"

"Yes!" Elle squeaked, fat joyful tears rolling down her cheeks.

"Yes!" Clayton shouted as he jumped up, lifting her into his arms to the clapping and hoots of other patrons. "How did I get so lucky?" he asked, drinking her in before kissing her to even louder cheers from people in the room.

"I was just wondering that myself," Elle sighed as they broke their kiss.

"See girls, a man with a good fortune is always in want of a wife." The Mrs. Bennet look-a-like chimed in with a high-pitched British accent. The older woman stood observing

Clayton and Elle from a corner of the room with two women dressed in period outfits.

Elle glanced at them smiling from Clayton's arms. The entire room was watching them with happy faces, clicking cameras, and even an iPad videoing the scene.

"Do you want to see the ring." He set Elle back on her feet.

"Yes, please."

There was a tiny click as the box opened revealing a silver ring with an emerald cut purple ruby framed in tiny intricate clear sapphires in the shape of starfish. Elle didn't like diamonds, she never had. She loved that Clayton remembered that. The ring was gorgeous. It was unique. It was special.

"I had it designed for you. I'm not going to lie; Viet and Willa helped." He took the ring out of the box slipping it on to her finger. It fit perfectly. The stones glittered as the overhead light hit it.

"I love it." She kissed him. "And I love you."

"Let's see it!" Mrs. Bennett demanded as she approached Elle and Clayton, her younger companions in tow.

The famed overbearing mother was joined by look-a-likes of her sweet daughter Jane and the original romance heroine, Lizzie Bennet. The Bennet ladies stood around Elle cooing about the ring and her strapping young man, as they called him. After several congratulations from the staff and fellow Jane Austen enthusiasts, they walked up the narrow wooden stairs toward the tearoom, Elle jokingly grumbled that she couldn't believe Viet and Willa had kept this from her. Clayton followed behind with a chuckle.

"I'm going to have to give them a piece of—"

"*Surprise!*"

The boisterous greeting startled Elle as she walked into

the rose-wallpapered tearoom with its maze of white linen tables adorned with full tea service sets.

"Oh my god!" She cried, for the second time in twenty minutes, covering her face in shock.

The room was filled with her people, all her people, lifting cups of tea, ready to toast. Everyone in shades of purple. Viet and Noah beamed from the center of the room. Aunt Janet blew her nose loudly into a tissue. Standing next to her was Pete, his blue eyes glistening with happy tears. Ryan, Viet's husband, snapped pictures of Elle and Clayton as they took in the sight of all their loved ones in the room. Willa rocked her lilac earrings and a matching sundress as she leaned against Tobey and Jerome in matching dark purple polos.

An iPad in Jerome's hands with several familiar faces dialed in virtually for this moment including Summer and Liam, who were staying at the farmhouse watching Fitz and Lizzie while they were gone. Both dogs were licking a giggling Liam's face.

Todd flipped them thumbs up from the screen as he sipped a cup of coffee. Carmen and Mathew were center square, baby Fischer sleeping on his daddy's shoulder.

Braedon held a *Congrats Boss Lady* sign in their hands from the lower left corner of the screen.

Nat wore a bedazzled shirt that read *Elle + Clayton 4EVER* as she blew them kisses from the Little Red Barn, where she was now living since she'd returned home in May to join her father's practice.

Elle's mom mouthed *I love you*. Elle mouthed it back and meant it. They'd come so far.

The entire tearoom was just them and their people. Clayton's parents stood by one another. Chris rocked a lavender bow tie along with a giant grin as he looked at his son and future daughter-in-law. Heidi sniffled next to him, dabbing her eyes with a cloth napkin.

"I can't believe you're here," Elle gaped.

"Oh, honey we love you two so much." Heidi gushed, tugging Elle close. "Thank you for choosing my son. He needs a strong woman like you."

"Oh, Heidi."

"Ok. Now I'm going to blubber to my son." She laughed before kissing Elle's forehead and letting go.

"I'm happy to get another daughter." Chris enveloped Elle, his bow tie brushing against her head as they embraced.

"Dad, you should get mom; she's a mess." Clayton warned placing a hand on his dad's shoulder. They turned to a sobbing and cackling Heidi who was being soothed by Noah.

"Oh dear." Chris' jaw went slack.

"I don't know if I should ask this, but was she like this the last time you got engaged?" Elle tipped her head and considered Heidi.

"Nope." The father and son said in unison.

"She liked Marianne. She was a nice girl. We both did, but she wasn't you. She wasn't our daughter." Chris said, his blue eyes warm with affection before he shuffled to his wife.

"He's right, you know? I know I've been married before, but this is different. With you it all feels like the first time." Clayton placed a hand on her cheek. "I think it's because it was always meant to be you."

"It's always meant to be us," she said, their eyes tethering as the voices in the room faded away leaving just them in their bubble. The twists and turns of her life leading her here to this moment with this man and these people.

"I always knew we'd end up here," Noah said, sauntering up with a gold rim teacup in hand.

Elle pressed a thankful peck to Noah's cheek. "Thank

you." Long before they'd known there was the possibility of an "Elle and Clayton," Noah had championed them.

Clayton hugged Noah in that trademark masculine back slapping hug. "You know this means your mom is going to harass you more about finding someone," Clayton chuckled.

Noah winced.

Elle and Clayton laughed.

"I am so happy." Janet barreled into Elle like a tiny bullet train, her vise-like arms pulling Elle in.

"Me too." Elle sighed, hugging her aunt back.

"Mom, let her go. It's our turn. Go hug Clayton," Tobey prodded. After one last squeeze, Janet let go and Tobey and Jerome swooped in to hug Elle.

"You know they're going to do a choreographed dance at your wedding, right?" Tobey rolled his eyes before kissing Elle's damp cheek.

Her laugh was watery. "I'm glad I'll have you to help me wrangle them." She ruffled his hair.

"Group hug!" Jerome boomed wrapping his arms around his husband and Elle.

"Bear, you're smothering us," Tobey grumbled, half-annoyed but a hundred percent enamored with his husband.

Escaping Jerome's embrace, she ran over to Viet and Willa nearly knocking them down to hug them giddily. Despite moving back home, Elle hadn't lost her closeness with them. The one week each month she was in town she'd stay with Viet and, sometimes, with Willa. They'd have happy hour, Thai Tuesday dinners, and brunch on the weekend.

Elle walked through the room of happy people toward Uncle Pete.

"Hey kiddo." His voice cracked.

"Hey." She stood in front of him. "So, I'm getting married."

"That you are." He nodded at her and then looked across the room where Clayton with a bemused look on his face stood talking to Noah, Willa, and Janet.

"Will you walk me down the aisle when I do?" Elle gazed hopefully at her uncle.

The tears in his glossy eyes overflowed as he looked at her. "Of course." He held her tight, and she held him back even tighter. "If I have to be replaced as the number one man in your life, I can't imagine a better man to be replaced by."

"There's no replacing you, you're my favorite uncle."

"I'm your only uncle." he said, his voice hoarse with emotion.

"My one and only." she inhaled him, taking in the love at this moment. "I love you, Pete."

"I love you, kiddo."

From the first day she was in this world, he had been there. In all the big and little moments of her life, he was there in some shape or form. He was hers and she was his. That's how it had always been and would always be. He wouldn't be Uncle Pete without Elle, and she wouldn't be Elle without her Uncle Pete.

"Ok, enough of this mushy stuff. I'm going to eat a scone." He cleared his throat and kissed her temple. "You got our girl."

Elle turned, following the flick of Pete's eyes toward an approaching Clayton.

"Always." Clayton assured as he reached her side.

"I know you do." Pete placed a hand on Clayton and then yanked him close for a tight hug. "You've been family, but now it's official. Although, if you break her heart, I will get Lt. Scout to help me bury you in the backyard."

"Noted." Clayton chuckled under his breath.

"Elle…" Pete pivoted looking over his shoulder at Elle. "…same goes for you. Don't break his heart."

"I won't." She loved that Pete felt as protective of Clayton as he did of her. The two men had gotten close since Elle moved home. So often she'd find them playing cards at the dining room table of the farmhouse or working on home improvement projects together.

"How are you doing?" Clayton asked, coiling his arms around her waist.

"Blissfully happy." She leaned her head back against his upper chest looking up at him.

"We're getting married." he said almost in shock. "You're going to be my wife."

"You're going to be my husband."

"We're going to have to change the sign I made for your office." When she moved in, he had a sign made for the door to his former study, now her office, that read *Elle Davidson, Sloan-Whitney East Office.* He'd had the words engraved on a smooth oak plaque then hung the sign over the center of the door.

"Changed to what?" she asked, a quizzical smile dancing on her lips.

"Elle Owens."

"I don't think I want to change my name. I love Elle Davidson," she said letting her words wash over her like the first refreshing burst of hot water. With the help of therapy, she'd come to love who she was. Elle Davidson was still and would always be a work in progress, but she could love who she had been, who she was and who she was becoming on her journey. She loved herself. She was worth the risk, after all.

"I get it. Elle Davidson is kind of fantastic." He nuzzled her neck. "As long as you're my Elle Davidson." He spun her around to face him.

"Always." She raised to her tiptoes and wrapped her arms around his nape.

"I love you, Mrs. Darcy." He leaned in close, his lips inches from hers.

"I love you, Mr. Darcy." She closed the inches between them.

It wasn't the end. It was the beginning…

Want to spend more time in Perry with Nat and Noah as their romance blossoms? Turn the page for a sneak peek of their story, *Coming Home* coming in January 2025…

Chapter One

"I want to do something splendid…something heroic and wonderful that won't be forgotten after I'm dead." ~Louisa May Alcott, *Little Women*

Nat Owen's jaw clenched as she worked to ignore the sour expression on Mrs. Lewis' face. *Don't give the octogenarian the stink eye.* "Your symptoms are consistent with a sinus infection, but—"

With pursed lips, Mrs. Lewis interrupted, "Is Dr. Owens coming in dear?"

The corners of Nat's lips straightened into a firm line. "I am Dr. Owens."

"Yes dear, but the *real* one. Your father," she said with a saccharine smile and dismissive flick of her wrist.

Do no harm, even to sexist old ladies. Well, especially to them. Tapping on her tablet to give herself time to drop into the Zen zone, Nat continued, "We'll have the nurse take a throat culture to rule out strep throat and I'll prescribe some antibiotics."

"I'd like to have Dr. Owens see me, dear."

Never had Nat experienced such a blood-boiling urge to say, "Bitch, please!" and flash her medical license proclaiming *Natalie J. Owens, Medical Doctor*. Eyes darting to the exam room door in surrender, she broadened her smile, even though it felt as if she were tightening an already too-tight sneaker. "Certainly. I'll see if he can step in."

Stepping out of the room, she controlled the force in her arm dying to slam the door, quietly eased it closed then leaned against it, closing her eyes. The door's reassuring stiffness soaked into her spine. "I am Dr. Owens. I am Dr. Owens," she murmured to herself.

It hadn't been like this in Boston during her residency. Not entirely. At first, there were a few people who saw her petite stature as *less than*. Distracted by her assortment of bedazzled, patterned, and bright-colored shoes, they soon learned underestimating Nat Owens was a big mistake. *Huge! Godzilla-sized!* It was as huge of a mistake as that summer she'd cut her own bangs. Yet, a few weeks into her residency, she became the go-to internal medicine resident assisting with big cases and presenting during grand rounds.

In Boston, she only needed to overcome a first impression. In the tiny hamlet of Perry, NY, there was a lifetime of impressions, a lifetime of being the youngest daughter of the popular Dr. Chris Owens.

For nearly one-hundred-years, there had been a Dr. Owens caring for the residents of the sleepy village, tucked between corn fields and cow pastures. A common trait shared by each former Dr. Owens was that they had all been the eldest son. Not the youngest daughter. That's how it had been since Nat's great grandfather, Jacob Owens, had first established the clinic in 1925. His eldest son, her grandpa, took over, and then her dad. With two older brothers, Clayton and Evan, it was never meant to be her.

I'm not who these patients think should be here. Still fuming, she found her dad and asked him to stop in to see Mrs. Lewis. Then she sought sanctuary in her office.

More of an alcove than an office, though. The space opposite the exam rooms was generally reserved for interns or residents from the medical school in Buffalo. She plopped into the swivel chair. It wasn't a fancy office like her dad's with its wall of windows and leather chairs. With its glittery framed photos, knickknacks, and an assortment of squishy stress balls shaped like animals, it was her refuge from the Mrs. Lewis-types of the world.

"Thank you, Dr. Owens. I'll stop by the pharmacy on my way home to pick up the antibiotics. When will the results of the throat culture come in?" Mrs. Lewis' voice drifted into Nat's open office door.

Seriously? Frustration sighed through Nat. She swiveled in her chair, listening to Mrs. Lewis and her father's softening voices as they shuffled down the hall to the clinic's reception area. Picking up a squishy hot pink pig-shaped stress ball, she clenched it. *I am Dr. Owens. I am Dr. Owens.*

A few minutes later, a throat cleared, pulling her attention to the open doorway where Dad stood. "Dr. Owens." Happy crinkles kissed the edges of his blue eyes.

"Dr. Owens," she said, lips quirked in a small smile.

Dad never ceased to be amused with having two Dr. Owens in the clinic. Even if some days he seemed to be the only person who remembered that she was a Summa Cum Laude graduate from medical school. He'd chuckle saying, "Dr. Owens" as he greeted her in the morning or asked, "Which one?" when staff said, "Dr. Owens."

Nat wondered if the amusement was pride in working

alongside one of his children or astonishment at it being her. The memory of his blank expression when she announced she was declaring pre-med at Boston College, often made her wonder. There were so many "Are you sures?" uttered, that just for a moment she questioned it herself. She had been sure and for the last ten years, she navigated her charted path to arrive here. She just never counted on feeling like the unwelcomed third cousin at the party.

A smile stretched across his face. "You were spot on with Mrs. Lewis' assessment."

"Thanks," she muttered.

He always gave these verbal pats on the back. It was like being a little girl with a not-yet-dry fingerpainting that he placed on the fridge, proudly proclaiming that she was the next Picasso.

"Dad—"

He raised his hand, halting her words. "Honey, it will take time. The patients are just used to me. Soon, they'll tire of the rusty Dr. Owens and want the shiny new one," he assured in a soft and encouraging tone.

"Both my Dr. Owens." Mom's gray eyes twinkled as she stepped beside Dad and pressed a peck on his cheek. "Hello, handsome."

Pink bloomed on his cheek.

The exchange both swelled Nat's heart at the effortless affection between them and churned her stomach. They were her parents after all. The idea of them still gettin' busy after forty years of marriage horrified her. Even if it was something she secretly hoped for herself.

"Boss." He winked and lifted a flirtatious brow at his wife.

"Don't you forget it." Mom wiggled her hips and adjusted his bow tie dotted with tiny yellow teacups.

"Gross! I'd go to HR about the two of you, but since

Mom is HR, there's no point," Nat groaned, watching the pink escalate to crimson across his face.

Who knew bow ties were a turn-on? Mom seemed to enjoy them. Ugh.

No wonder her dad had an army of fun bow ties. The teacup bow tie had been a gift from Elle Davidson, Clayton's fiancé.

"Oh, hush Natalie Joan," Mom chided with a grin. She turned to her husband. "Are you going to wear this bow tie to Clayton and Elle's engagement party tonight?"

"It might be a little fancy for a brewery," Nat offered.

The Farmer's Ale, a local brewery owned by Todd Krueger and her brother's best friend, Noah Wilson, would host the happy couple's engagement party. Since opening in May, it had become one of the hot spots in the village. Granted, there were only four other "hot spots" opened past eight, including the VFW, the Sea Serpent Restaurant and Lounge, and the Wine Down, but she'd argue the new pub rivaled any hip brewery in Boston. Even if she was a little biased.

"Oh, I have a *special* bow tie for tonight." Dad's eyes filled with mirth.

"Oh?" Mom purred, waggling her eyebrows.

"Seriously. I'm going to need a therapist to wipe away *this* image of the two of you from my psyche." Her face scrunched up as she gestured to her parents.

"Don't be dramatic." Mom waved her hands. "Anywho, Mrs. Jarvis is here. LeAnne is weighing her and will put her in exam room two."

"Thanks." Nat picked up her tablet and stood. The pregnant mother of three was her next patient.

With a sorrowful wince, Mom held her hands up. "Sorry, sweetie. She'd prefer to see your dad. He was her doctor with her other pregnancies and she's…just more comfortable with him."

Sinking back to her seat, Nat forced her lips upward. "Totally get it."

"It will take time, honey. Change is difficult. It's slow, but it always happens," he said, placing an encouraging hand on her shoulder before turning to leave.

I am Dr. Owens. I am Dr. Owens.

If she repeated that mantra, maybe it would come true, vanquishing the fear that in Perry, she may always be Dr. Owens's daughter and not *the* actual Dr. Owens.

Subscribe to Melissa's newsletter for important release information: www.melissawhitneywrites.com
And keep turning the page for a look at her exciting next release, *At First Smile*

In the Hello and In The Goodbye, a second chance romance that proves love can span time and distance.

SNEAK PEEK- AT FIRST SMILE

Chapter One

Cane Austen and Me

Pen

"Mommy, what's she doing?" The small chirping voice draws my attention.

I can't help but make the comparison between this small question and my mother's typical question of "Have you met someone yet?" But I know I am not the aforementioned "mommy". Still, my head tilts toward the tiny human anyways. There's something in the shock and awe in their voice telling me there is a small finger pointing at me.

"It's her stick—"

It's a cane. I don't correct the wrong terminology. Instead, I tighten my smile and tap my cane ahead of me as I stroll down the not-yet-fully awake Buffalo-Niagara Airport terminal.

"It helps her see."

Ah, if only it were that magical. It's barely seven a.m. After spending a week at home with my mother and husband number four –no wait five— I lack the temperamental bandwidth to explain to this woman and her child the intricacies of being legally blind. It's a cane. It doesn't help me see, but rather a tool allowing me to use nonvisual cues to get from point A to point T. Right now, the point T I'm destined for is the Tim Hortons tucked into the airport's food court.

Aunt Bea always said I was a shining light illuminating the darkness in the world's understanding of what it means to be blind. It's why I've dedicated so much of the last ten years to educating people through my social media page, Cane Austen and Me. To my ten-thousand followers I'm the "It" blind girl, documenting my every day and big adventures with Cane Austen, my white cane, helping the non-visually impaired world's knowledge be just a little less obscured about vision loss.

The knowledge that I'm longer Aunt Bea's little light aches deep in my heart. I can almost feel her plump arms folded around me as she cooed, "Pen, you'll help them understand." No matter how tired I was, she'd have expected me to stop. Explain how the cane works. Tell the child that not all blind people can't see. Set his mommy dearest straight on the blind people facts, helping their little human grow up without misinformation and ensuring that other little humans – ones like me with failing vision – don't repeat the storyline I'd faced as I grew up.

Clear their vision, Aunt Bea's sing-song words dance in my heart.

Sighing, I pivot on my strappy, wedge sandals and head toward the sound of the mother and child. A little boy sits, feet kicking, beside a woman, her long hair gathered into a messy bun, at a half-full gate.

"Hi. I'm Pen." My free hand gathers my long auburn hair, brushing it onto my right shoulder. The action soothes the pulse of anxiety. No matter how many times I do this, it's still awkward as fuck. Good thing I love you, Aunt Bea.

The little boy tips his head to his mom, whose forehead puckers in confusion.

Yep, I'm weirding them out. Frankly, I don't blame them. Most people don't have a lot of interactions with the legally blind. Let alone one who walks up to them and introduces themselves. Thanks to Aunt Bea, that is exactly who I am. Even if there are days – like today – where I wish I wasn't. Where I'd rather fade into the crowd, unseen and forgotten.

"I heard you asking questions about my cane," I say, lacing as much sugar into my words without sending anyone into a diabetic coma. "This is Cane Austen. I'm legally blind and I use her, so I don't trip or fall. Also, tapping [GB1] it makes noises that helps me figure out where I'm at."

"Are all canes girls?" The little boy's face twists into a pout.

A genuine smile spreads across my face. "Not all, but this one is."

"Why did you name it Cane Austen?" The woman's eyebrows knit.

"So she'll help me find my Mr. Darcy," I quip, making the woman snort with laughter.

It was the same reaction Aunt Bea had. This is my tenth Cane Austen. I've had a new one every year since I was sixteen. While everyone else was getting their first car, I was getting my first cane. The eye condition I have, retinitis pigmentosa, progressed to the point that a cane is necessary to keep me safe. I'd been diagnosed at age six, so I knew my vision was fading to black at a glacial pace…slow but unstoppable. Knowledge didn't lessen the painful realization that while classmates were getting their licenses and cars, I was facing just another way in which I wasn't like them.

Not allowing me to wallow, Aunt Bea presented me with my first white cane. Blindfolding me – which she found hilarious – she dragged me into the driveway where she gifted me a white cane tied up with a giant red bow. She'd even put a Porsche sticker on it, winking as she affirmed that her niece would travel in style. "You gotta name this bad bitch," she'd crooned, explaining that the cane was my car, and everyone named their vehicles.

The little boy worries his lower lip, as If considering his words. "What does 'legally blind' mean?"

What, indeed? To the world blind means you can't see, but unsuspecting civilians didn't realize that blindness is served on a spectrum. The majority of legally blind people are like me, with some usable vision. There's a whole medical explanation that Trina, my ophthalmologist bestie, would bore people with at parties. I keep it simple, saying I have enough vision to get myself in trouble but not enough to always get myself out of it. Which is why I avoid trouble. As adventurous as Aunt Bea raised me to be, I don't take uncalculated risks.

After finishing my impromptu blindness in-service, I leave the smiling mother/son pair and redirect myself toward Tim Hortons. My flight to LAX doesn't board for another hour, so I have ample time to secure my sought after spoils [GB2] and make it to the gate to lose myself in my steamy romance audiobook. There's something delightful about listening to the swoony and sometimes illicit words of a favorite hot guy voiced by a male narrator in public places. The idea of exposure makes the risk so much more rewarding. Whoever ends up sitting next to me on my flight home would, no doubt, turn a violent shade of red if they only knew what I was listening to.

Grinning, I tap my cane as I stroll toward Tim Hortons. Bless the airport gods! I fight the urge to wiggle my hips, spotting only one other person in front of me. The sweet ecstasy of a multigrain breakfast sandwich and apple cinnamon tea is within my grasp. Besides seeing Trina, Tim

Hortons was the only thing bringing me joy on this trip back to Buffalo. After moving to Seal Beach, California with Aunt Bea at seventeen, this world renown coffee shop was the only thing I missed. That includes my mother, already on husband number two, and who'd had no problem letting her teenaged daughter move cross country without her.

Whenever Aunt Bea and I went home, the first thing we'd do was hit Tim Hortons. Each Christmas, Mom sent us an assortment of teas, coffee, and hot chocolate from the retailer. Even this last Christmas. Though there's no longer a coffee drinker in the house.

I swallow the growing lump in my throat. Adjusting the large weekender bag on my shoulder, I force my focus to the back of the head in front of me. Only, in order for my gaze to actually land on the back of the man's head requires craning my neck. How tall is he? I'm five eight, but he's a giant.

"The card machine isn't working," the peppy cashier says to the tall man.

"Oh." His large hand slips to his pocket.

No doubt the action is to grab the wallet bulging from his back pocket and not to call attention to the way the faded jeans hug his firm backside. One that Trina would joke that she could bounce a quarter off. Although, I could think of far more pleasurable things to do with that ass.

Stop checking out his butt! Pushing my red-frame glasses atop my head, I twist my now extra foggy vision away from the tall man's cute butt. I mean, how would I feel if he was ogling me like I was the last cupcake?

That might be a nice change. It's been a minute since someone looked at me with the same kind of covetous gaze that I'd used when looking at baked goods after that ill-begotten month I tried to give up carbs. Life's too short to not eat a cookie or ten.

"Shit!" he grumbles, closing his wallet. "You don't accept Canadian money, [GB3] do you?" The little hitch of hope in his question is adorable, reminiscent of a child wishing there'd still be dessert even after not finishing their vegetables.

"Sorry." The frown is audible in the cashier's apology.

"Is there an ATM around?"

My cheeks flush with second-hand embarrassment for him. Few people carry cash on them. I wasn't one of them. My always prepared motto meant I never left home without cash. No matter what country I found myself in, my wallet remained stocked.

The cashier taps the counter. "I think there's one down by gate twelve."

"Thanks. I'll run down and come back," he says, slipping his wallet into his back pocket.

Poor guy. My lips drag into a pout. Traveling is frustrating enough but to toss in an unnecessary trip across the airport terminal is obnoxious. Plus, if all he has is Canadian money it likely means he traveled from Canada. I could hear Aunt Bea's sweet voice chiding me to always be neighborly. Well, Canada is our neighbor to the north.

"No need, I got this," I offer, pulling my glasses back down. "I have cash."

"No, it's—" His words halt as he spins to face me. Beneath the brim of a blue cap, a smile curls his lips. Its brightness is accentuated by his tidy dark beard.

A sudden swoop seizes my stomach, causing an explosion of butterflies. That's new. Am I into men with beards?

A navy Henley molds to his muscular frame. A fresh woodsy scent wafts from him, eliciting scenes of a pre-dawn walk through a dew-kissed forest. His entire aesthetic screams sexy lumberjack. Like someone who would press you against a tree, its rough bark biting into your bare ass, while even rougher hands held you in place.

Good lord, perhaps I need to cut down on my dirty audiobooks.

"That's kind of you, but I have cash. It's just Canadian… or in the bank." A gentle, barely-noticeable Irish lilt mingles with his low gruff timbre.

I love the way unique voices tingle along my nerves. Perhaps my dulled vision heightens the way I hear the world, but I revel in the musicality of voices, picking out the unique notes that make each one distinct.

"Those pesky banks holding our cash hostage," I joke. My smile lifts, just a little bit more, with his soft chuckle. "It's really no big deal."

"Are you sure?"

"This will give me at least five karma points for the day." I step up to the counter, joining him there.

"Are you in need of karma points?"

"Well, I did send my mother to voicemail this morning." Three times. But he doesn't need to know that.

This trip I lasted four of the five days I'd planned to stay at my mother's house, a new record, before I sought refuge. On day four, I retreated to Trina's, feigning that she had more reliable Wifi for me to work from than the farmhouse my mother lives in with Charlie, her latest husband.

He grins. "I wouldn't want to get in the way of you reaching Nirvana."

"Thanks." I brush my long hair behind my ear, facing the cashier. "Can I get a large apple cinnamon tea and bacon, egg, and cheese breakfast sandwich on a multigrain bagel."

The cashier shakes their head, a big laugh bursting. "That's two apple cinnamon teas and bacon, egg, and cheese breakfast sandwiches on a multigrain bagel."

An eyebrow arched, I face the tall man. "Tea?"

He wags a finger. "That judgy eyebrow may cost you some of your karma points."

I gesture at him. "You just don't seem the tea type."

"What type do I seem?"

I frown and cock one hip. "Like 'drinks gasoline while eating a burger made out of the grizzly bear he just killed with his bare hands' type."

"That's preposterous," he scoffs. "Everyone knows black bears make better burgers."

"I stand corrected." I laugh, pulling out my wallet.

After paying for our food, we slide down the counter. Drinks in hand, we stand waiting for our breakfast sandwiches. Other customers file up to the counter, while we remain in silence. Not uncomfortable or awkward silence, just companionable. Sipping my sweet, spicy tea, my eyes flick between the staff preparing our food and the sexy lumberjack beside me.

I play the game we all play when meeting someone. Using the little external clues to put together a picture of who he is. His clothes are comfortable and well-worn, but clean. One hand grips the to-go cup, while the other brushes the back of his head as if he's nervous.

Do I make him nervous? No, that can't be. Men like him make people nervous, not the other way around.

Gnawing on my lower lip, I try to think of the last man I made nervous. Besides Cael, Trina's fiancé who was terrified that her oldest and closest friend wouldn't give him the stamp of approval, the last man with a wisp of nerves around me may have been Alex. Ugh, Alex.

"Pen," I burst out.

His head tips to the right. "Pencil?"

Laughter bubbles out of me. "My name is Pen. Well, it's actually Penelope Meadows, but my friends call me Pen."

He grins. "Rowan."

Of course, his name is Rowan. That name radiates big D hot guy energy. Not a Herman or Stanley vibe about him.

"Nice to meet you, Pen." His hand envelops mine, sending a jolt of something zipping along my nerves.

I try not to fixate on that little tingle but have to admit failure. When was the last time my body reacted to someone?

"So, are you coming or going?"

Seriously? Coming or going? Who am I? I school my features into a pleasant smile stamping out the blooming wince at my non-stellar verbal skills.

"Excuse me?"

"Are you coming into town or leaving?"

"Both."

"Overachiever," I tease, twisting towards him, my arm brushes against his. My senses hum with the quick caress of his muscular body against mine. "So, where you heading to?"

"L.A."

"Me too!" I say with far too much pep.

What is wrong with me? I'm like an overexcited puppy. I should be cool and indifferent, not exclaim with the fevered devotion of two ten-year-olds exchanging friendship bracelets on the first day of camp.

"Well, not L.A. I don't live there. I live in Seal Beach, but LAX is a direct flight getting me the hell out of here sooner."

Why am I sputtering? Awkward, party of one. What the actual fuck is happening? I'd love to blame the sexiness radiating off this man, but in truth it's having spent any length of time with my mother. A few days in her presence and I lose the ability to function like the very capable twenty-six-year-old that I am.

"Not a fan of Buffalo?" He shifts, turning to face me.

"I have nothing against Buffalo as a city. People are nice. Love the wings. It's just…"

Stop talking, Pen! Do not emotionally vomit on this poor man. All he wanted was breakfast, not to have you overshare.

"…just prefer being home." I tighten my hold on Cane Austen's handle.

"Buffalo's not home?"

"Not anymore." I shake my head.

Rowan's hat brim shadows the upper half of his face, making it hard to read his expression. Reading facial expressions isn't my forte. Even with the limited vision I do have, it's often difficult to make out the tiny cues that can be found in someone's face. Aunt Bea always talked about the stories in the eyes. Those are stories I'm unable to read. If I'm close enough and the light is just right, I can make out some of the little eyebrow ticks, lip quirks, or forehead wrinkles.

My stories come from the voice and energy. Everyone has a kind of energy they exude. It may make me sound like the lady with a different crystal for each day of the week, but it's something I've learned to trust.

Right now, the energy coming off Rowan telegraphs annoyance, but I don't think it's directed at me. Despite my oversharing, his broad frame remains mere inches away. His obscured gaze fixed on me.

Clearing his throat, he nods. "I get it. I drove in from Hamilton. I grew up near there. I've only lived in L.A. for three years and it feels more like home than my hometown."

"That explains the Canadian currency." Smirking, I raise my tea to my lips. "So, how did a nice Canadian lad end up in L.A.?"

His hand rubs his neck. "Work."

"So, what do you do for wo—"

"Christ," he groans, yanking out his cell from his back pocket. "Sorry, this is the fourth call in a row that I've ignored. I need to take this."

"Sure." I smile.

Holding the phone up, he grumbles, "This best be important." Pivoting, he strides away from the counter.

"Ma'am." The cashier holds up two bags with what I suspect are our breakfast sandwiches.

Thanking the barista, I take them. In literally five seconds, I've lost Rowan. Scanning the now bustling food court, he's disappeared into the crowd. Do I wait? Do I try to track him down? Do I just take his sandwich in hopes that I run into him again? What if he comes back and thinks I stole his sandwich? Although, I paid for it, so it's not stealing.

"Excuse me, do you see that man I was with?" I ask the cashier.

"He went over there." She points.

"Where? Can you verbally explain?" I hold up Cane Austen in a nonverbal reminder that pointing is not the best form of direction giving for the visually impaired.

"Oh, sorry." The blush can be heard in her voice. "Far right corner... My right, not yours."

"Thanks."

Turning, I set off listening for his voice. Moving through the crowd, I make my way toward the far-right corner. Voice recognition is the best way for me to find people in large gatherings. Although, it's not ideal with someone I just met, but there's something about Rowan's voice that has imprinted on me, both distinct yet familiar. Like nothing I've heard before but somehow something as well-known to me as my own.

"Damnit, I told you I don't want to do that." Rowan growls.

I halt. Not because I've found him, but due to the frustration underscoring his words. He's pissed.

"This is fucking bullshit."

Really pissed.

With his back to me, he carries on in an annoyed mutter

with no idea I'm standing behind him, eavesdropping. It's not intentional, but I'm listening, nonetheless. Granted, my relationship with Rowan is five minutes old, but this anger reads wrong on him. Like an ill-fitting Halloween costume. Also, I'm not going to overthink my use of the word "relationship".

Raking my teeth against my lower lip, I clutch the sandwich bag. I should turn, run away, and give the sandwich back to the cashier. Let them give it to the angry man. Not because I'm scared. There's no nip of fear telling me to stay away. Rather, it's more like witnessing someone do something they don't want to do.

"You're being a real motherfucker," he snarls, causing a few onlookers to clear their throats.

Ouch. I don't blame them. His tone is harsh.

Dropping his duffle by his feet, Rowan's rigid stance slumps. His free hand grips the back of his neck, knuckles white as he digs in his fingers. The movement telegraphs regret.

"I'm sorry. That was uncalled for." Scuffing his sneakers along the floor, he lets out a beleaguered sigh. "I know. You're my motherfucker."

Aw. It's almost sweet the way it rolls off his tongue.

"We can discuss this when I get back. My flight gets in…" Pivoting, he comes face-to-face with me, mouth gapping. "Pen." It comes out almost pained.

Crap! "I wasn't listening…well I was, but not intentionally. I—" I hoist up the Tim Hortons bag. "Breakfast!"

"Thanks," he says, drawing out the word and taking the offered bag.

"Sorry."

The muffled voice of whoever is on the other end of the call crackles between us.

"I should go." Frowning, I turn and hurry away.

So fricking embarrassing. Rowan is clearly having a day and I'm all like "Here I am holding your breakfast sandwich hostage while eavesdropping on your conversation with someone you fondly refer to as motherfucker."

Finding my gate, I fold myself into an uncomfortable plastic chair to devour my breakfast sandwich and fall into my latest audiobook. The sultry timbre of Wesley Williamson – my favorite narrator – helps me escape into the world of thousand-year-old hot vampires with Mr. Darcy vibes. The story being weaves helps me leave the last week behind. Letting go of why I came back to Buffalo, the tension with my mother, and the awkward meet/cute with Rowan.

Rowan. My stomach flip-flops between a sigh and a flutter at the thought of him. I hope everything turns out okay with he and motherfucker. It seemed to have turned the corner before he'd caught me listening in. I scan the boarding area, wondering if he's here. He's not. At least, I don't see him which doesn't mean he's not here. He's bound for L.A. Are we on the same flight? The Buffalo-Niagara Airport is small, but not that small. There are several airlines flying direct to Los Angeles in this time window.

"Penelope Meadows, please see the agent at gate eleven's counter." A voice crackles over the sound system, interrupting the vampire/awkward girl meet cute.

Hitting pause, I sling my bag over my shoulder and shuffle with Cane Austen to the counter. "I'm Penelope," I say, reaching the agent.

"Ms. Meadows." The agent beams. "Your seat has been upgraded. I have a new boarding pass for you."

"Upgraded?" I blink.

"You're still in a window seat, but you've been moved to first class. Seat one-A. We'll start pre-boarding in a few minutes for our passengers with disabilities. Would you like assistance going down the jetway?"

First class from Buffalo to Los Angeles? Perhaps I had earned some karma points after all. Thanking the agent and telling them I wouldn't need assistance, I head back to my seat.

Pulling my phone from my pocket, I shoot a quick text to JoJo, my West Coast bestie. Trina is insistent that I'm allowed two best friends if I designate them by coasts. Trina Lyons, who is two years older than me, was my first bestie due to forced proximity. She lived next door until I moved with Aunt Bea to California. I met JoJo Rivers a year later as freshmen in undergrad.

Pen: Flight is on time. You still picking me up at the airport?

JoJo: Does a hobby horse have a hickory dick?

Pen: A simple yes would do.

JoJo: Then I wouldn't be me. Tongue out emoji.

I snort just a bit. Even with the magnification program on my cell, I have the worst time with GIFs and emojis, so JoJo spells them out for me. It's both sweet and totally self-serving because I'm a hundred percent positive that a majority of the GIFs and emojis that she spells out do not exist.

JoJo: How are you doing, BTW?

God, that's a loaded question. My heart aches just thinking about the many, many responses rattling around in me. How does one respond when their entire world as they know it has been ripped away in a single moment?

Pen: Okay.

JoJo: Acceptance smiley face when your friend is pretending they are okay when their not emoji.

Pen: Middle finger emoji.

JoJo: Gasp emoji.

Pen: These aren't real emojis emoji.

JoJo: I love you emoji.

Pen: I love you too emoji. We'll have all the LAX to Orange County traffic to dig into how I'm doing. I promise.

JoJo: Excited social worker friend emoji.

Hearing them announce pre-boarding, I text goodbye to JoJo and slip my phone into the pocket of my denim jacket. The late June weather is warm, allowing me to pull on my favorite pale pink cotton sundress, but the jacket will keep me warm on the plane.

I won't pretend that excitement doesn't crisscross inside me at turning left while boarding the plane. The first-class lifestyle isn't something I've indulged in. Outside of that all-inclusive resort Aunt Bea took me to in celebration of my Master's degree. As first-class as I typically get is getting to skip the wait at Bread, my favorite breakfast spot in downtown Seal Beach, because Aunt Bea and I've gone their every Saturday for the last nine years. Almost every Saturday.

Ignoring the twinge in my heart, I follow the flight attendant to my seat in the front row, which means more leg room. It also means all my things have to go up top. Pulling out the things I'll want quick access to – bottled water, bag of trail mix, phone, and earbuds – I toss my oversized weekender bag into the overhead bin and plop into my seat.

Head pressed against the window, I lose myself in my audiobook which drowns out the flight's boarding sound-track – murmured apologies, cleared throats, and muttered words, "I think that's my seat", and the repeated chastising of a passenger for blocking the aisle.

Someone takes the seat beside me. The furnace of their body laps against my skin. A fresh woodsy scent makes my eyelids flutter open. Straightening, I turn my face toward my seat mate.

"Pen," Rowan drawls.

At First Smile will be available for purchase in October 2024
Subscribe to Melissa's newsletter for important release information: www. melissawhitneywrites.com

IN THE HELLO AND IN THE GOODBYE
ABOUT THE BOOK

In the Hello and In The Goodbye is a sweet and sexy second chance romance that proves love can span time and distance.

Through distance and pixelated screens, a struggling couple fights to give their relationship a second chance with a series of virtual dates.

Colm and Evie never made sense on paper. She's like a comforting pumpkin spice latte. He's a straightforward large black coffee. Despite their differences, their love was like a fairy tale. Until a tragic accident drives an emotional wedge between them. Now, Evie's smile no longer reaches her eyes and Colm's seat beside her often sits empty.

When Colm accepts the opportunity to teach in Costa Rica for sixty days, their relationship seems doomed. Unwilling to say goodbye for good, Colm proposes an experiment to Evie. They agree to plan a series of elaborate virtual dates to bridge the chasm of distance between them. Will their experiment be enough to find their way back to each other again, or do second chances only exist in romance novels…and not in real life?

Available Now!
Buy the book wherever you get ebooks and paperbacks

ALSO BY MELISSA WHITNEY

In the Hello and in the Goodbye
(Available wherever you get e-books and paperbacks)

The Home Series
Finding Home - Book One
Coming Home - Book Two– January 2025
Making Home - Book Three –October 2025

At First Series
At First Smile - Book One – October 2024

Stand Alone Titles
Happy Ever Afterlife, – April 2025

ACKNOWLEDGMENTS

It's strange to sit here and write acknowledgements for my second published novel. It still seems a foggy dream to call myself an author, especially a published one. I would not be here without the help of so many beautiful people who I am truly blessed to call friend.

First, I must thank Milo, my pug. Yes, he gets top billing this time. Not only is he the inspiration for Fitz (don't tell Coco or Marvin) but my ride or die writing partner. Since I started this journey, he's sat beside me or at my feet as I've drafted, written, edited, scrunched my nose, and cried over the things I've written. Milo, you'll get all the treats and belly rubs you want.

Thank you, my husband, Liam. Even though Milo got top billing, you are the first in my heart. I love you so much and am so deeply lucky to have you as my Mr. Darcy.

I want to acknowledge those that have experience sexual trauma. You are not alone. I see you. I love you. I am you. I support you. I hope you see yourself in Elle's story, especially in her reclaiming of her heart. Sexual trauma may be part of your story, but it is not your story. You are more than your trauma, as am I.

Meghan Fischer, I remain in awe of your amazing heart. This is the story we started with and you read all 300,000 words, helping me get it from dumpster fire to lit candle.

Gemma Brocato, you are my writing mama bear. I am truly blessed to have you as my Yoda, guiding me on my author journey. Thank you for your amazing editing on Finding Home and all the other stories we're working on and the ones to come.

Thank you to Su from Earthly Charms for this AMAZING cover. You are the BEST in the game.

Thank you to Happily Booked PR (Florence, Jamie, and Jela) for your support, mad marketing skills, and proofing. You ladies offer so much support to indie authors and our depth of gratitude knows no limit.

Thank you to Autumn Belvins for your copy-editing skills, hype work, and overall awesomeness.

Uncle Mike, Aunt Jody, Cassie, and Ryan thank you for opening your family up to this stray cat. I love you all so very deeply. In many ways this book is a love letter to you all. Although Mike and Jody, you cannot read the sexy bits! Cassie, please blackout those pages!!

This story takes place in my hometown of Perry, New York. There are so many people and places there that helped shape me to who I am, but I want to highlight a few special people and places. Robin Finley, my eleventh grade English teacher, and Linda Tiuch Carmody, my fifth grade language arts teacher, for believing in my writing and encouraging me to write.

Pilar McKay and Heather Parfitt Jackson, the ladies that made up my Charlie's Angels trio from high school, for your support then and now. There'd be no Elle without her Carmen and Beth. Just as there'd be no Melissa without her Heather and Pilar.

Daryl's Pizzeria for feeding my belly and soul, then and now (let's face it, I wrote this book in hope of free pizza... Did it work?).

I am sure there are people I am forgetting. Please know that you are all in my heart and, lucky for me, I have a chance to thank you all in my book coming this fall!

Finally, thank you to my readers. If this is your first or latest Melissa Whitney novel, there'd be no Melissa Whitney the author without you, the reader. Your support of my stories not only *makes me feel loved, supported, and seen but allows me to tell these stories. Thank you from the bottom of my heart. I love you all and only hope I can bring you all the feels for many more books to come.*

ABOUT THE AUTHOR

Melissa Whitney hails from Western, New York, but lives in Southern California with her husband and three rescue pugs. When not brewing the perfect cup of tea, hunting for a pastry, or listening to her latest audiobook, she writes swoony and steamy romances. Melissa's work explores themes of trauma, disability, grief/loss, and the complexities of human emotions and experience told through a romantic, sometimes comedic, swoony, and steamy lens.

To learn more about Melissa visit www.melissawhitney writes.com to sign up for her newsletter. As well, you can follow her on social media @melissa_whitneyauthor (Instagram), @melissasuewhitney (Tik Tok), or Melissa Whitney Author (Facebook Page).

Printed in the USA
CPSIA information can be obtained
at www.ICGtesting.com
LVHW020005081024
793227LV00036B/1177